PRAISE FOR TESSA

—⚭—

JEWEL OF THE NILE

"Afshar's excellent latest follows a young mixed-race woman in
the first century CE as she embarks on a quest to find a father
she thought long dead. . . . Exquisite plotting and outstanding
historical details set this apart. Afshar's fans will be overjoyed
with this tale of love lost and found."

PUBLISHERS WEEKLY, STARRED REVIEW

"Tessa Afshar's novels are well worth waiting for and *Jewel
of the Nile* is certainly no exception! What a lovely book and
what a beautiful message."

CHRISTIAN NOVEL REVIEW

—⚭—

DAUGHTER OF ROME

"With meticulous research and a vividly detailed narrative
style, *Daughter of Rome* . . . is both an emotive biblical love
story and an inherently fascinating journey through the
world of first-century Rome and the city of Corinth."

MIDWEST BOOK REVIEW

"This is a lovely slow-burning, faith-filled exploration about
overcoming trials and accepting past mistakes."

HISTORICAL NOVELS REVIEW

"Afshar brings in a thoughtful consideration of whether or not there are behaviors that cannot ever be forgiven, and her intricate biblical setting will engross readers. This is [her] strongest, most complex scripture-based story yet."

PUBLISHERS WEEKLY

"Tessa Afshar inhabits the world of early Christians with refreshing clarity. From life under the threat of persecution to domestic details and her characters' innermost thoughts, she makes early Christianity spark."

FOREWORD REVIEWS

"Tessa Afshar has the rare gift of seamlessly blending impeccable historical research and theological depth with lyrical prose and engaging characters."

SHARON GARLOUGH BROWN, author of the Sensible Shoes series

"Tessa Afshar's ability to transport readers into the culture and characters of the biblical novels is extraordinary. . . . *Daughter of Rome* is a feast for your imagination as well as balm for your soul."

ROBIN JONES GUNN, bestselling author of *Becoming Us*

—— ❧ ——

THIEF OF CORINTH

"Afshar again shows her amazing talent for packing action and intrigue into the biblical setting for modern readers."

PUBLISHERS WEEKLY, starred review

"Lyrical . . . [with] superb momentum, exhilarating scenes, and moving themes of love and determination. . . . Afshar brings to life the gripping tale of one woman's struggle to choose between rebellion and love."

BOOKLIST

"Afshar's well-drawn characters and lushly detailed setting vividly bring to life the ancient world of the Bible. A solid choice for fans of Francine Rivers and Bodie and Brock Thoene."

LIBRARY JOURNAL

—— ❧ ——

BREAD OF ANGELS

"Afshar continues to demonstrate an exquisite ability to bring the women of the Bible to life, this time shining a light on Lydia, the seller of purple, and skillfully balancing fact with imagination."

ROMANTIC TIMES

"Afshar has created an unforgettable story of dedication, betrayal, and redemption that culminates in a rich testament to God's mercies and miracles."

PUBLISHERS WEEKLY

"With sublime writing and solid research, [Afshar] captures the distinctive experience of living at a time when Christianity was in its fledgling stages."

LIBRARY JOURNAL

"Readers who enjoy Francine Rivers's Lineage of Grace series will love this stand-alone book."
CHRISTIAN MARKET

"With its resourceful, resilient heroine and vibrant narrative, *Bread of Angels* offers an engrossing new look at a mysterious woman of faith."
FOREWORD MAGAZINE

———— ༄ ————

LAND OF SILENCE

"Readers will be moved by Elianna's faith, and Afshar's elegant evocation of biblical life will keep them spellbound. An excellent choice for fans of Francine Rivers's historical fiction and those who read for character."
LIBRARY JOURNAL

"Fans of biblical fiction will enjoy an absorbing and well-researched chariot ride."
PUBLISHERS WEEKLY

"In perhaps her best novel to date, Afshar . . . grants a familiar [biblical] character not only a name, but also a poignant history to which many modern readers can relate. The wit, the romance, and the humanity make Elianna's journey uplifting as well as soul touching."
ROMANTIC TIMES, TOP PICK REVIEW

"Heartache and healing blend beautifully in this gem among Christian fiction."

"An impressively crafted, inherently appealing, consistently engaging, and compelling read from first page to last, *Land of Silence* is enthusiastically recommended for community library historical fiction collections."

"This captivating story of love, loss, faith, and hope gives a realistic glimpse of what life might have been like in ancient Palestine."

THE HIDDEN PRINCE

TESSA AFSHAR

Tyndale House Publishers
Carol Stream, Illinois

Visit Tyndale online at tyndale.com.

Visit Tessa Afshar at tessaafshar.com.

Tyndale and Tyndale's quill logo are registered trademarks of Tyndale House Ministries.

The Hidden Prince

Designed by Jennifer Phelps

Edited by Kathryn S. Olson

The author is represented by the literary agency of Books & Such Literary Agency, 52 Mission Circle, Suite 122, PMB 170, Santa Rosa, CA 95409.

The Hidden Prince is a work of fiction. Where real people, events, establishments, organizations, or locales appear, they are used fictitiously. All other elements of the novel are drawn from the author's imagination.

For information about special discounts for bulk purchases, please contact Tyndale House Publishers at csresponse@tyndale.com, or call 1-855-277-9400.

Library of Congress Cataloging-in-Publication Data

A catalog record for this book is available from the Library of Congress.

ISBN 978-1-4964-5821-6 (HC)

ISBN 978-1-4964-5822-3 (SC)

Printed in the United States of America

28	27	26	25	24	23	22
7	6	5	4	3	2	1

To Laurence:

Brave. Loyal. Caring. Honest. True.

My beloved nephew.

You will always be a prince in my heart.

REGIONAL MAP

N

CAUCASUS MOUNTAINS

BLACK SEA

CASPIAN SEA

ARMENIA

Aras River

TARUS MOUNTAINS

Tigris River

MEDIA

Ecbatana

MEDITERRANEAN SEA

Euphrates River

Babylon

Susa

ZAGROS MOUNTAINS

Jerusalem

Anshan

PERSIA

Nile River

EGYPT

RED SEA

ARABIA

PERSIAN GULF

– – – ROADS

∧∧∧ MOUNTAINS

PROLOGUE

Then the king gave Daniel high honors and many great
gifts, and made him ruler over the whole province of Babylon
and chief prefect over all the wise men of Babylon.

Daniel 2:48, ESV

The Twenty-Ninth Year of King Nebuchadnezzar's Reign

My father tightened his grip on my hand as we hurried past the ziggurat, the golden shrine of Marduk at its top gleaming in the morning sun. He always felt uneasy when we came too close to one of Babylon's many temples. But this one, the most renowned and opulent, made his Jewish heart downright agitated.

The ziggurat had occupied the center of Babylon for centuries, growing dilapidated with the passage of time. When Nebuchadnezzar ascended the throne, he spent a fortune on repairs to the famous landmark, restoring the ziggurat to a magnificent height so that fifty men could stand upon one another's shoulders and still not touch the zenith. To stamp the monument with his personal seal of grandeur, the king had added the bejeweled shrine of the Babylonian god Marduk like a crown at the top of the lofty structure.

I stumbled as I stared over the walls, past the veil of palm fronds and verdant tree branches, following the slow progress of a white-clad priest as he ascended the ornate staircase, carrying a burning brazier.

"Pay attention, Keren. Stop staring at that abomination."

"Yes, Father," I said, my gaze still glued to the priest.

"You must not allow your mind to wander when you begin your service in Daniel's household. Stay your thoughts on the tasks given you."

"Of course."

"And do not ask impertinent questions."

"Who? Me?" I asked, offended. "Grandfather says my questions are the sign of a quick mind."

"As I said. Impertinent. You must quash that tendency."

"Yes, Father."

By now, we had left the main thoroughfare by crossing a bridge over one of the canals that watered the city and found our way to a narrow, unpaved lane. Most of Babylon's roads were made of packed dirt, though some were wide enough to accommodate two chariots.

Without warning, Father stopped and turned to face me. I was tall for my age. But he still had to bend his head to look me in the eyes. "Keren," he said, his voice growing faint. "You know we love you. Your mother and I."

"And I love you. Stop worrying about me."

"Daniel is a good man. You will be safe in his household."

I patted my father's shoulder reassuringly. Years ago, the king had elevated Lord Daniel to the position of chief amongst all the wise men, and governor over the province of Babylon, the wealthy capital of the nation of Babylonia. In one fell swoop, Nebuchadnezzar had made a young Jew ruler over many of his own countrymen.

Not all of us captives from Judah were so honored.

Many of my people served as slaves. Others had been sent to live in Babylonian lands previously uninhabited. Some, like my father, occupied more menial positions in Babylon. My father's skills had earned him the post of assistant to a scribe. Though my mother and sisters wove baskets for a merchant in the market, and my brothers worked in the docks, my father's salary was the mainstay of our home. His meager income had to stretch eight ways and was never enough. In a moment of desperation, my father had borrowed from a money lender at an exorbitant rate. And now, he could not pay it back.

He had wept when he had approached his kinsman Daniel. Wept with sorrow and, I suspect, no little shame. Though he had my blessing, offering to sell his youngest daughter to his wealthy cousin nearly broke my father's heart. Of course, we all hoped that my family would save enough to redeem me within the year. But I suspected our hope to be more of a vain dream than a realistic plan. In all the years we had lived in Babylon, my family had yet to save a single silver shekel.

To our relief, Daniel had graciously offered to buy me from my father. Only to return me to my family, immediately, as a kinsman-redeemer would.

My father had hung his head. "We cannot afford to feed her, you see. We simply do not have enough. Would you allow her to work for you? She will earn her bread, I promise. Send her home to us every Sabbath so we can see her and rejoice."

Lord Daniel had agreed. He might have been a cousin to us, but he was as many times removed from my father's bloodlines as my fraying tunic was from the sheep that had been shorn to weave its fabric. Daniel did not have to act as my redeemer by Law, nor did he have to multiply his generosity by feeding and housing me at his own expense.

I understood how important it was that I repay my master's generosity with useful labor. I patted my father's shoulder again.

"I will work hard, Father. You need not worry. I will not shame you and Mother."

He laid his warm hand on my cheek. "We never worry about that."

Lord Daniel's house was everything you might expect in a nobleman's residence. Years ago, he had lived at the palace, but he received permission from the king to move into his own house when his sons were born. Three stories tall, the building had walls of expensive oven-baked bricks, whitewashed to battle the brutal heat of Babylonian summers.

This palatial dwelling had little in common with our tiny rectangular reed home and its reed-mat doors. The front door of Daniel's sumptuous home, along with its frame and lintels, was made of sturdy timber, a commodity Babylonia had to import at great expense.

"Cedars from Lebanon," my father breathed, probably remembering another door from a home long since lost.

I had few such memories. My mother had barely weaned me when the siege of Jerusalem began. I had just turned four when it ended in a tide of fire and blood. Sometimes I fancied I could still hear the echo of hideous wailing in my dreams, the kind of grim, animal howls only a war can squeeze out of human throats.

I had come along when my mother had believed herself too old to bear more children. She named me Keren-happuch, after Job's youngest daughter. I suppose everyone in Jerusalem had felt a little like Job by then. But, rather too hopefully as it turned out, she had chosen the name of a daughter conceived after Job's troubles had ended. Ours were only about to begin.

Our family was one of the blessed. Save for my eldest brother, the rest of us had survived the butchery of angry Babylonian soldiers who were fed up with Judah's repeated treachery. We had survived Nebuchadnezzar's sword, the fires of war, the gnaw of famine, the waves of pestilence.

Only to be carried to Babylon as captives.

Ten years had passed since the day my family sat by the waters of the Euphrates, exhausted by their long, merciless march, and wept for the home they would never see again. Some wounds cannot be healed by the passing of time. They fade, only to gape and bleed again at some unexpected provocation. Which was why my father would stand and stare at strange times, eyes welling up abruptly as they did now, coming face-to-face with memories trapped in a door made of rare cedars.

I pressed his hand in comfort. He smiled, trying to steady his quivering chin, and raised his knuckles to rap reverently upon the amber-colored planks. A slave dressed in a neat, short tunic invited us in. "The master is expecting you," he said with a bow of his head.

Though he spent most of his time at the palace, Lord Daniel had a whole chamber set aside for his work at home. Bent over a pile of clay documents on his otherwise neat table, he was so deep in thought that our entrance did not rouse him. We stood quietly near the door, waiting to be acknowledged. Behind him, a partitioned case housing numerous clay tablets and cylinders spanned the full length of the wall. In one corner of it, he had stacked scrolls of papyrus, which were not as popular in Babylonia as clay documents.

My fingers itched to look at those tablets, to try and decipher them and see how well Grandfather's teaching had served me. In Babylonia, girls were usually not taught how to read and write. But my grandfather had other notions.

By the time I started to toddle, Grandfather had become afflicted with the start of his shaking disease and could no longer serve as a scribe. For the first time in his life, he had the luxury of free time. And he was bored. He discovered quickly that I found his stylus and tablets fascinating and began to teach me. We bonded together over what we both liked best. The knowledge and power of words. I would miss him, living away from home.

My new master lifted his head and blinked as if awakening from a dream. "Asa! Forgive me. I did not hear you come in." He rose from his seat, the folds of his long sea-green tunic falling about him in an orderly wave.

"And this must be Keren-happuch." He studied me with a glint of surprise. I was skinny for my age and as flat as the timber roof on his house. Womanhood, if it ever intended to visit me, had proven reluctant to bless me with any obvious charms. *Yet*, as my mother was fond of reminding me.

Father bowed his head. "We call her Keren, Master Daniel." My parents had realized early that if they wanted to keep me from getting into trouble, a shorter appellation would be necessary. I would be halfway down the road, chasing whatever had taken my latest fancy, before they pronounced the full cartload that was my given name. "You can trust her to work hard," Father added. "She is stronger than she looks."

I nodded to emphasize his words. My eyes fixed on the mounds of clay cylinders behind my new master. I wondered how many of them I could carry in my arms at one time.

"I am sure we will find something to suit her. Now, please receive this as a token of my appreciation for allowing your daughter to serve my household." Daniel dropped a cloth bag jingling with silver shekels into Father's palm. "I will arrange for her to visit you at home every Sabbath. We wouldn't want her mother to miss her too much, would we?"

The door swung open behind us and the most elegant woman I had ever seen entered on sandaled feet. Her long, royal-blue tunic danced at her ankles as she walked deeper into the room to stand next to Daniel. Two pale-blue shawls decorated with the golden fringe so admired by Babylonians draped diagonally across one shoulder, held in place by a jeweled belt. Someone had arranged her hair into a perfect, ornamented creation of loops and crimps, adorned by gold rings. But by far the most glamorous thing about her was her face, with its sharp, short nose, cool brown eyes darkened with kohl, and curved lips that dipped into a deep wedge at the center.

Those lips betrayed no expression when Lord Daniel introduced me. "Mahlah, my dear," Daniel said with a smile. "Here is your new charge, Keren. I am sure you will find some useful task for her around the house."

This, then, was my mistress. I would not be spending my time serving Lord Daniel in his study, it seemed. I hid my disappointment and bowed respectfully before the elegant woman.

My new mistress regarded me in silence. If she were a scroll, I was illiterate. I could read nothing from her expression, which remained bland as she scrutinized me. "Let us try the kitchens," she said.

My heart sank. This might not be an auspicious beginning. My mother and sisters rarely allowed me near the place.

"Excellent idea," Daniel said, immediately returning to his pile of clay tablets, and I barely had time for a hurried goodbye embrace from my father before Lady Mahlah led me out of the chamber.

"My husband tells me you are fourteen," the mistress said as she guided me through the corridor into the rectangular court-yard. Above us, a partial roof of palm wood planks and packed earth kept the climbing sun at bay.

"Yes, mistress. I am tall for my age, and the rest of me still has to catch up."

The elegant face remained impassive. But I fancied I saw the tiniest sparkle in the brown eyes as she turned to study me for a moment. "The kitchen is here" was all she said, leading me to a chamber in the far corner of the courtyard.

A rotund man with dark hair stood by the open door, sharpening his knife. He bowed when he spied the mistress. I kept an eye on him, worried he might poke his flesh on the point of his blade as he bent down. He proved dexterous, however, portly fingers nimbly tucking the knife away.

"My lady, how may I be of service?"

"I have brought you additional help, Manasseh. This is Keren. See if you can train her to be useful around the kitchen."

"Yes, lady." He bowed again, not straightening until the mistress began to walk away. I followed his example, though it seemed excessive. If I had to bow every time someone above my station came and went, I would spend the whole day bent over my shoes.

Manasseh sized me up. "Scrawny little rat, aren't you?" He lifted a huge iron bowl full of unshelled, dried walnuts from a shelf and shoved it into my chest. I staggered under the weight, barely managing to hold on.

"Shell," the cook barked. He pointed a corpulent finger toward the corner of the room where a hammer awaited on a stool. "When you finish, I have a bowl of almonds."

I sat on the floor, the bowl tucked between my legs, and started breaking shells. It was dull work, and soon my attention began to wander. On the low, three-legged stool where I had found the hammer, I spied a small clay cylinder resting on its wobbly side. A scrap of papyrus lay open near it.

Writing instruments held a great deal more charm for me than every manner of nut under the sun. I slowed my hammering as I slid to the right and craned my neck to have a better look. Enough light streamed through the door for me to make out the words.

The clay cylinder was a royal list of provisions. I recognized it immediately as resembling the ones my father sometimes prepared for the palace scribes. My brows knotted as I sounded out the wedge-shaped Akkadian syllables for oil, barley, dates, and flour.

Lord Daniel had been amongst the first wave of deportees from Judah—one of the talented young men of noble family that Nebuchadnezzar had carried off to Babylon nineteen years before the rest of us had been taken into captivity. As a high courtier in service to the king of Babylonia, he received monthly provisions of food and oil, of which the scribes kept careful records.

Next to the neatly prepared royal tablet lay a dirty scrap of papyrus with an additional list, this one in Aramaic. No royal scribe had prepared this atrociously spelled piece of workmanship. Quickly, I scanned the contents. Plums, emmer, prunes, fish, frankincense. It took some imagination to understand the words, they had been so mangled by poor penmanship.

My feet scrabbled a little closer to the three-legged stool, the pot of walnuts entirely forgotten now. This list included purchase prices as well as weights. It wasn't my intention to be nosy. But my bored brain found the sums too inviting to resist. I added them up in my head, first the weights, then the prices. The total on the paper did not tally with my additions.

The account became a wrinkle in my mind, a challenge I couldn't resist. I added the prices again more slowly, compared them with the weights, and went back over the list. It took only a moment to find three mistakes.

Scratching my nose, I stared at the cook's back, bent over as he vigorously pounded a piece of mutton. No doubt this list was his handiwork. As chief cook, he had charge over purchases beyond royal provisions. A household this large and wealthy would need to buy more than the basic staples the palace provided. But he had spent a lot less than he claimed on his list.

I bit my lip in thought. Judging by the man's inadequate writing skills, I assumed this was an honest mistake. Any half-educated scribe would be able to pick out his errors within moments, as I had. At best, he would find himself extremely embarrassed. More likely, he would be accused of attempted theft.

I cleared my throat. "Master?"

The cook's large head pivoted on his short neck. "Aren't you finished with those walnuts yet?"

"Not quite."

"Get a move on," he barked before returning to his pounding.

"It's only that . . . I have found a mistake, you see."

This time he turned more slowly, pinning me with an unblinking gaze. "Mistake?"

I nodded toward his list. "I couldn't help noticing. You added them wrong."

The portly cheeks, glistening with steam from a boiling pot, turned the color of the plums on his list. "You *read* my list?"

I shrank back. "I didn't mean to pry."

"You read *my* list?"

"The papyrus was practically under my nose." I scooted backward cautiously. "Naturally, I added the columns up. I can show you where the mistakes are. We can correct them in a blink. Give me a bit of ink and . . ."

The corpulent finger pointed at me again. "Up!" he bellowed. "Up!"

I scrambled to my feet. "I only meant to help."

"Out of my kitchen! *Out*, I say!" The bellows were getting louder. Now the other hand lifted, waving a bronze mallet stained by blood and mutton gore.

I gulped. My feet stumbled over themselves as I turned to obey the cook. I must not have moved fast enough for his liking. A booted heel landed squarely on my bottom and shoved hard. I tripped, lurching through the door, and, barely regaining my balance, dashed out of the kitchens as fast as my skinny legs could carry me.

Unsure where to go, I headed for the main house, looking over my shoulder every few steps to ensure Manasseh had not followed me with his bloody mallet. I had barely walked through the door when I collided with something soft, wafting with the perfume of roses.

The mistress.

She steadied me with an arm. "What is this uproar?" she asked calmly. "I heard shouting from the kitchens. Why are you not where I left you?"

"The cook requested my departure, mistress."

She gave me a look that scared me more than Manasseh's gruesome mallet. "And why is that?"

"I tried to help him," I squeaked.

"You tried to cook?"

"No, mistress! That would not be advisable for anyone's health." My mouth turned dry. "I tried to . . . That is, I made a suggestion."

One perfectly shaped brow rose. "Don't take a step until I return."

I stood motionless, sweat staining my woolen tunic. A few moments later the mistress reappeared from the direction of the kitchens, her golden fringes flapping against her soft leather sandals.

"He refuses to have you back," she said, her face blank of expression.

My heart sank. I wondered if she would return me to my father's house, disgraced, after less than half a day in her service. But she merely said, "Come. We will find you a new place to serve."

She led me into the bowels of the house, guiding me to a chamber in the south end of the property. My eyes widened as for the first time in my life I saw a bathing room—a whole chamber set aside for the purpose of personal ablution. I had heard of such places but had never had occasion to enter one. In my home, when we needed to bathe, we headed for the river.

With interest, I noted that the tiled floor sloped slightly toward the center of the room. Before I had time to examine this oddity further, a faint movement in a dark corner of the room made me hop back in alarm. I realized that the mistress and I were not alone in the chamber.

A woman walked toward us from the shadows. She had a round face, flushed and beaded with sweat, wisps of dark hair sticking to her forehead. Her arms were bare and pink. It dawned on me that she must be the household washerwoman.

She bowed to the mistress before picking up a wide bronze bowl full of water and emptying it upon the tiled floor. As the contents of her bowl flowed toward us, I took another hasty step away, worried that the foul water would seep into my only pair of sandals. But the water merely rolled into the center of the floor and disappeared down a small hole I had not noticed until then.

"Why, it's a marvel!" I cried.

"I am glad you approve," the mistress said dryly.

"Is that drain attached to a pipe, mistress? It must lead away from the foundations of the house. Where does it go? My guess would be into a canal, and there . . ."

The mistress held up a hand and I managed to swallow the rest of my words. "You don't need to figure out the architecture of it, girl. You merely have to make use of it." She turned to address the woman with the pink arms. "Rachel, this is Keren. Our new servant. I am placing her under your tutelage. See if you can make a good laundress of her."

"Yes, lady." Once the mistress withdrew, Rachel said, "I'm glad you are here. "My daughter used to help me with the heavy loads. But she is big with child and cannot manage it anymore." She fetched a load of wet garments from the corner of the chamber and, dropping them into her now empty bowl, handed them to me. "Follow me."

I shifted the bowl and found it not as heavy as I had expected. At one end of the courtyard, someone had strung up a length of rope, and Rachel helped me quickly hang the garments from it in an orderly row. A few linen tunics and short skirts such as those women wore under their garments, a dozen men's loincloths, and light summer shawls.

I smiled to myself. If this was the heavy work, my job as the laundress's helper would be simple.

"Come," she said. "Time to fetch the bedding."

"Bedding?"

She nodded. "Once a month, we wash the sheets and blankets.

Every blessed one. We start with the master and mistress's bed, followed by their sons' beds, and then the bedding used by guests. And there are always guests! Of course, we set aside another day for the servants' bedding."

I gulped, realizing that what we had just hung on the line was the lightest load I would likely encounter in this household. It took Rachel and me a good hour to strip the beds and gather the wool and linen fabric in two baskets. I thought she would head back to the bathing chamber. Instead, she headed for the street.

"Where are we going?"

"To the river," she said. "These are too big to wash indoors. I only launder the family's clothing there. The mistress is very particular and does not wish her intimate garments flapping in the wind by the banks of the Euphrates for everyone to ogle."

I did not answer. I could not. I had already grown winded from carrying the enormous basket, which contained more linens than I had ever seen in one place. When we arrived by the river, I collapsed on the shore and took a relieved breath. I could have taken a nap right there on those sheets, be they washed or not.

Rachel pulled out one sheet and showed me how to look for stains and to treat them with a bar made of fat boiled with ashes. After soaking the sheet in the river, she beat it with a smooth rock to remove the dirt.

"Now take this and rinse it," she instructed. "Then you can start on the next one."

I nodded as I took the sheet a little deeper into the river to allow the water to rinse over the linen. My eyes widened as I spotted a clump of reeds. I noticed amongst them several stems that would yield a perfect stylus for writing on clay.

If a reed was too thick, it yielded poor symbols; if too thin, it broke easily. If it was too old, the nib would shatter under pressure. It took experience to pick just the right reed. I loosened my hold on the sheet, reaching with one hand to the stem closest to me. My father would appreciate the gift of a sturdy reed for a new stylus. The stem proved stubborn, and I twisted further toward it to take a firmer grasp.

The unthinkable happened.

I lost hold of the sheet and it began to float, carried away by the currents of the river.

"Gah! The sheet! The sheet!" Rachel shouted from the shore, gesturing wildly with her arm.

My attention might have been a little lacking, but at least I knew how to move quickly. I ran down the shallow riverbed before the undulating sheet could go too far and lunged. A smooth stone jutting from the sands hit me squarely in the chest, and for a moment I lost all the breath in my lungs. But my fingertips twisted into the linen and I managed to grab it and pull.

I came to my knees, panting and wet. With a shaking arm, I lifted the sheet into the air. "I have it," I called.

Rachel patted me on the head as she retrieved the runaway linen. "Good thing you run fast."

After that, she would not let me come anywhere near the river with the laundry. She had me sit in the sun and apply her lump of boiled fat and ashes to any stains I found.

As I rubbed, I berated myself. How could I have been so inattentive? Why had I not kept my mind on the task at hand?

We ran into the mistress when we returned to Daniel's house.

"How did she do?" the mistress asked Rachel.

The laundress shook her head. "She is a good girl and she

works hard. But she was not meant to be a laundress. No doubt, you will find something more suitable to her talents." To Rachel's credit, she did not divulge my stupidity.

The mistress raised a perfectly plucked brow after the laundress left us. "What did you do? Make another suggestion?"

"No, mistress." I dropped my head. "I let go of the sheet in the river."

"One of my embroidered ones?"

"I fear so."

"Then you can help embroider another to replace it."

"You won't need to replace it. I caught it before it swam too far."

"In that fast current?"

I rubbed my chest. "I dove after it."

Again, I thought I caught the palest twinkle in her cool brown eyes before she signaled me to follow. "I trust you will have no need of diving with my weaver."

I swallowed a groan. Weaving, sewing, and embroidering were not my strong suit. But I was determined to do better. This time, I would not disappoint my mistress.

The weaver, Haggith, had the responsibility not only for weaving fabric, but also for sewing new tunics, repairing old garments, embroidery, and ornamentation for the whole family. She spoke Aramaic with the distinctive Hebrew accent that tinged my father's and mother's speech.

It dawned on me that most of the master's servants were from our country. Some, like the cook, out of religious necessity; others, no doubt like me, here because of an act of kindness. Who knew how many of us they had saved from starvation or prevented from falling into the hands of cruel overseers.

"Do you have experience?" Haggith asked, lifting her head

from the vermillion tunic that lay before her on the sheet she had spread over the carpet. Expertly, her fingers gathered the loose, delicate threads fringing the hem and tied them in exactly equal segments.

I bit my cheeks. "Not so you would notice. I am willing to learn."

"Let's see what you can do." She handed me a man's tunic with a tear near the hem. "Can you mend that?"

I took the ivory needle she offered me and did my best to bring the tear together with tiny stitches. The fabric bunched as I pulled the thread. Looking over my shoulder, Haggith shook her head. "Don't pull so tight."

I loosened the thread with the next few stiches, and the fabric gaped. "Not so loose!" the weaver snapped and took the tunic from me.

"Let's begin with something simpler." She laid a handkerchief on the sheet next to the vermillion dress. "Hem that. Keep it spread on the sheet so you can see what you are doing."

I nodded. Placing my fingers where she had shown me, I began to take tiny stitches, pretending to wield a stylus on wet clay. In truth, writing Akkadian was much more complicated than taking even stitches. It required a delicate touch, rendered in syllables rather than with an alphabet like my mother tongue. I told myself anyone who could write the complex Babylonian symbols could certainly hem a simple kerchief.

Bending low over the square of gray linen, I took tiny stiches and kept a close eye on the gauge of my thread. I left the kerchief flat on the sheet to ensure the fabric did not grow bunched and sewed with more patience than I had ever shown my mother at home.

"Finished?" Haggith asked.

I leaned away so she could examine my handiwork. She frowned and tried to pick up the kerchief. The sheet came up with it. I had sewn the seam all the way through to the sheet. I might have been given another chance if the red dress had not also grown trapped by my stitches, which had picked up a few of the delicate strands of the fringe.

After that, Haggith consigned me to a corner of the chamber as far away from her as possible. Giving me a hank of freshly dyed yarn, she ordered me to wind it into a neat ball.

"My mother usually assigns me the same task," I said morosely, fingers twining the yarn round and round. The ball was finished by the time the mistress came to ask after my progress.

Once again, I followed her down the long corridor of the main house. I did not dare ask if she intended to send me home. She came to a stop before Lord Daniel's chamber and after a brief knock entered with me in tow.

Daniel lifted his head from his work and gave her a slow smile. "Mahlah! Is it dinnertime already?"

"Not quite." She drew me forward. "I am returning this one to you. I have tried everything under my purview and found no fit. See if you can do something with her."

"I?" Daniel seemed lost for words.

Mistress Mahlah did not smile, exactly. But her eyes danced. "You, my lord. I will leave you to it." And promptly, she turned on her heel and left the chamber, leaving me standing like a tent pole in the middle of the room.

Daniel stared at me for a moment. Then, waving a hand, he motioned me to sit before returning his attention to what lay before him. I realized he was writing on a small tablet of wet clay no larger than the palm of his hand. Halfway through the first line, the nib of his stylus snapped.

"Not again!" he murmured. Pulling forward an alabaster cup full of reeds, he searched for a fresh stylus. Finding them all in disrepair, he expelled a long sigh before retrieving a short knife from the cup.

Gingerly, I came to my feet. "My lord? May I sharpen that nib for you?"

He looked up as if he had forgotten my existence. "I can repair your stylus," I said. "My grandfather taught me."

Daniel studied me for a moment. Without a word, he extended the broken stylus to me. He hesitated a little before handing me the knife as well. "You aren't going to cut off your finger, are you?"

In answer, I took the broken stylus and examined it in the light of the lamp. "The reed is poor quality. It keeps breaking because its walls are too thin and cannot bear the pressure of your hand." I pointed toward the middle. "If I cut it down to here, will you still be able to wield it comfortably? The reed walls thicken here."

Master Daniel nodded. I pulled the clay tile sitting on the corner of his table toward me and laid the reed's broken tip on it. Taking a firm hold of the stylus, I made a clean, diagonal cut across the top. Satisfied with the result, I made a few quick slashes, until the reed had the right contours at the tip, perfect for creating the wedge-shaped symbols of Akkadian.

The wet clay of the tablet had been marred when the nib had broken. I pointed to the damaged clay. "Would you like me to repair the tablet as well, my lord?"

Daniel pushed it toward me without comment. I dipped the tip of the stylus into the cup of water resting near the master's hand and carefully applied the wet, polished curve to the surface of the clay, smoothing it out with a few swift strokes.

"Will that serve?" I asked, washing the clay from the nib before passing the stylus to him.

He examined the freshly cut stylus. "Admirably. My thanks." Without comment, he returned to his writing, dipping the tip in water and wiping off excess clay on the rag he kept for that purpose. He had not dismissed me, so I sat on the carpet and waited in silence. When he finished, he pushed the tablet aside and turned his attention to me.

"It seems you know your writing implements." he said. "The stylus worked well."

I scrambled to my feet. "I saw a sturdy patch of reeds by the river earlier this morning. I didn't have a chance to examine them closely, but I suspect they would yield at least a dozen fine styli. Would you like me to fetch them in the morning? I could sharpen them, ready for your use."

Daniel frowned. "You can't go alone. I will send one of our men with you."

I could have clapped. His consent meant I wasn't being sent home. Tonight, anyway. "Thank you, master."

He hesitated. "Can you read and write?"

"Yes, lord. Though my Aramaic is better than my Akkadian."

"Everyone's Aramaic is better than their Akkadian," he said dryly, making me laugh.

Most people in Babylon spoke Aramaic, but the language of the court, and therefore of scribes, remained Akkadian, the archaic tongue belonging to ancient Babylonians and Assyrians. Aramaic was a simpler language to write, because like Hebrew, it had an alphabet, whereas Akkadian used six hundred syllabic symbols, requiring the memorization of a dizzying array of combinations.

"How do you know so much? Most women cannot read, let alone sharpen a stylus."

"My grandfather was a royal scribe in Judah." I smiled. "He is the talented one in the family. But he contracted the shaking disease and can no longer use his skills. I am fortunate that he passed some of his knowledge to me."

"Has he not trained any of your brothers?"

"They were too old and set in their ways before he had time to teach them." I shrugged. "He trained my father. But Father's fluency in Akkadian is limited, so he serves as an assistant to a senior scribe." In Babylonia, a well-trained scribe could grow wealthy working for one of the temples or the palace. An assistant scribe only scraped by.

Daniel pointed to the chair facing him across the table, and I lowered myself to the edge of the cushioned seat. He plunked something before me. I swallowed when I realized what it was.

A wooden tablet, covered with soft wax—the kind scribes used for writing a rough draft. On top, he laid a bronze stylus. "Write," he commanded.

I drew the tablet toward me and picked up the stylus, holding it at the ready. "My lord."

He began dictating Akkadian words in quick succession, faster than I could inscribe on the wax, so that I had to retain the memory of each in order to write all the words in the sequence he had spoken. *Eat. Drink. Earth. Heaven. Joy. Plough. Pig.*

I realized quickly why he had chosen this seemingly random list for his dictation. The word for *eat* required a combination of the symbols for *mouth* and *food*, a rather fiddly grouping of lines and triangles. The word for *drink* was very similar and could easily be mistaken for the first. The word for *pig* required sixteen different symbols. He was testing my dexterity as well as my knowledge.

He reached for the tablet when I finished and glanced at my handiwork. "No mistakes. And legible, which is no mean feat."

From the wooden case behind him, he fetched a small roll of papyrus along with a brush and a pot of black ink. "Now, let us test your Aramaic."

The hot, arid conditions of Babylon were not kind to papyrus. The clay from which the city's skeleton had risen, on the other hand, had proven the perfect foil for the climate of the valley lying between the Tigris and Euphrates rivers. That was one of the main reasons for the popularity of clay tablets.

My grandfather had taught me how to write Aramaic on papyrus. But in Babylonia, papyrus was relegated to the drab business of everyday life, not used for important documents. I was surprised that Daniel wished to test my knowledge of it.

"Ready?"

"Yes, master."

He began to dictate, his Aramaic crisp and cultivated. This time, I kept up with him more easily, though he dictated a rather complicated passage concerning astronomy. I finished the last word with a flourish and handed the papyrus back to him.

He raised a dark brow. "Neat hand."

Desperate to prove myself truly useful so that he would not send me back home, I cleared my throat and said, "Your ink is low. Would you like me to make some?"

He looked up. "You know how to make ink, too?"

I nodded. "Red and black."

"You're quite accomplished for fourteen."

I beamed. "My grandfather trained me well."

Daniel leaned back in his chair. "It seems my wife could not find a good fit for you in the household."

I gulped. "I can try harder. If you give me another chance . . ."

Daniel held up a palm. "I have several Babylonian scribes who work for me at the palace. But I rarely invite them to my home. This is my place of rest. My personal refuge. Having palace officials underfoot does not suit me. Which means I have no one to help me when I work here." He leaned forward. "How would you like to work for *me*, Keren? It would require long hours of training as well as service."

I jumped to my feet and almost shouted *hallelujah*. "I would like that very much!" I cried. In my excitement, I slapped my hand on the table, right where the wax tablet lay. My index finger went through the soft wax. I looked down and saw that in my eagerness, I had obliterated the word *joy*.

Daniel rose, grasping a walking stick. Most Babylonian noblemen carried one, with jewel-embellished heads and carvings that symbolized power, like lion heads or flying eagles. Daniel's had been made simply, devoid of precious stones, the head carved in the likeness of a deer.

Seeing me looking at it, he smiled faintly. *"The Sovereign Lord is my strength! He makes me as surefooted as a deer, able to tread upon the heights."*

"The prophet Habakkuk?" I guessed.

"Indeed. Do you understand it?"

"No, my lord."

"You will." He tipped that carved deer at me, indicating that I should to follow.

"I have no time to train you," he explained as he walked down the hallway with me shadowing his heels. "And clever as you are, you shall need a great deal more tuition. I have a solution to that problem. My two sons and their friend receive private tutoring at the tablet house we have set up for them."

Babylonians used the term *tablet house* in reference to public schools that served the sons of the nobility. There, wealthy young men learned literacy as well as incantations, prayers, astronomy, and numeracy. Daniel had set up a private one in his own home.

"In the mornings," he said casually, "you will work for me. In the afternoons, you will attend their classes."

"*Their* classes?" I squeaked, trying to imagine myself fitting in with three aristocratic boys. "But . . ." Babylonians did not train their women formally, save for a princess or two, destined to become priestesses at some high temple. "I mean to say, my lord, I am not a man!"

Daniel waved a dismissive hand. "The God who called Deborah to be a judge can surely provide for a girl in a tablet house." He came to a sudden stop and waved his stick at me. "Why do you think I have a deer carved on my cane?"

"To remind you of that verse every time you hold it."

"To remind me of that *promise* every time I hold it. I am leading you to one of those impossible places that life sometimes demands of you. A hard, precipitous path you have to ascend. A tablet house for a Jewish girl.

"The question is, will you let God give you the strength to climb this mountain? Will you trust him to give you feet like those of the deer?"

Before I could respond, he pulled a door open and greeted the thin man standing at the front of a long chamber.

"Forgive my intrusion, Azarel. This is Keren. She will be working for me in the mornings and joining your tablet house in the afternoons." The master delivered this truncated introduction without so much as a blink, before leaving me to my fate.

My throat constricted as the teacher turned to me. I tried

to stand straight and look like I belonged. To give him his due, Azarel's meek face betrayed no annoyance. If he felt any qualm at having to instruct a young woman, he did not show it.

Daniel's eldest son, Johanan, had his mother's good looks and enigmatic face. His younger brother, Abel, scrutinized me openly, not bothering to hide his curiosity. But his smile was friendly when Azarel introduced me.

Their friend Jared, lounging comfortably next to Johanan, looked the youngest of the group. I guessed him to be shorter than me by a head, and boyishly slim, with a face as smooth as an egg. I slipped onto the bench behind him, thinking him to be the safest occupant.

He turned to face me fully. "What kind of girl attends a tablet house?"

My eyes widened at this unexpected challenge before I even had time to settle. "My kind."

Azarel banged the tips of his fingers on the edge of his desk. "Attention, please." I ignored Jared's stare and glued my eyes to the teacher. Azarel had drawn the outline of an irregular piece of land on a tablet and was showing us how to calculate the yield of the apple trees growing upon it.

"Now, here is another piece of land bearing apple trees," the teacher said, giving us various measurements. "Who can calculate the land area and the yield of its fruit?"

"Ask the girl to do it, Principal Azarel," Jared said, turning his impish grin on me. "Let's see if she can keep up."

The scribe nodded slowly. He handed me a wooden practice tablet with clean wax. "Do you think you can try?"

"Yes, Teacher." My desire to prove myself to my classmates, who had by now turned fully in their seats to study me with undisguised interest, added speed to my calculations.

Principal Azarel examined my work over my shoulder. "Excellent work, Keren. Well done." From a basket in the corner of the room he fetched an apple, red enough to tempt a water buffalo. "Here is your prize. Since the others watched you as you worked, you can now take a well-earned rest while they figure out the problem for themselves."

I feared my smile lacked humility. I took a great bite of my apple, taunting Jared as I chewed with relish. He grinned, undeterred by my complacent expression, and turned to his tablet. The three boys were obviously competent, for in no time at all, they arrived at the correct answer.

By the end of the afternoon, we all had the measure of each other. Accustomed to brothers and sisters who had more love for the outdoors than the studious work of scribes, I found the competence of my new companions a refreshing challenge.

When the teacher left for the day, Johanan addressed the others. "Ruben is not coming today. We're short one man for sword practice."

"I can help," I said.

Johanan raised a brow. "You have proven you have a supple mind when it comes to numeracy, girl. Be content. Leave swordplay to us."

I shrugged. "I only wanted to lend a hand. My brothers taught me the rudiments since there are three of them and they are permanently short of a fourth."

Johanan came to his feet. In spite of my height, he towered over me. His younger brother, Abel, stood up next to him, topping him by two fingers. "Still think you can ply your sword against us?" Johanan said.

"You? Maybe not. But I can practice against him." I pointed my chin at Jared.

The boy rose slowly. His head only reached my chest. "You can try."

I nodded. "I can try." My brows furrowed in thought. "How old are you, anyway?" I did not want to press him too hard if he turned out to be younger than twelve.

"Sixteen."

I blinked. His amber eyes had a fierce cast to them, as if daring me to tease him about the lag in his body's growth. I had no desire to. Having looked like a tree trunk for a whole year when other girls my age had turned all soft and cushiony had taught me many a worthy lesson in humility.

"I'm fourteen," I said. "I hope to live to see fifteen. So don't wield your sword too savagely at me."

Jared flashed a brilliant smile. "I will show you mercy."

And a good thing he did. For Jared proved a wily opponent, as ferocious as he was small. Though nature had thus far withheld from him the advantages of manhood, he made up for his lack of stature and muscle with speed, employing a swift and sly strategy the likes of which I had never seen.

The third time my wooden sword went flying into the air, with the dull edge of Jared's sword at my throat, I held up my hands in good-natured surrender. "I see I need a lot of practice," I said, massaging my bruised hand.

Jared examined my sword. "This hilt is not a good fit for your fist. You see?" He pointed to the rounded grip. "The wood is too thick. I have an old one at home that will fit you better. I will bring it for you."

He kept his promise. The next day he showed up with a practice weapon that fit my small hand perfectly and spent a few moments demonstrating several new maneuvers. Before leaving for home, he taught me how to wrap my hand with scraps of fabric to protect it from the worst of the blisters that had started to form. Watching him ride away on his well-tended horse that afternoon, I had a startling realization.

God had sent me a friend to accompany me on my high places.

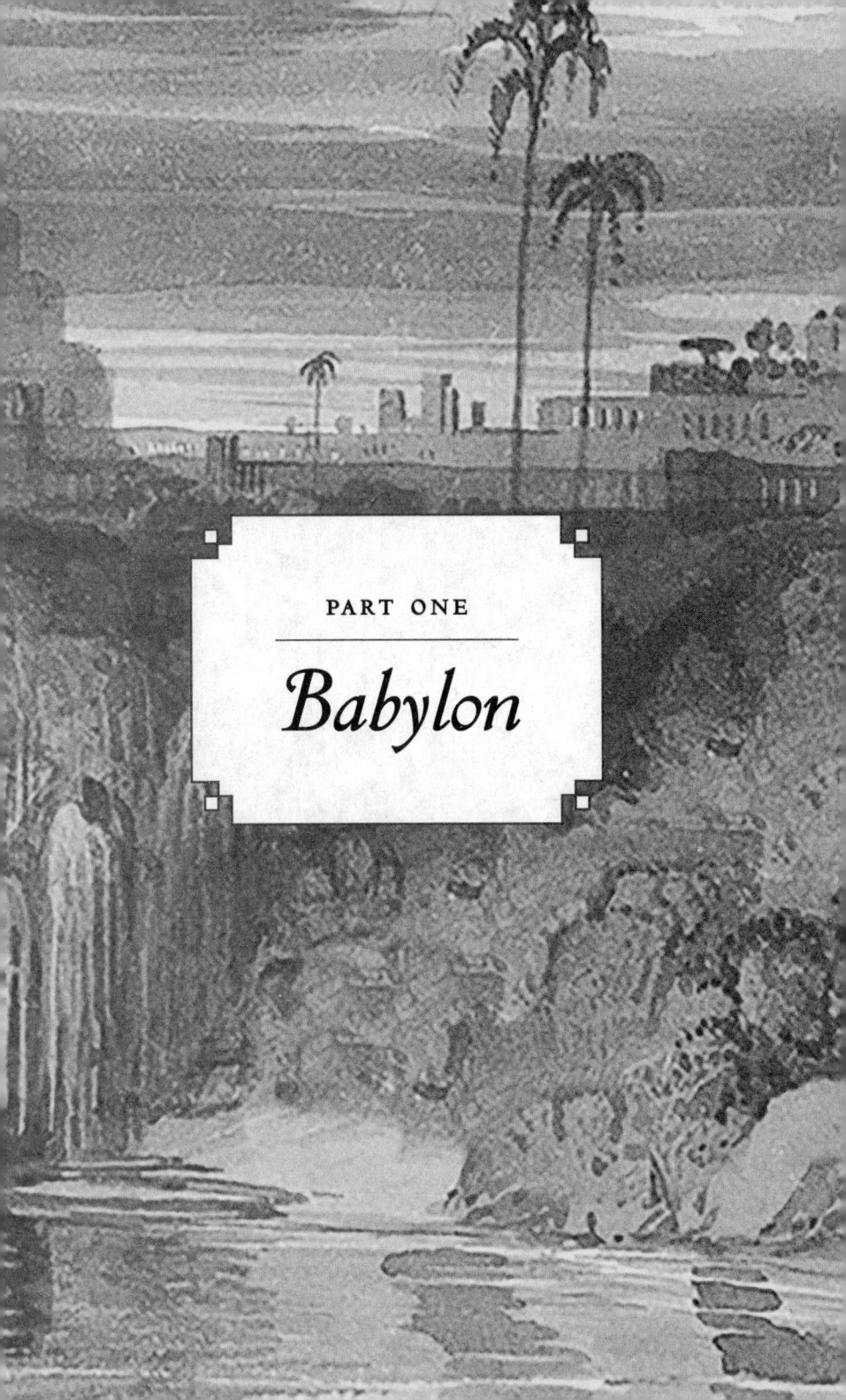

PART ONE

Babylon

CHAPTER ONE

Guard your heart above all else,
for it determines the course of your life.
Proverbs 4:23, NLT

Three Years Later
The Thirty-Second Year of King Nebuchadnezzar's Reign

I awoke before sunrise per my custom, for my master was an early riser and on his knees by the windows of his upper chamber, already in prayer, by dawn. It took no more than a few moments to fold my sheets and blanket, roll up my pallet, and tuck everything in a chest, which sat in a corner of Lord Daniel's workroom. Like the other servants in the house, I did not have my own chamber. But I fared better than most since I had the privilege of sleeping in my master's airy room and did not have to share it with a snoring mate.

Sorting through the day's tablets, I placed them in order upon Daniel's desk. He had dictated several letters the previous day, and I sat at my chair to make him additional copies for his personal records. By the lunch hour, when he arrived from the palace, I had completed my tasks.

Daniel always tried to eat at home. On the occasions when sharing the king's table became unavoidable, he had made arrangements to be served vegetables, grain, and water only, lest he break the Law of the Lord. My master ruled *in* Babylon, a world utterly counter to our faith. But he was not a man *of* Babylon.

He examined my work, made a few minor corrections, and dismissed me for the day. Making my way to the kitchen, I knocked on the open door.

"Shalom, Manasseh!" I called and dropped the list I had prepared for him on the counter.

Without comment, he swept up the neat roll of papyrus and placed it in a pocket before shoving a clay plate toward me. The smell of warm barley bread and chickpeas spiced with cumin, coriander, and leek made my belly rumble with hunger. Manasseh stretched a hand and added a pale-blue, hard-boiled duck egg to the plate.

I grinned. "You spoil me." We had long since made up our differences. Seeing that the master trusted me with his own sensitive documents, Manasseh had learned to seek my help with his lists and expenditures. It was an arrangement the mistress had welcomed with relief.

"You're still too skinny," he said.

I pushed the tail of my bronze stylus into his belly. "We can't all be so well-cushioned."

"Go on with you." He threw a green fig at me, which I managed to catch in midair. Stuffing the fruit wholesale, peel and all, into my mouth, I made my way to the opposite side of the courtyard. Sitting in a corner, I made quick work of Manasseh's delicious repast, dipping the last of the warm bread into the aromatic chickpeas. I looked at the angle of the sun and sighed. I would be late for Azarel's class if I did not hurry.

For three years, every afternoon I had attended the tablet house alongside Johanan, Abel, and Jared. But Jared and Johanan rarely attended our classes anymore, having both secured important positions in the city several months earlier. Only upon rare occasions, when their work allowed, did the two friends join us for an hour or two of learning.

My belly did an odd little flip when I saw Jared occupying his old seat. Quietly, I slipped into my sun-brightened bench behind him.

"You have a piece of lettuce hanging between your teeth," he whispered, turning toward me. "Right here." He pointed at his front tooth and shook his head as if in despair, amber eyes full of laughter.

I did not fall for the bait. I had eaten no lettuce. Besides, teasing me was Jared's favorite pastime. Since the first day when I had walked through the door of the tablet house and occupied the same seat, I had received an endless supply of good-natured harassment.

I stared at the broad shoulders and tall torso that blocked half the room in front of me and smiled. Jared looked nothing like the runt of a boy I had first met. Sometime that year, he had started to shoot up with the swiftness of an arrow. Over the months, his short, willowy stature had caught up to his age, growing enough height and muscle to now interrupt my view of Principal Azarel as I sat behind him.

I flipped a coil of his fashionably long hair. "Move your pretty curls. You're in my way."

He shook his hair and shifted his bulk so that he blocked me worse than before. "Not my fault you're a shrimp."

A blatant lie. I was still tall for a woman, though I had finally received those feminine blessings which had eluded me for so long. And while I could not claim to be quite as blessed as some, I had learned to be grateful for what I did have.

Johanan, sitting on the other side of Jared's bench, swiveled his head and hushed us. I offered him a dazzling view of the full set of my teeth and he rolled his eyes. Having recently celebrated his betrothal, he considered himself too grown-up for our juvenile teasing.

The one thing that drew Johanan back to the tablet house in spite of his newfound solemnity was his fondness for languages, and a talent for them that rivaled mine. Whenever Principal Azarel offered a class on advanced Sumerian or Akkadian, Johanan tried to make an appearance.

Since he and Jared had been inseparable from childhood, Jared always came along, though he preferred mathematics to technical vocabulary. Jared's loyalty anchored him to his bench when he would rather have spent his rare hour off riding or engaged in an exciting hunt somewhere in the wilderness.

One thing that their age and elevated status had not changed was their weekly weapons practice. "Bow and arrow," Johanan said in his usual pithy manner when our lesson on classic Sumerian concluded.

"You free?" Jared pointed his chin at me.

"I am."

"Let's start with swords, then."

I smiled my thanks. In spite of no lack of enthusiasm on my part, I had never mastered the bow and arrow. Its composite formation of glued wood, bone, and sinew made its tensile strength too much for my arms. I could pull the string. But my aim betrayed me. Fortunately, my companions still welcomed me for basic sword practice, where I could prove useful in helping them maintain form and speed. But they had outgrown and outmatched me long ago in most other weaponry.

"How is your brother?" I asked. Jared's younger brother, Joseph, had turned seven a few weeks ago. I had seldom seen a more doting brother than Jared. It was as if he intended to make up for the mother the child had lost, and the father who paid him little attention.

Jared smiled. "Joseph is growing like a weed. He is definitely taller than I was at his age."

"You have more than made up for it."

"Yes. But it took me a year to grow accustomed to my fast-changing size and stop knocking into things."

I laughed. "We were all relieved when you ceased to break everything in your path."

Jared tied his hair back with a strip of hide, his attention on the cluster of shields hanging from the wall. "I can still break things." He threw me a look of mock threat.

I ran my finger along the shaft of an iron-tipped spear. "You can try." I grasped the slender wooden sword I always used just as he reached for a heavy, round shield. For a moment, our arms connected from shoulder to elbow. A jolt of reaction shot through me. I jumped away, feeling breathless and hot.

Jared inhaled sharply. His lips tightened for a moment. "It's too cold for that tunic. You need a shawl." Turning, he flung a sword to Johanan. "You, with me."

I felt my cheeks flame. I knew my tunic had grown ragged and thin, its short sleeves reduced to mere flaps over the curves of my shoulders. I could neither afford a better one nor purchase a shawl. When my mistress had given me one of hers, I had gifted it to my mother, whose garments were even more frayed than mine.

Abel twirled his sword in my face, gesturing me forward with a wave. He had donned armor not because he felt afraid of the nicks and bruises I might give him, but because he needed to grow accustomed to the added weight of the hammered metal. I found myself too distracted to give Abel much challenge, my eyes following Jared as he thrust and parried against Johanan.

If I could kick myself, I would. For months I had been gazing at that man like a motherless puppy, unable to stop myself. He made my heart do odd things in my chest. Blood rushed to my face at the strangest moments. For three years, he had been my friend. A companion for my soul. Then without warning, something had shifted, and I could not press it back to the way it had been.

I suspected his absence from my life had altered the way I saw him. When he had been a regular part of my days, I barely spared him a thought. Now that he was gone, I had learned to long for him.

In spite of myself, I turned my gaze to Jared again, and for a tiny moment our eyes caught and held. My mouth turned dry. Jared flushed. Something whacked into my ribs.

"Ahh!" I doubled over, holding my side.

"Your mind is wandering." Abel shrugged. "That should have been an easy block."

I rubbed my side. "I am done for the day."

"So am I," Jared said, replacing his sword neatly in its slot against the wall.

"A few quick shots for target practice, before we return to work?" Johanan selected a bow and grabbed a quiver of arrows.

Jared nodded. The two of them had been appointed to the

position of canal supervisors, an important post for men so young. The system of canals that irrigated the city of Babylon and its surrounding farmlands kept the capital alive. But the waterways tended to become clogged with rushes and water weeds and mineral deposits, leading to disastrous flooding. Even the Euphrates, which divided the city of Babylon into two, silted up regularly, withholding its bounty from the thirsty city. Officials such as Johanan and Jared were appointed to supervise the waterways, protecting the residents from terrible floods.

I lingered to watch them practice with their bows, all three deadly accurate with each shot in the relatively short distance that the garden allowed, though I had seen Jared maintain perfect aim from a distance five times as long.

As he was leaving, he hesitated in front of me. His mouth opened and closed. His jaw tightened, emitting no sound. He blew out a long breath and left without a word. At times like this, I wondered if he had become as addled as me.

Then I remembered who Jared was. Son of the aristocracy, his father a minor prince of Judah, with the blood of kings in his veins. He had no room in his life for a girl like me, barely above a slave, and that by Daniel's grace. The miracle was that he had offered me friendship. Anything else belonged to the realm of dreams.

Guard your heart above all else, Lord Daniel had drilled into me from the first week of my employment. Good advice for those who could manage it. Somewhere, I had lost my way to those wise words.

CHAPTER TWO

——————— JARED ———————

The hour spent plying his sword, followed by the bow, did what his mind could not manage. It calmed his heated blood. She had had this effect on him since the day he set eyes on her, her regal neck bent down to accommodate his short stature. *I hope to live to see fifteen. So don't wield your sword too savagely at me,* she had said, not a shekel of sarcasm twisting the words into something cruel.

Over the years, he had come to know everything about her. Know the way her brows dipped when she missed home, the way the corner of her mouth tipped when she was teasing, the way she bit her lip when she focused on a particularly difficult arithmetic problem.

He knew the way she moved when she felt harried—wide,

rapid strides, with her hands tucked into her belt—and the way she moved when she felt happy—strides just as wide, but slow, with a tiny, unconscious swing to her hips.

He could close his eyes and tell the moment she entered a chamber by her scent. For two weeks out of the year, she picked pink rose blossoms at Daniel's farm for the annual rosewater and oil production. In appreciation, Mahlah gave her a few bottles of rose oil. She used a drop of the perfume every day, and its sweet, heady fragrance mingled with the clean scent of the river where she spent so much time and took on hints of the scholarly smells of ink and clay, creating something utterly irresistible and uniquely Keren.

Every part of her made something in him flutter to life. But lately, the response had grown more explosive, more impulsive, so that the accidental brush of her bare arm against his during practice had overwhelmed him with the desire to pull her into his arms and declare his love for her.

He repressed a sigh as he settled himself at the dinner table. As always, his father kept the family waiting, which meant no one could eat, no matter how hungry they felt. When Hanamel finally arrived, he motioned for the dinner to be served, forgetting to speak a blessing over the meal.

Jared's younger brother asked for the plate of vegetables, his voice soft. But not soft enough to hide his stutter, an affliction that had begun after the sudden death of their mother six years earlier. He had hardly been out of swaddling clothes at the time and still clinging to the affectionate mother who had doted on him. Losing her warm protection overnight had shaken the boy. The grief of it had roosted in his tongue. An unfortunate weakness as far as their father was concerned.

Hearing the stutter, his father's mocking voice rose to batter the boy like a sharpened axe against a sapling, deriding his small disability with such vivid cruelty, the poor boy could barely hold on to his tears.

"Father!" Jared said, the simple appellation turning into an objection.

"And you," his father growled, turning his attention to Jared. "When do you plan to marry? When I was your age, I had a princess for a wife, belly out to here." He held his hands out to the table. "What's wrong with you?"

Jared's face remained expressionless. "I plan to save a bit of money first. Enough to rent a house. I don't wish to be a burden to you."

His father's lip curled. "What are you now? You eat my food, drink my beer, sit at my table. What is that, if not a burden?"

Jared refused to point out that he now brought his own rations into the household and had contributed the silver shekels needed to repair the crumbling roof his father had neglected for a year.

Lord Hanamel leaned forward. "Find yourself a wife with a rich father and a fat dowry. And be quick about it, or I will do it for you."

His father's wives, two women he had wed after his mother's death, lowered their heads, recognizing their own stories in that statement. They were nothing to Hanamel save a sizable dowry. Jared felt pity well up when he regarded their reddened faces.

He pushed aside his beer, untasted. He was nothing like his father. The thought of marriage to a woman he had no interest in turned his stomach into a sour knot.

He could imagine his father's reaction if he discovered Jared's feelings for Keren. Which was why he had never spoken of his love to her. What good was love, if he could do nothing about it? He would merely dishonor her, and himself, by declaring it.

CHAPTER THREE

The LORD is on my side; I will not fear.
What can man do to me?

Psalm 118:6, ESV

The next morning, I took inventory of Daniel's writing materials. Over the previous weeks, he had gone through every single stylus at his usual alarming pace, and I realized I had to fetch more reeds. Donning my sandals, I went in search of Hanun, the male servant assigned to accompany me whenever I left the house. The old man pulled a hand through his beard, a big yawn splitting his face.

"What's your hurry?" he said, lifting the bar from the gate and opening it.

"I am conducting an errand for the master."

"Aren't we all," the old servant murmured and shuffled forward.

Regardless of how desperately I tried to hurry the man up, he seemed capable of only one speed. Shuffle. Over the years, it had been a contest between us, trying to make the other's pace shift. I had never won. Short of moving behind him and shoving, my only remaining option was to match his shambling gait.

We had a mutual understanding, Hanun and I. He considered me an inconvenience and I returned the compliment.

I crossed the old stone bridge over the Euphrates and wended my way to an outcropping of thick reeds on the western bank. Taking my sandals off, I handed them to Hanun and padded down the hilly embankment into the shallows, giving the stalks careful scrutiny.

In my preoccupation with the reeds, I missed the *kelek*, the simple Babylonian riverboat made of hides stretched over willow branches, that floated dangerously close to me, its single male occupant eyeing me as I scrambled amongst the skinny stalks.

When a powerful hand wrapped about my calf and pulled, I let out a yelp of surprise before falling on my behind. The hand pulled hard, dragging me toward the buoyant *kelek*.

I began to struggle, kicking my feet, trying to free myself from the man's hold. But no matter how hard I twisted and kicked, he managed to retain his bruising grip and hauled me ever closer.

My feet and ankles were in the boat now, the rest of me dragging in the mud. The man's hand slithered up my calf, getting a pinching hold of my flesh. My skin crawled at his touch. One more pull, and he would have me on board his boat, bound for who knew where. Everything had happened so fast that Hanun had not even seen the struggle from his vantage point farther up the shore.

Finally, hearing my cries, he scampered toward us, shaking his wooden staff at the man. "Let her go!" he yelled.

"Get away, old goat," the *kelek*'s skipper hissed, not loosening his hold.

Hanun would never reach us in time. Even if he did, he would be no match for the boatman, who at half his age would no doubt have twice his strength. "The staff," I cried, beginning to realize the hopelessness of my situation.

The old man pitched the staff at me in a wild arc. I grabbed at the roots of some reeds with one fist, holding on with all my might. My other arm reached out and managed to pluck the flying staff from the air.

I let go of the roots and allowed myself to be drawn toward the boat. As soon as I came face-to-face with my assailant, my legs stretched all the way onto the *kelek*, I raised the staff, holding it like a sword. All those years of practice came to my rescue. I did not even have to think through the movements of my arm, my wrist, my fingers. They danced with a will of their own, thrusting my makeshift sword down against the man's chest and belly.

Gasping, he let go of my leg but twisted his hand into my tunic and pulled. I shrieked at the top of my lungs and brought the staff down in a sideways swipe. At the last moment, he sprang back, missing the worst of my strike. Still, the tip of Hanun's staff bashed against his teeth, his mouth spouting a fountain of blood.

Finally, the hand wrapped around my tunic like an iron manacle loosened, and I dragged myself off the boat, heaving, crawling out of the river and onto the higher bank. The *kelek* driver spewed a stream of obscenities, one palm wrapped over his mouth, the other using his paddle to get back into the deep. In a moment, he disappeared around the bend of the river.

Hanun knelt by my side. "You all right?" he asked, eyes round.

I took a deep breath, trying to calm my wild heart. Handing

him his staff, I said, "I am sorry. I broke it." The top had fractured in the melee.

Hanun studied the ragged wood silently. He raised a brow and shook his head. "I think Master Daniel should send you to protect *me*."

I grinned weakly. "Thank you for coming to my aid. If not for your staff . . ." I did not even want to finish that thought.

There was no dearth of nefarious characters loose on the waters of Babylon's rivers, including slavers. I had come so close to being another man's property. Or worse.

I swallowed a sudden desire to burst into tears and rubbed my calf. By morning, I would have a mighty bruise. "I didn't fetch my reeds."

"Lord Daniel won't mind waiting a day or two. We best get you home." His voice sounded surprisingly gentle.

I noticed the river's traffic was already picking up, broad-bottomed sailboats and long rowboats with multiple oars drifting south with the wind and currents, expertly avoiding collision with one another on the greenish waters. The increasing congestion added a layer of safety to the shoreline. No one would dare attack a woman with so many witnesses abroad.

I stood on shaking legs and hesitated. Grinding my teeth, I turned back toward the reeds. "Come, Hanun. We are going to get what we came for."

The old man gave me a measured look. His lips twitched, and for just a moment, I thought I caught something akin to respect on his face. The expression faded too quickly to be certain.

I grabbed his hand and matched my steps to his shuffling ones as we descended to the water's edge. I might have been determined to accomplish what I wanted, but I was not foolish enough to let the old man out of my sight this time. Hastily cutting several handfuls of the best stalks I could reach, I shoved them under my arm and helped Hanun back up the bank.

* * *

An hour after arriving home, I still had not managed to make a single stylus. My fingers were trembling too much. Something in me had shaken on the banks of that river. Something deep I could not name.

For the first time I had discovered how the course of my life hung by a fragile thread. This had been a lesson my parents had learned well in Jerusalem. But I had been too young when Babylon's siege shattered our world. Too young to feel the sorrow of being taken into captivity. The hardest circumstance of my life had been coming to Daniel's house, and in many ways, that had turned out to be a blessing.

By the river, a core, sleeping part of my heart had awoken to a stark reality. I could not keep myself safe from pain or danger.

With her usual catlike quiet, the mistress entered Daniel's chamber, startling me into dropping the knife I had been using to carve the stylus tips. She took one look at the pile of reeds I had ruined and said, "Come. Those can wait."

With relief, I left the few salvageable stalks and trudged after her. She led us to the courtyard, where she had spread a blanket under the shade of a tall mulberry tree. Settling herself on the blanket, she arranged her tunic about her in an elegant fan and motioned for me to join her.

An enormous wooden bowl piled with a mountain of dates sat between us, and she began pitting them after rinsing her fingers in a bowl of water. I followed suit, pulling out the ovoid pits from the sticky flesh and discarding them in a bucket someone had set up next to us for the purpose.

It was the kind of tedious work that normally drove me to distraction. But on that morning, I welcomed the dull, repetitious nature of it. Sitting next to Mahlah, her every movement radiating an odd, self-assured serenity, the alarm left over from the attack slowly began to fade.

We were halfway through the pile of dates when the door from the street opened, revealing Johanan and Jared.

Mahlah raised a hand in greeting. "This is an unexpected pleasure." It was unusual to see them return from work before noon.

Johanan knelt to kiss his mother on the cheek. Before the mistress could object, he had grabbed a couple of pitted dates and shoved them into his mouth. "We finished our project early," he said when he had swallowed the sweet morsels. "The supervisor rewarded us with a free afternoon. We thought we would celebrate with Manasseh's cooking."

Jared stared at me, his brows knotting. "What's amiss?"

He had an uncanny ability to read me. Over time, some invisible filament of his heart had wormed its way into mine, so that he could sense my every mood before I said a word.

I shook my head and did not reply. The fragile thread that had been pulled in my depths might unravel completely if I tried to explain what had happened that morning.

"A man attacked Keren at the river," the mistress said. "He grabbed her when she was collecting reeds and tried to carry her away in his *kelek*."

I dropped my eyes, unable to look at anyone. For an inexplicable reason, I felt a blaze of shame burn through me, as if the man's actions were somehow my fault. As if his very touch had left a smudge of dirt on me.

"What?" Jared, who had bent to one knee next to me, sprang up. "I'll kill him! Where is he?" He turned toward the door as if he would walk right out and grab the man off the bend in the river and pummel him with his bare hands.

"Calm yourself, Jared," Mahlah said, her voice dry. "Keren already dealt with him. All these years of sword practice proved useful. She used Hanun's staff to give the man a few good whacks. He was spitting out teeth and lisping curses from his bleeding lip when he sailed off with his tail between his legs."

The old man had apparently given the mistress a full report of the morning's misadventure.

Johanan burst out laughing. "I wish I had seen that," he said, his voice warm. "Well done, Keren."

Mahlah's face softened. "I wish it had never happened." Her hand fell in a rare caress over my hair, and she gave me a reassuring smile.

Jared returned to my side, no doubt realizing the futility of trying to find an unknown man on a river teeming with a thousand *keleks*. Kneeling again, he reached a tanned finger to play with the leather thong of my sandal, which had come undone and lay next to my foot. "Are you well?" he asked and stared at me, hard.

I realized with surprise that I was, indeed, well. Somewhere between his burst of angry outrage and Mahlah's singular show of affection, that hot flame of shame had turned into a pile of ashes.

CHAPTER FOUR

There is one whose rash words are like sword thrusts,
but the tongue of the wise brings healing.

Proverbs 12:18, ESV

JARED

He turned restlessly on his narrow bed, twisting the sheets into a knotted mess. Sleep was impossible. He sat up, drawing a hand down his face. The thought of what might have happened to Keren made a rare flame of fury blaze through him. He curled his hand into a fist and squeezed, wishing he held the neck of the brute who had meant her harm.

He had been about his work, directing laborers to dredge a portion of the canal, his mind focused entirely on the task at hand when it had happened. Too far away to protect her.

He grinned weakly. She hadn't needed his protection.

The grin turned into a chuckle as he pictured her beating the man with the staff, putting him to flight.

Instead of running home afterward, she had squared her shoulders and gone back to retrieve the stalks she had come for. Bruised and shaken, she had held fast to her purpose.

His heart gave an odd twist. There was an exquisite quality to her courage. The bravery that rose from fragile roots. She seemed to him as stable as the ground itself. Unshakable.

He grabbed the cup of water sitting next to his bed and took a long swallow.

He thought of the way, every day for the past three years, she had stood up for him. Spoken in his defense. Tried to protect him from every shadow of pain.

Growing up under his father's roof had taught him to expect little safety in the world. His father's tongue could be as hard as his lash. Jared had outgrown the lash, but the brutal force of his father's words still struck without warning. Keren had always known how to soothe the pain that came after the onslaught of his father's callous criticisms.

Daniel had given Jared his first real taste of the kind of dependable affection you could rest your weight on. Johanan had offered constancy in unbreakable friendship.

Keren had also given him those things. But she had given him something more. She had championed him. He never felt so safe as when he was with her. Her very presence felt like a shelter.

His throat turned dry. Things could have ended very differently by the river. He could have lost her today.

CHAPTER FIVE

Their life shall be like a watered garden,
and they shall languish no more.
Jeremiah 31:12, ESV

The Sabbath began at sunset the day after the incident by the river. I made my way home as soon as I finished the last of my chores, with Hanun dogging me like a shadow. I picked my steps carefully down the narrow alleys, dodging animal droppings and the piles of garbage discarded haphazardly along the way. Unlike the Hebrews, Babylonians frequently abandoned their rubbish in the streets. Not that they wasted much: what they did not use, their animals did, and what the animals could not eat, they frequently burned for warmth. Still, enough was left over to make for an unpleasant stroll.

Every few years, fed up by the mounting shards of broken pottery, bones, and indigestible bits of various sizes, the city officials commanded the streets be covered in a new layer of packed dirt. This meant that the older houses found themselves a step or two below street level. Then again, a step or two seemed a small price to pay in exchange for a fresh road free of sharp, smelly objects.

Father and Mother enfolded me in their usual embrace, four arms wrapped around me like grapevines, and just as sweet as their fruit. I laughed as my mother buried me in kisses, her lips leaving a trail of love over my forehead and making a mess of my tidy hair.

"My beautiful girl. You grow lovelier every time I see you," she said with a sniff. She said that every week when I came home. It didn't count, seeing as she was my mother.

My father tapped my shoulder like he was trying to ensure I wasn't an apparition. "Our clever girl is home!"

He imbued the word *clever* with a breathless gravity, pouring into it a weight of admiration, as though in his eyes I had become Babylonia's foremost scribe. I poked him in the ribs and he snorted through his nose. My father had always been ticklish. Sometimes, when I was a little girl, he would threaten me with tickling fingers and bend over laughing at the mere thought.

I offered the sack I had carried from Daniel's house to my mother. "The mistress sent you these with her greetings." That morning, the master had received three bushels of apples from his orchard in the country, and the mistress had set aside a dozen juicy ones for my parents.

My youngest brother, Benjamin, grabbed them from my hand. "Your timing is impeccable. My stomach thanks you."

Before I could scold him, Grandfather approached, hand sliding against the wall to support his quivering frame. I clasped him to me gently. "Grandfather!"

He grinned at me. "Did you forget all about me now that

you have the great Lord Daniel to keep you company?" His voice was breathy and weak. But to my ears, it sounded more glorious than the king's singers.

"I miss you every day."

His grin widened. "Let us see." He took hold of my hand and noted the dark ink stains. "Hard at work, are you?" From his pocket, he extracted a small, clay amphora. "I made you this. It will take the stains right off. Won't do for a pretty girl to walk around looking like an old scribe."

I laughed and tapped his bearded cheek. "Thank you, Grandfather."

"Hanun, join us for the Sabbath meal," my mother said.

The old man, who had just finished drinking the cup of water my sister had fetched him, shook his head. "Thank you. But I best return home before the start of Sabbath." Hanun tried never to miss a meal prepared by Manasseh's skilled cooking. Especially not the Sabbath feast.

"Thank you for bringing my girl home to us. You are a good man."

Hanun blushed under my mother's praise. I chortled as his back straightened and he marched out of our house, his steps more vigorous than he ever managed with me.

My mother spread our best cloth on the floor and the family gathered around it, our bodies packed in tight in the small space. We began with the traditional songs of Sabbath, followed by Father's prayer over the small cup of wine. Mother passed the clay urn and bowl so that we could wash our hands ceremonially, and Father spoke the blessing over the bread, which we dipped in salt and ate, before starting the rest of the meal in earnest.

I settled into the familiar, noisy companionship, filled with the sounds of hearty laughter and eager conversation. Time had a way of playing tricks on me as soon as I walked into this simple house, as if I had not been absent from its walls for six days.

And yet, in the midst of that familiar cacophony of affection, I realized a tiny sliver of disconnection. From week to week, nothing seemed to have changed. But in the slow gathering of months into years, part of me had grown more entrenched in Daniel's home than here.

This would always remain my family, my root, my settled place. But there were no tablet houses here. No letters to grand officials or sealed palace documents to work on. No bathing chambers and elegant dinners. Our morning prayers were simple. They lacked the brilliance and vision of Daniel's teaching. And though I had my pick of friends amongst my siblings here, there was . . . no Jared.

My shoulders drooped. I wondered if I would ever find the feeling of home—unbroken, uninterrupted home—again. But the flash of despondence sloughed off quickly as I shared my experience by the river with my family and received the balm of their care. By the time I returned to my master's house the following evening, I felt more clearheaded and lighthearted, loaded only with the weight of love, seven times over.

* * *

The following morning, I noticed a few tablets had been stacked haphazardly in one corner of Daniel's chamber, and another sat abandoned under the table, the typical detritus of my master's activity in my absence. If he did not keep the Sabbath, the piles would heap much higher. I returned the tablets to their rightful place, knowing Daniel thrived in an orderly environment. When he arrived an hour later, he found me seated on my chair with my wax tablet on my lap, ready to take down his notes for the day.

"Aah!" He smiled. "There is an empty spot when you leave us, Keren. It does me good to see you here, at the ready, knowing I can rely on you, as always." He looked around as if at a loss. "I've been searching for that tablet from the palace architect. The one concerning the roof. Do you know where it is?"

The last time we had worked on anything concerning architects had been a year ago. Fortunately, I kept the records in good order. It took just a moment to find the one he wanted.

He gave it a quick glance and nodded. "That's the one. Well done, Keren." Blowing out a long breath, he settled behind his desk. "A small portion of the palace roof has sustained damage, and the matter needs to be addressed quickly. This patch of roof supports the southern portion of the Hanging Gardens."

"The Hanging Gardens?" I gasped, eyes widening.

"Have you ever seen them?"

"Only from afar, looking up over the walls that surround them."

Daniel, who had personally walked along the tree-lined pathways of those gardens many times, nodded slowly. "No matter how many times I visit them, their beauty never ceases to astonish me. The head gardener tells me that the great oak tree where the queen walks every morning will be damaged if we don't undertake the roof repairs quickly."

The Hanging Gardens of Babylon were one of the world's wonders. It was rumored that Nebuchadnezzar had built the architectural marvel for his wife, princess Amytis of Media, to remind her of the verdant forests of her homeland.

Creating a lush, leafy park in the middle of the blazing sun and unforgiving arid winds of Babylon presented enough of a challenge. But Nebuchadnezzar had decided to build his garden on the rooftop of his palace.

The average homeowner considered himself blessed not to have a leaky roof when the rains came. To go so far as to build a park on a rooftop surpassed the imagination, not to mention skill, of most. Undaunted, the Babylonian king had built a foundation of arched vaults with baked bricks and water-proofed them with bitumen. Upon those vaulted ceilings, the architects had loaded enough soil to support the roots of massive trees and flowering shrubs and to accommodate the clay irrigation pipes that watered them.

I was not likely to ever see a place so exotic as Media, but if it resembled the lush verdure of the Hanging Gardens, it must be a delightful place.

In his usual proficient manner, Daniel dictated a letter to the architect, and another to the builder. As soon as he finished, he put on his turban and grasped his walking stick, preparing to leave for the palace. I began work on a fresh clay tablet, knowing Daniel liked keeping copies of his correspondence.

To my surprise, he lifted a detaining hand. "You can do that later. Would you like to come to the palace with me?"

I shot up from my seat. "The *palace*?"

He offered me a wide smile. "Yes, Keren."

I ran a hand along my faded tunic and gulped. "I would like that very much."

For the first time in my life, I rode in a one-horse chariot, clinging to the bronze bar in front of me as Daniel expertly handled the reins. The swift black horse, golden jewelry sparkling down the length of its mane and tail, clipped along the narrow road at a swift pace, making my body jostle up and down like an abandoned skiff on the waves of a blustery sea. By the time we drove through the double doors of the southern palace, my belly had moved somewhere into the vicinity of my throat.

In spite of the bouncing, I had managed to hold on to the bag of Daniel's tablets, which he had entrusted to me for safekeeping. "Come," he said, throwing the reins to a boy who had appeared out of nowhere with a bow.

What else could I do? I went.

My jaw hung over my knees as we passed through two courtyards paved with glazed tiles of dark blue. It was as though some artisan had captured the night sky and spread it over the earth like a carpet. Square pools of clear water sparkling under the sunlight occupied the center of each courtyard. Potted flowers waved lazily in the breeze.

The southern palace stood on the edge of the Euphrates. Daniel's office, where he led me, had a high brick ceiling, with light pouring in through the wide window overlooking the pebbled banks of the river. At his gesture, a long-robed scribe rushed to my side and relieved me of the tablets.

"You will find two letters in the bag, LuSalim," Daniel explained. "They are already sealed and need to be delivered. Right away, yes?"

LuSalim bowed, his head touching his knees. If that was the proper way to show respect to my master, I owed him several hundred cubits in bows.

Daniel's chin gave me that slight, dignified nod I had come to recognize as an invitation to follow, and I fell into step behind him. A long corridor led to a wide, open chamber with arched ceilings, each curve blending into another, forming a continuous weaving of vaults. Lining the walls were hundreds of shelves, embellished with ivory, gold, silver, alabaster, and filigree work. But that was not what captured my attention. On those shelves lay thousands of tablets and cylinders of clay. Standing frozen in the middle of the chamber, I could see that some were very old, containing Sumerian writing.

I gasped. "Is this . . . ?"

"The library. Yes. It holds records from as far back as a thousand years ago." Daniel tapped his walking stick on the floor tiles before pointing its carved tip toward a staircase. "You can gaze upon its wonders later, Keren. First, we must climb."

I had to peel my feet from the floor to climb the narrow stairs. My mind remained in that extraordinary place, however, and I wondered if I might be allowed to pass an hour or two amongst those fascinating shelves.

I blinked as I came to the top of the stairs, a flare of sunlight blinding me for a moment. At first, I assumed Daniel had brought me to the rooftop. My breath hitched as I realized my mistake.

Birdsong filled the air, and the smell of something sweet and exotic tickled my senses. I stood on a path lined with short fruit trees. Pink roses and purple salvia grew amongst clumps of mint. A carpet of tall grasses swayed lazily in the breeze next to large balls of allium.

The ground itself rose up in a gentle swell, at the top of which stood a solitary oak that looked to be a hundred years old, a marvel in itself, given that the place had been built less than two decades earlier. I took a few steps forward, inhaling the scent of a verdant world not belonging to Babylon, and certainly not belonging on a rooftop.

"It's breathtaking," I whispered.

Daniel leaned into his walking stick. "I wanted you to see it. To have this memory in your heart. To understand what God meant when he promised, *Their life shall be like a watered garden, and they shall languish no more*. Whenever you are languishing or weary, whenever you are tempted to give up, I want you to remember this place. This watered garden. For this is the Lord's promise to you, Keren. One day, this shall be your life, though you live as a captive now."

I turned in a slow circle and looked around me, absorbing not so much the undeniable beauty of the place but its impossibility. A garden in an arid land. Green hills on a rooftop. Water flowing up instead of down. Flowers blooming where nothing but beams and bricks should lay. This was God's promise. No arid land could stay his hand. A garden awaited, even for a captive like me.

CHAPTER SIX

The LORD says,
"The women of Zion are haughty,
walking along with outstretched necks,
flirting with their eyes,
strutting along with swaying hips,
with ornaments jingling on their ankles."
Isaiah 3:16, NIV

It was afternoon by the time I returned home from the palace. As soon as I finished copying the letters from the morning, I grabbed my clean tunic and headed for the bathing chamber.

Working for Daniel had placed me in a unique position within the household. He treated me more like a young niece than a servant. The mistress, too, bestowed upon me unusual privileges, such as free use of the luxurious bathing chamber, or like tonight, the invitation to have my evening meal with the family.

Still, I called them *master* and *mistress*, a verbal reminder that although they treated me as family, I was not quite their equal.

I washed quickly and changed into the fresh tunic, another thin woolen affair the color of dried mud. Twisting my long, straight hair into braids, I tucked them about my head in a poor imitation of one of the mistress's elaborate coiffures. We were expecting guests later in the evening, and I wanted to look presentable.

Maybe it was because of my odd place in this house, the not-quite-equal place, the always-a-little-out-of-step place, that I tried so hard to fit in. I labored over my hair as long as I could and adjusted my tunic to fall modestly about my ankles. After Jared's criticism of my poor garments, I felt especially ill at ease about my appearance. Finally, I had to admit there was little else I could do to improve my apparel and headed for the dining room.

The family had invited Deborah, Johanan's betrothed, as well as her parents and her younger sister for the evening meal. I had met Deborah a few times, a sweet girl whose exquisite looks were at odds with the shy smile that widened every time Johanan came near. She had extended that smile to me as well and spoken to me without the stiff airs she might have assumed with someone who occupied such a dubious place in the household.

Deborah's sister, Zebidah, on the other hand, had never visited us before. She came as something of a shock to all of us.

Though she lacked her sister's marked beauty, she suffered none of her shyness.

Her figure, which enjoyed more curves than the Euphrates and Tigris put together, was placed on display to such advantage that all the young men in our company were hard pressed not to stare. I was a girl, and *I* stared.

Her pretty tunic with its speckled design and tightly wrapped, fringed shawl revealed far more than my old tunic, for all its thinness. Zebidah's brown eyes had been expertly enhanced with kohl, the lids sparkling blue thanks to a liberal application of powdered lapis lazuli. I had never seen a woman so . . . womanly. Her anklets tinkled delicately as she made her way down the table to a bench.

It seemed to me, as I watched her with fascination, that Zebidah represented everything a man might desire in a woman. Judging by the way the young men grinned at her like drooling babies, they agreed with me.

The dining room in Daniel's house featured a narrow wooden table with claw-shaped feet and several rectangular benches designed for sharing. Zebidah gave me a sharp glare when I sat next to her on the bench.

"What are you doing?" she hissed, not so loud as to make a commotion, but enough to make her displeasure known.

My back stiffened. "Sitting."

"Here? Shouldn't you play with reeds, or dust tablets, or undertake whatever it is you do?"

I reddened. "I was invited."

Jared must have heard the exchange. He extended his hand to me. "Come and sit by me, Keren." To my delight, his admiring glances changed to a glower as he addressed Zebidah. "On this night, she is a guest, like you."

A perfectly plucked brow rose. "Pardon. I am not accustomed to eating with servants."

I moved quietly to the other side of the table to settle beside Jared. The space next to him was narrow, allowing no room between us. My hip pressed against his, and our legs connected, knee to thigh, through the thin linen and wool of our tunics. For a moment, we both froze.

Then Jared took a sharp breath and, with an abrupt move, shifted so fast he almost knocked Johanan off the bench. I scooted the opposite way myself, so that half of me hung over the edge. The air between us seem to crackle and hiss.

Fortunately, no one noticed. Zebidah kept everyone distracted, entertaining us with a seemingly endless stream of amusing comments. She addressed Daniel by his Babylonian name, Belteshazzar, as though she were attending a palace function rather than enjoying a family gathering.

On the table, servants placed steaming platters filled with leg of mutton cooked in shallots and red beets, garnished with crushed leeks and garlic, along with a stew of lamb, poached with barley and vegetables. The Babylonians cooked this dish in milk. As the Jewish Law forbade the mixing of meat with dairy, Manasseh adjusted the recipe for our household. Whatever his method, the lamb emerged as tender and delicious as anything the Babylonians might produce.

Silently, I passed the emmer crackers that were served with the lamb to Jared. He took the basket, careful to avoid my fingers. Clearing my throat, I tried to think of some clever comment that might break the excruciating awkwardness that had risen between us like a wall. But I felt as witty as a walnut shell. "The mutton is delicious."

Jared grunted.

He crushed an emmer cracker delicately over his lamb the way the Babylonians did, managing to avoid spilling the crumbs on his lap. I brushed surreptitiously at the copious crumbs that had spread over my tunic.

"Isn't the lamb succulent?" I tried again. "The sheep arrived from Lord Daniel's farm this morning."

Another grunt met my brilliant effort at conversation. I dipped my bread into the rich stew and stuffed it in my mouth. It tasted like canal sludge to me. I turned away from Jared's stony profile, my gaze riveted on Zebidah as she regaled us with the story of a well-known courtier whose wig had fallen over his sandals when he had bowed to the king.

In comparison to her hilarious anecdote, my first visit to the Hanging Gardens and the ancient palace library sounded insipid even to my own ears. Most people did not find libraries as exciting as I did.

Thankfully, the musicians entered the room, jostling their harps as they lined up against the wall. At least their songs saved me from having to further compare my dull conversation with Zebidah's amusing remarks.

CHAPTER SEVEN

*Why then has this people turned away
in perpetual backsliding?
They hold fast to deceit;
they refuse to return.*
Jeremiah 8:5, ESV

JARED

On the way home after work, Jared passed the temple of Inanna, the popular Mesopotamian goddess of war and sex. Her priestesses wielded great power and were not known for their chastity. Shock slowed his steps as he recognized a familiar face in the crowd of worshipers. Zebidah!

He wondered if he should try to extract her from the place and decided against it. She seemed an enthusiastic participant. He doubted that she would appreciate his interference. If she called the guards down on him, he would be the one in trouble. No Babylonian would understand an Israelite's antipathy for one of their favorite deities.

Sighing, he decided to bring the matter to Johanan. He wondered if Deborah knew of her sister's proclivity for worshiping the gods of Babylonia. He doubted it. The two sisters were fish and fowl, with little in common.

Zebidah's decision to worship one of Babylonia's prolific deities should not have shocked him. Even before their captivity, the people of Judah had cavorted with the gods of their neighbors. One glittery idol or another had drawn their attention and lassoed their hearts away from the Lord.

Babylonia had been the fork in the road. The place of decision.

The travail of captivity had awakened some of the Judeans from their moral slumber. A small remnant had seen their destruction as a call to repentance. An invitation to seek the ancient paths of the Lord.

Others had chosen to sink deeper into Babylon's ways. You could barely tell them apart from the other residents of the land anymore. They were slowly being absorbed into the world around them.

Lost, forever.

For Deborah's sake, it saddened him that Zebidah had chosen to be amongst them.

No sooner had he arrived home than his father sought him out. "Have you met Zebidah?"

Jared's eyes widened. *"Zebidah?"*

"She is the younger sister of the girl who is betrothed to Daniel's son."

"How strange that you should mention her! I was just thinking about her." He wondered if his father had also seen the girl at Inanna's temple.

Lord Hanamel grinned. "Were you, now? A tasty morsel, that one."

Jared took a cautious step back, surprised by his father's enthusiasm.

His father's grin widened, making him look like a wolf. "She would make a good wife for you, I have decided."

Jared's head snapped up. *"Wife?"*

"You are welcome."

"Father, no!"

"What do you mean *no*, you ingrate?"

"For one thing, I saw her worshiping at the temple of Inanna this evening."

"So?"

Jared's mouth dropped open. He was aware of his father's lax attitudes when it came to faith. Still, he found it jarring that even a man like his father would consider the worship of Inanna acceptable.

"You can't mean it," he said, his voice hard.

"Of course I mean it. The girl is charming. Charming! You'd be lucky if she looked upon you twice. Plus, her father is a wealthy merchant. Plenty of money for an acceptable dowry in those pockets. Not to mention that marriage to her would make us relatives of the great Belteshazzar, the favored of the king." Father rolled his eyes.

Heat snaked up Jared's chest, spilling over his cheeks. Grinding his teeth until his jaw ached, he refused to disgorge the words that were dancing at the tip of his tongue. Years of living with his father had taught him self-control. He knew he would regret an impetuous word. This new scheme brewing in his father's head must be met with a considered response.

"Go and change," Lord Hanamel commanded. "Be quick about it."

"Why?"

"They are coming to dinner, that's why. And you better win her over, or I will make you sorry."

"*Zebidah* is coming?"

"Along with her parents."

In his chamber, Jared dragged a clean tunic over his head and shoved his feet into a fresh pair of sandals. Binding a silver belt about his waist, he noticed the trembling of his fingers and tried to still them.

His father would never accept Keren as his daughter-in-law, regardless of her loyalty, her brilliance, her courage, her kindness, her godliness. But he was willing to open his arms wide to Zebidah's idolatrous ways for the sake of her dowry. The tang of nausea crawled up his throat at the thought.

During dinner, sitting across from Zebidah, he was surprised to discover himself enjoying her company. He had to acknowledge one thing: the girl *was* charming. In spite of himself, she had him laughing, engrossed in her amusing stories. She bent toward him to whisper some fatuous comment, and the pull of her hit him like a hammer. The sheer force of her sensuality, an amalgam of her musky scent, her bold gaze, and the heated intimacy of her attitude, wrapped around him and tugged.

He inhaled sharply, leaning away.

She adjusted her shawl knowingly, revealing more curves with every practiced movement. Something in Jared turned cold.

He thought of Keren, who, with a single smile, made him feel warm to the marrow of his bones. Exhaling, he let the sensual hold loosen. Dissolve.

Zebidah might make him laugh. She might charm his eyes. She might even fool his body for a few moments. But Zebidah and her dowry could go jump in the Euphrates for all he cared. His heart had known a true woman. And Zebidah simply could not compare.

CHAPTER EIGHT

For the LORD is good;
his steadfast love endures forever,
and his faithfulness to all generations.
Psalm 100:5, ESV

Twice a week, Daniel taught us the Scriptures before leaving for the palace. He began the lessons early, forcing me to rise an hour before my usual time. Droopy with sleep, I still would not miss a moment of his engaging instruction. Even Johanan and Jared, with all their newfound responsibilities, managed to attend Daniel's tuition.

The master greeted us with a Hebrew blessing. The ancient language of my people, Hebrew was rooted in my very blood, and I felt each distinct syllable flowing over me like balm.

As always, Jared and Johanan had settled next to each other, though I sensed something different about them that morning. A subdued quiet that seemed weighed down. They sat, heads bowed, shoulders drooping, lips flattened, not acknowledging the rest of us.

"His steadfast love endures forever," Daniel began, not bothering with a preface. He had a habit of doing that, of dousing us, without preamble, into the deeps. "Where is that from?"

"Chronicles?" I said, brows knotting.

"It's a psalm, isn't it?" Abel sat up. "The one that repeats the same phrase over and over again."

"No, it's that short psalm." Jared raised his chin. "I remember. The one that says to serve the Lord with gladness."

"Yes," Daniel responded.

The three of us leaned forward. "Which?" we said in unison.

"All three of you are right, as it happens. This is a phrase that is repeated in Scripture. Again and again, God reminds us of this truth, because he does not want us to misplace it. The Lord's steadfast love endures."

Daniel waited a beat. "*Endure.* A hard word. A grit-your-teeth and bear-the-pain kind of word. A strength-in-the-midst-of-storms word. We think of hardship when we think of endurance."

His gaze landed on Johanan, lingered, softened, and moved to Jared like a caress. "But sometimes, when God whispers *endure*, he isn't talking about pain. He is talking about love. His *love* for you endures."

A shaft of moonlight pierced the room through the single window and settled on Daniel like a mantle. He smiled. "God's care for you in this captivity endures. The warmth in his voice as he guides you endures. His melting affection as he looks upon you endures. His companionship, his shelter, his provision, his help, his counsel, endure."

Jared and Johanan were sitting up now, backs ramrod straight, mouths softened, as if Daniel's words had poured strength into their spines, while at the same time emptying the bitter words that had been locked behind their lips.

It occurred to me that Daniel had chosen this specific message on purpose. He had an alarming prophetic knack. Dreams and visions came to him, sometimes revealing the mysteries of the distant future, and at other times, speaking to a present need.

Daniel drew closer. "God wants your hearts to learn to endure, too. Endure in love. Love him even when he seems absent. Love him when he has offended or disappointed you. Love him when you feel he has not protected you."

"That is no easy task," Jared said, his voice subdued.

Daniel adjusted the filigreed belt at his waist. "No. Then again, it is no easy thing to be a captive and yet live as if you were free. You may occupy high positions, but as captives you will be ridiculed, challenged, insulted, ignored. You will labor harder and better than the rest and still find that, sometimes, your reward is a scolding you did not earn. Others lower than you will climb higher, and you will have to swallow the acrid taste of injustice. If you do not learn to lean into God's enduring love, in time, you might become slaves to bitterness. And that's a far worse slavery than merely being captives in Babylon."

Jared cleared his throat. "Surely you never felt that way, my lord?"

"My companions and I had our share of struggles. You know the story of my three friends, Hananiah, Mishael, and Azariah."

I smiled. The story of the three men known to Babylonians as Shadrach, Meshach, and Abednego had become one of my favorites. "They were thrown into a furnace of flames," I said, "because they refused to worship the golden image that King Nebuchadnezzar had set up."

Hananiah himself had recounted the tale for us over dinner

one night as we had peppered him with questions. What was it like to walk in an inferno and not be burned? Had the fourth man in the flames spoken to them? How did they feel when they emerged from the furnace? Hananiah did not have many answers. His memories of his time in the flames were hazy.

"They had done nothing wrong," Daniel said. "Still, they faced death." He leaned forward. "Your generation, too, will face its own fiery furnace in this realm. And each of you must cope with your own personal trials."

A shiver ran down my spine, like a physical foreboding of a blazing fire headed my way.

Daniel looked at each of us in turn, his expression grave. "That is why you must learn to endure. Endure in the fire, because God's love for you endures. Trust in his plans for you, my sons and daughter." His hand glanced over my head. "Let him give you the strength to bear the flames."

Though Daniel's exhortation ended on a note of hope, on a reminder of God's trustworthiness, I could not shake the uneasy feeling his words had wrought in me. The near disaster by the river had taught me that life was unpredictable. Daniel's fire was a shadow that hung over every one of us, a flame that could burn without the slightest warning.

When he finished our time with another blessing, I tried to shake off the odd disquiet and forced myself to focus on the practical duties of the day. Mundane activity was the cure for all the fears that chased me.

"We are short on envelopes," Daniel told me, while the boys chatted quietly in the corner.

A peculiar aspect of using clay tablets for correspondence was that you could not merely roll them up and seal them in order to keep their contents private. We had to create thin containers of clay that the tablets could sit in during transit. These containers were called envelopes and were often broken upon receipt. Which was why I was forever running out of them.

"I am heading to the river," I said, "to collect mud for a batch." The minute mineral deposits in the river yielded the best clay for tablets and envelopes.

Daniel tapped his cane on the table. "I forgot to tell you that Hanun is ailing and cannot accompany you. Nothing serious, Mahlah assures me. But you must wait to go to the river. I don't like the thought of you alone on its banks. Especially after what happened."

Jared cleared his throat. "I can accompany her, my lord. I do not report to the chief engineer for another hour. Besides, it will give me an opportunity to inspect the eastern moat."

Babylon possessed several powerful fortifications. The city lay encircled by a double row of defensive walls, punctuated with crenellated watchtowers. Beyond them, a deep moat had been dug, which surrounded the outer wall. Fed by the Euphrates, the moat provided Babylon with what its flat topography could not: an unbreakable defense. However, like every other body of water in Babylon, it was subject to silting and blockage and, as such, under the purview of canal supervisors.

Daniel smiled his acquiescence, and Jared and I set off for the river. Pale twilight illuminated our path as we walked in silence, though questions whirled inside my head faster than one of the eddies in the Tigris.

There had been a time I would not have squirmed before asking Jared anything that came to my mind. But so much had changed over the last few months. What had been easy and natural now squeezed out of me with a twisting awkwardness that turned my stomach into a pool of acid.

I cleared my throat and dove in like a water buffalo in the shallows. "Is all well with you and Johanan?"

"It will be." I thought Jared would leave it at that, my face pressed firmly against the closed door of his secrets. A stone sank in the pit of my stomach.

As if sensing my thoughts, he flashed me his old smile, full of cheek and confidence. "We received some harsh words from the engineer who is in charge of the canal supervisors. I brought certain concerns to his notice, and Johanan supported me. Instead of thanking us, he censured us publicly. Our pride was a little bruised. Nothing we won't recover from."

I remembered Daniel's words, warning that in this captive world, we would find insult and challenge. In a way, working for Daniel had spoilt me. I had been spared the cold severity of answering to Babylonian masters.

"I am sorry," I said. "I thought you were happy with your work."

He shrugged. "Happy enough." He sidestepped a pile of broken shards. "I don't see myself supervising canals for the rest of my life."

"What do you see yourself doing?"

"That's the trouble. I don't know. Here I am, head stuffed with more knowledge than most people receive in two lifetimes, and still I feel lost. Like God meant me for something more. Something . . . different from this."

"Have you told Daniel about it?"

He nodded.

"What did he say?"

"That he did not find his way to his own calling until he was almost killed. Nebuchadnezzar would never have put him in charge of Babylon if he had not placed him in an impossible position first. Requiring that the wise men tell him his dream before interpreting it!"

"And you thought *your* master was unreasonable."

Jared grinned. "True enough. Daniel had to face a mountain, not the molehills that irritate me. He clung to God, as he always does, hoping not only to save himself, but to spare the lives of his friends. He never thought that the sword pointed at his throat would open the doors to his future. He is a gifted administrator, the likes of which only come once in a generation. But he would not have known that if God had not allowed death to cast its shadow over him first."

"Sounds like a hard way to find your calling."

Jared laughed. "I said the same."

I had asked myself similar questions about my future. Most women knew their call in our world. We were made to marry and bear sons. To nurture our children and help our husbands. Yet, thanks to the unexpected threads of my life—Grandfather's unusual training, my father's unsettled debts, my education in Daniel's house—I had been schooled more as a scribe than a wife. Except that as a woman, my skills would not be welcomed in the conventional manner. I wondered if I was meant to be a helper to Daniel all my days.

The thought of being a wife and mother seemed more a torment than a hope. I could have those things. But not with Jared. I did not merely want to be a wife. I wanted to be Jared's wife.

A sweltering wind arose with sudden force, plastering my tunic against me. With a self-conscious shake, I plucked the formfitting fabric loose.

Jared came to a sudden stop. "I forgot." He reached inside the bag he carried and from it pulled a folded square of fabric. "For you," he said.

I stood, baffled. He pushed the fabric under my nose until I took it. It was my favorite color, the pale blue of a summer sky. Unfolding it, I discovered a shawl in softest wool, fringed with silver tassels along its edges. "What is this?" I held the elegant shawl, bemused.

"A gift."

"From your stepmother?" I asked, confused, thinking that perhaps one of his stepmothers had passed her old garment to me. But the material looked new.

"Not from my stepmother," he said, sounding offended. "What kind of gift would that be? From *me*. I bought it for you."

Jared took the shawl from my nerveless fingers and shook it loose. His large hands took the corners, and for a moment the blue wool flapped in the air like the wings of an exotic bird. Then, still facing me, he wrapped it around my shoulders and pulled the edges forward. His hands lingered at my waist over the shawl and my tunic, the warmth of them sinking all the way into my bones.

Jared's fingers tugged softly on the ends of the shawl, drawing me closer. Blood turned hot in my veins. Jared's head bent low. I could hear his breath, ragged and slow. His lips lowered until they almost touched mine.

A chariot drove behind me, big wheels churning in a bit of mud, and the sound startled me into taking a half step forward. Deeper into Jared's arms. For a moment I stood frozen, pulse exploding, bones turning liquid where my body brushed against his.

Jared exhaled as if he had forgotten the air that had sat trapped in his lungs, and the sound of it broke the spell between us. "I can't!" he whispered, his voice anguished, and leapt away, hands and lips and limbs separating from me in a scrambling rush.

I grabbed the shawl just before it fell to the ground and wrapped it around me tightly, feeling the absence of the gentle hands that had abandoned me and the soft lips that had not kissed mine.

"It's beautiful," I croaked, trying to sound as if nothing unusual had taken place between us. "Thank you."

Jared pulled a hand through his long hair, and I saw with satisfaction that those sword-trained fingers were shaking. Under his breath, he said, "You deserve it, and more."

That was the last thing he said until he deposited me at the house, before rushing off to report to work. I clung to the shawl he had bought me, purchased with his own hard-earned money, and tried not to dream of the heat of his hands at my waist.

And failed.

CHAPTER NINE

Wrath is cruel, anger is overwhelming,
but who can stand before jealousy?

Proverbs 27:4

That evening, Jared's father, Lord Hanamel, came to dinner. The jewels in his ears and on his fingers flashed as he took his seat next to Daniel. Everything about Hanamel reminded me of stone: the flat lips, the hard jaw, the cold gaze. The unfeeling heart.

I had once asked Daniel why Lord Hanamel had fared so well in Babylon even though he had royal blood. So many members of the different branches of the royal family had suffered great loss under Nebuchadnezzar.

Of the three kings who had ruled in Judah during Babylon's long invasion of the land, the first, Jehoiakim, a vindictive prophet-killer who burned Jeremiah's warning scroll, died before the first siege of Jerusalem ended, his body dragged and dumped beyond the gates of the city. His son, Jehoiachin, surrendered to Babylon after merely three months of rule, a fact that probably saved his life. He was even now enjoying the king's hospitality in captivity somewhere in Babylon. The last king of Judah, Zedekiah, who had switched allegiance as swiftly as a royal princess changes clothes, had watched as his sons were lined up before him and put to death one at a time, before being blinded himself and carried off in chains. All the nobles of Judah with any hint of allegiance to Zedekiah had been slaughtered. But Lord Hanamel had survived the culling of the royal family.

Daniel had merely told me that Lord Hanamel had done the king a service and refused to expand on his explanation. Which left me to draw my own conclusions.

There were two kinds of Judean nobility who prospered in Babylon. On the one hand, there were men like Daniel and his friends, who, having been carried away from their homeland in their youth, had served our masters while clinging to God. Such men used their influence to give aid to our people.

On the other hand, there were those who found success in the land of our captivity, but at the expense of our countrymen. They revealed secrets. Betrayed trust. Stepped on the backs of the fallen to pull themselves up. Lord Hanamel had that kind of dark cloud hanging over him, though no one ever dared accuse him outright.

I watched him settle in his chair like a potentate, fastidiously brushing the table with the edge of his napkin. As though you could find a speck of dust on Mahlah's furnishings!

"How is your Joseph?" Daniel asked. "He must be almost seven."

"God has cursed me with a stupid child," Hanamel said coldly.

"Surely not!" Daniel sounded shocked. "I saw him only last month. He seemed bright as a summer's day. Why, he even quoted some Hebrew Scripture Jared had taught him."

"Boy can't even speak a sentence in Aramaic without stuttering ten times. Forget Hebrew."

Mahlah's serene face grew blank. Daniel covered his wife's hand with his own. "A childhood affliction," he said with an easy smile.

"He's old enough to outgrow it. The boy simply refuses, in spite of all my efforts to correct him."

"Ah. But you and I are men of the court, Hanamel. We are trained for sophisticated matters of the world, not the affairs of children. They need a different kind of expertise. Azarel is a marvel in such matters. Why, he helped Johanan outgrow a similar affliction."

"He did?"

"Indeed. In fact, I have a proposition for you. With Johanan and Jared out of the tablet house, Abel spends too much time alone. He still requires two years of training. It would be a great help to me if you sent Joseph over to the tablet house. Azarel can easily divide his time between the two boys. And I am certain Abel will enjoy the companionship of the little fellow. He has always been the youngest in the tablet house. He will relish the chance to play big brother for a change."

The conversation stopped for a beat as a servant carried in trays of drinks. As a rule, with the evening meal, we drank weak beer served with long straws to avoid the barley hulls floating to the surface. Grapes did not grow in the harsh climate of Babylon, making wine and raisins extremely expensive. But in honor of Hanamel, Mahlah served wine, poured into cups carved out of thin alabaster decorated with silver.

Hanamel took a sip and curled his lip, as if he found the contents dissatisfying. "I will think on your offer, Daniel."

"Thank you, Hanamel. Indeed, consider allowing Joseph to remain with us for three months. That will give Azarel more time to work with him."

"Three months, you say? Living here?"

"At my expense, of course."

Another sip, this one longer. "I will let you know what I decide."

I saw Jared's hand turn into a tight fist. I knew he longed to pull Joseph out from under the shadow of his father. Daniel's offer was an answer to prayer. But only if Lord Hanamel accepted.

The talk turned to Jared and Johanan's work as canal supervisors, and we laughed when Johanan admitted to falling into the river on his first day while trying to impress his comrades with his dexterity.

"You must be pleased with Jared's accomplishment," Daniel said to Hanamel. "It's rare for a young man his age to attain such a position."

"What is there to be pleased about?" Hanamel sneered. "Canal supervisor! At his age, I was a proper courtier, eating regularly at the king's table."

Daniel's smile faded. "Those were different days, Hanamel. A different time."

"So you say. Yet you were younger than my son when you rose so high. You need not excuse his failures to me. They are before me every hour."

Jared had turned ashen. Though this was far from the first time that Hanamel had belittled his son in our presence, it never became easy.

I drew my new shawl close about me, caressing the soft wool. What I really wanted was to caress Jared's back, wrapping my arms around him and never letting go. No doubt such an outrage would have toppled Hanamel right off his royal rump.

What a pleasure that would have been to watch. Under the cover of the tablecloth, I stretched to give Jared's fist a quick, reassuring squeeze.

* * *

A week later, Jared arrived at Daniel's house in time for dinner. Clutching his arm was his little brother, Joseph. Lord Hanamel had decided to allow him to stay at Daniel and Mahlah's house for three months.

"My father's youngest wife is with child," Jared shared as we enjoyed our vegetable and lentil stew. "He had given up hope of ever having another son. Now he is convinced she will bear him one."

"Congratulations!" Mahlah said, who always perked up when she heard news of a coming babe.

Johanan groaned. "Another younger brother. You have my sympathy."

Abel cuffed him on the shoulder, making us laugh.

"I have been blessed with this one." Jared wrapped an arm around his little brother. "I am sure another will bring even more joy." Handing Joseph a piece of bread, he added, "The important thing is that this news convinced my father to part with Joseph for a few months. With a new child coming, his focus has shifted elsewhere."

Abel leaned toward Joseph. "Well, whatever the reason, I am glad you are moving in. We will show these two louts what younger brothers are made of, won't we?"

Joseph squirmed as he became the focus of everyone's attention. "Y-y-y-yes." His face turned crimson as he stumbled over the simple word.

Mahlah leaned toward the boy. "Good answer. Now, why is your bowl empty?"

As Joseph realized that no one would punish or diminish him in this household because his tongue stuttered, the tense line of his back loosened.

Watching him, Jared beamed with pleasure. I leaned close to his ear. "You're a good big brother." He squirmed with the same fidgety movements as Joseph, and though he was not a little boy, I found it just as endearing.

* * *

It was a month before Johanan and Jared joined the tablet house again. A festival celebrating Marduk, the city god of Babylon, had provided them with a free day. After Azarel's lecture on Sumerian literature, they decided to unwind with a bit of sword practice, while Joseph remained in the tablet house so he could receive special tuition from Azarel.

My face felt hot as we walked to the armory. I rarely spoke to Jared these days, catching only brief glimpses of him during morning prayers. He never lingered with me, dashing away to some assignment or another as soon as Daniel blessed us for the day. When he could, he joined us for dinner in order to spend time with Joseph. Even then, he often had to cut his time short.

"Shall we use real swords today?" Jared suggested.

I frowned. This was a new side to my old friend. Of the four of us, he was usually the most cautious, thinking through his every decision with care. Jared and Johanan sometimes used real swords, but only when they were alone. They never included Abel or me, since both of us lacked their skill and experience.

Abel leapt in the air. "Yes!" He hated our wooden practice swords.

I shrugged. I had used a real sword while going through basic exercises by myself. I felt familiar enough with the weight and balance of the metal to enter into the fray with these wide-shouldered men. "I can keep up," I said, trying to sound confident.

Jared handed me the lightest sword in the armory, a thick blade made of bronze. "With me," he said, and I grinned.

Johanan grabbed a double-edged sword, blade shimmering with fresh oil, and handed another to Abel. "You two—" he pointed the weapon's tip at Abel and me—"keep your proper distance, and watch your footwork."

Abel laughed. "I scare you, do I?"

"I mean it. We break all manner of rules when we use the wooden swords. You can't do that with these. Mind your distance. One mistake, and you aren't merely going to have a bruise. You will need needle and thread."

Jared led me through a simple warm-up routine, blades up, down, at an angle, knees bending, thrusting forward, moving back, and beginning again. Finally, we were ready to engage.

Balance and timing required all our focus. In order to block Jared's attacks, I had to watch his every move and keep enough distance so that the tip of my sword did not draw too close to Jared's fingers.

"Halt!" Johanan cried, and we all took a step away. He sprinted to the corner of the courtyard and I realized why he had stopped the practice. Deborah and her sister, Zebidah, had stopped by unannounced.

Johanan's cheeks turned the pink of spring blossoms as he faced his betrothed, making me grin. Zebidah walked toward us slowly, curves swaying, her tight red and gold tunic accentuating every movement.

She pressed her fingers delicately to her nose, an old Babylonian greeting. "Hail, Jared," she said, leaving the rest of us out.

Jared nodded. Johanan sauntered our way, his fingers wrapped around Deborah's. "Shall we call it a day?"

I was about to put the sword away when Zebidah spoke. "No, please! I was enjoying watching you spar. Do go on for a little longer."

At Deborah's smiling nod, Johanan picked up his sword again, and I faced Jared once more. The way Zebidah smirked at me made me determined to prove my skill. I might not walk on heels and shake my hips like a tambourine. But I did know how to hold a sword.

I faced Jared, and once again, we began with the routine of basic exercises before slipping into spar form. Every once in a while, Zebidah would call out a word of encouragement with a tinkling laugh, and Jared's eyes would slide her way. I took a tiny step closer and another, determined to keep his attention on me.

Determined to keep his attention off her.

My back was to Abel and Johanan. Zebidah said something I did not catch. Jared grinned, his attention wavering from me. I took a determined step toward him, forgetting Johanan's caution about keeping a safe distance. Forgetting that I wielded a real sword.

I lifted the tip high, pointing at Jared's face, intending to wean his drifting eyes away from Zebidah and back to me.

Behind me, Johanan stumbled.

His tripping feet brought him backward and he collided into me. The force of his body, heavy with muscle and armor, caused me to lurch forward. Sword still raised, pointed at Jared's face.

I had violated the rules. Come too close. There was no safe distance between us. My body careened into Jared.

Bronze sword extended, unhampered.

CHAPTER TEN

I sink in deep mire,
where there is no foothold;
I have come into deep waters,
and the flood sweeps over me.
Psalm 69:2, ESV

In the tumble of that tiny, frozen moment, I had no time to change direction. No chance to turn the sword. It shoved its way into Jared's face with the force of Johanan's body added to that of my arm.

The bronze tip found Jared's left eye.

At the last moment, I managed to pull my arm back a fraction, enough to keep the sword from going all the way into the skull. But it was too late to shield Jared entirely.

The blade pierced his amber-colored iris.

Everything came to a standstill. Jared stood frozen, beyond pain, beyond response.

Slowly, his hand traveled to his face, covering his eye. Blood spurted between the fingers, mixing with pale liquid that flowed upon his cheek.

He screamed, a tortured sound of anguish forever tattooed in my mind. Falling to his knees, he bent over, keening.

The sisters were shrieking. Johanan had sprung to his friend's side, repeating his name over and over. Mahlah ran into the courtyard and dropped next to Jared.

"Send for Lord Daniel," she cried, addressing the watchman at the gate, for once beyond calm. "Tell him to bring the palace physician. Tell him to hurry."

I bent over and vomited, dropping the bloody sword from nerveless fingers.

"Come, my dear," Mahlah crooned to Jared. "Let us bring you inside where you can lie down."

Jared did not seem to hear or understand. He whimpered as Mahlah took his arm and raised him, Johanan on his other side. Fingers stained with blood hid his eye from me. But I did not have to see the injury to know what I had done.

I moaned and fell to my knees. If heaven had smitten me at that moment with a long shaft of lightning or a protracted plague, I would have been grateful. Grateful to stop the dawning torment of what I had done.

Whatever pale thread of hope I had held onto vanished when the palace physician came. Jared's screams must have carried all the way to the Hanging Gardens as the physician plied his wares on him.

Finally, Mahlah emerged, leaving Daniel to sit vigil at the sickbed. One look at her colorless face and I knew.

I collapsed, my face in the dirt, beyond words or tears or prayers.

"Come," Mahlah said and tried to raise me up.

I shook my head.

"You cannot stay here, Keren. His father will arrive any moment. He must not find you."

He would want to kill me, she meant. I raised my head, wild hope taking hold of me. "Let him! Please, mistress. Let him have his way."

"Get up, I say!" she shouted and pulled me up with a strength I had not suspected her of having. Before I knew it, she had dragged me into the bathing chamber and sat me in a dark corner.

Knees pressed to my chest, I crouched, trembling violently. Mahlah wet a towel and wiped my face and neck, her fingers unsteady. Our bodies knew the world had shifted, and there was no going back.

"Will he die?" I asked, teeth chattering.

"The physician does not think so."

I swallowed bitter bile. "Is he blind?"

Silence. Then, "In one eye. The other . . . may be saved."

"May?" I was shocked. The sword had only pierced one eye.

"If the wound does not become putrid and spread."

I felt as though someone were twisting my entrails and whimpered helplessly, a feral animal caught in a trap I could never escape.

The sound of shouting penetrated the closed door of the bathing chamber. An angry voice hollered.

Hanamel.

Through the fog that had descended over my mind, I made out Lord Hanamel's words. "Where is she? Where have you hidden her?"

Footsteps dashed in our direction, doors opening and banging shut. Daniel's voice reasoning. More hollering. Footsteps approaching the door of the bathing chamber.

Mahlah pressed me into the wall. "Stay!" she hissed, her face close. "Not a whisper. Not one fidget! Understand?"

I nodded, shocked into awareness by her unusual ferocity. Mahlah leapt toward the door. The single lamp in the middle of the chamber, which hid me in shadows, revealed her form. She loosened her hair and untied the corner of her shawl, looking for all the world as though she was preparing for a bath.

The door banged open. Hanamel stood at the threshold.

Seeing the vision of Mahlah, her hair in disarray, shawl undone, apparently silenced whatever words he meant to screech.

Mahlah drew herself up into the queenly posture she had perfected. Though she remained modestly attired, the outrage on her face accused the man of a thousand indiscretions.

"Lord Hanamel! I shall attribute this intrusion to your understandable agitation. Now, if you don't mind?" She gestured with her fingers for him to leave.

Hanamel took a hasty step back as the mistress shut the door in his astonished face. The shock of his unintentional encroachment upon Mahlah must have shaken him, for his steps receded more quietly than they had arrived, and soon we heard the front gate closing.

The mistress returned to my side. "He will come back, Keren. You must remain hidden until he has calmed."

"May I see Jared? Please?"

"His father arranged for him to be carried home. I am sorry. He is gone." She knotted her hair hastily at her nape and retied her shawl. "Come."

Numbly, I stumbled behind her as she led me to Daniel's chamber.

I stood and watched her pluck my folded pallet and blankets from the chest. She made my bed with her own hands, while I, offering no help, remained motionless, tears flowing hot and salty down my chin.

The mistress drew me gently onto the bed and, after untying my sandals, pressed my shoulders into the wool-stuffed mattress. "Poor child. Try to rest," she whispered as she pulled the blanket over my shivering form.

I curled on my side and did not answer.

* * *

Skinny and curved like an old Assyrian dagger, the moon was shining thriftily when I stole out of Daniel's chamber. I had visited Jared's house once before, when we had stopped there for provisions before an impromptu trip to the countryside with Master Azarel.

For all Hanamel's hauteur, the house was half the size of Daniel's, a brick-and-mortar reminder of its inhabitants' captivity rather than their grand bloodlines.

On that memorable visit over a year ago, I had not been allowed inside. But as I had waited in the narrow courtyard, Jared had hung out of a window to throw a cake of dates my way, and through the open shutters, I had had a glimpse of his chamber. I still remembered the exact location.

Midnight had come and gone by the time I arrived at the house. A prickly juniper tree stood sentinel outside the courtyard wall. I climbed it, scratching my face and arms in the inky darkness.

It was too far from the trunk to the wall. But one long branch hung over the edge. I crawled along its lanky length, hoping it would not snap under my weight, and dropped to the top of the wall.

With a quick shimmy of my hips, I was hanging over the courtyard by my fingertips. Letting go too quickly, I landed on the stones with a thump. My foot twisted under me awkwardly, and I swallowed a cry as pain shot up the side of my leg. Limping, I made my way to the window of Jared's chamber. I saw with relief that the shutters had been left open.

Another climb, another descent, and I found myself in the chamber I had always dreamed of visiting. Someone had left a small lamp burning on a table.

On a feather-stuffed bed lay a still figure, bandages wrapped tightly over one eye.

In the dim light, I could make out his features. The skin beneath his left eye was inflamed and red, screaming at me in angry accusation. In contrast, every other part of him had a bone-white cast, as if all the color in his body had leached into that tiny tract on his cheek.

His head lay unmoving on its Babylonian pillow, a delicate rectangle of ivory supported by four carved legs. I tiptoed to his side and sank to my knees. If my entrance had disturbed his sleep, he showed no sign of it. His chest rose and fell in an even, steady rhythm. I found myself counting each breath, clinging to the numbers as if they were life.

Perhaps I made a sound, my tunic rustling as I watched him. Or maybe my very presence disturbed him, like a dark shadow that chased into his dreams. His uninjured eye snapped open without warning. It widened as he saw me, and for a moment a veil of panic settled on his pale features.

"Jared!" My voice emerged a croak. I stared at him like a dying fish, my lips moving without sound.

"What are you doing here?" he asked coldly. For the first

time since the day I met him, I noticed Jared's resemblance to his father.

"I . . . I had to see you."

"Get out."

I straightened. "Jared, please!"

"I said leave, Keren! I don't want him to find you here."

I scooted closer. "Does it hurt?"

He drew his hand toward the bandage, fingers hovering in the air before dropping back on the bed. "Get out!" he whispered with a sudden vehemence that made the words sharper than a scream. "Get out!"

Leaping to my feet, I took several steps away. "I wish it had been me."

He went still. "Why, Keren?"

"I didn't mean to."

"Why were you so careless with my life?" A bitter laugh seemed torn from his throat. "But then, we both know the answer to that, don't we? Now leave, before they find you here."

"Forgive me," I begged.

"Forgive you?" He closed his eye. "You've ruined me."

CHAPTER ELEVEN

For thus says the LORD:
Your hurt is incurable,
and your wound is grievous.
Jeremiah 30:12

—————— JARED ——————

Pain shot through his eye socket and into his head. The ground, the ceiling, the walls, and everything that was the world spun from the intensity of it, so that he could barely breathe. It was as if the tip of Keren's sword returned again and again to pierce him, a hundred times a day.

The moment haunted him. That one unredeemable flash of metal and agony and blood and loss. Keren's irreversible decision.

The thought of Keren made him frown. Dreamlike, he recalled her face, here, in his room, kneeling by his side.

It was no dream, he realized.

She had snuck into his chamber sometime in the night. The

little fool. If his father had caught her here, she would have found herself blinded in a flash, just as he had been, thanks to the ancient Code of Hammurabi, the law that still ruled in Babylon. His father had been screaming for justice since he discovered the source of the accident.

Eye for an eye! Eye for an eye!

Not a religious code, subject to grace. But an unbreakable law. An unrelenting punishment.

Then it occurred to him that she had seen him. Like this, helpless in his bed. Weak, and blind, and ugly. He had ordered her to leave, he remembered, unable to bear the thought of her seeing him so diminished.

Broken.

Another memory came to haunt him. Her face crumpled, her hands held out in entreaty. *Forgive me.*

He recalled the words and felt heat spreading over his face. He had refused her the one consolation he could have offered her.

Another stab of pain brought him to the edge of oblivion but did not drop him over into its comfort. When it had passed, the pain left behind something cold and hard.

Why should he console her? She had robbed him of sight. Of future and hope. He would never be whole again. The one person he thought he could trust with his life! The one person he felt wholly safe with.

She had betrayed him.

His father's words reverberated through him, a fresh wound that ached every bit as badly as the empty socket in his head. *You are ruined. Good for nothing.*

That's what he was. A ruin.

Why should he forgive her that? Keren had stepped too close with her cursed sword because she had been jealous of Zebidah.

Another flash of memory haunted him for a moment. Keren limping to the window.

The fool. Had she injured her foot climbing into his room? Had she broken her ankle? He hoped someone had noticed and looked after her.

He grimaced. What did he care?

Another dart of pain pierced through his head, making him groan. Making him forget everything but his mounting misery.

CHAPTER TWELVE

Woe is me because of my hurt!
My wound is grievous.
But I said, "Truly this is an affliction,
and I must bear it."
Jeremiah 10:19, ESV

Daniel found me in his chamber, crouching in the corner of the room, cradled against the wall. I found solace in the cool touch of the brick, the only solid thing in a world that had turned into a stormy sea.

He knelt before me. "Come, child. Time to eat."

I looked at him, chiding him without words. How could he imagine that food held any appeal?

He understood my unspoken admonishment. Without comment, he left me, only to return bearing a cup. "No food, then. But you must drink."

I opened my mouth and let him pour something warm and sweet down my throat. He covered me with a blanket and tucked the corners in, anchoring them against the wall behind me.

"Hanamel is claiming the Code of Hammurabi. He says Jared wants justice."

I stared at him, not comprehending.

"*Eye for an eye*. He is threatening to go to the king with his complaint."

Comprehension dawned. "He deserves it," I said, eyes filling with tears. I felt those tears tickle two eyes, spill from two lids, and watched my master through two lenses. All the things I had taken from Jared. "I owe it to him. Please take me to Lord Hanamel that I may pay my debt."

"Keren, this is no time to make rash decisions. We must allow for time to heal Jared. Heart, body, and soul. Time for tempers to cool. For now, you are to remain here. Don't leave the house. Not even to step into the courtyard. Hanamel has set men to watch my home and your father's, also."

"My father?" I asked, shaken. "You told him?"

"I did. Your parents would be here now, except we do not want to draw Hanamel's attention. It would only boil his ire if he thought they had come to bring you solace."

I thought of the river of misery I had brought to my family and covered my face with my hands. "Please. Bring me to Lord Hanamel so he can do what he wishes."

"No! I forbid it, Keren. We must wait. Lord Hanamel may yet change his mind. Promise you will abide by my will."

I dropped my hands. "I blinded my best friend."

"I know. I am sorry. It was a terrible accident. Now we must do what we can to bring healing to everyone concerned."

"There is no healing for Jared."

"There are many forms of healing. More important even than an eye." He dropped a scroll into my lap. It was encased in silver filigree. "These are the prophecies of the prophet

Jeremiah. I have been waiting for this copy for a year. It arrived today from a relative of Baruch's, the scribe who took them down originally. Read through them as you wait."

I placed the scroll on the floor beside me.

* * *

The hours curled into each other, growing muddled and indistinguishable. Day and night lost their order as I hid in Daniel's chamber, Jared's words echoing in my mind. *You've ruined me.* Now he wanted me blinded. Like a knife in my flesh, that demand twisted and twisted. I had to leave this room. I had to pay my debt to Jared! But Daniel would not allow it.

When he returned to see me, I jumped to my feet. Not bothering with a greeting, I cried, "Our own Scriptures demand it! *If anyone injures his neighbor, as he has done it shall be done to him, fracture for fracture, eye for eye, tooth for tooth*," I quoted.

Daniel did not even blink. Smooth as butter, he countered, "Moses also said, *You shall not take vengeance or bear a grudge against the sons of your own people, but you shall love your neighbor as yourself.* This is not the Code of Hammurabi, Keren. It's the Word of God, and it always makes provision for grace."

"I should know better than to try and best you with Scripture," I said bitterly, collapsing back against the wall.

Daniel crouched before me, his embroidered tunic bunching at his knees. "I saw Jared this morning. He seems better. Stronger. The wound has not gone putrid, which means he will not lose his sight in the other eye."

I jerked my head into a nod.

"He told me he has no desire to pursue vengeance against you, Keren. He never did. He is not claiming the Code of Hammurabi."

"He is not?"

"Not at all. That is his father's doing."

A small weight lifted from my chest. I felt like I had gone from drowning in an ocean to drowning in a pool. But I was still drowning.

* * *

That evening, Johanan slipped into my room, looking disheveled and pale. He sat on the floor, legs knotted into two long triangles. "It's my fault too," he said. "If I hadn't tripped, if I hadn't knocked into you, it wouldn't have happened."

His misery drew me out of mine. "It is not your fault," I said, my voice heated. "If I had kept the proper distance, you could have knocked into me and I would still have managed to divert the sword."

He slashed a hand into the air. "Even if you had the reflexes of a gazelle, a hard knock would have pushed you too far, too fast. I share this blame."

I pulled my knees tighter into my chest. "Have you seen him?"

Johanan nodded. "He is better. The injury is healing well, God be thanked. We have been praying for him night and day."

I had been praying myself, though I doubted that the jumble of my desperate supplications counted for much. "That is good news."

"Keren." Johanan leaned toward me, his shoulders a rigid bar. "You must leave here."

"Leave?" It dawned on me that Daniel and Mahlah must want to be rid of me. I had brought trouble upon their household. Hanamel was not a man to let go of his grievances easily.

"Of course." I heaved myself up and turned to gather my things. "I will leave your house at once."

Jared is not satisfied, I will tell him where you are, and he can come and fetch you back himself."

I felt like someone had pulled my spine out of my back. With a wobble, I collapsed on the floor. "Banishment?"

Johanan pulled a hand through his hair. He nodded once. "It's the only way to save you. I am trying to arrange it now."

"Where?"

"I will tell you once I know for certain." He knelt and grasped my hands. "Keren, I believe Jared will one day forgive you. I believe it with all my heart. He only needs time to remember."

"Remember what?"

"Remember who you are. His dearest friend."

I pulled my hands out of his. My sword had severed everything that had once knit me to Jared.

Johanan's crack about remorse had stung me. After years of studying the Scriptures with Daniel, it surprised me how few of them I could remember. Grief had wiped them from my mind like a flood cresting upon the sands of my memory, erasing the words that had once comforted and guided me.

For the first time, I picked up the scroll Daniel had entrusted to my keeping. The prophecies of Jeremiah, the son of Hilkiah the priest. At the time, I had not appreciated Daniel's generosity in leaving his new book with me. He already owned a scroll containing a small selection of Jeremiah's prophecies. But he had wanted to get his hands on the full collection for as long as I had known him.

And now, having finally received the scroll, he had left it with me, like an unopened invitation.

Slowly, I unrolled the crisp, new papyrus. My hand slipped and the scroll unfurled further than I had intended. My eyes fell upon the Hebrew words:

> *But I said, "Truly this is an affliction,*
> *and I must bear it."*

My breath hitched. I felt as if the Lord himself had placed these words into my hands. As if he wanted me to know that he understood my affliction. And he was telling me that I must bear the burden of it. The ache of it. That I must learn to endure. Like Jeremiah did.

I read on, and the next sentence made me drop the scroll.

My home is gone.

CHAPTER THIRTEEN

My times are in your hand;
rescue me from the hand of my enemies and from my persecutors!
Psalm 31:15, ESV

"Media?" I gasped. "That . . . that's on the other side of the world!"

"Not quite so far." Johanan's lip tipped up. "On the other side of the Zagros Mountains, certainly. Babylon's queen is from Media. Ecbatana, the capital city of the Medes, is famed for its beauty."

In a sudden rush I remembered my visit to the Hanging Gardens and how I had thought that I would never see so exotic a land as that. "Who is this Harpagus?"

"He is a nobleman in the court of Astyages, king of the Medes. He travels to Babylon quite often, which is how my father knows him. In fact, he has been a guest in our home. His current visit is a short one. He has come to deliver a few of Media's fine horses to the queen as a birthday gift from her brother." Johanan straightened a clay tablet on his father's desk. "He is a good man, Keren. He won't mistreat you."

"Lord Daniel . . ."

"Cannot know. Once it is discovered that you are gone, Hanamel is sure to blame my father. He must be innocent of all wrongdoing when he is questioned. And if he does not know your location, he cannot reveal it."

I hung my head. "He will think I repaid his kindness by abandoning my work. I may not be a slave, but I owe him my lifelong service."

"He will want you safe, Keren. Both my parents do. They would approve of this scheme, I assure you, or I would not undertake it."

I tried to swallow past the swelling knot in my throat. Johanan wanted to bundle me off to a faraway land with a man I had never met. Save for a few basic words, I could not even speak the language. All my years of study, all the languages I could navigate my way around, and I had never considered learning Median.

"Will I be a slave?"

"No! A servant, as you were here. When I spoke to Harpagus, he assured me that you will be free to leave if you choose."

"What use can he possibly have for me?"

Johanan tapped the top of the desk with two fingers. "You will serve him as you served my father, I assume."

"It will be a challenge, considering I speak no Median."

"Scribes with a fluent knowledge of Akkadian are sought after, even in Media. You will learn their tongue quickly enough. Besides, Harpagus speaks Aramaic."

"When is he leaving Babylon?"

Johanan hesitated for a beat. "Tomorrow."

I had been sitting in my favorite corner. At that final pronouncement, I sprang to my feet. "*Tomorrow? Are you mad?*"

"The day after that, Hanamel is due to have an audience with the king. You must be gone before then."

"But . . . but, Johanan! I haven't even seen my parents since I injured Jared! Daniel will not allow them near this place. You want me to go away without taking my leave of them? Without . . ." I choked, thinking of their vine-like arms, clinging to me with love.

Johanan held up a hand. "We must slip you out of this house without being noticed. I will send your parents a message to meet us outside the city walls. You can speak to them before joining Harpagus's train."

"How can I sneak out of here without being seen?"

"With some ingenuity."

That night, Daniel and Mahlah came to bid me good night and pray for me, a habit they had established since the accident. Aware this might be the last time I ever saw them, I sat mute with misery, a tight band of pain crushing my chest. The uncertainty of my future took on a new reality, like the utter darkness of night that follows a bleeding sunset.

They might not be aware of Johanan's scheme, but Daniel and Mahlah knew Lord Hanamel's intentions. Daniel's forehead had turned into a permanent gnarl of lines. Even Mahlah's usually unflappable expression was more empty than serene, as if she had pulled a curtain to hide behind.

"Keren, this business is not going away. Lord Hanamel is still frothing at the mouth."

I nodded. "I ruined his son. It's understandable."

"Jared is not ruined!" Daniel expelled an exasperated breath and presented me with his back. He stood unmoving for a long while. Then squaring his shoulders, he faced me again.

"Our great ancestor, Jacob, became lame. By the hand of

God's own angel. That infirmity never stopped him from fulfilling God's will for his life. I would hardly call Jacob a ruin. Jared is blind in one eye. But the Lord's plans for his life remain as firm as ever. Does that sound like a ruin?"

I shook my head. Daniel saw the world through a unique lens. He had known of a dream before anyone shared it with him. He had seen his friends walk into a furnace of fire and emerge whole. He had spoken to an angel and glimpsed into future mysteries. His perception of life had been shaped by these things. The rest of us ordinary mortals bore the fiery arrows the world hurled at us and sank in defeat. He always found his way to hope.

I would miss this man.

His eyes narrowed. "God's plans for you are not vanquished either, Keren." He rubbed his hands together with sudden vigor. "Not at all. In fact . . ." The lines on his face smoothed out. "In fact, you remind me of myself."

"You, lord?"

Mahlah regarded her husband with a strange stillness.

"I was seventeen when Nebuchadnezzar took me amongst the first wave of captives to Babylon. Young and full of glorious plans for my life. None of them included living in a palace full of idols. When the rest of my countrymen were allowed to remain in Judah, I had to navigate my way around serving a Gentile king. I thought my future a wreck. Yet the Lord had guided my steps here. He had intended that I be here at this time in our history.

"He has a special call on your life, also, Keren. I have always felt it. Your path to that call may be hard. At times grueling. But trust me when I tell you that your mistake has not destroyed God's ability to fulfill his will in your life."

He laid his hands on my head, joined by Mahlah's soft fingers, and prayed for me. Before leaving that night, Daniel bent and, for the first time in our acquaintance, kissed me on the crown of my head. Mahlah embraced me in trembling arms, her eyes shimmering in the lamplight.

As I watched them leave, I brooded over Daniel's conviction that God still had a plan for my life. I had longed to be a wife and a mother. But that longing had set its roots in Jared, and so I had not watered it. Why grow a desire that could never be? I had assumed God had called me to help Daniel for the rest of my life. Now that, too, had been taken away. There was no purpose left for me.

* * *

Although most Babylonians threw their garbage into the streets, a small portion of Babylon's residents maintained more fastidious habits. In Daniel's house, for example, we collected our rubbish in a large, old basket with a lid and once a week carried it to a heap outside the city.

At suppertime, Johanan told his father that he would empty the garbage the following morning, since the hill used as a trash heap was on his way. Although this was not a chore usually assigned to him, Johanan had a habit of offering help in the house, and as such, his suggestion did not raise any eyebrows.

Early the next morning, before anyone had roused from sleep, Johanan slipped into Lord Daniel's chamber and threw a ragged sheet at me.

"What's this?"

"Your disguise."

I held my bundle of belongings against my belly as Johanan wrapped the sheet around me loosely, covering me from head to feet. He then had me sit, squeezed into a tight ball, head shoved into knees, arms knotted together, making myself as small as possible.

Wrapping his arms around me, Johanan picked me up and carried me out of the room as if I were a heap of old fabric.

My body protested against this uncomfortable ride, but not nearly so much as when Johanan shoved me into the basket of collected garbage, adding another load of foul-smelling rubbish over my head. The smell of rotting fish bones and entrails nearly gagged me, and I squawked.

"Hush," Johanan ordered in a loud whisper.

The basket was lifted and placed on the back of a tiny two-wheeled handcart, barely wide enough to accommodate it. If Johanan hit a large bump, he would end up spilling me and the garbage into the street. Which might not be a bad ending, considering the stench that surrounded me. My arms were wrapped so tightly about me, I could not even loosen them enough to cover my nose. Helplessly, I tried to draw breath into my lungs as Johanan started to pull the cart. It struck me as apt that I should leave my master's house hidden with the refuse.

I was dizzy and sore by the time we passed through the glazed blue tiles of the Ishtar Gate, and emerged onto the street the king had named Aibur-shabu, "the enemy shall never pass." Another bone-jarring ride brought us to the trash heap, where to my eternal relief, Johanan spilled the basket's contents gently on the ground, and I came rolling out. Hands helped untangle the sheet from around me. I thought them Johanan's. But when I had shoved the hair out of my eyes, I saw two beloved faces a moment before I was swallowed up in embraces.

My Imma and Abba.

CHAPTER FOURTEEN

"For I know the plans I have for you," declares the LORD, "plans to prosper
you and not to harm you, plans to give you hope and a future."

Jeremiah 29:11, ESV

I was an inarticulate limpet clinging to them, my tears mingling with theirs. After a long, wordless embrace, I stood back. "Grandfather?"

My mother shook her head. "Too far for him to walk, Keren. He could not keep up."

I pressed a shivering hand over my mouth to silence the sobs that wanted to erupt. *Grandfather!* To leave without seeing him almost broke my heart. His fragile health meant that I might never see him again.

"And we could not bring the others," Father added. "That might have tipped off Lord Hanamel's watchers that we were on our way to you. As it was, we had to leave separately to keep them off our scent."

I nodded. "I am grateful to see you both." Turning to Johanan, I added, "Thank you for making it possible."

Johanan rubbed the back of his neck. "I have done little enough. I will arrange for someone to carry letters between you. Hopefully this exile is of short duration. Lord Hanamel will forget about his revenge, and you will be able to return to us quietly."

"Please, God!" My mother drew me back into her arms.

"I stink," I said.

My mother smiled. "I shall not soon forget the sight of you rolling out with the trash. Come. Let us wash you in the river lest your new master be tempted to make you a swineherd."

Father's horrified stare tugged a grin out of me, though my heart felt like a stone sinking under the waves. Mother and I slipped to the riverbank and did our best to wash the stench of moldy garbage from me. I returned shivering and wet, but at least smelling human rather than of dead fish.

We rushed through our final goodbyes as Johanan urged me to hurry. I was still weeping when we navigated our way east to meet with my new master's train. Just before arriving at our destination, Johanan pushed his handcart to the side of the road.

"I forgot. I have something for you." He handed me a small jingling bag. "It isn't much. But it will help you in a crisis."

"I cannot take your silver."

"For my peace of mind, you must. It would be madness to send you to Media with empty pockets. If you need help, write me. I will do what I can to come to your aid."

I shook my head. "I am too much in your debt already, Johanan. I shall never be able to repay you."

"Nonsense. You are like a sister to me." He snapped his fingers. "You will also need this." He retrieved a thick fold of fabric, which he had tucked under a narrow shelf in the handcart.

"What is it?"

"My old winter cloak. Ecbatana is much colder than Babylon. Even now, in late spring, you will find the nights chilly."

I took a step back. "No, Johanan. Keep your cloak. I have my shawl."

"That will hardly see you through the spring. It snows there in winter, knee-deep at times, I am told."

"Knee-deep?" I squealed. I had never seen snow in the flat, sandy plains of Babylon, though the old Babylonians claimed that once, in the days of their youth, there had been a squall that had covered the city in a blanket of white. The flakes had melted by the following day and never returned.

Johanan pushed the gray cloth toward me. "Which is why you need this cloak. Besides, I have a new one."

Under the circumstances, I could not afford to cling to the remnants of my pride. I would freeze in the snow-covered heights of Ecbatana. I received the thick fold of wool and slipped it under my woefully small bundle.

"I have something for you, too." I offered Johanan the clay tablet I had made him, tucked snugly in its thin earthen envelope. "An early wedding gift."

I had worked on the tablet for over a month, since Johanan and Deborah's betrothal had first been formalized. It was a copy of the Shema, written in Hebrew, and painted with gold and silver detailing. Daniel had allowed me to take on a few extra jobs from the palace to pay for the expense of the paint.

Good thing it had been completed before the accident, or I would have nothing to offer Johanan now. I had been a useless mess over the past ten days, my hands shaking worse than Grandfather's.

Johanan's inscrutable expression cracked as he opened the

envelope, and for a moment his eyes glittered in the light of the rising sun. "It is beautiful, Keren."

I held out a papyrus scroll to him. It lacked a seal, since I did not possess one. Instead, I had simply rolled it tightly and tied it carefully with a length of blue ribbon. "This one is for Jared."

Johanan took the scroll.

"He'll probably throw it in the fire, unread. But I had to try. Give it to him when you think he can . . . bear to look at it." My voice trembled worse than my hands. I hoped Johanan would put it down to my battle with guilt and not suspect my true feelings for Jared.

This might be my greatest punishment. Being forced to leave without seeing Jared one last time. I felt something in me unravel at the thought, like a braid coming undone. Dropping my head, I hid my tears from Johanan.

Then, pasting a smile on my face, I said, "Shall we? I best not be late for my new master."

* * *

Harpagus's athletic bearing shouted military training. But something about the exquisite formality with which he greeted us marked him a courtier as well as a warrior.

I bowed as Daniel had taught me, addressed him as lord, and tried to display Daniel's influence on my manners. I expected him to inquire about my training or test my knowledge. Instead, he merely asked in heavily accented Aramaic, "Can you ride?"

"No, master."

The corner of his thin mouth quirked upward. "You'll learn. We saved you a mule."

He signaled one of his men to lead a brown mule with white

forelegs to my side. I had never noticed how big mules were. Now, standing next to one and knowing I would have to ride it all the way to another kingdom, the beast appeared enormous.

Johanan rubbed the mule's neck. It turned its face into Johanan's shoulder and bumped him gently. "He's a friendly one."

"You think so?" I asked hopefully.

"Stay away from his backside, show him you aren't scared, and you will get along fine."

"I may have a small problem with that bit about not being scared."

Harpagus, who had been whispering with one of his men, came over to us. "My men are ready. We will be leaving in a few moments. Say your goodbyes."

For a moment, I felt a wave of panic. Harpagus had seven men riding with him. I would be the only woman in their midst. I threw an alarmed look at Johanan. Perhaps I should take my chances with Jared's father. At least I knew the evils that awaited me at home. This flight into the unknown seemed entirely foolhardy.

As if reading my thoughts, Johanan bent forward and looped his hands. Without thinking, I pressed my foot into the cradle of his fingers, and he threw me over the beast's back. Grabbing the bridle, he handed the worn leather to me.

"The Lord watch over you, Keren. I will write you as soon as I can."

Helplessly, I gazed on as the final cord to my old life severed when Johanan walked away, his tall form disappearing in the bend of the road that led to Babylon.

I was now truly alone.

Harpagus adjusted the straps on his felt saddlecloth and,

grabbing his stallion's withers, mounted with a great leap. He sat the chestnut with the comfort of one who had spent endless hours on the back of a horse.

Though I could not ride, Azarel had educated me alongside my classmates on the fundamentals of good horseflesh. My new master's horse was a Nisaean, the most highly regarded breed in all the world. Only the truly wealthy could afford them.

The magnificent Nisaean horses had for centuries been raised and trained by the Medes. The whole world clamored for the steeds of Media, many of which found their way to Babylon. But the Nisaean line, taller, swifter, and stronger than their smaller cousins, fetched the greatest price.

Harpagus guided his horse next to my mule. Wordlessly, he adjusted the reins in my hands.

"Do you speak any Median?" he asked me.

"No, my lord." To drive the point home, I added, "Not one word." I hoped he would be so disappointed by that news, he would send me home.

Instead, he pointed to the sky and told me the Median word for it. He corrected my pronunciation and taught me the word for stallion. I was learning the word for clouds when we began our journey toward the city of Ecbatana.

Harpagus traveled simply, lacking the cartloads of baggage I had seen other courtiers lug about. He had a mule train for his gear, which he pressed at a good clip over the Royal Road. Just before sunset, the road split, and we took the branch leading northeast, into the passes of the Zagros Mountains. By the time we stopped for the night, I felt dizzy with exhaustion. For hours, I had bounced on my saddlecloth like a sack of old apples, stopping only when Harpagus called short breaks to rest the animals.

His men unpacked plain tents and set up a small one for me next to Harpagus's larger one. He traveled like a soldier, I realized. Ambulatory and simple. With my bundle shoved under an arm, I crawled into my tent and, for the first time in ten days, fell into a deep, dreamless sleep.

Pain awakened me in the morning. Every muscle, joint, bone, and freckle hurt. Groaning, I grabbed my bundle to search for a washcloth. I frowned when I noticed a fat scroll of papyrus. I gasped with horror. It was the new Jeremiah scroll, the one Daniel had acquired recently.

I must have mistakenly shoved it into my bundle the night I had packed. How could I have been so careless? I was relieved to note that its light silver cover had protected the papyrus from getting damaged.

A small scrap had been tucked into a seam of the silver cover.

Curiously, I tugged it loose and instantly recognized Daniel's writing. When had he concealed this note inside my jumble of things? Then it dawned on me. Daniel must have known I would be leaving!

My daughter, Keren,

Let the words of the prophet accompany you on your journey. May they serve as a reminder of our love for you. Cling to God, and let him lead you. Remember, he has not forsaken you, and neither have we. Wherever your journey leads you, know that our God safeguards a future and a hope for you.

I pressed the note to my heart and felt the weight of terror lift.

CHAPTER FIFTEEN

If we are thrown into the blazing furnace, the God we serve is able to deliver us from it, and he will deliver us from Your Majesty's hand. But even if he does not, we want you to know, Your Majesty, that we will not serve your gods.
Daniel 3:17-18, NIV

JARED

While everyone slept, Jared slipped out of his own home like a thief. Tired of his father's fits of anger, his incessant demands for vengeance, and his bitter threats, Jared longed for a few hours of calm. His father's rages only served to keep his loss constantly before him.

To add insult to injury, Lord Hanamel had banned Daniel and his sons from visiting Jared, closing off the only source of sanity in his capsized life.

Like a homing pigeon, he headed for the one place that offered him comfort. In the predawn darkness, he made his way to Daniel's house.

He hoped he would not run into Keren by accident. He was

not ready to see her. According to his father, Lord Daniel had hidden her somewhere in his house, refusing to bring her out even when the king himself had demanded it. Though relieved to know her safe from his father's clutches, he had no desire for an encounter with her.

Perversely, as the sleepy servant accompanied him into Daniel's chamber, he felt a sharp pang of disappointment to find the room empty, with no trace of Keren in sight.

Daniel wrapped him in a warm embrace as soon as he came into the room. "How are you?" he asked.

"Better, now that I am here."

"How is the pain?"

Jared shrugged. "Sometimes bearable. Sometimes . . ." He shrugged again.

"It has only been three weeks. Give it time. We are praying for you."

"Yes." It was hard to explain to a man like Daniel that pain eroded the roots of faith; it ate away at the fabric of hope.

"You have hidden Keren?" The words slipped out before he could recall them.

"No."

Jared felt a frisson of alarm. "No?"

"I know what your father believes. But she is not here, Jared. The king's men have already searched the place."

A shard of pain twisted in Jared's temple and he winced. "I am glad she is safe from my father."

Daniel remained silent.

"She *is* safe?"

"I do not know where she is."

"Her parents?"

A quick shake of the head. "She is not with them."

Jared rubbed his temple. "Where can she be?"

"I do not know. But my guess is that she has left Babylon."

Jared sank slowly into a chair. "Left Babylon?"

"As long as your father thirsts for revenge, she cannot be safe here."

"But where has she gone? She knows no one but you and her family."

Daniel touched the carved deer at the end of his walking stick, which leaned against his work table. "I suppose that means she is amongst strangers."

"She's all alone?"

"I did not say that."

"Who went with her?"

"The Lord, our God."

A strange sound escaped Jared's throat. He pointed to the eye patch covering his empty eye socket. "The one who allowed this, you mean."

Daniel gave him an unflinching stare. "The same."

"That's not very reassuring, Daniel."

"I told you that you would face your own fiery furnace one day. If you want a taste of reassurance, you have to begin where Hananiah, Mishael, and Azariah began."

"And where is that?"

"*But even if he doesn't . . .*"

Jared shook his head, confused. "I don't know what you mean."

"That morning, when they were dragged before the king, they told him that our God was able to save them from his hand. But they did not stop there. They went on. *Even if he doesn't*, they said, hanging their lives on the hook of possible disappointment.

"Where do you draw the line for God, Jared? Even if he does not take away this pain? Even if he does not restore your independence, your strength, your health? Will you still choose him, even if? Choose him every day?"

Daniel picked up his walking stick. "Because if you want reassurance, then you have to sort out your *even-ifs*."

Jared swallowed. The problem with spending time with Daniel was that sometimes you got slapped instead of coddled.

PART TWO

Ecbatana

CHAPTER SIXTEEN

Then Jacob awoke from his sleep and said, "Surely the
LORD is in this place, and I did not know it."
Genesis 28:16, ESV

On the high slopes of the rugged Zagros Mountains, I saw snow for the first time in my life. Like the fleece of a thousand lambs, it covered the gray shelves of rock and transformed their sharp edges into something soft and pristine.

Riding through the passes in the mountains as we climbed ever higher, I spent my time learning Median and memorizing the book of Jeremiah. I found myself huddling in the folds of Johanan's old cloak, grateful for its warmth as our route took us into icy elevations. My Babylonian-trained flesh, accustomed to soaring temperatures in the spring, shivered to find what felt like the depths of winter instead.

I became slowly familiar with Harpagus and his men. They treated their horses as friends and, when the terrain allowed, entered into friendly races against one another. They kept their beasts' manes cropped but every morning combed the long forelocks with such tenderness, you would think they were braiding a sweetheart's tresses, festooning the horsehair with bright-colored ribbons. Their horses owned more ribbons than I ever had.

Though the men ignored me for the most part, after a few days they began to extend a distant civility bordering on courtesy. They offered me a share of the roasted rabbit and dry bread instead of expecting me to grab it for myself and gave me the first turn in the woods.

My body, pressed to the limit by the unfamiliar activity of long, daily rides, grew so exhausted by the end of the day that for the first time since the accident, I started sleeping well at night. Even my thoughts became clearer.

Jared was never far from my mind. But memories of him no longer crippled me. What I discovered was that although the healing of my shattered heart remained a long way off, I could press on with life. I had no joy. No taste of happiness. But I could function.

It took us three weeks to arrive at the lands belonging to the Medes. By then, I had made peace with my mule and even learned to enjoy its constant bids for affection. Like a toddler, that beast demanded to be petted at every turn.

As we entered Media, the plains grew verdant with forests and the air bright and crisp. Then, trees gave way to waving grasses. Fields of clover and alfalfa dotted with wildflowers and shallow brooks stretched before us as far as the eye could see. No wonder Nebuchadnezzar's queen missed home. The Hanging Gardens had found their inspiration here in this green place of rolling hills and rivers.

On our last day, the meadows turned into orchards bursting

with pink and white blossoms as we approached Media's capital, the ancient city of Ecbatana.

The city had been built on a gentle hill at the foot of Mount Alvand. I had thought Babylon's two rows of walls and deep moat an imposing defense. Ecbatana boasted *seven* concentric walls wrapped around the heart of the city. Each circuit of massive wall had been built of mud bricks at gradually elevating heights, so that the tops of all seven walls were visible upon approach.

It made for a dramatic welcome, especially since the battlements of each wall had been painted a different color: white for the one closest to the road, then black, followed by scarlet, blue, and orange. The final two battlements had been gilded with silver and gold. I stopped my mule for a moment and stared as we approached the first set of gates.

A village had sprung up just outside the city to accommodate farmers, artisans, servants, and other residents who could not afford the prices of the expensive homes built within the city proper. The ordinary folk could easily take shelter within Ecbatana if the enemy ever chose to attack. With seven walls and a mountain to protect them, the residents of the Median capital must feel safe, indeed.

As we rode past the gates and filed by seven different sets of guards, it dawned on me that my new master was a man of greater influence than I had realized. The guards treated him like royalty. Even his large stone and mud-brick house sat within view of the domed ceiling of the palace, as if proclaiming its master's favor with the king.

Upon our arrival, Harpagus handed me off to his wife, who handed me off to a housekeeper who handed me off to a servant girl named Aryanis.

Aryanis gaped at me for a long moment before bursting into rapid-fire Median. I had learned many words in the past three weeks. But my conversational skills were still lacking.

"Do you speak Aramaic?" I asked.

She frowned and shook her head. "Hungry?" she asked, making eating motions with her fingers.

I recognized the word. Before I could answer, my belly made a noise a lioness might not be ashamed of. I rubbed my stomach and said, "A little."

Aryanis grinned and motioned for me to follow. In the kitchen, she filled two bowls with broth, grabbed a piece of fresh bread, and drew me to a corner where we sat down to eat. A whiff of mutton and onions rose from the bowl, assuring me the contents would not defile a Jew.

When we finished our meal, Aryanis introduced me to the other members of the staff before leading me to a narrow alcove jutting out of the formal living area.

"You sleep here. Next to me." She tapped her chest.

With relief, I nodded. I had been dreading the thought of sleeping alone in this great house, surrounded by strangers. She handed me a thin pallet and a couple of old blankets.

As I made a bed next to the one already stretched out in the diminutive alcove, I thought of my ancestor Jacob. He too had traveled far from home. In the deepest wilderness, he had laid down his head on a stone pillow and discovered that he was not alone. God himself had stretched his ladder from the heavens to the earth, so that his angels could ascend and descend amongst the lonely and brokenhearted. In that forsaken place, God had promised Jacob, *I am with you and will keep you wherever you go.*

I tapped the ground next to my head. "Set the foot of your ladder right here, my Lord. Be with me and keep me."

* * *

I awoke to a pair of large green eyes staring down at me. I bolted up in surprise and exhaled when I realized my watcher was only a boy. He pressed a finger to his lips. His clothes were odd, suited more for a walk in the wilderness than the house of an elegant courtier.

I managed to untangle myself from the linens. Noticing that Aryanis had already risen and made her bed neatly before leaving, I began folding my own blankets. The boy made himself at home on my mattress as if it were his personal chair.

I raised an eyebrow. "Please, have a seat," I said in Aramaic, not expecting him to understand.

He leaned against the wall and stretched his legs, crossing his feet at the ankles. "A little lumpy," he pronounced as he wriggled into the pallet, finding a more comfortable spot.

"You speak Aramaic!"

He jerked down his chin. "You move slow, girl."

Before I could ask who he was, and why he had a problem with my speed, Aryanis pushed open the curtain that divided the alcove from the large chamber. Spying the boy, she burst into a volley of rapid Median, most of which I missed. Clearly, she did not appreciate his presence, and just as clearly, the boy knew it. He darted out of the alcove, easily avoiding the broom Aryanis held aloft.

When he was far enough to be out of Aryanis's reach, he stopped. "See? I said you are too slow. Now I have to wait longer for my horse. He'll be toothless by the time you're ready." Before I could ask what earthly connection I could have to his horse, he disappeared. I caught him scrambling out of a window, nimble as a little cat.

"Who is he?" I asked Aryanis.

She curled her lip. "Trouble." Between her words and gestures, I understood that I was to bathe and change before going to see the master.

If Harpagus had an indoor bathing chamber, I was obviously not going to be invited to use it. Instead, Aryanis led me to the well, where we fetched water. Stringing up a sheet in a corner of the garden, she handed me the jug of water and a lump of lye. Pointing to a shallow oval cask with pointed edges at either end, she made a sitting motion. This must be a Median bathtub, I realized.

On my journey through the mountain passes, I had learned that the Medes, like their Persian kin, considered bathing in rivers and streams bad manners. Instead, the bathers were to draw water and carry it away for their wash, lest their filth should pollute creation. Over the past three weeks, I had not managed to have a proper wash, not while in the company of eight men.

Now I tried to fold myself into the narrow wooden tub and scrubbed the dust of long travel from my hair and skin. My tunic needed a good wash too, and I did my best to scour it, though the end result would not have passed muster with Rachel's exacting standards.

Pulling on the tunic I had brought with me, I hung my dripping garments from the clothesline. Adding a few drops of precious rose water to my wet hair, I combed the thick tangles and braided them into a simple rope down my back.

"Ah. Good," Harpagus said when I arrived at his chamber. "You smell better."

I felt heat travel up my neck. Thanks to my mode of transportation from Daniel's house, I had not exactly smelled of a garland of lilies when I first met Harpagus. Three weeks of rough travel must have added to my bouquet.

Harpagus himself had changed from his simple riding trousers and padded tunic into formal attire. His long carnelian-red tunic had wide sleeves adorned with narrow pleats, and another bank of delicate pleats hung from his left hip to the floor. His hair and beard had been curled and anointed with perfume, topped by a domed hat made of felt. He looked a courtier through and through.

I studied his chamber, which was much smaller than Daniel's, containing a fraction of the books and scrolls I was used to looking after. His desk seemed disappointingly empty. I wondered how I would ever find enough work to occupy my hours in this depressingly undersupplied room. Why exactly had Harpagus agreed to take on the expense of feeding and sheltering a scribe if he had so little use for one?

CHAPTER SEVENTEEN

I shall not die, but I shall live,
and recount the deeds of the LORD.

Psalm 118:17, ESV

—————————— JARED ——————————

Jared reached for the cup and missed, his fingers knocking the goblet over. Pale golden beer spread over the luncheon table. He gasped and sprang back as liquid dripped off the edge and onto the floor.

His father cursed. The single harried slave serving their lunch did his best to mop up the mess, but the damage had been done. The beer dribbled into his father's lap, making the man swear louder.

"If you can't eat like a civilized man, get out of my sight."

"Leave h-h-him alone!" Joseph cried. "He c-c-can't help it."

All eyes turned to his usually mouse-quiet brother. Their

father had pulled him out of Daniel's house for pure spite. Until he had returned home, Joseph's stutter had been reduced to an occasional slip.

"What did you say to me?" Lord Hanamel said, coming slowly to his feet.

Joseph swallowed. "I said he c-c-can't help it."

Jared's heart melted at the courage it had required for the boy to stand up for him.

"Get out of my sight!" his father roared. "Get out of my house! I don't want you near me. I don't want you under my roof. You are not my son!"

Paling, Joseph rose and made his way out of the room. Jared slithered out of his chair and followed. Halfway down the hall, he caught up with the boy and pulled him into a fierce embrace. "What got into you?"

"It's wrong, wh-wh-what he does."

"I know."

The wide brown eyes filled with tears. "What d-d-do I do, Jared?"

"I'll take you to Daniel's house. You can stay there. Come to think of it, Joseph, this is the best thing that could have happened. Life in this house is not good for you. Mahlah will take good care of you. And I will try to visit you when I can."

They walked to Daniel's house together, their steps slow, more for Jared's sake than Joseph's. As he had expected, Daniel and Mahlah welcomed his brother with open arms. At least now, Joseph was safe from his father's tyranny.

The way back home proved slower even than the trek there. Twice, Jared stumbled on a pothole he had missed and sprawled ignominiously in the dirt. He had assumed that having the sight of one eye would mean that he could function the same as before, even if he did not look like a whole man. He had been sadly mistaken.

Small accidents served to continuously remind him of his loss. He kept bumping into walls, especially on his blind side, misjudging the distance. Again and again, particularly when in a hurry, he would reach for an object and grasp air. He had lost the speed and accuracy he was once proud of.

Even riding had taken on a menacing quality. He could not perceive, with any real precision, his distance from the object ahead of him and had come close to disastrous collisions several times.

Sneaking past his father's door when he arrived home, he headed straight for his chamber. Sinking into the sole chair in his room, he bent to wipe the dirt caking his tunic where he had fallen. He saw that he had torn a hole as long as his finger in the fabric.

Fisting a hand, he crashed it on top of the scarred table. Neither the clattering noise nor the sting in his flesh helped banish the weight of frustration. He blew out a breath, trying to clear his mind. Trying to find a way through the maze that had become his life.

He had two stories to live. In the first, God had saved his eye. In the second, God had taken his eye. Both were true. God had allowed Keren's sword to take the sight of his left eye. And yet, God had also shielded the sight in his right eye. The physician had warned him that often, with this kind of injury, the damage spread to both eyes, causing total blindness. Even death was a common occurrence.

Two stories, both true.

It was up to him which story he chose to live out every day. The lost eye or the saved eye. The blind man or the sighted one. The God who had abandoned him or the God who had saved him.

He knew which story his father was living.

Jared tightened his fist. He would not turn into his father.

His world had become hard. His heart did not have to follow suit.

Grabbing a handful of disparate objects, he lined them up on his table. A cup, a jug of water, a shoe, an amphora of perfume, a comb, a silver belt buckle. With rapid-fire movements, he tried to grab each one. Half the time he missed. He lined up the objects again. The second time, he knocked down the jug, spilling water all over his shoes.

The third time, he managed to miss fewer objects, but at the expense of speed.

Again and again, he set up the objects. After the twentieth try, he noticed that if he moved his head from side to side, his right eye could make up for the vision missing in the left.

Excited with this discovery, he made his way to the barn and fetched his horse. It was just before the dinner hour and the streets were at their most crowded. After his last near disaster on the road, he had not tried to ride again, afraid of causing harm to others. His hands grew moist with sweat as he directed the beast.

Remembering to frequently move his head from side to side, he plodded along until he arrived at the main canal before heading home again. By some miracle, he had broken nothing, except perhaps his pride, which had resented the slowness of his pace. He had ridden like an old man. But he had ridden. And speed could always be improved.

CHAPTER EIGHTEEN

Let the favor of the Lord our God be upon us,
and establish the work of our hands upon us;
yes, establish the work of our hands!
Psalm 90:17, ESV

"As you may have surmised, I don't have much use for you. Not as an assistant." Harpagus indicated his small case of scrolls with a manicured finger.

My mouth turned dry.

"However, there is a task I have in mind for you. A rather . . . delicate matter."

My mouth turned even dryer.

"I want you to teach a boy."

Relief made me sag. That did not sound so bad. "Your son, my lord?"

"A shepherd boy."

I had never managed to train my face to hide my emotions. No doubt Harpagus read the shock on my visage. Shepherds were rarely literate. For an aristocrat to take an interest in the education of one bordered on eccentricity.

"A shepherd boy?"

"His father, Mitradates, is one of the royal shepherds." The wide sleeve of his robe floated like a ship's sail as he moved his arm. "The son, Artadates, is clever. He will learn quickly. And I have given him good incentive to study hard."

I had a sudden memory of the green-eyed boy who had taken over my pallet earlier that morning. "By chance, is the good incentive you mentioned a horse?"

"Why, yes! How did you know? I have promised the boy that he can choose his own horse from my stable if he learns his lessons well. Since he is as horse-mad as other boys his age, he is keen to study."

Not wanting to oust the boy, I kept my silence.

"He was here, wasn't he?" Harpagus's lips tightened. "The boy has a propensity to forget instructions when they prove inconvenient to him. I have impressed upon him that he is not to come to this house unless I send for him. I fear his audacity will prove his undoing."

I tucked that bit of information in the back of my mind. "What would you like me to teach Artadates, my lord?"

"Educate him as the sons of aristocracy are educated."

A bit of spittle found its way into my lung and I coughed.

"He speaks Aramaic, though he cannot write it. I want him perfectly fluent, as if for court. Also, teach him numeracy, and some basic knowledge of Akkadian."

"You must have very clever sheep in Media," I said, wondering if the sheep here responded better to Akkadian than Median.

Harpagus glared.

I bit my lip. In truth, my curiosity had raised its monstrous head and was baying to be satisfied. Why did Harpagus want me to teach a shepherd boy ancient Akkadian? Except for scribes and men concerned with the running of nations, it was a useless skill.

"One thing."

"Yes, lord?"

"I assume that working for a man like Belteshazzar has taught you some discretion, in spite of all evidence to the contrary?"

I reddened at this well-deserved put-down. "Some, lord," I said.

"I don't want anyone to know about this. Do you understand me?"

"You want me to teach the boy in secret?"

"Precisely."

"Not in your chambers, then?"

"Absolutely not. I have prepared a small cottage outside the city for the purpose. Every morning, after seeing to my letters, you will meet Artadates in the cottage and instruct him until afternoon.

"When you return to the house, look for Aryanis. I have assigned her to teach you our tongue. The quicker you learn Median, the less you will stand out."

He bent to collect a basket from under his desk. Inside, he had piled several wooden tablets covered in wax, a couple of bronze styli, a knife for sharpening reeds, a mold for creating clay tablets, a pot of ink, and a thick roll of papyrus.

"Artadates will show you where you can find reeds and good clay. I assume you can create your own tablets and cylinders?"

"Yes, my lord."

"And, Keren? Don't fill the boy's head with tales of your God. He has been taught to honor our gods. You understand?"

I bowed my head. The Medians revered Mitra, the god of

light and truth, as their chief deity. Lord Harpagus had said *gods*, however. My Jewish ears were attuned to the difference, and I wondered what gods the boy had learned to worship.

With a wave of his hand, my master dismissed me. I was about to ask him how I was supposed to locate my pupil when he turned, making the pleats in his tunic fly like a wind-borne thunder cloud. "I forgot one more thing I want you to teach Artadates."

I stopped and turned to receive this final instruction. I was expecting an exotic topic, like ancient Sumerian. It seemed entirely fitting to this strange assignment, especially since the Sumerians had two hundred different words with which to describe sheep. Even Babylonian poetry wouldn't have surprised me. But I had underestimated Harpagus's ability to shock me.

"You know your sword, I understand. Teach the boy sword craft."

The blood drained from my face. "Sword craft, lord?"

Harpagus nodded. "He has the ability of a born athlete, but not the technique. Teach him the rudiments. Improve his overall physical conditioning. Help him develop good form, rhythm, timing, distance."

I barely stopped myself from laughing hysterically. He wanted me to teach *timing* and *distance*?

"I don't think I am the one to teach him sword craft, my lord."

The pleats of his sleeve floated in the air again, as if wiping away my words. "Nonsense. Belteshazzar's son told me of your little accident. These things happen. You must overcome."

These things happen? Was he mad? My mouth opened and closed like a silver carp caught in a fisherman's net. Finally, I managed to croak out, "I cannot teach the boy sword craft, my lord."

"You can and you will." Harpagus lowered his head like a wild boar ready to charge. "Otherwise, you best pack up your bundle and get out of my house."

I offered him some more of my silver carp impression. "My lord, couldn't one of your men . . . ?"

"No!" He pulled a hand through his perfumed hair. "There are a dozen men I could have given the task to, before now. Two dozen teachers better qualified than you to instruct him. But I cannot risk it. You are an outsider. I can trust you not to have other ties. Other ears to which you report. It has to be you. Work out the tangles in your mind, girl. Artadates is growing too old to keep roaming the plains as a shepherd. At this rate, he will fall too far behind his peers to catch up. Teach him the sword. Also, the bow and arrow."

His hand came to rest heavily on my shoulder. "The boy needs your help. Will you give it?"

This was my undoing. This cry for help, naked of excuses.

Harpagus was anxious for his shepherd boy; I could see that. And though I did not understand why it seemed so important to him that the boy should be educated like the son of an aristocrat, I did understand the desperation that leaked through that hand and sank into my bones.

"Yes, Lord Harpagus. I will give him my help."

CHAPTER NINETEEN

He will once again fill your mouth with laughter
and your lips with shouts of joy.

Job 8:21, NLT

———————————— JARED ————————————

Johanan looked at him like he had lost his mind. "I can't do it, Jared! I am sorry."

Jared pressed the practice sword firmly into his friend's grip. "You can. Think of it as a medicinal regimen. I cannot adjust to my blindness without practice."

Johanan groaned. "Couldn't we practice drinking beer or cutting roast lamb with our knives?"

"I can do those things alone." He lifted his sword and found his body falling into the old-remembered position. "We will start slow to ascertain what I can manage."

Jared did not disclose that his own belly was churning with a surge of nausea. He ignored the clamoring fear, which demanded that he walk away from this foolishness. The last time he had stood on this very spot, he had lost the sight in one eye. Jared grasped his wooden sword more tightly.

"Begin!" he cried and lunged.

He tried to remember to move his head from side to side to increase his perception, to attack with confidence. Most importantly, to resist the hesitancy that had begun to dog his steps.

They had slowed their movements to half the speed of their usual match. Still, he found himself missing strike after strike. He could not judge the distances with the same easy accuracy that he had once taken for granted.

He pushed himself, refusing to give up.

The physical activity was starting to loosen his disused muscles. It had been over a month since he had exerted himself. After an hour, he called a halt to the torture. He leaned against the wall to steady his wobbly legs. Wiping the sweat from his face with a corner of his sleeve, he found himself grinning. He felt he had improved by a hair's breadth.

"I may be blind in one eye, but at least my sword was not shaking." He pointed his practice sword at Johanan's still-unsteady weapon.

"My sword was the steadiest part of me," Johanan said, expression benign. "Everything else was shaking a lot worse."

Both men began to laugh, until they were bent over, hands on thighs, gasping for breath.

"I will take you up on the roast lamb and beer now."

Johanan shook his head. "I don't think I can cut soft cheese with these hands."

Jared raised a brow. "Think we are too old to ask your mother to cut our meat for us?"

They bent over with laughter again. That easy mirth, poking at their weakness without judgment, loosened something heavy that had settled like a yoke beam across Jared's shoulders.

CHAPTER TWENTY

Harpagus had told me to meet Artadates at the gate of the seventh wall. I found the boy leaning against the white battlements, arms crossed, leisurely studying the crowds. The green eyes widened slightly as they landed on me. "Finally, you come."

He was a handsome boy, with a flawless complexion bronzed from spending endless hours in the sun and a sharp nose with curved nostrils. The strong brows, which had an odd raven-wing flip above the left eye, gave him a hawkish appearance.

"Have you already chosen your horse from Lord Harpagus's stables?" I asked as we passed through the gate.

"Yes!"

"Which is it?"

Artadates flashed a set of perfect teeth. "The tall chestnut."

"You mean Lord Harpagus's own horse? The *Nisaean*?"

The boy nodded enthusiastically. "That one. He's beautiful, yes?"

I tried not to laugh. "He is the master's personal horse. I doubt he will part with it even if you start writing in immaculate Aramaic with your right hand and solve an arithmetic problem with your left, while singing an Akkadian song in perfect pitch. You better set your sights on a more realistic goal."

"What does it mean, this *realistic*?"

"Means reasonable. Sensible." I raised a brow at him. "Sane."

"Ah. I understand now. You mean *little*. But if you set your sights on the realistic thing, then you only get the realistic thing. Me, I plan for better."

"Getting a priceless Nisaean horse from Lord Harpagus is not a plan, Artadates. It's a fantasy."

"You think?"

"Yes."

"You're wrong."

We were walking downhill, leaving Ecbatana behind us, Artadates leading the way. Although significantly shorter than me, he kept a clipped pace, so that I had to stretch my steps to keep up. "Convince me," I said.

He shrugged. "Lord Harpagus, he is a man of his word. What he promises, he does. You can trust him."

"Of course." In Media and their cousin nation, Persia, speaking the truth and keeping one's promise were the measure of a man. Harpagus's given word would be more binding to him than any legal document.

"So. Harpagus told me that if I studied hard and did well, I could have any horse in his stable. He did not say, *except for the Nisaean*. He said *any* horse. Maybe he did not *mean* any horse.

But that is what he said. Now he must honor that word. That is my plan. What do you think?"

I laughed. "Sneaky."

I wondered if Artadates could convince Harpagus with that argument when the time came to present his case. I studied the charming smile; the bright, intelligent eyes; the confident carriage; and had to admit he had a chance.

Artadates had been right. My thinking had been too little where he was concerned. I must adjust my expectations of him.

"First, you have to learn to read and write Aramaic."

The boy shrugged. "You teach. I learn."

"Where did you learn to speak it so well?"

"Lord Harpagus hired me to wash the stone wall outside his son's schoolroom. He was receiving private tuition in Aramaic at the time." Artadates led us off the main road and onto a dirt track. "When I finished cleaning the wall," he continued, "Harpagus had me paint it. Then he did not like the color and had me paint it again. After that, he wanted flowers. I was working outside that schoolroom a long time."

"You picked up Aramaic merely by overhearing it?"

"Can't read and write it, though."

"How old are you?" I asked.

"Ten. You?"

"Seventeen."

"You married?"

"No. You?"

Artadates grinned. "I'm too young. You're getting old, girl. Better find a man."

"Between you and Master Harpagus, I think I have plenty of male company to contend with."

Artadates led us onto another track and pointed. Apple trees lined a path to a modest mud-brick cottage. White and pink blossoms shed their petals over us in the breeze as we made our way down the path.

It dawned on me that this was no ordinary cottage. We were headed for a tablet house. And I was the teacher.

Like a dream, I remembered the first Scripture Daniel had ever quoted to me:

The Sovereign LORD is my strength!
He makes me as surefooted as a deer,
able to tread upon the heights.

I thought of the high places to which God had led me.

From the day I had walked away from Babylon, I had literally been climbing to heights I had never experienced, until the thin air pulled at my lungs and made me gasp. Now I slept in the foothills of imposing mountains.

Much more than that, God had asked me to ascend the impossible places of life. Places too hard and alien for me to have ever dreamed of. A new country. A new language. A new master. A new tablet house. Only this time, I was entering not as the pupil, but as the teacher.

For three years, Daniel had been training me for these heights and I had not known it.

"He makes me able to tread upon the heights," I whispered as I walked in.

The only furnishings in the one-room cottage consisted of a table branded with years of abuse, two wobbly chairs, and a wooden chest. Handing Artadates one of the wax tablets, I settled down and began to teach him the Aramaic alphabet.

I found in him a willing pupil with an exceptionally quick

mind. His questions displayed a keen understanding. His greatest gift, however, was his ability to focus entirely on the task at hand, rarely growing distracted.

When the sun had traveled to the middle of the sky, signaling the arrival of noon, I stopped the lesson.

"Time for a break," I said. "Can you go home to eat and return within the hour?"

Artadates flashed his easy smile and pulled out a small bundle from the folds of his cloak. "No need. My mother packed food." Unwrapping the bit of linen, he revealed a round of bread, a square of soft sheep cheese, and a handful of tarragon and mint.

"You came more prepared than I." I nodded my approval, wishing I had thought to ask Aryanis for a snack. Harpagus had so bewildered me with his request that morning that I had left his house in a daze.

"No food?"

I shook my head. "It's all right. I will prepare your next lesson while you eat."

"An empty stomach is no good."

Artadates stared at his feast with a forlorn expression. Then with a little shrug, he broke the bread into two. One half emerged slightly bigger. Using an iron knife, he cut the cheese more equally and, piling some herbs on top, placed the two morsels on the halved pieces of bread. He picked the smaller half and offered it to me.

Touched by his generosity, I accepted the offering. "Thank you, Artadates. That is very kind."

After muttering a blessing, I was about to take a bite when the boy's fingers wrapped around my wrist.

"No," he said.

I tried not to laugh. Clearly, he had thought better of his

beneficence. Placing the bread and cheese back on its hand-kerchief, I pushed it toward him.

My brows must have risen all the way to my hairline when Artadates pushed the larger half of the bread toward me. "You are bigger than me. You eat this one."

"Well." For a moment, I found it hard to speak. "Well." I cleared my throat. "Artadates . . . this may be the most gallant offer I have ever received." I pushed the larger bread back toward him and drew the smaller half to me. "However, you are a growing boy. I insist you have that one."

As I ate my delicious repast, I began to understand Harpagus's odd interest in the boy. He was a remarkable child.

Another possibility had also occurred to me. It seemed likely that this boy was, in fact, Harpagus's son. Not by his wife, who had given him a son three years older than Artadates. Or even a concubine. But a child sired on another man's wife.

Such an indiscretion would explain Harpagus's desire for secrecy, as well as his determination to educate the boy. Not that Artadates's parentage made any difference to me. I thought him well worth my time and tuition, regardless of what his parents had been up to behind closed doors. I could have been given many a task far less worthy and thanked God for the opportunity to bless this bright child.

After we finished our meal, Artadates sprang to his feet and pointed to a shadowy corner of the chamber. I turned to follow his finger just as a ray of sun found its way into the darkness. Leaning against the wall stood several wooden practice swords, a couple of bows, and a quiver full of arrows.

"Swords," my pupil breathed, enchanted.

"Swords," I spat, tormented.

"Now? Harpagus said I was to learn."

I walked slowly to the corner where Harpagus had left us the cache of weapons. Instead of the swords, I reached for one of the bows. It had been made in more diminutive dimensions than a regular bow, clearly with a child in mind. I examined it closely. In spite of its size, the bow had been well made, using a composite of materials that made it both flexible and powerful. I judged the draw weight and length appropriate for my pupil.

"Do you know how to use this?"

"I am the best!"

"That remains to be seen. Who taught you?"

"My father. A little."

"Let's see what you know, shall we?"

I might not have had an accurate aim, but after three years in the company of ardent archers, I knew all about the posture, the stance, and the anchor point of a good bowman. I grabbed both bows and the quiver of arrows, a thumb protector made of horn, and one of the wooden tablets.

Surveying the grounds around us, I chose an apple tree, then changed my mind and headed for one that stood closer. Better play it safe on our first try.

Tucking the wooden tablet against a branch, I handed Artadates the smaller bow and thumb protector. "Try to hit that tablet."

Artadates curled his lip and pointed at the apple tree. "Is this realistic?" Before I could object, he strode to the tree, grabbed the tablet, and walked beyond the first apple tree I had considered, until he reached the wall that ran around the perimeter of the cottage. He positioned the tablet upon the wall and walked back to me.

I crossed my arms. The distance was much too far. "You will have to collect your arrows," I warned. "Wherever they land."

Ignoring my warning, my pupil took aim. The first thing I noticed was that in contrast to the original location, he had cleverly placed the tablet where the sun would not interfere with his vision.

I could also see that he had not received proper tuition. He had placed his feet too far apart, hip twisted forward, torquing his upper body out of proper balance. Still, he managed to land the arrow into the corner of that tablet, which I had not expected.

He looked at me in triumph. "*This* is realistic!"

I clapped. "I will have to adjust my definition of that word when it comes to you. Come with me." I walked him to the southern wall of the cottage. Pressing his shoulders and back into the bricks, I said, "Try again. Only, this time, keep your shoulder and back connected to the wall. Right leg behind, left leg forward."

We spent a few moments on correcting his posture as I explained why each adjustment was necessary. "Extend your left arm like a pillar of plaster. Straight and steady. Right arm at the level of your lips. All right, draw until you reach your earlobe."

Artadates practiced his draw as I repositioned the tablet. This time, the arrow flew with fluid ease, landing closer to the center. With a nod of approval, I adjusted the boy's middle and ring fingers against his thumb. "Feel the blood pooling in your fingertips? Good. Now, when you step forward, keep your left shoulder and back aligned with the wall."

He looked at me thoughtfully and, after a moment of concentration, loosened his arrow. It landed dead center of the tablet. As did the second and the third. He gave me a confident smile and lifted the bow again. I could see that his left arm was starting to tremble from the strain.

"Enough," I said gently. "Exhausting the hand will cause you problems in the long run. We will build your strength every day. Remember, you will not always be standing as you shoot. Sometimes you will kneel, or discharge your arrows from the back of a moving horse. We must build your strength and accuracy, so that you will be able to master each position."

Artadates lowered his bow and regarded me with something close to adoration. "I think I'm going to like you."

CHAPTER TWENTY-ONE

But you, O LORD, are a shield about me,
my glory, and the lifter of my head.
Psalm 3:3, ESV

JARED

The pain came for him, piercing his barren eye socket and storming through his head. Jared lay on the bed, trying not to twitch a single muscle. He had found that if he lay very still, the pounding abated a little, becoming one hammer instead of a host of stonemasons beating against his skull.

After weeks of battling headaches that came without warning—sometimes attacking with a sharp-toothed brutality that robbed him of sense, arriving like a pugilist's unexpected fist, and sometimes almost benign, tolerable, until it turned on him and became vicious again—he had learned a few lessons.

He had learned that he suffered the pain in three different time spans. In the present, as it hounded him, snapping at his flesh. That was the simplest to understand, the suffering of the body.

But the present pain also hooked into previous pains, nights he had wept in shame because he could not bear the torment. The pain now might not feel like that, might be weaker and more tolerable, but it held the fear over him, always reminding him that it could be brutal again. Every past defeat came to visit him with every new pain, magnifying its power.

Then again, there was the future, in some ways the most powerful torment, for with every episode of recurring pain, the questions arose, demanding answers: What if *this* is my life? What if I am never healed? What if I grow worse? What if I can never work or be useful to anyone?

His bed had become a veritable battleground. A striving against three monsters that returned again and again, day or night, alone or accompanied, uncaring of convenience or need, sometimes lasting hours, sometimes stretching over days.

One simple truth had risen, lifting up out of the storm, to become the rock that was higher than the pain. Higher than the fear. Higher than the unanswered questions.

He would choose to cling to God.

His love for you endures, Daniel had said. *God wants your heart to learn to endure, too. Endure in love. Love him even when he seems absent. Love him when he has offended or disappointed you.*

In the midst of the pain, the disappointments of his life, the chronic nature of this immovable beast and the terrors attached to it, he had decided to cling to that truth.

I choose to trust you. I choose to believe you. I choose to love you.

It took every pinch of valor in his soul to stay faithful to that resolve.

There were times when his faith was a ladle full of water on the blazing conflagration of pain. It availed nothing, and pain emerged shouting with smug victory. Lately, though, he had noticed that the more he stood his ground, refusing to give in, the less discouragement ruled over him. Pain was starting to lose its power over his soul, if not his body.

Motionless on his bed, he engaged in the now familiar battle, pounding back against the ache in his head with a different fist: The fist of faith. The fist of trust.

As he did so, he felt a shift in his soul. Where his body had grown weak, his spirit began to rise in strength.

For the first time since the accident, he felt a glimmer of hope for his future. Even if the worst came to pass, God would look after him.

> But you, O LORD, are a shield about me,
>   my glory, and the lifter of my head.

He whispered David's words again and again, until sleep consumed him.

CHAPTER TWENTY-TWO

My eyes long for your promise;
I ask, "When will you comfort me?"
Psalm 119:82, ESV

"Why does he make me study this poxy language?" Artadates pressed his back against the chair with a huff. "I want to be a general! I will never use Akkadian!"

I could not blame the boy. Akkadian was a clunky old language that no one spoke anymore. Its history lay at the root of its lingering influence. After the long centuries of Assyrian rule in the region, followed by the relatively young but dazzling reign of the Babylonians, Akkadian had grown deep tentacles into the administrative structure of every powerful land in the area. You needed Akkadian to have access to past records. And it had become a sign of civilization, a mark of superiority.

In truth, Akkadian was the language of scribes and officials. Even Nebuchadnezzar, who had been raised as a beloved prince and groomed to rule, had only a glancing familiarity with the written language, enough to know if someone was trying to cheat him.

I shrugged. "Perhaps one day you will find it handy on the battlefield, Your Generalship."

"Bah." My pupil crossed his arms and stared at the clay tablet mutinously.

"I see the chestnut galloping further and further away." I made a fluttering motion with my fingers.

"He is a Nisaean horse. He is fluent in Median. That horse is too smart to speak Akkadian."

The boy had worked hard all day. I could see that he needed a break from the monotony of study.

"How about a turn with the sword?" I suggested, trying to hold back the dread I felt.

He jumped off his seat so fast, the birds congregating outside the window took flight in a noisy explosion.

I had come up with a temporary plan for teaching him sword craft. It still made my stomach churn to think of going near the cursed things. But my strategy made it more tolerable.

I stood next to Artadates, our toes aligned, and began by demonstrating the correct grip on the hilt, progressing to proper balance. I never faced him. Never stood before him, pointing my weapon at his sturdy little body. Instead, I trained him side by side, going through the motions, correcting his mistakes.

When I taught him a simple combat move, Artadates lunged with the enthusiasm of a lion cub. Even the repetitious nature of the exercise did not daunt him. For a whole hour, he bent his knee as he bounded forward, lifted the wooden sword, pointed, and pulled back.

But I knew the boy would not be content with drills that taught him basic skills. He would want to spar. To learn to engage an opponent with skill. And that was one thing I could not offer him.

In spite of all my precautions, that night I was haunted by nightmares.

Again and again, I saw Jared's face, one hand covering his eye, blood spurting between his fingers. The echo of his screams besieged me until I awoke, gasping, shivering, and nauseous.

I untangled myself from the drenched blankets and crept out of the little nook I shared with Aryanis, feeling like I could not breathe in that oppressive darkness. On bare feet, I made my way to the garden and sat on the stoop.

That dreadful moment would not let me go. The horror of it would not release me.

I dropped my head in my hands and wondered afresh how to get past what I had done to my closest friend.

Unexpectedly, a dim memory of Daniel inserted itself into my anguished thoughts, like a bead of perfume splashing into water. I could hear the warm timbre of his voice, feel its velvety comfort.

Endure in the fire, because God's love for you endures. Trust in his plans for you . . . Let him give you the strength to bear the flames.

"Lord, I don't know how to endure this fire. Give me the strength to bear the flames!"

Somehow, crying out to God helped. It helped loosen the load of unendurable guilt. I spent the rest of that night praying for Jared. Real prayers, not the sad, blubbering, guilt-ridden offerings I had managed thus far. Instead, I prayed for the friend I loved. The man I adored. I prayed for his well-being. His faith. His future. And for the first time since the accident, I wondered if God's plans for Jared might be able to survive the devastation I had dealt him.

* * *

A few mornings later, just after I had collected my lunch on my way to the cottage, Harpagus summoned me. "You are needed at the palace."

I gaped at him. "My lord?"

"The senior scribe is in bed with fever. Several of his assistants suffer from the same malady. Cursed luck. The Lydian delegation has arrived to work on a new treaty. Which means charters and documents that require the expertise of learned scribes. We are shorthanded, and the king is in a foul temper about it."

"You want *me* to serve at the royal palace?" My voice came to a squeaky stop on the last syllable.

Female scribes were not completely unknown in Mesopotamia. But they were very rare and most often served other women. You were more likely to discover a horse capable of flight than find a female scribe in the court. In all my years working for Daniel, he had taken me to the palace once, and on that occasion, he merely showed me the library and the gardens. The Medes were just as conservative as the Babylonians when it came to their women.

Harpagus did not even blink. "We'll hide you in a back room."

"Lord Harpagus, I have never worked in such a capacity. I couldn't begin to know the procedure."

"You can write the copies." Every royal document was copied at least once, so that a record of the transaction could be kept by both parties. "You have surely made copies for Belteshazzar."

I gnawed a short nail. "Many," I admitted.

"That will serve."

At least he did not make me go to the palace in my thread-bare old tunic. Instead, he asked for his wife's help. With some hasty assistance from the lady's handmaiden, my hair was loosed from its long braid and arranged more formally, tucked into wide rolls against my neck as I yelped from the sharp pins that scraped my scalp. Without a by-your-leave, the handmaiden stripped me of my ragged tunic.

Harpagus's wife gave me one of her plainer tunics made of dark-blue wool, with an attractive short cape that hung from the shoulders like loose sleeves.

I was bundled on top of the same mule that had carried me from Babylon. Grabbing the beast's sides with my thighs and holding on for dear life, I dashed off after Harpagus's chestnut as we headed for the palace.

Having lived in Babylon most of my life, I was no stranger to wonders and grandeur. But the palace at Ecbatana had a different feel from the obvious riches of Babylon. The building, diminutive in comparison to Nebuchadnezzar's palace, offered a subtler elegance, with dove-gray stone walls and a delicate domed ceiling in the center that was as uniquely wondrous in its own way as the Hanging Gardens. Porticos and colonnades gave the whole building a sense of lightness, and since most of the columns were plated with gold or silver, by sun or candle-light, the whole place sparkled as if someone had pulled down a habitation from the stars and planted it on earth.

Every green handspan in Babylon was a wonder, gained by dint of war with the elements. In the city of Ecbatana, with its mild weather and rich rainfall, gardens grew lush with little help from human hands. Now, in the height of spring, the palace wore a verdant mantle in every shade of green. Red and white flowers spread their perfume with such abundance that for a moment I stood like a drunkard, stupefied by the extravagant beauty of it all.

In the days since my arrival, I had discovered that Harpagus had been born to one of the most prominent of Media's clans and was related to the king himself. Not long ago, he had commanded the Median army to a decided victory against the Lydians, helping to end a five-year war. As a result, every military man in the place looked upon him with awe, and at times, downright adoration.

His elevated position in the palace meant that we were received with bows and chest thumps from soldiers and civilians alike. Grabbing me by the elbow, he led me through a gold-plated door.

I had a dizzying impression of an entrance hall covered in silver tiles before he guided me down a narrow corridor. Here, silver tiles turned to ordinary mud brick, and the gold-plated doors to exposed cedar. By the plainness of our surroundings, I knew we must be closer to where the worker bees of the palace made their home.

Leading me into a narrow, windowless chamber, he bid me sit at the table that took up the length of one wall. A harried-looking, bald, beardless man entered, arms piled with clay tablets. At the sight of me, he took a tripping step and almost dropped his mountainous burden.

"Here is the help I promised you, Axarys," Harpagus said.

A small puff of air escaped the man's chest, followed by another. And another. "But . . . But . . . My lord!"

I looked on amused, oddly comforted by Axarys's reaction. At least I was not the only one alarmed by the prospect of my having to serve in the palace.

"She worked for one of the highest officials in Babylon. I

think you will find her adequate. Keep her here, out of sight, and let her handle the Akkadian copies."

Axarys gave me a wild look. Finally, unable to bear the weight of his towering burden, he deposited the pile on the table next to me. Without a word, he pulled out a tablet. "Copy this," he said and, bowing hurriedly before Harpagus, left.

Harpagus smiled and followed him, leaving me with my work. I searched and found fresh clay tablets and reeds on a shelf and went to work. Carefully, I laid out the text in proportion to the size of the tablet, ensuring the inscription was centered and pleasing to the eye. An hour later, when Axarys returned, I had completed the copy.

"Let me see." He held out a hand, and I slid my tablet toward him on the table. He perused my work for a moment. Slim eyebrows knotted. Pulling the original close, he began comparing the two documents.

Slowly, he straightened. "I see you know your business."

"I can make a copy."

He nodded. With dexterous fingers, he pulled five more tablets from the pile on the table. "Set to work on these. I will bring you fresh clay tablets."

I lost count of the number of documents I copied that day. No sooner had I finished one pile than Axarys arrived with a new batch. By the evening, I had a crick in my neck, my fingers were tingling, and my stomach had a few choice remarks for the way I had neglected it.

At the sight of Axarys returning, I tried not to grimace. Finding his hands empty, I breathed with relief, hoping he had come to dismiss me.

"You have done marvelous work today," he said with a smile. "The scribes are stopping for the evening. But we want to invite you to join us for supper. It is the least we can do in return for your service."

"Oh!" I rose to my feet. "Join the other scribes?" I felt a rush of pleasure at the request.

While I had enjoyed many pleasant hours with dear friends over the past three years, I had never known the companionship of colleagues. To be included in a gathering of scribes meant an acceptance that transcended my gender and youth. "I wish I could," I said wistfully. "But my master will no doubt wish me to return home with him."

"Lord Harpagus has already given his permission," Axarys said in the tone of a man accustomed to supervising details.

In a daze, I found myself following Axarys down the familiar narrow corridor with the mud-brick walls. He stopped in front of a plain cedar door and pulled it open.

And that is how I came to meet the king.

But I go ahead of myself.

CHAPTER
TWENTY-THREE

You shall eat the fruit of the labor of your hands;
you shall be blessed, and it shall be well with you.

Psalm 128:2, ESV

A dozen scribes sat around the broad rectangular table in the center of the chamber. The hum of conversation came to a standstill as its occupants turned to stare, cups frozen in the air, hands paralyzed midgesture, words abandoned half spoken. In short, like a mighty magician, I turned the men in that chamber into living statues. But it was a spell I did not know how to break.

I adjusted the little cape across my shoulders and took a half step backward toward the door.

"This is Keren," Axarys said. "Lord Harpagus's scribe. She completed all the Akkadian copies today."

The silence stretched for a beat. A skinny eunuch in the corner slapped his cup on the table and began to clap. To my astonishment, every scribe joined in, until the place boomed with their ovation.

Axarys held up his hands. "Make room. Make room. And get her a cup of wine."

I found myself sitting next to the skinny eunuch as someone pressed a chalice brimming with ruby wine into my hand. "My name is Spitamas," the eunuch said. "Count me as your friend. You should know that you have saved our necks. We owe you a great debt."

I chuckled. "I merely made a few copies."

The little eunuch lowered his voice and drew closer. "The king was in a terrible state when he discovered we might not be able to produce the royal records in a timely fashion. He would have considered it a humiliation before the Lydians, you see. A sign that he presides over a shoddy court." Spitamas's head swiveled right and left. He bent even closer, and his voice dropped to a whisper. "The king had threatened to . . ." He drew a finger across his throat.

"No!"

He nodded somberly. "If we had not performed." He shrugged. "Without the senior scribe and several assistants, we had no hope of succeeding. You saved us. If ever we can return the favor, just say the word."

"It was my pleasure."

Spitamas topped off my still-full cup. The scribes began to pass every platter on the table my way. Though hungry, I carefully selected bread and vegetables only, adding a spoonful of stewed quince, hoping to avoid dishes that might break Israel's dietary laws.

The conversation quickly turned technical, dissecting phrases in the Akkadian translations. I found myself consulted upon several points, a sensation that felt as foreign as it was pleasant. Working for Daniel had meant that I remained ever the student. Here, they treated me as a reliable expert.

A slight commotion at the door drew my attention. Two of the royal guards entered, followed by Harpagus and a man I had never met. He needed no introduction. As everyone scrambled to rise from their seats, I had a moment to study the potentate who ruled Media.

Astyages.

Embroidered linen and wool rustled at his feet as he stepped into the room. The golden diadem at his brow and the jewels on his chest and adorning his fingers sparkled in the lamp light. He was as perfumed, curled, pampered, and spangled as you would expect a king to be.

But before I dropped to my knees and lowered my head like the other scribes, I caught an expression on his face I had not expected to find on a king. He surveyed every shadow, every angle, every bowed figure with an odd suspicion, as though he expected a tiger to peel itself from the shadows and pounce on him.

"I came to congratulate you," the king said in a bored voice as he stepped farther into the room.

Axarys bowed deeper, his forehead touching the floor, and replied for everyone. "We live to serve, lord."

"Harpagus tells me you had help. Who is this new scribe? I should like to thank him personally."

I almost toppled on my face. Axarys might have felt the same. Those little puffs of air I had come to recognize escaped his lips. Without a word, he pointed my way.

The king's gaze followed the shaking finger leading in my direction. I kept my head bent, trying to melt into the floor, a strategy that clearly failed since a sweaty hand hooked under my chin and pulled.

I forgot to breathe as I looked into the face of the king. The one who had threatened his scribes with death should they prove dissatisfactory.

The king's eyes widened slightly. "Well." He let his tongue sit on that word, stretching it out as if he were playing a note on a harp. "I see why you keep this one to yourself, Harpagus." He laughed at his own jest.

Harpagus bowed smoothly.

The king's fingers released their hold on my chin. From a pouch, he pulled out two pieces of silver and held them out to me. "In appreciation for your work today."

Astounded, I raised my palm to receive the unexpected offering.

"You see," he said, "I am more generous than Harpagus. You should come work for me."

I gulped, unable to think of a suitable reply.

"My lord already has the most beautiful women in his household," Harpagus drawled, "and the most talented scribes in his court. Surely he cannot begrudge me one servant who is neither the one nor the other?"

Astyages laughed. "Very good. *Neither the one nor the other.* No. I suppose she is not." To my relief, he turned his back and walked out.

That, I hoped, was the last time I would ever come face-to-face with the king. Like so many of my hopes, it came to nothing.

* * *

In the morning, Harpagus dictated a short letter and dismissed me with a wave. Before leaving, I tried to return his wife's dark-blue dress with its pretty cape. But he told me to keep it in case I had need of it again.

I wondered if Harpagus would be as generous if it were *his* tunic he was giving away and hoped his wife would not resent this free use of her belongings. Or me for receiving them.

Thankfully, she seemed in great spirits when I ran into her that afternoon. She was also wearing a new tunic with wide, pleated sleeves. I assumed Harpagus had rewarded her enforced generosity with a more fashionable garment.

I had not touched the silver Johanan had lent me, determined to save it for emergencies. Now, having made a little silver of my own thanks to Astyages, I finally purchased a roll of papyrus and, after mixing a pot of black ink, sat down to write my first letters home. I wrote a letter to my parents, another to Grandfather, and one to Johanan.

I tried not to weep as I told them how much I missed them. But my tears slipped down to mix with the ink.

CHAPTER TWENTY-FOUR

You shall be like a watered garden,
like a spring of water,
whose waters do not fail.

Isaiah 58:11, ESV

JARED

It was almost like the old days. Dinner at Daniel's house with his dearest friend seated on one side of him and Joseph on the other.

Except it was nothing like the old days.

Johanan's betrothed, Deborah, along with her sister, had joined them for the meal. Zebidah had reddened when Mahlah had seated her across from Jared, turning her face away to look at anything but him. After a great deal of fidgeting, she had swapped places with her sister, saying the cushion was too hard.

Jared had received the message. If she had ever felt an interest in him, the desire had certainly waned. She could not even bear to look at his face, not with that ominous black-leather eye patch.

A part of Jared sighed with relief. Zebidah's attentions had always caused him a squirming embarrassment. Another part of him tasted the larger rejection underlying Zebidah's response. She was like a signpost of what everyone else felt. Out in the world, away from the safe haven of his closest friends, he could expect a daily barrage of cold shoulders, turned faces, and wriggling awkwardness.

This was his life now. He had better make peace with it.

He jumped when, without a word, Deborah rose from her seat and settled herself next to him. Grinning, she stared into his eye without flinching. "You look very dashing with that eye patch, Jared. You remind me of one of King David's mighty men of war, or a general from an exotic land. If I weren't almost a married woman, I might have to set my cap at you."

The rigid line of Jared's back relaxed slowly.

"Hey!" Johanan interrupted. "What am I? Dried parsley?"

"Not at all, dear," Deborah assured him with her sweet smile. "You are very handsome, too."

"Just not a mighty warrior from an exotic land," Jared said with a smirk.

After the servants cleared the dinner dishes and the musical entertainment ended, Daniel asked for a private moment with Jared. In his chamber, Daniel settled himself behind his desk.

"The truth is—" he indicated four piles of clay tablets on the table before him, and another mountain of papyri on the shelf behind him— "I am drowning. Over the past three years, Keren learned to anticipate my every need. Now . . ." He shrugged.

Jared nodded. By the end, she had run the place so smoothly, Daniel had grown reliant on her help.

He knew how Daniel felt. Losing her had made him realize

just how much *he* had come to rely on her friendship. Her encouragement. Her warmth. Jared ground his teeth.

Daniel's fingers brushed over a clay envelope, removing a fine layer of dust. "I was hoping you would help me."

"Me?"

"Not permanently, of course. I know this would not suit you. But while you are recovering physically, would you consider assisting me? You have the training and knowledge. Four hours a day?"

The thought of leaving his increasingly depressing home for several hours a day, not to mention feeling useful again, made him want to clap. And he would be able to see Joseph every day!

"My headaches . . ."

"You can rest when one strikes you. Work at your own pace." Daniel raised his brows temptingly. "I offer a fair wage!"

Jared laughed. "I would do it for free."

"No, you will not." Daniel rubbed his hands together. "Splendid. I look forward to a bit of order around here." Daniel's smile faded as he leaned forward. "Your father will not be pleased."

Jared kneaded the back of his neck. Lord Hanamel would receive any offer from Daniel as an affront. "True."

"It may not come to this, of course. But I want you to know, like Joseph, you will always have a home with us. You are like a son to Mahlah and me, Jared. Having you live with us would be a blessing."

An odd sensation spread through Jared's chest. A warmth that made its way to his throat and turned into a walnut-size lump that made words impossible. His single eye filmed over with a curtain of moisture.

* * *

Johanan insisted on riding home with Jared, an offer he did not refuse. Though riding was becoming easier, navigating his way on this overcast evening offered a greater challenge. They spent the time speaking of Johanan's upcoming wedding and his joy at the prospect of having Deborah move into his father's house.

They had been building an addition to the back of the home where the couple could have their own small apartments. Johanan hoped that the building and furnishing would be complete by the time of the wedding in six weeks.

Outside the house, Jared stopped at the small stable, where he handed his horse to the solitary servant. Johanan tied his own mount to a stone pillar and accompanied Jared into the empty courtyard. He would not be welcome any further and only came this far because the late hour meant he was unlikely to run into any of the residents. Jared bid his friend a warm farewell, knowing Johanan had accompanied him as far as possible to ensure his well-being.

In his chamber, he lit a lamp, and froze. At the center of his bed lay a papyrus scroll, tied neatly with a length of blue ribbon.

Frowning, he untied the looped knot and unfurled the scroll. His heart skipped a beat as he saw the name. For a moment, he considered crushing the delicate papyrus in his fist and pitching it out of his open window.

In spite of the sudden surge of anger, he found himself seated on his bed, the roll of papyrus on his lap. Open. His thumb traced the ink on the fibrous surface of the letter. Against his will, he began to read.

To Jared, son of Lord Hanamel, from Keren-happuch,
daughter of Asa:

May the Lord bless you.

Weeks ago, Lord Daniel took me to the Hanging
Gardens. You have seen them several times, but it was my
first visit. I was astonished by their beauty. Lord Daniel
told me that he wanted me to have this memory in my
heart, so that I could understand God's promise.

Daniel said, "Whenever you are languishing or weary,
whenever you are tempted to give up, I want you to
remember this place. This watered garden. For this is the
Lord's promise to you. One day, this shall be your life."

I want to pass that promise to you, Jared. Your life shall
be like the Hanging Gardens in spite of what I did. Beauty
and strength growing out of an impossible ground. God
can do this, for his redemption far surpasses my sin.

I am leaving Babylon tomorrow. I will not burden
you by asking for your forgiveness again. I write only to
say that you deserve a full life. And I believe the Lord will
bless you with one. May you languish no more, my friend.

Jared rolled up the letter and set it carefully on the table next
to him. For the second time that night, he felt the odd sensation in his chest, and the walnut-size lump in his throat, and
the confounded curtain of moisture in his eye.

CHAPTER
TWENTY-FIVE

I know that you can do all things,
and that no purpose of yours can be thwarted.
Job 42:2, ESV

After two months in Lord Harpagus's household, Aryanis had drilled enough Median into my brain that I could carry on a conversation without sounding like a toddler.

My life had settled into a familiar routine. Light scribal duties in the early mornings with Lord Harpagus, followed by my time with Artadates, ending with a haphazard lesson in Median life and language from Aryanis.

But the comfort of my routine met with an unexpected surprise.

One morning, I arrived at the cottage and found it empty. Usually Artadates would be waiting for me by the door, pouncing on me with a slew of questions.

We had gotten into the habit of moving our table outdoors to enjoy the fresh air as we worked. I started dragging the table toward the shade of an apple tree, wondering what had become of my usually punctual student.

At the sound of hooves, I shielded my eyes against the sun. Artadates often walked to the cottage, though upon occasion, he borrowed his father's mount, so that he could practice archery on horseback. This morning, he had come on his horse. But he had not arrived alone.

Riding before him sat a boy I had never met.

I studied my pupil as he vaulted off the back of his mare with the natural grace of a gifted athlete. He had once told me that his father had taken him for his first ride a week after his birth, and I believed it. I had rarely seen anyone so at ease astride a horse.

But today, my eyes were glued to the stranger who remained on the mare, making no effort to dismount. He seemed to be of the same age as my pupil, though his rich clothes marked him as a member of the nobility. I bit my lip, knowing Harpagus would not be pleased to hear of Artadates's friendship with an aristocratic boy. And worse yet, bringing him to our cottage! Above all things, my master valued secrecy when it came to this child.

Artadates waved me over. "Who do we have here?" I asked.

"This is Tigranes. I found him on the way to the cottage. He has injured his ankle and can't walk well. Tigranes, this is my teacher, Keren."

The boy gave me a regal nod.

"What happened to your ankle, Tigranes?"

"My silly stallion happened, that's what. At the mere sight of some slithering serpent, he reared and threw me," the boy said in disgust. "That craven, lily-livered deserter didn't even have the decency to return for me. Left me on the ground with a twisted ankle and abandoned me."

"He was hobbling when I found him," Artadates said. "Seemed wrong to leave him that way."

Which explained why he had ignored all of Harpagus's warnings about keeping the cottage a secret and decided to bring the boy here in broad daylight. Artadates was not one to leave someone in need behind.

"Perhaps we best take you home right away, Tigranes," I said, hoping to diminish the damage. The boy would probably not even remember how to return to this place.

Tigranes's shoulders drooped. "I was hoping I could rest a little." His voice sounded strained. "It has been such a long morning, and I could use a bit of water." Brown eyes stared at me pitifully.

"Please, can he stay, Keren?" Artadates bounced on the balls of his feet.

Unable to resist the double plea, I helped the boy down from the horse and led him to one of our chairs. As he drank from my cup and inhaled the last crumb of the bread and cheese I had brought for lunch, I tried to discover more about our unexpected guest. The boy proved slippery, answering every question so vaguely that by the time he finished, I knew no more about him than I had when I started.

Clearly, this required a deft touch. "Tigranes," I said. "That is not a Median name. You must be Babylonian." I knew full well the boy did not hail from Babylon. Neither his garments nor his speech or name indicated any connection to the land of my captivity.

"Certainly not!" he objected. "That is an Armenian name."

"Ah! You come from Armenia. And your father must be . . . a perfume seller?"

The boy sat up straight, all pretense of weakness forgotten. "Perfume seller! Fire and lightning! My father is the king."

We were all rendered silent by this confession. Tigranes turned pale, flustered by his own disclosure. That the boy spoke truth, I did not doubt for one moment. I realized, however, that this revelation held a number of unfortunate ramifications for both sides.

If Tigranes was the son of the king of Armenia, that meant he was staying at the palace. I happened to know that the king of Armenia was not visiting Astyages at this time.

Which meant Tigranes was a hostage.

Keeping young hostages was not an unusual practice amongst royal houses. Armenia was under the yoke of Media and obligated to pay their conquerors an annual tribute. To ensure the process went smoothly, one of the sons of the king resided as a permanent guest of Astyages.

Such hostages received rigorous tuition, so that they could return home properly trained for their position. A boy like Tigranes had no business roaming outside the city gates on horseback. He was probably not even allowed outside the palace walls.

I crossed my arms. "I believe a lot of people are searching for you at this very moment, Prince Tigranes."

The boy shrugged. "Possibly."

Artadates leaned against the table. "Why are they looking for Tigranes?"

"Because he is a hostage."

Artadates whistled. "Were you running away?"

"I was going for a ride."

I expelled a long-suffering sigh. "We have to return you to

the palace. What's more, you must promise not to speak of Artadates or me or this place to anyone."

"I won't," the boy said, brightening, "if you don't take me back."

"You can forget that. Back you will go," I said, my voice hardening. "Besides, how far will you get with a limp and no horse? We will try to sneak you back into the palace. How you explain your absence is up to you. Just don't mention us."

"Fine," the boy said. "If you let me stay for another hour."

Artadates, who had been studying this bargaining exchange with interest, clapped. "That seems like a reasonable request. Can he stay, please?"

It was not often that my pupil enjoyed the company of another boy his age. Not one who had received the advantages of proper tuition. He was hungry for companionship.

"One hour," I said.

Of course, I had to wave my planned lessons for the morning goodbye. Artadates challenged the prince to a seated archery contest. I could tell my student was holding back, making allowances for Tigranes's injury. When the prince landed a shot dead center of the target, Artadates threw himself into the game, and the boys finished the contest at a tie. I wondered what Artadates would be capable of, should he receive proper training and practice as his new friend had clearly done.

The boys discussed the merits of Artadates's mare. The beast, though no thoroughbred like the chestnut he longed for, nonetheless displayed all the qualities of a good Median horse, with a powerful chest and elegant lines.

"She is serviceable. But no warrior's horse," Artadates admitted.

"At least she does not run at the first sign of danger," the Armenian prince said with a huff.

When our hour came to an end, I expected the boys to put up a fuss, begging for more time. Instead, they held up their end of the bargain without demur. Artadates hopped upon his horse and, gathering up the bridle, tucked it under the felt blanket. Using his legs to keep the mare still, he held out his arm to help Tigranes settle before him as I lifted the boy.

The Armenian prince treated me to a fierce scowl.

"I am sorry. Did I hurt you?" I asked.

"A mere girl, hurt me? Fire and lightning! It is merely galling to be lifted into the saddle by a woman, like a bawling babe."

We kept an old blanket at the cottage. I fetched it so that our guest could wrap the brown wool around himself, hiding his fine garments from curious eyes. I signaled for him to remove his gold earrings and muss his neat locks. Now the boys looked like two ordinary shepherds.

Artadates nudged the mare forward, keeping the pace slow enough for me to keep up on foot. I had worried about returning Astyages's hostage to the palace without anyone being the wiser. To my astonishment, the Armenian prince led me to a gate in the garden, which farmers used for food delivery.

"It isn't locked during the day," he said with a satisfied grin. "It's not as if there is an army at our door. They only secure the place after sunset."

"What will you tell them?"

"That I fell. Which I did."

"Outside the palace."

He shrugged. "They don't need to be privy to all the details."

I allowed the boys to whisper their goodbyes privately. They were not likely to set eyes on each other again. But it had been a memorable day for both.

The events of the morning had placed me in a quandary. Should I report the prince's visit to Harpagus or protect Artadates from my master's censure? In the end, I chose to tell Harpagus about the king's hostage. I suspected that his primary motive for the many rules he insisted upon was to keep Artadates safe. If my failure to disclose the prince's unexpected visit placed my pupil in some unforeseen danger, I would not forgive myself.

When I described the events of the morning to my master, the blood drained from his face. After a long silence, he whispered, "You cannot stop the hand of fate." Without another word of explanation, he walked away.

I did not believe in fate. The purposes of God, however, were a reality that I clung to. While I could not understand Harpagus's strange words, I felt pressed to pray for Artadates. After two months of spending most of my waking hours with him, he had wormed himself into my heart. In the absence of family and friends, I had poured my affections into the boy and found him an easy child to love. He had become far dearer to me than any ordinary pupil.

I crawled into bed early, knowing Aryanis would be late with kitchen duties that night. I had just unfurled my Jeremiah scroll when a soft sound drew my attention.

"Artadates!" I gasped as the boy slinked toward me on bare, silent feet.

He pressed his finger to his lips to hush me and settled himself at the foot of my pallet.

"You know you are not allowed here!"

He shrugged. "I brought you a present." He pressed a round object covered by a ragged kerchief into my hand.

"For me?"

He nodded enthusiastically. Before I had a chance to open the kerchief and inspect the contents, his hands untied the knot for me, revealing a flash of golden pastry. "It's stuffed with walnuts. My mother made me two. I saved one for you. She is the best cook in all of Media!"

I had a tantalizing whiff of butter and yeast and honey. Astonished, I shook my head. "But why?"

"To thank you. For letting Tigranes stay today. And for helping him return."

The boy gave me an awkward pat on my hand and scampered off into the dark before I could acknowledge my gratitude.

CHAPTER
TWENTY-SIX

JARED

Once he had read Keren's letter a second time, Jared grew occupied with a question that had nothing to do with the contents of the scroll.

Who had delivered the letter to his chamber?

Because, presumably, the person who had brought this missive had received it from Keren herself. In her message, she had said that she was leaving Babylon. But before her departure, Keren had handed that scroll to someone. It followed that the same someone must know her whereabouts.

Did he *want* to know her whereabouts?

Jared beat the end of the rolled papyrus against his palm as he considered the question. He had no intention of pursuing the girl. Of coming face-to-face with her, even. But he needed to ensure that she was safe. Know that she had found sanctuary.

Daniel had told him weeks earlier that he suspected Keren had left the city already. Yet the letter indicated that she was leaving Babylon *tomorrow*. Which either meant that Daniel had mistaken Keren's timing or that this letter was old.

Upon careful inquiry, Jared discovered that no one in the household had knowledge of the messenger who had delivered Keren's scroll to his chamber. It seemed to have appeared out of nowhere.

Then he remembered the open window of his room. Remembered also that Johanan had walked into the courtyard with him. Had lingered as Jared bid him good night and entered the front door.

It had taken him a few moments to walk the length of the dark hallway and enter his chamber. Could Johanan have placed the letter there in so short a time?

He strode to the courtyard and, standing by the open window of his room, looked within. It quickly dawned on him that his friend would not have had to crawl into the chamber. As an accurate marksman, he could have pitched the letter through the window and watched it land on the bed.

Someone had to have helped Keren leave Daniel's house all those weeks ago when she had disappeared like smoke, leaving Lord Hanamel cursing with frustrated fury. Daniel and Mahlah had not been involved with that rescue.

With a sudden flash of clarity, Jared realized that his friend had been the source of Keren's escape. Instead of feeling betrayed, he only felt a rush of relief. With Johanan at the helm of Keren's flight, he could at least know that she was safe, somewhere far from Babylon's walls and his father's rage.

* * *

That rage, as it transpired, exploded in Jared's face not long after. Lord Hanamel refused to even consider the thought of Jared working for Daniel.

"You are the one complaining about the cost of feeding me and my horse," Jared said through gritted teeth. "Until I can return to work as a canal supervisor, this is the perfect solution."

"Nothing is the perfect solution if it involves that man! Had he not meddled, the girl would have received her just punishment by now."

Jared's voice grew ominously quiet. "Lord Daniel had nothing to do with Keren's disappearance."

"Don't be a fool. Of course he did."

"What is more," Jared continued as though his father had not spoken, "I do not want Keren punished. I am asking that you drop this persecution."

His father took a threatening step forward. *"Eye for eye, tooth for tooth,"* he ground out. "You are mad if you think I will allow that girl to walk away without paying her debt to me."

Jared ignored his father's familiar rant. "I will start working for Lord Daniel in the morning."

"Don't bother returning to my house if you do!" Spittle flew out of Hanamel's mouth as he shrieked, his threat followed by a voluble string of curses.

CHAPTER
TWENTY-SEVEN

Thus says the LORD to his anointed, to Cyrus,
whose right hand I have grasped,
to subdue nations before him
and to loose the belts of kings,
to open doors before him
that gates may not be closed.
Isaiah 45:1, ESV

One afternoon I arrived home only to discover that I had mislaid my blue shawl at the cottage. I would have left it there, except that this was Jared's gift. The one he had bought me with his hard-earned silver. The one he had wrapped around my shoulders with his gentle hands.

I was not about to be parted from it for even one night.

Sighing, I slipped on my sandals and headed out once more, trudging down the main road that led through the seven gates of Ecbatana, past the surrounding village, and curving into the paths that led to the cottage. I thought I had left the shawl on the back of my chair. Not finding it there, I turned to the chest where I stored our school supplies and sighed with relief when I spied a flash of blue.

My brows knitted as I picked up the shawl. One of the practice swords was missing from the chest. I had stashed it there myself following our lesson that afternoon.

An unexpected noise made me freeze in my tracks. There was someone out there!

The cottage and its land belonged to Lord Harpagus. A low wall encompassed the property, marking it as private, clearly discouraging outsiders. He did not allow anyone but Artadates and me to step inside the place. Whoever was whispering out there had no right to be on this land.

Forgetting about the missing sword, I tiptoed to the back of the cottage where the voices seemed to be loudest and pressed my ear to the wall. I could distinguish the voices of two men, speaking softly.

"He is never home anymore!" one said.

"You knew this day would come. He is not just any boy. You are raising a prince of royal blood. He must be educated accordingly. One day, he will have to take his rightful place."

"But, my lord, he is my son!"

"You have raised him like a son, you and your wife. And you love him, I know. For the sake of that love, you must hold him loosely, Mitradates."

The sound of muffled weeping came through the wall.

"We may call him Artadates. But remember his true name. He is Cyrus, the son and grandson of kings."

I pulled my ear from the wall and gasped. I knew the voice that had spoken those last words. It belonged to my master, Harpagus. And the man whom he had called Mitradates must be my pupil's father, the royal shepherd.

Or *not* his father, as I had once suspected.

Except that I had been wrong.

Harpagus was not my pupil's natural father. Not if the boy was the son and grandson of kings!

None of these revelations had the power to make me stand there, paralyzed like a startled doe, however. What had turned me into a statue was a name. For my pupil was not Artadates at all.

His rightful name was Cyrus.

A name with which I had some familiarity.

I frowned, trying to remember the passages I had once studied under Daniel's tutelage. The prophet Isaiah had mentioned a king named Cyrus by name in several prophecies about my people. He was the only person not of Israel's lineage to ever be called God's *anointed* in our Holy Scriptures. Bits and pieces of the prophecy came to me like shards of a Mesopotamian mosaic.

> *Thus says the LORD to his anointed, to Cyrus,*
> *whose right hand I have grasped,*
> *to subdue nations before him . . .*

> *"He is my shepherd,*
> *and he shall fulfill all my purpose."*

The prophecies foretold that Cyrus would rebuild Jerusalem and lay a new foundation for our shattered Temple. And he would set the exiles free.

Could Isaiah's Cyrus be this same boy that I had been tutoring for over two months? Could the shepherd boy that sat a horse as though born to it, and loosed an arrow like a warrior, be the king who would one day set my people free?

Was it even possible that the child who had shared his bread with me might one day become the ruler who would release my people from their bondage?

What a far-fetched dream it all seemed! What an impossible outcome that I, having been cast out from my home for the magnitude of my sin, should now find myself tutor to the one God had chosen as a savior of my people!

And yet, I could not shake this growing conviction. I could not persuade myself that the name would turn out to be a mere coincidence.

I collapsed on the chair, having forgotten the two men who conversed outside. I thought only of the boy I had come to love.

When the door creaked open, I sprang up with a squeal.

"I thought I saw you come in," Harpagus said.

"I left my shawl." I held up the blue fold of fabric I still clutched in nerveless fingers.

"You heard?"

I did not pretend ignorance. "Yes, lord."

Harpagus nodded his head. I realized that if he had seen me enter the cottage, he could have stopped the conversation with Mitradates. Clearly, he had wanted me to overhear his revelations.

"But, lord," I said, "how can Cyrus—"

Harpagus cut me off hastily. "You must never speak that name aloud! It endangers us all."

I pressed a hand to my chest, trying to slow the drumbeat of my heart. "How can Artadates be the son of kings?"

"I will tell you his tale. First, you must promise to hold every word shrouded in secrecy. The boy's life is at stake, as are yours and mine."

I jerked my head into a nod. "I would never put Artadates's life in danger, my lord."

"Yes. I believe you have grown fond of the boy."

Harpagus began to pace. "Perhaps I should begin our story with the king's father, Cyaxares. Our people call him Cyaxares the Great, for after a strong rule and many a successful siege, he came to be known as our most capable king. Being blessed with long life, his reign lasted several decades. Meanwhile, Astyages waited and waited for his turn on the throne."

"Ah."

He stopped. "You begin to understand? Perhaps the waiting proved too much. Perhaps he was born with a possessive nature." Harpagus waved an arm. "Whatever the reason, Astyages has always been exceedingly jealous for his crown."

I remembered the odd look on the king's face the night I had met him. The way he had examined every shadow with an intense suspicion.

"Astyages has no sons. His eldest daughter, Mandana, was a beautiful princess of marriageable age when Astyages had a dream that disturbed him greatly."

Having lived at Daniel's house, I was no stranger to the dreams of monarchs, and the power they could wield. Nebuchadnezzar's dream had almost cost Daniel his life, before God interceded. I nodded my comprehension.

"Summoning the magi, Astyages demanded an explanation. The magi told him that his dream spoke of the future greatness of his daughter's progeny. Instead of celebrating this good portent, the king began to fret. What if this unconceived grandson should grow great, but at Astyages's expense? What if he were to wrest his kingdom from him?"

"He feared a child not yet born?"

"Precisely." Harpagus paced a straight line from the back wall to the front door. "Astyages's solution proved simple.

He married Mandana off to the Persian crown prince, Cambyses."

I shook my head, not understanding how this marriage helped Astyages feel safe.

"The Persians pay tribute to us, having been conquered by the Medes years ago. But they have been rattling their chains. Growing in power and independence, which has worried Astyages. Their kingdom lies too far to the south for us to fully control. By foisting Mandana upon Cambyses, Astyages killed two birds with one stone. He ensured the Persians' good behavior. And assumed his grandson's greatness would now be someone else's problem. Let the Persian king deal with a powerful grandson. They live too far away to pose a problem for us."

Harpagus dropped into a chair and motioned for me to sit as well. "This strategy worked for a season. Until, at Astyages's demand, Cambyses sent his pregnant wife with a delegation of the Persians to Media, so that she could pay homage to her royal father."

"The king had another dream while she was here?" I guessed.

Harpagus gave me a surprised look. "Precisely. This dream proved more dire. The child in Mandana's womb would one day rule over many nations, including Media."

In spite of the coolness of the air, I felt sweat drench my brow.

"The king insisted that Mandana remain at Ecbatana until she had delivered her babe, claiming the superiority of our physicians to those in Persia. The princess obeyed, of course. What else could she do?

"In a few months, she was delivered of a healthy boy. Cambyses came for the birth. He remained long enough to hold his son in his arms. When he received an urgent message from

Anshan about an imminent attack from one of the mountain tribes, Cambyses had to hurry home.

"Astyages refused his daughter permission to return with her husband, declaring that she had become weak from childbirth. He insisted that she remain in Ecbatana for a lengthy rest, until she was fully recovered. Mandana told me she felt more like a hostage than a cossetted daughter. But again, she had no recourse. Neither as a daughter nor as a princess who owed her allegiance to the king of Media.

"In a rushed ceremony, she and her husband named their son Cyrus, pointedly honoring Cambyses's father rather than Mandana's. The prince kissed his little family and left his wife in the care of his father-in-law, before heading back to Anshan."

I leaned forward. "So that babe was the grandson of two kings: Astyages the Mede and Cyrus of Persia."

"Precisely." Harpagus dropped his head, and his voice with it. "That is where my part in the tale began."

In the same low tones, Harpagus told me the rest of his story, his words so vivid, I found myself traveling in time and experiencing every scene as though I had lived it . . .

CHAPTER
TWENTY-EIGHT

Though they plan evil against you,
though they devise mischief, they will not succeed.
Psalm 21:11, ESV

Harpagus bowed before the king, surprised to find himself the only person present in the audience room. He felt a foreboding tingle travel up his spine. Everything from the grim cast of Astyages's mouth to the purple tinge in his complexion warned his visitor of an impending calamity.

But nothing could have prepared Harpagus for what Astyages demanded.

"I want that child killed," the king spat.

Confused, Harpagus kept his expression bland. "That child, lord?"

"Cambyses's brat. I want him dead," the king said, impatience making him slur.

For a moment, Harpagus stood frozen, certain he had misunderstood the king's intent. "You mean your grandson, lord? Mandana's babe?"

"Who else could I mean?"

Harpagus did not know how to respond. As a military leader, he had killed his share of men. War was a messy business. He had seen women and children suffer and die. But the thought of murdering a babe of his own people made his skin crawl.

And not just any babe.

The great-grandson of Cyaxares, the most admired monarch who had ever ruled over this nation! It seemed a betrayal to even think of it.

Harpagus swallowed hard. He could not commit such a base crime, not even at the behest of his king. Yet, to disobey was to die.

He wiped a trail of sweat from his brow. "You wish me to murder your grandson, my king?" He said the words carefully, slowly, hoping to shock Astyages with the plain brutality of what he planned.

It did not work. "Of course we must make it look like an accident. I don't want a horde of Persians knocking on my door."

"What kind of an accident?"

"He does not walk or crawl yet, so we cannot stage a runaway chariot. Our options are limited."

Our options. A churning nausea rose up in Harpagus's belly. He wanted no part of whatever plan Astyages had hatched. He did not want any share in this *we* or *us* or *our* villainy.

The king continued, unaware of the displeasure darkening Harpagus's thoughts. "My daughter insists that the child sleep with the windows unlatched, believing the fresh air will make him strong. This works to our advantage. We can steal the child from his cradle after the wet nurse feeds him in the evening.

I will send the woman a gift of the wine from my own table. It will contain a special powder that will cause her to sleep heavily."

"Who would consider the disappearance of a child from his cradle an accident, lord?"

The king held up a finger. "It's a tragedy, Harpagus. A wild dog roamed into the chamber through the open window and grabbed the babe. A few drops of blood in the cradle, the bristle of a dog hair or two, and the sighting of a wild dog prowling about the palace several days in a row. Why, I myself had a glimpse of it only this morning." The king sneered.

Harpagus felt his throat tightening. He pressed the bridge of his nose. "My lord king, I am your humble servant."

"Good."

"And as your humble servant, I advise that you carefully consider this grave step you are about to take. Think of your daughter's suffering."

"Bah! She can have other children. Think of *my* throne, man. My dreams do not lie. That innocent babe lying peacefully in his mother's arms will, in a few years, wrest my kingdom from me!" He pounded a fist into his palm. "I say no! I say never! The boy must die. And you are the one to do it."

Harpagus bowed smoothly. "As you command, lord."

He felt his blood churning, every beat an accusation in his chest. If he committed this atrocity, how could he ever look into his own son's eyes, the sturdy three-year-old boy who romped about his house and gazed upon his father with worshipful admiration? Everything he valued—honor, truth, goodness— rose up in rebellion against such a contemptible act.

After the king dismissed him, he began to concoct the rudiments of a dangerous plan. Instead of going home, he headed for the modest cottage occupied by Mitradates, one of the royal shepherds. It took several knocks before the man answered the door. In the harsh morning light, he looked at his visitor through red-rimmed eyes. Recognizing Harpagus, his mouth fell loose.

Drawing a hand against his stained tunic, he gave an awkward bow. "Forgive me, master. We were not expecting company."

"My wife told me of your sad news," Harpagus said. "I am sorry for your loss."

The shepherd's chin wobbled. "Your lady is most kind. We have not told anyone yet. But she came to our door yesterday, bearing gifts of bread and cheese just after it had happened. She thought she would be celebrating a birth with us."

Tears streaked the ruddy face. "It's that we are so old, you see. What a miracle to discover my wife was with child. I never knew such joy. And now, the babe is dead. One breath only we had with him, before he was lost to us."

Harpagus stood frozen for a moment. No going back, if he set this thing into motion. No undoing this thread. He squared his shoulders.

"Mitradates, I believe I have a solution for your problem."

CHAPTER
TWENTY-NINE

I cry out to God Most High,
to God who fulfills his purpose for me.
Psalm 57:2, ESV

I stared at my master with rounded eyes. "Does Artadates know?"

"He does not. The only parents he has ever known are Mitradates and his wife."

"But . . ."

"Yes. We should tell him the truth. One day. For now, I consider him too young." Harpagus removed his round hat as though the weight of it felt too great. "A slip of a tongue and all of us will be subject to Astyages's vengeance."

You, most of all, I thought, and realized I had spoken aloud.

He leaned back against his chair. "Now you understand why I welcomed the opportunity to bring you to Ecbatana. The boy deserves an education."

"Do his parents know their son lives?"

Harpagus shook his head. "I could not risk it. The king has spies everywhere. Letters can be intercepted. Besides, if they knew, they would gather their armies and be here before Astyages had time to finish his dinner. It would be a bloodbath. One they will lose. Media's army is far greater, not to mention better equipped, though I have no doubt they can deliver a mighty strike against us. Neither kingdom would benefit from such a war."

"Why not just deliver the boy to his parents yourself?"

"I cannot simply ride off to Persia without the king's express consent. My movements are a matter of state. Astyages has kept me from going anywhere near Anshan for ten years. Mandana has never returned to Ecbatana since she lost her child. Astyages wishes to ensure I do not ever come face-to-face with her. He fears I may slip and tell her what he did. He knows I never agreed with his decision."

"Could you not have sent the boy to Anshan with the shepherd?"

"Mitradates and his wife dote on him. If I sent them off on that long journey, I am not certain they would find their way to the child's rightful parents. The temptation to keep him for themselves might prove too much."

Harpagus drew a weary hand over the crown of his head. "Let us say they resist the enticement of holding on to the boy. Let us even believe that, by some miracle, they avoid every danger as they travel without the benefit of guards and arrive at Anshan without falling prey to bandits or wild animals. How are Mandana and her husband supposed to believe the outlandish claims of a shepherd that this child is none other than the babe they supposedly lost ten years ago?"

"You could write them a letter."

"Why should the king and queen of Persia accept the word of a Median general over the claims of Mandana's own father? It would smack too much of political intrigue."

Harpagus snapped to his feet and began to pace again. "A thousand times I have determined to send the boy off. A thousand times I have reconsidered. Perhaps if I had managed to return him years earlier, it would not be such a great dilemma. Now, it seems too late. Cambyses and Mandana have had no other children. When Cambyses became king after his father's death some years past, they named his nephew the heir to the throne. Sending the child into that tangled mess with no one to watch for him would place him in grave danger. A possible pretender to the throne? How many daggers will point at his throat, do you think?"

I could not argue with his reasoning. Yet the cost seemed too great. He had saved Cyrus's life. But he had not salvaged the boy's identity or rightful place.

"You understand now why I have forbidden you from filling his head with talk of your religion? He is already an outsider. Raised in Media. If he arrives home, worshiping some Jewish deity, he will have no chance at the throne. I have seen to it that he venerates Ahura Mazda, the god of the Persians, while paying homage to the Median god as well."

I fidgeted with the blue shawl in my lap. Unbidden, the words of the prophet Isaiah came to me: *I call you by your name, I name you, though you do not know me.* God had foreseen this moment. He had known I would sit here and have my hands tied. My mouth gagged. Unable to tell the boy about the wonders of the one true God. Cyrus would do the Lord's bidding without knowing him.

"Do you believe he still has a chance to ascend that throne?" I asked.

"For now, all we can do is to try to keep him safe," Harpagus said. "You have met Astyages. Did you notice something familiar about him?"

"Familiar, lord?"

Harpagus motioned to his face. Frowning, I tried to recall my brief meeting with the king. I gasped as I realized what concerned Harpagus. The king had the same forest-green eyes as Cyrus. Worse, above the left eye sat a strong brow with an odd raven-wing flip at its end. The similarity was subtle. You might miss it if you were a casual observer like me. But the king himself would not overlook that eerie similarity.

It finally dawned on me why Harpagus wanted to keep the boy away from the palace at any cost.

A sudden clatter at the door made me snap to my feet. The subject of our discussion stood at the door, his mouth hanging open. I assumed he had overheard our conversation.

But he banged his forehead with the heel of his hand and gasped, "Fire and lightning! Now you are trying to teach *him* Akkadian?"

Harpagus strode toward the boy. "What are you doing here, Artadates? You should be home."

The boy shrugged. "I came to practice. The teacher says my handwriting looks like drunk ants."

Something about the boy's excuse smelled fishy. I noticed the way he leaned against the doorframe and realized the little rascal was hiding something.

"What do you have there?" I pointed to his side.

"A door."

"Next to the door."

Artadates expelled a sigh. Without a word, he dragged the practice sword from where he had tucked it between his body and the frame and proffered it to me. "I was just bringing it back."

"And why did you take this?"

"To practice, of course." He gave a pointed look at Harpagus and said no more. I realized he did not want to complain in front of my master about my unwillingness to engage him in a proper fight.

In a different time, a different life, I would be bowing before this boy and offering him my allegiance. Instead, he stood there in shepherd's garb and defended my honor with his silence.

I accepted the wooden sword and packed it neatly in the chest. "Run along now," I said tiredly. The untidy knot of Harpagus's revelations was burning a hole in my belly. "Your mother is probably worried."

"She is accustomed to his scampering ways," Harpagus said. He mussed the boy's head and gave him a small shove out the door. "We better return home ourselves. The city gates will soon be locked."

I plodded after Harpagus, my mind a whirl of questions. Then it dawned on me. Artadates's words had been nagging at me, though I could not determine why, exactly. Now I remembered. If it had not been for the fog of shock my master's secrets had induced in my mind, I would have seen it right away.

Artadates had said, "Fire and lightning!" Those had been Tigranes's words the day he had visited the cottage several weeks earlier. And now, they occupied such a comfortable place on Artadates's tongue that they flew out at a moment's notice.

I knew what that meant. I swallowed past my dry throat.

My pupil was spending time with Tigranes. I had refused to spar with him. So he had found himself a playmate who would fill the void.

The grandson of Astyages and Cyrus had found himself the son of a king to befriend. And, in the process, he had found a way to slither into the palace of a man who had plotted his murder ten years earlier.

I wondered again about Artadates, this hidden prince.

More than the son of kings, could he be the promised liberator of my people? The Cyrus foreshadowed by the prophet Isaiah?

God had called *his* Cyrus a shepherd. I had always assumed the word to be symbolic. A metaphor for a king who would lead and protect God's people. What if, like David, this Cyrus had his beginnings as a true shepherd? Ambling through fields, guarding lambs, and sleeping under the stars?

The prophets had foretold that the captivity of my people would last seventy years. That placed Cyrus at the right age. Thirty-five years from now he could be a seasoned warrior, and yet still young enough to lead armies in his wake.

Or he could be the most well-educated shepherd that ever lived.

I put one foot in front of the other as I trudged up the hill toward Ecbatana. I knew what my heart said. Knew it to the marrow of my bones.

My Cyrus and God's shepherd were one and the same.

This was the reason God had brought me here, to this faraway land. My banishment in Media was not merely a punishment for my sin against Jared. God had led me here for Cyrus. And for my people.

Daniel had been right all along. I had a call on my life.

Far from destroying God's purpose for me, the sword that had taken Jared's eye had, like Jonah's fish, swallowed me only to disgorge me on the shores of the land where I was meant to come.

CHAPTER THIRTY

This is an easy thing in the eyes of the LORD.

2 Kings 3:18, NIV

―――――――――― JARED ――――――――――

"Where is she, Johanan?" Jared pressed Keren's letter against his friend's chest.

Johanan placed the practice sword he had just grasped back on the rack. "In Media," he said woodenly.

"Media?" Jared had never considered that Keren might have fled so far away. "Are you insane?"

Johanan inhaled. "You can fetch her back, if you choose. She made me promise that I would tell you where she went if you wanted her punished. She only agreed to leave when I assured her that you did not want to claim the Code of Hammurabi."

"The Code of Hammurabi? You *are* insane!"

"Then why are you angry?"

"Because Media is a foreign land with . . . with . . . foreign people. She knows no one there. She doesn't even speak the language!"

"She has learned it by now. You know her with languages."

"The point is, she is all alone," Jared shouted. "Why did it take you so long to give me that letter?"

"You were ill, at first, and in no condition to worry about her. As you began to improve, your anger grew. I did not want you to simply tear up her scroll without reading a word. I had to wait until you had calmed."

Jared sighed. "I see."

"I know you are worried for her. But in Media, she is safe from your father's vengeance. Not a day goes by when Lord Hanamel does not seek a fresh audience with the king, hoping to pester him into a wider search. If she had remained in Babylonian territory, she would likely have been arrested by now."

Jared went still. "I realized he was enraged. But I had no idea my father had continued his pursuit of vengeance with the king."

"He has never given up. I had to get her far away from here."

"I need to see the king before my father does."

"You can forget that idea. Nebuchadnezzar has grown more withdrawn and elusive in recent months."

Jared shook his head.

"It is almost impossible for an ordinary man with no real connections to the court to gain permission for a royal visit," Johanan insisted. "This has helped us in a way, since it has kept your father from being able to converse with the king a second time. But Lord Hanamel could soon gain permission for a second audience, given his royal ties. You, on the other hand, would be more likely to grow a pair of wings and fly."

Jared grabbed a sword. "First, we practice. You might wish *you* had a pair of wings when you see how much I have improved."

Johanan groaned. "Oh, please! Must we?"

"Yes, we must. I think better when my hands are busy."

"You can think all you like, Jared. But some things are simply not possible."

"For you and me, perhaps." He flashed a smile. "But this is an easy thing for the Lord."

CHAPTER
THIRTY-ONE

Moab has been at ease from his youth
and has settled on his dregs;
he has not been emptied from vessel to vessel,
nor has he gone into exile;
so his taste remains in him,
and his scent is not changed.
Jeremiah 48:11, ESV

I pressed the edge of my wooden sword against Artadates's neck. A shocked breath whistled from his lips. After a short hesitation, he leapt away. I threw my weapon on the ground and crossed my arms.

"You would be dead now, if I was a palace guard," I said, keeping my voice low.

"How did you find me?"

"You're not that hard to follow." Silently, I apologized to God for the fib. In fact, I had found it a considerable challenge to keep up with him. "The more imperative question is, what are you doing sneaking into the palace?"

"Just having a bit of fun."

"A bit of fun?" I spat the words. "A bit of fun is going apple picking. Or enjoying a long walk in a meadow. Or a good ride on a well-trained horse. This . . ." I pointed at the stone he had managed to dig out of the base of the garden wall. "This is what gets little heads separated from their skinny necks."

Artadates rubbed his skinny neck. "Long walks in a meadow? Fire and lightning! Remind me never to try and have fun when you're around."

"Where is he?"

"Where is who?"

I tapped my foot. "Where is your princely friend, that hostage of King Astyages you have been sneaking off with?"

Artadates grimaced. Wordlessly, he pointed at the wall. "In there somewhere."

Before I could respond, the head of said hostage appeared through the hole created by the loose stone Artadates had removed.

"Uh-oh," he mumbled when he saw me.

I gritted my teeth. "You might as well get yourself all the way out."

The Armenian price grinned and slithered out with the agility of a lizard. He peeled a shriveled leaf off his cheek as he straightened, beating mud from his tunic. "I came to see what was holding you up," he told Artadates.

My pupil pointed at me. "Watch out, or she will have you taking long walks in meadows and learning Akkadian."

"Fire and lightning!" Tigranes gasped, as if I had threatened to hang him on the gallows.

"You two are in a heap of trouble. You are going to *wish* for an Akkadian lesson when I finish with you. What do you mean by sneaking in and out of the palace?"

"We didn't do anything bad," Artadates said. "We are merely practicing our swords. Drilling with you isn't enough, Keren. If I am to learn, I need a proper partner."

Every heated word of caution and correction evaporated at Artadates's explanation. Because the boy before me was, in fact, *not* Artadates. Here stood Cyrus, a prince who would one day lead armies into Babylon. He needed to learn the use of a sword. And he was right. My daily drills, though vigorous, were not enough.

"Well, you can't do that in the palace," I said. "You will be caught and punished." Not to mention possibly recognized. "Nor can you practice in the cottage. Lord Harpagus would never agree to it."

The boys groaned in unison, sounding like a disgruntled choir.

"We need to find you two a concealed spot," I said, ignoring their moans. "Where you will not be discovered by anyone."

Cheers met my new pronouncement. Before they grew too enthusiastic, I plunged ahead.

"Three times a week only," I cautioned. "Tigranes, you must ensure no one follows you when you leave the palace. And Cyrus, you will not return to this place again. Understand?"

"Who is Cyrus?" Artadates looked at me, his open face filled with curiosity.

Heat stained my cheeks. "Just a trip of the tongue. I meant you, Artadates. Now, do you know an abandoned spot we can use? A place no one is likely to stumble upon accidentally. You know this area better than Tigranes or me."

Artadates grinned slowly. "I know the perfect place."

* * *

When I returned to the house, I found a pile of letters awaiting me. Johanan had kept his promise and found a way to send me a satchel full of missives from my family. Nothing from Jared, of course. I had known not to expect a response from him. Still, the knowledge had not prepared me for the pang of disappointment that twisted in my belly.

I opened Grandfather's letter first and stared at the wobbly lines on the papyrus and wept as I remembered the quivering fingers that had made them.

My tears turned to laugher as I read about my brother, who in his frantic haste to get ready for his job at the docks had accidentally swept a pot of Grandfather's red ink off the table. But when he had dropped to his knees to retrieve the overturned pot, he had been confounded. The ink pot had vanished. After ensuring that no ink had spilled on my mother's prized carpet, he had shrugged and dashed to work.

An hour later, when my mother had reached for her basket-weaving reeds, she had a surprise in store.

To create her baskets, she soaked the reeds in a tub of water for an hour in order to make them pliable enough to use. That morning, she discovered that every single reed had turned a delicate shade of pink!

She sat and stared at this unexpected wonder in dismay. Having promised five new baskets to the merchant in the market, she came to the conclusion that she and my sister would have to use the blighted pink reeds since they did not have time to soak and soften fresh ones in time.

Thankfully, the merchant had liked the appearance of them so much, he had ordered ten more. Now my brother was demanding a share of her income, saying he had invented the color.

I read through every word my family had written several times and kissed their names where they had signed the papyrus. Home seemed the same as ever. Nothing fundamental had changed. I longed for that sameness now, in my topsy-turvy life. That indefinable security which only the presence of these people seemed to provide.

Yet I also knew that I was exactly where I was meant to be.

I remembered a verse in Jeremiah's writings, which seemed to apply to my present circumstances. Speaking of Moab, the Lord had complained to the prophet that, like bad wine, the nation had settled on its dregs, never emptied from vessel to vessel.

The juice of grapes needed to remain in its original vessel until the dregs settled at the bottom. But in time, the vessel had to be emptied into another, leaving behind its impurities. The process was carried out several times, until the wine aged properly, growing purer with every emptying.

Empty the vessel too quickly, and the wine would lose its flavor. But leave it too long, and it would sour.

I had been like that vessel, settled in the security of my family and Daniel's household. The Lord had kept me there, steady and unchanged, shielded from harm.

But in his chosen time, God poured me out of my family. Out of my home. Out of the companionship of my friends. Out of the only land I had ever known.

He hadn't poured me out to destroy me. The reverse, in fact. If I had remained in Babylon, I would have become like Moab, soured and useless. This great upheaval would somehow lead to a fruitful life. I had lost the vessel of home, only to find new purpose in the vessel of Media.

Tenderly, I rolled up the letters and tied them with bits of ribbon before tucking them on the tiny shelf that Aryanis and I shared. Harpagus found me wiping tears from my cheeks.

"Homesick?"

"Yes, lord."

"I am sorry for it. How does the boy progress?"

"Exceptionally well. Lord Harpagus . . ." I hesitated. I had never told him of the prophecies about Cyrus. Yet I had come to trust this Gentile who held the boy's life in his hands. Perhaps it was time I told him what I knew. "May I tell you something curious? In confidence?"

He motioned to the garden, and grabbing the scroll of Jeremiah, I followed. A small vineyard grew at the bottom of the plot, where an old stone bench had been worn smooth by visitors over long years. Harpagus sat on the bench while I stood before him, my eyes lowered.

"My people, as you know, lord, live in exile. Our homeland lies in ruins. But there are several prophecies that speak of the end of our captivity. According to our prophets, there is one who will set us free from bondage to Babylon."

"Yes, yes." Harpagus crossed his legs. "I am sure there is."

"His name is Cyrus."

Harpagus froze. "Whose name?"

"The name of this coming savior. This Gentile king who will one day defeat Babylon's empire. His name is Cyrus."

"It says that in the prophecy?"

"Yes, lord. He is named Cyrus in the prophecy. More interesting to you, perhaps, another of our prophets wrote this." I unrolled the scroll of Jeremiah. Finding the appropriate passage, I translated it for Harpagus. "This is what the Lord says: *For the Lord has inspired the kings of the Medes to march against Babylon and destroy her.*"

"What?" Harpagus came to his feet.

"The kings of the Medes, lord. This Cyrus, who shall one

day defeat Babylon and set my people free, is a king of the Medes."

Harpagus paled. "It says that in there?" He pointed to Jeremiah's scroll. He had not missed the salient point of my revelations. If you put the two prophecies together, it was clear that one day, a man named Cyrus would sit on the throne of Media.

Harpagus sank back on the bench. "Have you told the boy any of this?"

"No, lord."

He nodded. "Best keep it that way, for now. He is still a child. He need not carry the weight of prophecies on his shoulders, should you prove wrong."

I closed my eyes. "Or should I prove right."

CHAPTER THIRTY-TWO

──────── JARED ────────

Jared considered asking Daniel to arrange a meeting with Nebuchadnezzar but thought better of it. Given the thorny situation his father had created, the further he kept Daniel from the matter, the safer his mentor would be should things go awry.

He could think of no other way to gain an audience with the king, however. He felt as though he were trying to open a door of heavy bronze with a feather. Short of sneaking into the palace, and likely getting himself killed, he had run out of ideas.

Then, to his amazement, he received a letter from the court, which Daniel delivered to him.

Holding up a small clay cylinder, Daniel twirled it one revolution between thumb and forefinger. "I did not realize you had connections in the palace."

"Neither did I." Jared took the cylinder from Daniel's hand. Breaking the seal and outer envelope, he read the message quickly. His jaw slackened.

Months ago, he had sent a letter to one of Nebuchadnezzar's royal scribes. He had thought the missive lost in the mighty coils of bureaucracy which was the royal court and forgotten all about its contents. After his accident, so much of ordinary life had slipped his mind. Consumed by the loss and pain he had suffered, he had never thought of the letter again.

Now that forgotten message, and the incident that had instigated its composition, seemed to have opened the impossible door he had been searching for.

He had been summoned to court!

Of course, he had only been given an audience with a royal scribe, which was a long way from meeting with the king. But he had managed to get his foot in the palace door. And God, who had used an old, forgotten letter to bring him this far, would be able to carry him the rest of the way.

"Well?" Daniel asked.

Jared grinned. "I'm off to the court to meet with one of the royal scribes."

"Which one?"

"It does not say."

"You are not in trouble, are you?"

"I hope not." Jared's grin widened. "I believe I have been summoned on a matter pertaining to the new bridge."

"The one the king loves like a newborn son?"

"The very same."

By the age of fifty-seven, Nebuchadnezzar had ruled in Babylon for thirty-two years. He had spent his youth forging military conquests, culminating in the dazzling defeat of Egypt's famed army at Carchemish. Though a few battles and skirmishes still occupied the Babylonian king's attention, in these middle years of his rule, he had turned the bulk of his attention to rebuilding Babylonia. Daniel had once told Jared that the king was proudest of these achievements, his large public works, including the rebuilding of Babylon's fortifications and enlarging the royal palace and temple of Marduk.

Most recently, Nebuchadnezzar's engineers had completed a mighty bridge spanning the Euphrates. The king, according to Daniel, had a deep affection for this wondrous new structure, built at his bidding, connecting old and new Babylon with impressive grandeur.

This bridge, Jared hoped, would offer him an entrée into the king's presence.

He returned to his chamber to change into more formal attire, adjusting the wide fringe across one shoulder. Taking a quick peek in the silver mirror to ensure his eye patch had not dislodged, Jared headed to the stables.

He had been staying at Daniel's house for weeks now, since his father had dismissed him summarily from under his roof. The calm he had found here—working for Daniel in the mornings, spending the afternoons with Joseph, striving to regain his physical equilibrium with exercise, and ending every night with Daniel's hands on his head, praying—had helped with his pain. Though the headaches had never left him entirely, they had diminished in number.

He felt the slowness of the process of healing and restoration grating on him. Patience, which had never come to him easily, was learned in sedate increments, he found. He could only hope that a headache would not strike him now, just as he was about to embark on this important meeting.

Although he was not as lithe on his horse as he once might have been, he negotiated his way through the busy thoroughfares of the city with new confidence. At the palace, one of the guards led Jared to an airy chamber whose walls were covered from ceiling to floor in rich Egyptian tapestries.

A short, slim, beardless man looked up from behind an ebony desk. "Canal Supervisor Jared, son of Lord Hanamel, I presume?"

Jared bowed his head and pointed at his eye patch. "No longer canal supervisor, I'm afraid."

"Ah, yes. I heard about your accident. A tragedy."

Jared shrugged. "I am growing accustomed."

The scribe waved, indicating the chair facing the table. "I am Urshanabi, the king's senior scribe."

Senior scribe! Jared was stunned that his plain letter had opened the door to so high a personage.

Urshanabi placed a small clay tablet on the table before him. Jared recognized his own seal, now broken.

"Quite a letter," the senior scribe said.

"It is accurate." Jared lined his feet together and tried not to fidget. The last time he had attempted to explain what he had seen, he had been reprimanded severely.

Urshanabi leaned back. "At first, when one of the scribes brought your message to me to review, I ignored it. Your claim seemed hardly credible."

"At first?" Jared's brow rose.

"The details you included. They grasped ahold of me and would not let go. Tell me. How did you notice the problem with the new bridge? No one else had, not even our best engineers."

"When I served as a canal supervisor, I was assigned the area of the river surrounding the bridge. I noticed my men were having difficulty getting close to the pilings. The currents were too powerful. The workers kept getting slammed into the banks.

"Finally, I went into the river myself, intending to check the level of the silt. I am a strong swimmer and hoped to fare better than our men."

"Did you?"

"Yes. There wasn't a great deal of silt. But in the process, I noticed the current's direction remained persistent, slamming against the same portion of shoreline that supported the bridge's pilings. When I dove under, I noticed that the stone ledge on which the pilings had been built did not extend all the way into the riverbed. It was quite thin, in fact. And the current had been eating at the clay base underneath. I could already see the erosion."

"That's when you knew the bridge was failing?"

"I suspected it then. But I wanted to confirm my findings. I made some calculations based on what I thought the bridge must weigh and realized it was in danger of collapse. Unless, of course, you move the pilings further back."

"Why did you not report your findings to the chief engineer who heads the canal supervisors?"

Jared gazed at Urshanabi with an unblinking eye. He had no intention of becoming a snitch. The truth was, after consulting with Johanan, they had approached their supervisor together. The man had treated both to a dressing-down neither would soon forget. He accused Jared of growing too big for his shoes, thinking himself qualified to criticize the king's new bridge.

"I see," Urshanabi said with a slow nod. After his years of experience in the court, he must have learned to interpret silence as well as words. "You will be happy to know that I sent my top engineer to have a look."

"What did he find?"

"As you claim. The new bridge is in danger of collapse. Maybe not today or tomorrow. But in a year or two."

"Better you find out now, when it can be repaired."

"Indeed. The lord king is aware of your service. He has bid me to offer you whatever you wish."

Jared exhaled.

CHAPTER
THIRTY-THREE

The horse is made ready for the day of battle,
but the victory belongs to the LORD.
Proverbs 21:31, ESV

"You need trousers," Artadates informed me after we finished our morning lessons.

"Trousers?" I frowned at him. "Why would I need trousers?"

Median men wore ankle-length trousers under their long, narrow tunics. The pleats on the sides of their garments allowed them the freedom to move with ease. Their women, however, were not known for the practice.

"It makes riding easier." He pointed at my threadbare Babylonian tunic. "That thing is going to split when you mount a horse. If you are going to learn to ride, you will need trousers."

"I have no intention of learning how to ride a horse. I rode a mule from Babylon, and that was bad enough."

Artadates placed his hands at his waist. "If you want to keep up with Tigranes and me, you will need to ride. Tigranes is going to teach me proper archery while riding a galloping horse. Do you want to sit inside the cottage and twiddle your thumbs while we go off into the wilderness by ourselves?"

"Fire and lightning!" I said.

Artadates doubled over, laughing.

"Where am I going to get my hands on a pair of trousers?"

"Can't you sew them?"

"No, I can't."

"I thought girls are supposed to know such things."

"Not this girl. I know Akkadian."

Artadates nodded his head sagely. "I see why you aren't married. You probably can't cook, either."

"You would be right about that."

"My mother cooks better than the chefs in the court of Armenia. I know, because Tigranes told me when he tasted her food. My father is always smiling at dinnertime."

"I may not know how to cook. But I know how to organize an army."

Artadates froze. Without a word, he pulled his chair closer. "This is going to be so much better than Akkadian."

"Do you know who Cyaxares was?"

"Well, I never met him, if that's what you mean. But he was the father of the king."

I nodded. "He was a great general. Until he ascended the throne, the armies of Media had been organized according to their tribes. The men belonging to each tribe showed up and fought together in a mighty jumble, foot soldiers and cavalry all mixed together. Cyaxares put an end to that practice. Instead, he arrayed the army in organized detachments, dividing them by weaponry. Archers in one group, spearmen in another, and so forth. This allowed him to use each arm of his army strategically, increasing his control of the battle."

Artadates stared at me adoringly. "You've been holding out on me. You knew all these wonderful things, and you never said."

I crossed my legs. I had already reached near the bottom of my military knowledge. When the boys had studied warfare, tactics, strategy, and military history, I had been busy working for Daniel. My command of the topic was woefully limited. I gnawed the inside of my mouth. We had to secure a proper instructor for this child I called Artadates who was not Artadates at all.

He poked my side. "You still need trousers."

* * *

"My lord?"

Harpagus looked up from his clay tablet. "Well?"

"It's a delicate matter."

He threw his hands in the air. "What? You want me to fetch ostrich feathers and fan your face?"

I tightened my lips. "Do you have a pair of old trousers I may have?"

He raised a brow, awaiting explanation.

"For riding a horse. Artadates wishes to practice archery while riding, and I need to accompany him."

Harpagus leaned against the back of his chair. "In that case, you will need more than trousers. You will need a horse."

"That would be helpful."

The corner of Harpagus's mouth lifted. "You don't know how to ride."

"Artadates plans to teach me."

"Indeed? Well. Try not to break your neck."

"How hard can it be? I already know how to ride a mule."

Harpagus sighed. "What a barbarian you are." Like all Medians, his fondness for horses plumbed depths I had never understood. "I will arrange for you to have the use of a gentle mare. Try not to ruin her."

I gave him a morose look, unable to make any promises.

"As to trousers, I will fetch one of my son's. At thirteen, he is closer to your size than I. Although he is already taller than you," he said proudly.

One of the servants came to the door and bowed. "A messenger from the king, my lord." He placed a small clay envelope bearing a scarlet seal in front of Harpagus.

"Is he waiting for a response?"

"No, lord."

Harpagus dismissed the servant and, breaking the seal and envelope, extracted the tablet within. His brows knotted in thought. "The king asks that I bring you to the court tomorrow."

I frowned. "Is his senior scribe ill again?"

"So he claims."

"Claims?" I asked, alarmed.

"I believe you have . . . intrigued him."

I clutched my belly, trying to soothe the sudden shaft of searing pain. I would rather dance with a hurricane than intrigue a king. Unpredictable humans with unlimited power should play no part in any sane person's life.

* * *

To Lord Daniel, ruler of the province of Babylon, from his servant Keren,

You will wonder, no doubt, how this letter has found its way upon your table. Love, I have discovered, can carve a path, even across rivers and mountains. Also, secret couriers are not as scarce as I had feared.

Not a day passes that I do not miss you and Mistress Mahlah.

You were right, Master Daniel. God has a purpose for me. This banishment, too, serves his will.

Though I cannot reveal where I am, I can tell you that I have found the one Isaiah calls the Lord's shepherd. The one who will one day set our people free. His name you already know, though I have not set it down in this letter.

He is only a boy. An extraordinary child. But if I am right, he will grow up to rule.

Pray for me, Daniel. Pray that I will not fail him. Pray that I will not fail God.

I send you my prayers and my heart.

CHAPTER THIRTY-FOUR

Behold, I am the LORD, the God of all flesh. Is anything too hard for me?
Jeremiah 32:27, ESV

A lightning-fast thrust and Johanan stood disarmed, his sword lying uselessly at his feet.

"How did you do that?" he cried, breath coming in short bursts.

Jared grinned. "I have had more opportunity to practice since I started to work for your father."

Johanan retrieved his sword from the ground, rubbing his sore wrist gingerly. "I believe you are better than you were before the accident. You are certainly more ruthless."

"When I lost the sight in my left eye, I became hesitant about every step. Overcautious, lest I made a mistake. I have been battling that instinct for months. The experience may have made me a little fiercer than before."

Wiping the back of his neck with a rag, Johanan shook his head. "Will you tell me how your interview with the king went, or are you planning to finish the job and kill me with suspense now that you have wounded me with your sword?"

Jared laughed. His meeting with Urshanabi had finally led to an audience with the Babylonian king that morning. "I entreated Nebuchadnezzar to forgive Keren's crime so she could return home with impunity."

"And?"

"The king called me *noble* and said few would be willing to use their royal reward for the sake of another. He is quite wise for a Babylonian Gentile."

"And?" Johanan cried, exasperated.

Jared shrugged. "He agreed with my request."

Johanan expelled a long breath. "He did?"

"That is not all." Jared jingled the fat cloth purse the king had thrown at him before dismissing him. Loosening the strings, he gave Johanan a glimpse of the silver shekels within.

Johanan whistled. "That must be a year's worth of wages."

"Maybe two, given what I made as a canal supervisor."

Pulling a hand through his disheveled hair, Johanan leaned against the wall. "It's hard to believe you managed to secure Keren's pardon."

"Did you ever doubt it?"

"Every day!"

"So did I!"

The two friends burst into loud laughter. It had only a tiny tinge of hysteria to it.

Just then, Daniel's old servant, Hanun, happened to walk by.

He frowned, giving them a wide berth. "Mad!" he muttered. "The whole generation of them." Which only made Jared and Johanan laugh harder.

"I will write Keren a letter to inform her of the good news," Johanan said, still grinning. "She must be longing to return home."

"How will she travel?" He did his best to sound nonchalant. "Is Harpagus coming to Babylon soon?"

"I doubt it. I assume she will join a caravan of some kind. There are bound to be other travelers headed for Babylon."

"A caravan? You want her to travel with strangers?" Jared snapped to his feet. "Do you know what can happen to a woman alone on such a long journey?"

"Do you have a better idea?"

Jared ground his teeth, refusing to answer.

CHAPTER
THIRTY-FIVE

You have delivered me from death.
Psalm 56:1,3 NIV

In spite of daily practice, it took me weeks to learn to ride competently. I found in Artadates a surprisingly dedicated teacher. He was gentle with his correction, lavish with his praise, and exacting to a fault.

As his tutor, for months I had demanded the best from him. Now that the shoe occupied the other foot, I had to meet his requests without complaint, knowing that my own attitude would come to haunt me when he became my student again a few hours later.

It took a couple of days before he even allowed me to mount the horse. Instead, he drilled me on the right posture first.

"You have several bad habits to break. Unlearn that slouch, for one. Back straight," Artadates said, hands tucked at his waist. "Head up. Not like you are going to catch snowflakes in your mouth. Tuck your chin in."

"I have never even seen snowflakes, let alone caught them in my mouth."

He blinked. "For someone who knows a lot, you don't know much."

When I was finally allowed to mount my horse, my tutor would not permit me to actually ride.

"I am quite certain you said you were going to teach me horseback *riding*," I said, trying not to betray my exasperation. "Not horseback sitting."

"You can ride when you master a good seat. Your carriage should be in harmony with your horse."

To give the boy his due, he did make a good rider out of me. Of course, I had no idea as I plodded on Harpagus's gentle mare that Artadates's strict instruction would one day save my life.

* * *

My birthday came and went with no one to remark upon it. Other birthdays passed too. My mother's. My oldest brother's. And Jared's.

I kept myself as busy as my body could bear so that these reminders of home would not drown me in a quicksand of grief. I discovered the physical exhaustion that came from riding long hours an effective panacea for homesickness. I was simply too tired to feel.

My riding lessons were interrupted at least once a week, thanks to the king. Upon one pretext or another, he requested my presence at the palace. Some days, he allowed me to join the rest of his scribes, whereupon he would find an excuse to stop and loiter.

More often, he required my presence in his audience chamber. He would have me take down a letter in the presence of foreign dignitaries and then say that even his scribes were prettier than the royal ladies who occupied their court. I winced with embarrassment, knowing he had used me as a means of delivering an insult, but helpless to repudiate him.

Harpagus always came with me on these occasions, trying to shield me from the king's wandering fingers, which had a tendency to twirl in my hair or linger on my shoulder. I think my master's presence discouraged Astyages from going further. His eyes traveled much more boldly than those stubby, bejeweled hands. Sometimes he stared at me the way a thirsty man looks upon a bowl of chilled, sweet melons.

I always came home from these visits drenched in sweat and feeling slightly nauseous. How a man had the power to make me feel dirty with his mere gaze mystified and rattled me. At home, I had half a dozen people to confide in. Here, I had to bear the burden of this odd violation alone.

One early afternoon, I returned home from another such audience at the palace, fists shaking with frustration. I headed for my nook, intending to change out of my palace finery so I could ride to the cottage and spend the rest of the afternoon with Artadates. But Aryanis stopped me on my way.

"You have a visitor."

I stared at her, nonplussed. "I do?" It must be Artadates, I realized.

"Where is that boy?" I barked.

Aryanis smirked. "If that's what you call *boy* in Babylon, I should like to move there." She hooked a thumb toward the garden. "Waiting for you by the roses."

"The cheek!" I fumed.

It was one thing for Artadates to sneak his way into the

house. But to come visiting openly broke all the rules Harpagus had established. My steps slowed. Aryanis would have recognized Artadates and chased him away. That left the Armenian prince. Mercy! Those children were going to be the end of me.

My mouth turned dry with a sudden premonition. Tigranes would not have sought me openly unless something had gone awry.

I started to run toward the garden. My feet came to a jarring stop when I spotted him.

Even with his back toward me, I recognized him. It had been six months since I had last seen him. Six months of regrets and loneliness. Six months of missing him.

My breath hitched as it dawned on me why he had come.

Johanan had promised that he would reveal my whereabouts to Jared if he decided to exact his punishment. *Eye for eye.*

That was the debt I owed. One I intended to pay. My lips parted, and for a moment I found myself unable to breathe.

I forced my feet forward. Even though I had made no sound, he seemed alerted to my presence and turned. A black, convex leather patch covered his left eye. For a moment I could see nothing else, my gaze captive to that bit of leather.

The inadequate covering for my sin.

Then my vision glided and I took in the rest of him and frowned with surprise.

The last time I had seen Jared, he had been pale and sickly, lying helpless on a bed. But the man standing before me was muscle-hard and tanned from the sun. Everything about him save that uncompromising eye patch screamed health.

His long hair had been pulled back into a severe braid, tied into submission by a leather strip. At his hip hung an empty sword belt. He must have left his weapons with the gatekeeper, entering the house unarmed as a sign of peace. In spite of the barren scabbard and quiver, he looked more a warrior than the studious young man I remembered.

I swallowed the hard lump in my throat and forced my knees to bend until I fell at his feet. "You have come to claim the Code of Hammurabi."

"The Code of Hammurabi?" he snarled and crossed his arms.

"It is your right."

He ground his teeth. "I am not interested in that particular right."

"I don't understand. Then, why are you here?"

"Will you please get off the ground?" He waved his arm toward me. "I can't speak to you while you occupy that ridiculous pose."

I was certain that my face was pinker than the rose petals surrounding us. Slowly, I straightened. The initial shock of seeing him here in Ecbatana had started to recede, leaving me shivering with reaction.

"What are you doing here?" I asked, utterly befuddled.

"Johanan sent you a letter to explain."

"I never received it."

He shrugged. "Likely, I traveled faster than the courier and arrived before Johanan's message."

I stood and, for a moment, drank in the sight of him. Something had happened to Jared in the months since we last met. Beyond the eye patch. The blindness.

The physical changes were subtle. The shoulders were slightly broader, the chest thicker, the legs more muscular. But I felt the change most in his face. The features remained the same: same contours, same angles, same lips and nose and brow.

Only, everything seemed harder, as if the softness of innocence had fled.

That, too, was my doing.

"You've changed," I said, before I could stop myself.

"You, also," he said.

I had forgotten that I still wore my palace finery, my hair tucked into wide rolls against my neck, the dark-blue wool tunic with its dainty cape fluttering in the mountain breeze. "I only just returned from the palace," I explained.

"The palace?"

"The king requests the services of an additional scribe, sometimes."

"You have risen in the world." His voice betrayed the merest hint of bitterness.

"Hardly. He is an ogling buffoon, more interested in using me as a means of humiliating his visitors than any actual work I could do for him. I prefer my service to Master Daniel a thousand times."

"Ogling? Has he harmed you?" His lips barely moved as he spat the words.

"Not at all." My hands fluttered in the air between us. "Jared. Why are you here? In Ecbatana? In this house?"

He shrugged. "I came to fetch you, of course. You can come back home."

"Home?" I swallowed convulsively.

Jared nodded. "The king has granted you pardon. My father's demands for your punishment have been denied."

I felt as if someone had pulled out my spine and subsided to the ground in a nerveless heap. "I am *pardoned*?" In my wildest dreams, I had not expected this outcome. Knowing Jared's father, I had believed him incapable of forgiveness. Since he had the law on his side, I assumed my exile would last as long as he lived, at the very least.

"But how?"

"You have the new bridge to thank for that." Briefly, he told me how he had discovered the frailty in the structure. "The king felt he owed me a debt for rescuing his favorite project from destruction, not to mention saving him from the embarrassment of its public collapse." He lifted a careless shoulder. "When he offered me a reward, I asked for your freedom."

"You used your royal boon to gain *my* pardon?"

His jaw hardened. "For the sake of our old friendship."

I nodded, heeding the warning in the sharp words. He might not wish me punished. But neither had he absolved me. Our friendship was a thing of the past. I had lost him as surely as he had lost his eye.

"You can return to your family. To your work with Daniel. I am here to accompany you back home."

For a moment, I felt dizzy with relief and joy. I could go home! See Grandfather, hold my mother and father. Serve Daniel. Leave Astyages and his wandering eyes behind.

Then the truth set in. I might be released from the judgment of the law. But I had not been released from God's assignment.

Coming to my feet, I shook my head. "I cannot return home," I whispered.

CHAPTER THIRTY-SIX

I believe that I shall look upon the goodness of the LORD
in the land of the living!
Wait for the LORD;
be strong, and let your heart take courage;
wait for the LORD!
Psalm 27:13-14, ESV

JARED

Pain came like a roaring dragon that night as he lay in his cramped room at the inn. He was gripped by the unrelenting talons of agony, unable to move.

He had pushed himself too hard, riding through the passes of the Zagros Mountains, pressing the guide he had hired into an urgent pace. The shadow of a faint pain had trailed his every step, growing darker and more menacing as he had chosen not to heed the warning signs pounding in his head. He should have rested for a day. Should have slowed down.

Instead, he had striven harder, intent on arriving at Ecbatana as soon as possible. He could not even explain his haste to himself. What difference would another week have made?

Then he had come face-to-face with Keren. He had thought himself prepared for the sight of her. Immune to the old enchantment.

He had been wrong.

She still smelled of roses. Still managed, without a word, to turn his insides into a twisted maze. That elegant tunic with its short cape and the soft, dark, figure-hugging wool had been a shock. He had never seen her attired formally. She had knelt at his feet, like some exotic captive queen before a conquering prince, and laid her life in the palm of his hand. His heart had almost exploded in his chest.

The woman had blinded him, and he still melted at the sight of her. It made him want to spit.

It was only an odd physical response. The lingering potency of puppy love. He had left that boyhood love on the blood-stained dirt of Daniel's courtyard. But the wanting would apparently take longer to discard.

He pressed his hand against his temple and groaned. For days, he had ignored the nipping teeth of a slight ache. Since the accident, pain had been a common visitor. But with rest and prayer, he had managed to tame its severity. Managed to extract its teeth and live with it.

Now exhaustion, combined with the shock of seeing Keren and hearing her unexpected revelation, turned it into an unyielding noose, pulling tight, robbing his breath.

And to his dismay, Jared found himself unable to pray.

He had convinced himself that he was beyond this level of sickness. On his way to healing.

Instead, faced with the old, venomous fangs, the familiar fears returned with such speed, they left him reeling. He curled his lips and was shocked to find himself angry with God.

For not healing him yet. For allowing the worst of the pain to return.

He remembered Keren's extraordinary revelation. Could this boy truly be the promised champion of his people? Could he one day end Judah's captivity in Babylon?

Something in Jared believed Keren's conviction that her Cyrus was the same as Isaiah's Cyrus.

In which case, what was Jared to do? Return home and leave her to care for the child alone? Leave her to contend with all the dangers surrounding the boy, with no help save from a Mede who remained too bound up in the power of his king?

All his life, Jared had sensed that God had a special task set aside for him. Could this be the call he had longed for?

Yet here he lay in chains of pain, unable even to care for himself, let alone for a child who had earned the enmity of a king.

A bubble of resentment rose up in his chest. Why would God allow him to be reduced to such an impotent state? How was he to aid anyone when he lay here, more helpless than a newborn?

He tried to cling to the discipline he had learned over the months. "Even if you do not heal me," he gasped out, "you are still good." They were empty words. His heart refused to inhabit them. It stood apart and sneered, complaining of its weariness.

"Even if you do not heal me, I will trust you." Jared spat out the words through gritted teeth, battling self-pity and fear as well as pain.

"Lord, help me!" he cried. He pressed the tips of his fingers against his empty eye socket. *Help me respond faithfully to this journey of pain. Give me the strength to draw near to you rather than allow this agony to carry me away in its tide, separating us. Even if healing eludes me, let me find you in the midst of my pain.*

A singular thought seemed to find its way to the surface of his mind, like oil on water, refusing to sink. If he had an assignment in the land of the living, then he would find the courage to complete it. Sick, ailing, weak, broken—it did not matter. If God had called him to help the boy Cyrus, then he himself would provide the strength.

CHAPTER
THIRTY-SEVEN

In arrogance the wicked hotly pursue the poor.

Psalm 10:2, ESV

I watched Jared tie his stallion to an apple tree and make his way toward the cottage. The old graceful walk with its loping strides had gone, replaced with something more watchful. He took shorter steps, his head sweeping to the side as he moved. With shock, I realized that his single eye was trying to do the work of two.

He had asked to meet Cyrus when I explained why I could not accompany him back to Babylon. When I told Harpagus of Jared's request, unexpectedly, he relented.

"You trust him?" he had asked.

"With my life."

"He is not a Mede, so I need not fear he will spy for Astyages. It might be prudent to have a young warrior on our side. Do you suppose he will agree to help us?"

"I am certain he will not," I said, thinking of the warning in Jared's voice when he had mentioned our *old* friendship. "He will wish to return to Babylon." He would wish to be rid of me as soon as his conscience allowed.

Now, as Jared entered the cottage, his attention glued to Artadates, I noticed the dark half-moon under his eye, emphasized by the pallor of his face, and wondered if he had slept at all.

Clearing my throat, I introduced the boy. "Jared, this is my pupil, Artadates. Artadates, Jared is . . . an old friend." Best to stick to his own description, though I imbued the words with the warmth of cherished history, not the finality of an ending.

Artadates smirked. "You have a *friend*?"

The corner of Jared's lip tipped. "I like you already."

Artadates pointed at Jared's sword. "Are you any good?"

"I used to beat *her* regularly." Jared pointed his chin at me.

"Not that good, then. She doesn't even dare to *face* me. Just puts me through boring drills."

Jared shot me a hooded look before returning his attention to Artadates. "Those are fighting words, boy. You have to prove yourself now."

Artadates leapt to his feet, beaming. Before long, the two of them were in the orchard, plying their practice swords. Jared pushed Artadates hard to test the boy's mettle. Judging by his smile, what he found pleased him.

After their practice bout, Artadates asked to examine Jared's real sword.

Handing the weapon, hilt first, to my pupil, Jared said, "You're not too terrible. I might even have detected a glimmer of potential. Did your father teach you?"

"No. My father is one of the royal shepherds. He does not know sword fighting."

"Is that what you want to be when you grow up? A royal shepherd?"

Artadates looked up from his examination of the blade. "I want to be a general. One day, when I am all grown up like you, I plan to lead armies to victory."

Jared nodded with understanding. "And what do your mother and father think of this aspiration?"

Artadates returned the sword, his face shuttered. "They look sad when I mention it. They would prefer for me to be a shepherd. It's a noble profession, you know."

Jared nodded again. "Indeed. But it's not for you?"

Artadates looked at his shoes. He gave his head a small shake. The glow of excitement animating his features dimmed.

I watched this exchange with fascination. I had never thought to ask my pupil how his parents might feel about his dreams. Every day he spent with me, growing in his knowledge and education, was a day he moved further from the life his adoptive parents offered him. He was growing into a stranger before their eyes.

The familiarity of childhood allowed him to inhabit *their* world. But they could never enter into *his*. I might have served to educate the boy. Then again, I had also caused him to outgrow the only family he had.

For the first time, I saw that he felt like a stranger at home, and his loyal little heart was nagged by guilt for that division. Love bound him to the shepherd and his wife. But it could not bridge the gap of understanding, of dreams and ambition and desire that were daily being laid in Artadates's heart, like stones paving a road to an unknown kingdom where his parents could not follow.

Mitradates and his wife had been a pair of ducks who had raised a swan as a duckling. And now the swan had grown old enough to recognize that he did not belong in their pond. I shook my head. All of them would have to bear the pain of separation if Artadates returned to his birth parents.

What a mess Astyages had created with his possessive ambitions. What a tangle of painful threads he had woven around his own daughter and grandson, all to shield his throne.

I pushed these weighty thoughts away as we ate a brief lunch. I had packed enough bread, herbs, white cheese, and roasted pistachios to feed Jared as well. We were about to begin a lesson in Aramaic grammar when I heard the sound of hooves approaching. I made Artadates climb out of the back window as I went to the door.

Harpagus dismounted lightly from the chestnut. Seeing him, Artadates abandoned his hiding spot and came running.

"Oh, what a beauty!" he breathed, caressing the stallion's neck. "What a champion amongst horses you are."

Harpagus threw the lead to the boy. "You can go for a short ride. Mind you don't tire him. I have to ride back in a moment." The words had barely left Harpagus's lips before Artadates leapt on the back of the Nisaean and trotted off in rapture.

"My lord! I did not expect to see you here," I said.

Before answering me, Harpagus sized Jared up with an experienced eye. I introduced the men to each other and wondered if my master had ridden to the cottage merely to meet my childhood companion.

But when Harpagus turned his attention to me, he said, "The king asks for you."

I groaned. "Not again. I better go home and change."

"Astyages will be displeased if we delay too long. We can head to the palace from here," Harpagus said. "What you are wearing is acceptable."

With the arrival of autumn, the weather had turned cool. I had finally capitulated and spent a good portion of the income from my work with the scribes on a length of aquamarine wool. For a small fee, Aryanis had sewn the fabric into a tunic for me.

Wide, long sleeves in the Median style kept me warm against the icy mountain breezes, and the tightly woven wool, gathered at the waist with a belt, provided modest covering all the way from neck to toes. It was the first brand-new tunic I had ever owned. Perhaps seeing me garbed so plainly, with my hair in its usual braid, would put the king off calling me to the palace at the behest of every whim.

Harpagus addressed Jared. "Would you be so kind as to pay me a visit later this afternoon? Wait on me at my house. I wish to discuss Artadates with you." I suspected he wanted to ask Jared's help with the boy, though I did not know what exactly he had in mind. Unlike Daniel, Harpagus was not a man to open his heart easily.

Jared dipped his head. "It will be my pleasure to wait upon you, lord."

Watching this exchange made me feel discombobulated. Jared so naturally stepped into lordly manners. He seemed utterly different from the teasing young man I had come to know in the tablet house.

Harpagus signaled Artadates, and the boy cantered toward us, his seat perfect. With a flourish, he jumped off the stallion and handed the reins to Harpagus.

"Thank you, my lord." The boy raised his head regally. "My Aramaic is very good, don't you think?" His eyes twinkled. "I have studied hard. I write better than Astyages's scribes."

"Indeed?" The corner of Harpagus's lip twitched. "Keep up, and you may one day own a stallion of your own. Now, off with you. We must be on our way."

"I like the chestnut," Artadates hinted.

Harpagus rolled his eyes. "What a surprise."

* * *

Like everyone else at court, I spent half my time in the king's great hall loitering, waiting to be called upon. It required a great deal of patience to stand poised while my knees screamed for a chair and my mind squirmed with boredom.

That afternoon the audience hall was piled with foreign dignitaries from several lands, each with his own personal request, often beginning with a long, sycophantic appeal to Astyages. I spent the time counting the columns, then counting the flutes in the columns, trying to avoid thoughts of Jared.

The monotonous order of the royal visitations was ruptured when one of the lords of Media broke into the line. "My lord king!" he cried, bringing the low hum of conversation to a standstill. "A moment of your time, if you please! A great injustice has been perpetrated upon my son."

His hand wrapped around the arm of a young man, who, judging by his slouching frame, wanted nothing more than to disappear into the floor. Drawing him forward, the nobleman pressed the boy in front of him where the king could have a good look.

Given the smooth cheeks and the fuzzy shadow on the upper lip, the boy looked to be no older than thirteen or fourteen.

His tunic had been torn on one side, revealing an angry red welt. Having suffered from several like it in my younger years, I recognized the mark instantly as the work of a practice sword.

"See what has been done to him, and this at the hand of a shepherd boy?"

Astyages, who had been leaning negligently against the cushioned backrest of his throne, sat up. "A shepherd boy?"

"Just so. A shepherd boy dared raise his hand against *my* son. A lord of the land! Can you imagine such an outrage? I demand he answer for this crime."

My blood turned to ice.

I knew the shepherd boy in question, though he had not been named. That wretch must have made his way back into the palace in spite of my strictest instructions.

Astyages commanded that the boy in question be fetched immediately. I hoped that he had made himself scarce by now. But a fist tightened around my chest when a few moments later several guards walked into the audience hall, accompanied by a clutch of boys. At the center walked my pupil, back straight, chin held at a proud angle.

I threw a panicked look at Harpagus. He stared ahead, his complexion gray.

The king descended the steps from his dais. "What is your name?" he said, his voice imperious.

A lesser boy would have been cowed. Artadates bowed respectfully. But his mien remained calm. "I am Artadates, lord king, son of Mitradates, one of your royal shepherds."

"And are you the author of this disgraceful attack upon his lordship's son?"

"I am. But there was no disgrace to it. The boys here chose me to be leader in our game. This one—" he pointed at the boy—"did not approve of the decision. So we fought over the privilege. A fair and honorable fight, as any who saw it can tell you. But when he lost, he went crying to his father, who happened to be here. Now, if I have done anything blameworthy, punish me as I deserve, lord."

The king's eyes narrowed. "You are bold for a shepherd. How old are you, boy?"

"Ten, lord." He stood taller. "I will be eleven in two weeks."

Harpagus closed his eyes and swallowed. Astyages did not seem to pick up on the significance of the timing. Instead, he turned to the complaining father. "And your son? How old is he?"

"Thirteen, my king."

"How is it that a ten-year-old shepherd can beat the best of my young lords?" His eyes landed on Artadates again and narrowed. "How is it that a shepherd boy knows how to ply a practice sword at all?"

Artadates shrugged. "It is not so complicated to twirl a stick." Everything about him—the proud stance, the fearless tone, the touch of humor—was drenched in the confidence typical of him.

I closed my eyes and prayed with desperate urgency. He would do far better today if he could, for once, act the humble shepherd he was supposed to be.

Artadates, oblivious of the danger bearing down upon him, plowed ahead. "I have used a shepherd's staff all my life, and it's not so different."

Astyages stared at the boy as if mesmerized. He stretched a clawed hand and wrapped it around Artadates's collar to pull him closer. After an infinitely long moment, the claw loosened, and one finger hooked under the boy's chin, yanking it up. Astyages studied that visage, with eyes and brows so like his own; it must have been like a mirror that took him backward in time.

The king's head lifted abruptly. He searched through the faces in the hall until his gaze found Harpagus.

CHAPTER
THIRTY-EIGHT

For everything there is a season, and a time for every matter under heaven:
a time to tear, and a time to sew;
a time to keep silence, and a time to speak.
Ecclesiastes 3:1, 7, ESV

Harpagus stood frozen, his face a mask of horror. Although no one else understood the significance of this silent exchange, the king's rising rage was like a towering wave that fell upon the place, impossible to miss. The audience hall became as still as a tomb. Even the offended father was struck dumb.

Without warning, a voice interrupted the thick silence. A boy's voice.

"He is telling the truth, lord king!" Tigranes stepped forward and bowed. "Artadates, I mean." He took another step until he stood shoulder to shoulder with Artadates.

He bowed again, this time with a pretty courtly flourish, and pointed to his chest. "You may recall I am Tigranes, prince of Armenia. This shepherd boy is the best archer of us all. His swordsmanship is passable. Not so good as mine, but that can be forgiven since I am superior to the rest of the boys." With every word, Tigranes sidled forward, until Artadates stood in his shadow.

With his last step, the Armenian prince delivered a swift kick to Artadates, and my pupil finally realized his friend's intent. He took his bearings before melting into the shadows. Meanwhile, Tigranes droned on and on about Artadates's prowess on the horse, followed by a detailed account of his fight with the defeated Median boy, distracting the king with his exaggerated descriptions.

"Go," Harpagus hissed under his breath. "Find the boy and hide him. I will see you at home . . . if I am able."

I did not have to ask what he meant. The black look Astyages had given him said it all. I pushed aside the rising anxiety for my master. For now, my every thought had to center on Artadates. I had to try and keep the boy safe. He had no idea the danger that followed his every step.

Tigranes's ploy had worked long enough to allow Artadates to slip away. But I only had a short lead time. Any moment, the king would grow fed up with the Armenian prince's drawn-out story and discover the absence of the grandson he had long believed dead.

As my feet pounded their way toward the main road, it dawned on me that Astyages's first act would be to post extra guards at the city gates. They would be instructed to detain any boy who answered to Artadates's description. I could only hope Artadates was already heading out of the city. Both his parents' home and our cottage were outside the perimeter of Ecbatana's walls. If he had not headed that way already, he would likely be trapped inside the city, and easy prey for the king's spies.

I slowed my pace as I approached the first set of Ecbatana's gates, trying not to attract undue attention. The guards had seen me pass through these same gates every day for months and were familiar enough to barely give me a second glance. I expelled a relieved breath as I approached the final wall.

The sound of a commotion behind me made me turn. Looking back through the six open gates, I saw that several royal soldiers had gathered at the first one, questioning the guards. I grimaced. They were closer than I had expected! All eyes were on the freshly arrived detachment of soldiers, and no one paid any attention as I passed through the final gates.

I ran to the cottage first. It dawned on me, as I huffed my way up and down the hilly road, that Artadates could no longer be protected from the truth.

I would have to tell him who he really was.

His ignorance now placed him in greater danger, allowing the king's men to trail him with ease. As it was, he might have avoided going to the palace if he had known the facts of his birth.

Then again, telling him the tale of his grandfather's cruel plot meant robbing the boy of what little childhood he had left. He would be faced with the rupture of the only family he knew. Faced with the lies they had told him. Faced with the reality that another father and mother had loved him. Longed for him. Mourned him.

None of it could be helped. Artadates had to learn the truth. And he had to be hidden from Astyages's wrath.

I arrived at the cottage winded, only to discover it stood empty. I called out Artadates's name to be sure he had not hidden somewhere nearby. When I received no answer, I headed for his home.

Mitradates had left for the fields hours earlier. His wife opened the door to my pounding knock. In all the months I had tutored Artadates, I had only met her twice. Both had been tense occasions. I could not blame her. She was a simple woman who wanted to hold on to her child. I represented everything that threatened that desire. The education I offered her son would open doors to a life far different from the one she could give him.

"Is he here?" I said, wasting no words.

She paled. "I thought he was with you."

I shook my head. "Astyages knows. Likely, his soldiers are on their way here even now."

She staggered. A hand reached to her throat, clinging, as if she could not breathe.

"If you see him, send him away from home. Do you understand? Tell him to hide."

"My boy!" The words emerged broken.

The pain in her voice pierced the shell of anxiety and urgency that drove me. I wasted a precious moment to draw the poor woman into my arms. "I am sorry," I whispered against a tearstained cheek. "I will try to protect him."

And then I flew over the embankment that surrounded the little hut, heading east for our hiding place. The one Artadates had found for our riding practice. Although a beautiful dale, the locals avoided it, because years earlier a tragic accident had taken the life of three young women there. Now, everyone believed the place cursed. The boys and I had not found anything malevolent in the field. Being in a protected valley, it had offered a perfect answer to our need for secrecy.

I arrived there out of breath and doubled over, my hands on my knees. "Artadates," I wheezed, my voice a wisp. He must have been listening for me, for he came running right away.

He was grinning, that boy, enjoying his little adventure.

Love swelled in my breast as I took in that self-satisfied smile that had never tasted fear. And on the heels of it, rage, born of my own terror. How could he be so careless of his life?

"You rascal!" I hissed. "How dare you disobey Lord Harpagus's orders? You have been told again and again to avoid the palace. Yet what do you do? At the first opportunity, you head there."

The bright smile dimmed. He dropped his head. "I am sorry, Keren. Tigranes had arranged a competition, you see. He had told the other boys that I would beat them at every game. I could not let my friend down, could I? He would have been embarrassed in front of everyone if I had not shown up. Things would have turned out fine if that ninny had not run off to his father with his complaints." He patted my hand. "It's all right, Keren. No need to worry. All is well now."

I groaned. "All is definitely *not* well."

"Is the king very angry that I beat that sniveling fool?" He rolled those green eyes, which had betrayed him to his grandfather. "He should thank me for it. What is that boy going to do when an enemy soldier gives him a thrashing? Run home to his mama? Better to understand his weakness now." The grin returned. "You should have seen me, Keren! That practice sword was lightning in my hands. Let me show you what I did—"

"Stop, Artadates!"

What I was about to reveal to this child would change his life forever. Would haunt that smile. Would rob him of that easygoing assurance.

I considered delaying this painful revelation. Perhaps I could find Mitradates, and he could tell the boy. Or even Harpagus. Yet I knew, even as I considered each option, that they were out of reach.

Harpagus might even die this very day for his betrayal. Mitradates and his wife might fare no better. In any case, these were the very people to whom Astyages would send his spies. They would be the ones under observation. Artadates would have to stay as far away from them as the sun from the moon.

No. God had placed this painful responsibility firmly in my hands. I tried to swallow past the lump in my throat.

"Artadates, it's not so simple. Your life remains in danger." I drew him to a thicket of oaks and sank gratefully against the scratchy bark of a tree. The ground was cold; the sky had turned an angry gray. I shivered in the cooling air.

Artadates settled next to me. "Is the boy's father very angry?"

"I imagine so. But it is the king I worry about."

"He is offended that I beat one of his young lords?"

I shook my head. "He is offended for a different reason. Artadates, I need to tell you a story. And I need you to listen well, because it concerns you."

The boy watched me with curiosity as I unfurled the tale of Mandana and her father. When I reached the part about the king's demand that Harpagus kill the babe, Artadates's expression changed, growing grave and pale. He leaned away from me, as though expecting a physical blow.

Somewhere in that bright mind, he had already connected those dots. Connected Harpagus's unusual interest in him. But his heart was battling that truth. Denying it.

I pressed on with the tale, a cruelty I had no choice but to administer.

"Harpagus could not do it," I explained. "He could not kill the great-grandson of Cyaxares. He could not destroy the son of Mandana. He chose to disobey his king."

I dropped my head, unable to look the boy in the eyes as I

continued, thrusting this final implacable blade into the fabric of his life. "Harpagus knew that Mitradates and his wife had lost their newborn babe only hours before. No one else had heard the news yet. Harpagus decided to give Mandana's babe to Mitradates. He could think of no other way to save the child.

"*You* are that child, Artadates. You are Cyrus. The blood of kings flows through your veins. Your father is Cambyses, king of Persia, and your mother is Mandana, princess of Media and the queen of the Persians. Those are your real parents. And they have no idea you are still alive."

Cyrus scrambled to his feet. Wordlessly, he shook his head.

I reached out for his hand. "I am truly sorry."

He yanked his fingers out of mine. "It cannot be true! My name is Artadates, the son of Mitradates."

"Do you know why Astyages recognized you? Because your eyes and eyebrows are a mirror of his own."

Cyrus stood transfixed. He must have remembered staring into the face of the king. Remembered the shape of the green eyes, the odd upturned brow.

The truth shattered the fragile walls of denial he had been trying to erect around his heart. Slowly, his face crumpled. Layer after layer of hard truth and its implications wormed their way into his awareness, until there was nothing to hold him up. He fell on his knees, shivering, and still refused to weep. I held him tight as he battled his tears, and won.

CHAPTER
THIRTY-NINE

Before they call I will answer;
while they are still speaking I will hear.

Isaiah 65:24, NIV

Once, while riding in our dale, I had narrowly escaped driving my horse into a covered pit. Artadates and I had discovered that the pit led to an underground cavern. Now I concealed him in that hidden chamber, extracting his promise that he would not move until I came for him.

Just before the city gates were locked for the evening, I made my way to Harpagus's house, my mind in a whirl. What if my master was dead?

"Is Lord Harpagus home yet?" I asked Aryanis as soon as I arrived.

"No. And he missed supper. I don't know who is more vexed, his lady wife or the cook. He had promised to be home early. It's his son's birthday. Strange! I have never known him to miss it." She turned to leave. At the door, she whirled back.

"I almost forgot. That visitor of yours is here again. The handsome one. Although he asked for the master this time instead of you."

"Jared! Thank the Lord!" I had forgotten that Harpagus had asked him to return to the house that evening. Dashing to the garden, I found him, once again, waiting amongst the roses with his back to me.

I crashed through the last of the fall blooms like a runaway baggage camel. The noise of my desperate pursuit must have alarmed Jared, who turned, one hand reaching for his empty sword belt.

He was dressed for hard travel, his legs encased in the tight trousers favored by Median cavalrymen, his short tunic sporting long, tight sleeves. He had donned leather boots and a quilted vest over his tunic to keep the nip of the mountain winds at bay.

"What's wrong?" he said, alarmed by my haphazard arrival. "Where is Harpagus?"

As succinctly as my jumbled mind allowed, I told him of the events of that afternoon.

"And the boy?"

"He is safe for now. But I must return to him soon. He is bound to go looking for Mitradates, demanding answers. And then he'll be caught in whatever net Astyages is spreading for him."

I took a tortured breath. "Jared, I know this is not your concern. Although I believe this boy to be the Cyrus Isaiah spoke of, I am well aware that I may be wrong. He may be an ordinary boy with an extraordinary name. Either way, I cannot leave him."

I fisted my hands until my nails dug a row of neat crescent moons into my palms. "I have no right to ask this, especially after what I did—"

Before I could finish, Jared cut me off. "I will help you."

My jaw grew slack. "I don't think you understand what I—"

"If there is any chance that this boy is who you think he is, we must do everything in our power to preserve his life." He adjusted an iron-studded wristband. "On my way to Ecbatana, I had a sense of urgency. This odd feeling that I must push hard or I would be too late. That is why I arrived before the messenger carrying Johanan's letter. I rode like the wind to get here.

"Now I think perhaps the Spirit of God urged me on so that I could be here in time for this danger. I have been sent to help the boy, whoever he is."

My shoulders started to descend from around my ears. It was finally dawning on me that God had moved before we had recognized our need. He had sent Jared in time for an extremity we had not known to expect. Relief flooded through me. God would preserve us in the midst of this burning furnace.

"I don't have enough words to thank you, Jared."

His gaze tore from mine. He seemed to find his boots of grave interest. "There is one thing you should know. I suffer from headaches. They are a mere nuisance, usually. But sometimes they afflict me with such force that I become helpless. Unable to ride or even walk."

I felt those words like a blow to the chest. It took all my will to stand still. To not bend over and heave. "I am so sorry, Jared! Heaven have mercy. I am so sorry."

"I did not tell you to pile guilt on your head. It's a warning. Having me along may not always be useful. On the contrary. If afflicted by disabling pain, I will be more of a hindrance to your cause."

"We must trust God, both of us. He brought you here, just

as he brought me. Obviously, he must think we are somehow equipped for this task."

"I wonder at his sense of selection. Really, I do. A king and his troops are in pursuit of a helpless child, and all the Lord sees fit to send is a woman with more talent for a stylus than a sword and a canal supervisor who can at any moment become utterly incapable of performing even the simplest task."

I smiled. "You have had the training of a warrior all your life. And I think you will find Cyrus is anything but helpless."

Hearing light feet, I turned to find Harpagus bounding toward us. "Where is he?"

Relief swelled at the sight of him. "Safe for now."

I did not specify Cyrus's exact location. Although Harpagus had been allowed to come home, we could not discount the possibility that the king might arrest him at any moment. Torture could extract all manner of information, even from the bravest of men. Better that Harpagus not know too many details.

"What happened with the king?" I asked.

"He demanded to meet me in private. To my surprise, he said he was relieved the child still lived. His disappointment in me for my disobedience was outweighed by his joy at meeting his grandson, or so he claimed. He commanded that I bring the boy to him so he could have the pleasure of meeting him properly."

I frowned. "Do you believe him?"

"Not for a moment. That old fox merely wants to get his hands on the child. It's time you take him from here. Take him home to his mother and father."

"To Anshan?"

"To Anshan. I cannot delay any longer. Fate has forced my hand."

"Or perhaps the Lord has chosen the time."

Harpagus smiled. "Perhaps."

"Do you have a map?" Jared asked, already a step ahead of us.

"Does that mean you will help the boy?"

Jared glanced at me. "I will."

Harpagus exhaled. "I am in your debt. As for a map to Anshan, I possess a good one. In my younger days, I spent a year at the Persian court. I had to travel back and forth to Ecbatana every few weeks and made my own map. It's very detailed, though old."

"That will prove helpful."

Harpagus grasped Jared's shoulder. "I am asking a lot of you. But you are in a unique position to help us save the boy. Being a stranger, you will have the most freedom to leave the city and travel unhampered. I will give you three of my own horses. My house is being watched. You are bound to be questioned, once you leave it. With my horses in tow, you can claim to be a horse trader from Babylon. We will give you everyone's baggage so that Keren and Artadates can travel light."

Jared nodded. "Where will I meet them?"

"Ride east until you reach the crossroads where the Khorasan Highway meets the road south. A farmer owns a cottage in the eastern corner. He is loyal to me and will hide you if Astyages's soldiers are about. You can wait there until Keren and the boy arrive."

"How will I find my way?" I asked.

"I will show you on the map. Once it becomes known that the boy is the king's own grandson, his pursuit will be impeded. Astyages cannot move against a child of his own flesh openly. That will hamper his chase."

"Can you help spread that news?" I asked.

"I will do my best."

Jared frowned. "What then? What kind of company should we expect?"

"Instead of a troop of soldiers, you will be pursued by smaller bands of highly trained assassins who won't flinch at doing dirty work for money."

I gulped. "Excellent."

"Once you enter Persian territory," Harpagus said, "you will be safe. They will not risk being caught beyond that border. But until then, your every step will be shadowed by death."

Jared gave a casual nod as if he had merely received an assignment to inspect a particularly silted canal. "What of Keren and the boy? How will they make their way to me without discovery?"

Harpagus turned to me. "Did Artadates manage to leave the city?"

"Yes, lord."

"Good. Or else he would have been trapped in Ecbatana." He exhaled. "Keren's escape from the city will require more stealth. She is known to be my servant and has attended the court enough to be recognized by the king's men. If we can find a way to get her out of the city without being discovered, I have an idea how she and Artadates can travel the rest of the way to you without discovery."

Harpagus motioned for us to follow him to his chamber. He retrieved a bundle from the bottom of a chest. Opening the knot about the wrinkled fabric, he extracted a shapeless tunic, gray and ragged, embellished with coarse iron bells.

I gasped. "Lepers' clothing! Are those unclean?" I took a long step back.

"You mean did I strip them off a leper? Of course not. I

haven't nursed that boy from harm for ten years to give him leprosy with tainted garments. No. I had these made with old fabric. I always knew one day I might have to try and sneak him away in a hurry."

Tentatively, I reached for the tunics. Even knowing they were fakes, I cringed as my fingers came in contact with the threadbare gray material. The little bells were set to motion, tinkling an ominous warning at my touch.

Cyrus would hate this plan. But not nearly so much as I.

"Will you write a letter to Queen Mandana, my lord? She is more likely to trust you than two Jewish strangers arriving at her doorstep with a shepherd boy in tow."

Harpagus nodded. "As I have told you, I doubt she will place much weight on my word. It will be up to you to convince her. You will have to carry the letter, Keren. If they find it on you . . ."

"It will mean my death," I said. "I know."

"Lepers are not allowed within the walls of Ecbatana. So my plan is only good once you leave the city." He pulled restless fingers through the ornate, ringleted hairdo that had required his dresser two hours to perfect. "I don't know how to get you out, Keren."

I shoved my hands up my wide sleeves until they were swallowed by the warm fabric. "I have an idea."

By the time I returned from packing my meager belongings, Harpagus had made quick work of several documents. Two personal letters to Mandana and a bill of sale for three horses, which he gave to Jared.

"In case my horses are recognized, this will prove that you are not a thief." He removed a ring bearing his seal from his index finger and passed that on to Jared as well. "The farmer to whom I am sending you cannot read. But he will recognize this and offer you whatever aid he can."

Carefully, Jared hid the ring in a concealed opening of his padded vest. The padding served as the perfect cover for the delicate jewel.

Harpagus marked the map to Anshan, ensuring both Jared and I understood where we were to meet. To me, he gave the lepers' bundle. From the wooden chest he extracted a small pot. Delving two fingers into the white paste within, he rubbed it in patches on my hand and arm. Within moments, they looked leprous, skin dead and peeling. "Be generous on your faces and no one will look at you too carefully. It will wash off with warm water."

"Thank the Lord!" I cringed at the hideous sight my arm made.

Tucking the pot inside my bundle, I hid the incriminating letters to Mandana within the folds of my old Babylonian tunic. It was not nearly so effective a hiding spot as Jared's vest. A cursory search would reveal them. I must find a way to avoid being searched.

*   *   *

The city gates closed after sunset, to be opened with the rising of the sun. I left Harpagus's home after dark, making no effort to conceal my movements. In the stillness of the evening, I heard the whisper of a quiet pair of feet following in my steps. My pursuer must have been surprised to see me approach the palace. He lingered by a tree as I gave a name to the guard and waited.

A few moments later, a slightly disheveled Spitamas hurried toward me. The skinny eunuch and I had formed a friendship of sorts in the course of my visits to the palace. Still, he must have thought it strange to have me show up at the royal door at such an hour and ask for him by name.

"Is aught amiss?" he asked as soon as he spotted me.

"I need your help."

He nodded. "You shall have it. I told you, we owe you our lives."

When I entered the palace, my stealthy pursuer sat at the foot of his tree and made himself comfortable, assuming I must have a clandestine rendezvous with the eunuch. Such things were not unheard of either in Babylon or in Media. I breathed a sigh of relief as I followed Spitamas within.

* * *

Just before dawn, I found myself bundled between Spitamas and Axares in a covered litter, dressed in a palace eunuch's garb, my head hidden in the folds of a cloak. I had taken a chance, refusing to shave my head to blend in better with my companions. Hence the necessity for the hooded garment.

Now, as we approached the first city gate, my belly began to churn. Would that calculated risk deliver the executioner's axe to our necks? The guards had to take one look at me to know I was no eunuch.

In truth, it had not been mere vanity that had stayed my hand from putting the razor to my scalp. It was the thought of standing before Queen Mandana and her royal husband with a bald head. A shaven scalp was a sign of shame on a woman. How could I expect the royal couple to credit anything I said if I showed up looking like a disgraced maiden?

But at the sight of Axares and Spitamas, the guards waved

us through, never casting more than a cursory glance my way where I sat slumped, my neck lolling in pretend sleep, snoring like a hog in its sty.

Seven times we were waved through until I left Ecbatana, Harpagas's letters to Mandana safely strapped to my midriff. I have always maintained, since that harrowing sunrise escape, that scribes make the best of comrades and the bravest of friends.

As soon as we were able to turn down a side alley, I kissed my companions on their smooth cheeks, hopped out of the crowded litter, and legged it for the hills.

CHAPTER FORTY

The prudent sees danger and hides himself,
but the simple go on and suffer for it.

Proverbs 22:3, ESV

Cyrus proved every bit as horrified as I expected when I produced the disguise I had brought him. "You can't make me wear that thing. I would rather be captured."

"That can be arranged!" I snapped.

He set his jaw at a mutinous angle and stared me down. Which was quite a feat, given that his head only reached my chest.

"Look, Jared is waiting for us at the crossroads on the Khorasan Highway. Between here and there, the king's men will be swarming. Every one of them will be looking for a boy who looks like you. Once we reach Jared, we can shuck our disguises, don trousers, and ride on the horses Harpagus has sent."

Cyrus blinked. "Harpagus sent horses?"

I smiled slowly. In the midst of all the commotion, I had

forgotten to give him the good news. "I believe amongst them is a chestnut you have had your eye on."

"*My* chestnut?"

"It is now."

For a moment, the old grin flashed. "I told you it was realistic to want that stallion."

"You were right."

Cyrus dropped his head. "Chestnut or no chestnut, I cannot leave without speaking to my parents."

"It's impossible, Cyrus! Their every movement will be watched."

The mutinous gleam returned. "I will put on your leprous costume. I will even let you smear that repugnant paste on my face. But first, I will speak to my father."

I dropped to my knees before him so that we were closer in height. "Cyrus—"

"Don't call me that! My name is Artadates."

"Artadates is the name your parents gave you to protect you. Everything they have done since the day you came into their lives has been in order to shield you from harm. Do you think they would want to expose you to danger now?"

Cyrus remained mute.

"You know they would do anything to keep you safe. Including letting you go. One day, you will be able to see them again. Ask your questions. But that is not today. Today is the day you make sacrifices in order to live. Today is the day you begin to act like the soldier you want to become. Your first step as a future general is to say goodbye. And you must say it without seeing them."

Cyrus dropped his head. His chest caved in and began to shake. I had seen that boy bruised, tired, hungry, frustrated, and vibrating with emotion. But I had never seen him cry. Now he gave in to a storm of ugly, sniveling, whimpering sobs. I wrapped my arms around him, wishing I could spare him this terrible pain.

I knew how he felt. I, too, had had to walk away from my parents. Leave for an unknown future with no guarantee I would ever see them again. But I had been older, and at least I had been granted one final goodbye.

Cyrus took a step away from me. He dashed the tears from his face before holding out his hand. "Give me that poxy tunic with the stinking bells. But if you ever tell anyone about this, I will have to gut you like a fish."

I was not sure if he meant the weeping or the costume, though I discovered that the moisture of his tears made the paste work all the better, so that by the time I finished with him, he looked truly hideous. I did not think he would want me to share that bit of news either.

The wretched bells on our loose tunics tinkled as we made our way east toward the crossroads. Lepers found no more welcome in Media than they did in any other nation. Often, we were greeted by curses. Cyrus and I did our best to avoid people, crossing the road every time we saw someone approaching. Still, more than once, we became the object of a rain of pebbles, and on one painful occasion, a couple of sizable rocks.

But no one looked too closely upon us. Our disguises, though dangerous in their own way, also proved highly effective. The king's soldiers avoided us as assiduously as everyone else.

By the time we arrived at the crossroads, the sun had started to set. Taking my bearings, I pointed to the small farmhouse sitting on the edge of a brown field. "That's the one," I said, heading for the building.

Several steps before I reached the door, something hard hit me in the chest, making me stagger. Another projectile followed in rapid succession. I bent over, wheezing. "Fire and lightning!"

"Get off my land, leprous scum!" Something round whizzed by my ear, and I had a whiff of rotten apples.

"Stop!" I cried. I dared not speak the name of Harpagus too loud even here. I managed to capture the next flying apple in my fist. "We are friend, not foe," I said between my teeth.

A man walked out of the shadows, juggling brown apples. "I'm no friend of lepers. Get off my land, I said."

"They are not what they seem!" Jared cried in Aramaic and sprinted out of the lengthening shadows to stand next to Cyrus.

The farmer raised an arm as if to restrain him. "You fool! These are lepers. You can't come back into my house now. Not even for the master's sake will I welcome that!"

Jared took Cyrus's hand and poured a dribble of water from the cup he held. Wiping the skin with a corner of his cloak, he held up the now clean hand. "See? It washes off."

The farmer blinked and leaned forward as if he could not trust the evidence of his own eyes. Jared poured more water on my arm and gestured for me to wipe the gray blight off my skin. With relief, I complied, holding up the healthy limb.

"It was the only way for us to get away. Please," I said. "This land is too exposed to the road. Will you let us take shelter in your barn before someone notices us?"

Reluctantly, the farmer nodded his head. Grumbling under his breath with every step, he veered away from the large barn with the new roof and led us instead to a derelict building whose walls had more holes than planks.

To me, the neglected structure seemed more welcoming than a gold-rendered palace. We had made it safely out of Ecbatana.

The three of us had escaped with our limbs intact, and best of all, we were together. I breathed a sigh of relief for the first time in what felt like days.

*   *   *

We left the farm as soon as the somnolent sun lit the sky with weak, gray light. Cyrus and I had bathed, using the water in the creek that ran behind the barn, washing off every last vestige of our feigned leprous blight. Harpagus had packed his wife's old riding tunic for me, alongside a few of his son's garments for Cyrus. Though we lacked the expensive jewels, wigs, and servants necessary to mark us as wealthy, our clothing declared us respectable. But our horses set us apart.

We rode the horses Harpagus had given Jared, three stunning Nisaeans, plus Jared's old Babylonian mount, now relegated to act as a common packhorse. We traveled like the angels on our elegant mounts. The haunted look began to leave Cyrus's visage as he rode the chestnut he had for so long coveted. That stallion trotted like a conqueror, muscles bunching and releasing with unbelievable power, barely registering the weight of his new master.

We left the main road as soon as we could, aware that Astyages would most likely have sent men to patrol it. Riding through dale and forest presented many risks. Anything from a protruding root, a large rock, or even a curled-up snake could mean a horse with a broken limb. Bandits were more likely to attack three solitary travelers in an isolated meadow than on a road that served as a major artery between north and south.

The journey from Ecbatana to Anshan could take up to twelve days by horseback, and that was without mishap. The detour slowed our progress, an eventuality we regretted yet dared not alter. We expected to be on the road for two weeks, at least.

When we arrived at a sheltered copse, we decided to break our journey for the night. Cyrus had barely wolfed down the bread and yogurt the farmer had given us before he fell asleep. Jared and I took turns keeping watch. During Jared's last watch, I found myself unable to sleep and crept from my blankets to sit near him.

"I never thanked you properly. For coming to fetch me home."

In the darkness I felt the movement of his shoulder, a careless shrug.

"Why did you?"

Another shrug. "I have no real job at the moment. Traveling to Media seemed like a pleasant pastime."

"Why did you use your favor with the king to gain my pardon?"

A heavy sigh. "I told you. For the sake of our old friendship. For Daniel and Mahlah. For your heartbroken parents. There had been enough damage done already. Why add to it?"

Perhaps the dark made me brave. The pitch black of night, brightened only with pale moonlight and a few stars that had managed to escape the net of clouds, sinking us into deep shadows. He could not see me and that made me bold.

Besides, after so much loss, what could it matter? What could he say that would hurt me more? "Did you ever love me?" I asked.

He inhaled. "Did *you*?"

"Love you? Yes. I always loved you. As a friend, at first. And then . . . more."

A hard little sound escaped his throat. He touched the

leather eye patch. "Perhaps you only thought you did," he said dismissively. He presented me with a wide shoulder and refused to say another word.

*   *   *

The next morning, we were on the move before the sun rose, trusting the horses' superior night vision to guide us through the fields. By the afternoon, torrential downpours stopped our progress. We took shelter under the stingy protection of some skinny trees. Within an hour, we were sodden and miserable with cold. But the rain would not let up, forcing us to halt for the day.

After a sleepless night, we arose to gray skies and no rain. When we tried to proceed, we discovered the deluge had turned the terrain into a soggy mess, impassable for the horses. Rather than wasting another day waiting for the fields to dry, we decided to risk the peril of riding openly on the road for a few hours.

It was the worst mistake we made on that journey.

Only an hour into our trek, we realized we had been detected. The highway south was hilly in places. You could see the road from some spots all the way down to Elamite land on a clear day. When we looked behind us, expecting to find nothing but road, we spotted two riders, bodies glinting with metal from armor. We broke into a gallop and those men did the same. There was no doubt now that we had picked up a tail.

I thanked God for Cyrus's stringent training as I leaned close to the horse's neck, my body rising and falling with the rhythm of the mare's gait. At the sharp bend in the road, I held a tight line without having to decelerate, a trick Cyrus had taken days to teach me, and one only the best of horses could manage.

But even Nisaean horses, famed for their stamina, can only maintain that kind of flat-out pace for short bursts of time. Our best chance at eluding our pursuers was to head back into the fields. We veered off the road and made for the deep grasses. The ground squelched under the horses' hooves, but it had dried enough to support a careful canter.

Jared led us up a gentle hill and stopped. Dismounting, he pointed to a copse of trees on the other side. "You and Cyrus take the horses and hide in there. I will take care of our pursuers."

"No!" I could not draw enough air into my lungs. "You can't face them alone, Jared. I will stay and help."

He pushed his face close to mine. "Do as I say!"

I shook my head.

"Your job is to keep the boy safe. Now do it!"

I gave him an anguished look. He was right. I couldn't send Cyrus off alone and couldn't risk keeping him here.

Grabbing the reins of Jared's stallion and the packhorse, I wheeled my mount and headed into the copse of trees, Cyrus in my wake. Dismounting, I pushed the horses deeper into the woods. This served a double purpose. If horses aren't cooled down properly after a hard ride, they can suffer painful spasms, or even develop a deadly colic. The walk through the woods would help cool them down. Furthermore, the woods would provide a better cover if our pursuers managed to find our trail. Even though most of the trees had lost their leaves to the autumnal frosts, they still supplied more shelter than the open field.

Spotting a ring of ancient elms and broad-leaved evergreens, I came to a stop.

"Climb," I told Cyrus, pointing at an evergreen with thick branches and dark leaves. "Climb as high as you can and don't make a sound."

Cyrus turned to study the hill where we had left Jared. "I don't want to hide like a child. I want to help."

"That makes two of us. Now climb."

He must have sensed my frustration with our situation. My own desire to return to Jared's side. Seeing me resist that urge convinced him to do the same, though judging by the curve of his mouth, he was disgusted by our choice.

I watched him shimmy up the trunk to ensure he remained hidden from the casual observer before tying up the horses in a knoll to our west. They pawed the ground, steam rising from their nostrils, as if they sensed my dread. I calmed them with a few gentle caresses as I dropped their blankets over them. Trained by Harpagus for battle, they knew when to quiet down.

With nothing left to do, I returned to the tree where Cyrus had hidden, sank to the ground, and prepared for an excruciating wait.

CHAPTER
FORTY-ONE

The LORD will keep you from all evil;
he will keep your life.
Psalm 121:7, ESV

———————————— JARED ————————————

Jared lay stretched on the ground, his body hidden by a blanket of dead leaves. He had an arrow notched loosely in his bow, his thumb already encased in its ivory protector. Remaining perfectly still, he resisted the urge to brush off a small spider crawling up his sleeve. A sudden move at the wrong moment could reveal his position to the foe.

All his years of practice had never pitted him against sentient flesh and blood as a target. He had trained for battle as any son of nobility was expected to do in Babylon. But pointing his arrow at a man's chest was something else entirely. Cold sweat gathered on his brow in spite of the chill.

Then he remembered what those men would do to the boy if they caught up to him. Do to *her*. He cracked his neck to the left. To the right. Three fingers tightened on the bowstring. No one would pass through him this day. No one was going to harm her.

Her words returned, now of all times, to haunt him. Had it only been two nights ago? It felt like a lifetime.

Did you ever love me?

The words had loosed a storm of rage in him. How dared she ask it? After what she had done to him! How dared she try to unlock the secrets of his heart, as if she still had some claim to them?

The storm died a sudden death and another took its place as he recalled other words.

I always loved you. As a friend, at first. And then . . . more. More.

Extraordinary, how much one could pour into one word. A world of possibilities. He frowned. Possibilities that had been ruined by her. If there had been any depth to her affections, she would have put his well-being above her irrational jealousy. She would have kept him safe.

Abruptly, all thought came to a halt as he observed movement at the base of the hill. He forced his body to remain utterly still as he waited. His blood ran cold when he saw only one man ascend toward him. Where had the second man gone? Had he circled the hill and headed for the woods? Straight to Keren and the boy?

In a lightning decision, he changed his plan. He needed this man alive so he could question him. Loosening his grip on the arrow, he set the bow down.

He heard rather than saw the approach of the soldier. The

man was almost upon him before Jared made his move. His hand flashed out, fingers coiling around a leather-encased ankle, and twisted.

With a short cry, the man toppled.

CHAPTER FORTY-TWO

For I will restore health to you,
and your wounds I will heal,
declares the LORD,
because they have called you an outcast.
Jeremiah 30:17, ESV

A twig snapped, bringing me to my feet. I expected to see Jared. Instead, a stranger strode toward me, tall and wide-shouldered, with ill-kempt, long hair that was probably home to many happy lice. He didn't bother to raise the sword that dangled from his hand when he saw me. I suppose he did not feel threatened by a woman alone and unarmed.

I gasped and reached for the wooden practice sword I had hung from my belt.

He grinned. Someone had knocked out his two front teeth, turning his smile into a gruesome cave. "Well, now!" he said in Median. "How entertaining. I will keep you till later. First, where is the boy?"

I lifted my sword and lunged. He had not expected that, thinking perhaps that I would try to run in the opposite direction. His mistake worked to my advantage. Somewhere along the way, he had discarded his breastplate; the blunt wooden tip of my weapon found his chest, and I put my shoulder into the blow and rammed it home.

A wheeze of air escaped his lips. He stopped smiling. I delivered a sideswipe to his ribs and lifted my practice sword for another frontal assault. Thus far, I had managed to use the element of surprise. But that could only work for so long.

Just as I aimed my weapon at his belly, the man gathered himself enough to finally raise his sword. He delivered such a blow with his steel that the tip of my sword went flying into the muddy ground. Another blow, and another section of wood severed.

I could not give up. Lifting my short, cleaved weapon, I drove it toward his temple. He parried with a mighty thrust that landed at the hilt of my wooden sword, fracturing it into two useless pieces and almost hacking my fingers with it.

Callused fingers snaked around my neck and squeezed. "Where's the boy?"

"What boy?"

"Where is he?" the man shrieked, squeezing harder.

I clawed at his face, his hands, his arm. Kicking and scratching and biting anything I could reach, I did my best to overcome him. But he was too strong. I could not breathe. My vision began to swim.

I heard a whoosh, felt an odd whistling past my ear, and astonishingly, the choking hold on my neck slackened. The big man dropped at my feet like a brick.

Heaving big mouthfuls of air, I wrapped my hand around my aching throat and stared at the unconscious man. A little red lump was rising in the middle of his forehead.

Cyrus shimmied down the tree trunk and came to stand over the fallen warrior, a sling hanging from his grip. "Bah. Months of practicing my sword, months of sweating over my bow and arrows. And what do I have to fight this lump of lard with? A boring old sling."

My jaw hung loose. "You brought him down with a stone?"

He grinned. "Picked up a few good ones along the way. Missed the first couple of shots in all the excitement. Good thing you kept him busy for a while. I was on my last stone."

I shook my head. "Remind me to tell you about a king named David. Slings make a good weapon in royal hands, it seems."

Cyrus ignored my reference to royal hands and bent down to grab the man's sword. He held the steel in front of him like a proper warrior. "I would rather stick to swords. Next time, I will save you with this."

"First, help me pull off his trousers," I said, already at the unpleasant task.

Cyrus frowned. "Whatever for?"

"We need something to tie him up with."

It took some heavy maneuvering, but by the time the man started groaning, we had him trussed up, his ankles tied to his wrists, helpless as a little babe.

The sound of running made me snap to my feet. Shoving Cyrus behind me, I grabbed the sword from his hand and took on a defensive posture.

I wilted with relief when Jared came crashing through the trees, his own sword at the ready. He took one look at the man on the ground and froze. "I came to save you."

Cyrus pushed me to the side and stepped forward. "You can stand in line. But from now on, I want to carry my own sword and my own bow."

I mussed his hair. "You certainly have the heart of a warrior, and the aim of one too. But swords are a great responsibility. Allow me to bear that burden for you a little while longer." I tucked the sword where my wooden weapon used to hang. One thing this experience had taught me: I could not allow my squeamishness around swords to keep me from being properly armed. We were facing trained soldiers. My wooden weapon had almost gotten us killed.

"Where is the other man?" I asked Jared.

"Tied up on the hill. Between the two of them, we should have enough weapons to fill an armory."

We dragged the man on the hill into the woods to keep his friend company. They were making enough of a din to alarm the wildlife all the way to Persia. No doubt they would attract the attention of other men roaming the highway for us.

We tore off their sleeves, gagging and binding their mouths. They could still make sufficient noise to startle the birds. But not so much that it could be heard from the road. Leaving them a skin of water and a bit of bread, we figured with enough perseverance, they ought to wriggle out of their bonds in a day or two. Of course, we took their horses. We were merciful, not stupid.

"It gets cold here, at night," Jared said. "I suppose you could always cuddle if you feel like you're freezing."

One of Astyages's men screamed incomprehensibly through his gag.

"What did he say?" Cyrus asked.

I wrapped an arm around his shoulder. "I think he was complimenting you on your aim."

He grinned. "I thought so." The boy punched me gently on the arm. "My thanks."

"For what?"

"For not telling him where I was hiding. Even though he almost choked you to death. You never said."

"I tried to tell him. But that fool was squeezing my windpipe too hard."

Cyrus laughed. "No, you didn't." The green eyes became serious. "You were willing to die to keep me safe."

That afternoon, when we stopped for the day, Cyrus disappeared for a short while. When he returned, he had a handful of delicate purple flowers with six petals. At the center of each small flower were several red stigmas.

"Crocus!" I exclaimed.

He offered me his bouquet. "Saffron crocus. I picked them for you."

I had a whiff of the luxurious spice. "Hoping I will learn to cook?"

He shrugged. "A boy can dream. I am getting sick of old bread."

* * *

After a couple of blessedly eventless days, we came upon a small village in the distance. We needed to replenish our dwindling supplies of food and water. Still, we knew entering a village was too great a risk. We decided the safest course was for Cyrus and me to hide with the horses while Jared rode in.

He returned bearing fresh eggs and bread, cooked chicken, pomegranates, and a tub of white cheese. It had been a long time since I had eaten fresh food. That night we feasted like royalty.

An overfull stomach is a terrible burden when you are on watch. It took all my willpower to stay awake.

I spent the time thinking of my recent conversation with Jared. I had been heartsick over his dismissive accusation.

Perhaps you only thought you did.

Then, I sat up, hit by a realization. He had not denied it!

When I had asked if he had ever loved me, he had not denied it. Instead, he had left my question unanswered. A simple no would have sufficed.

The man had used his boon with the most powerful potentate of the world to clear my name. Had come personally to fetch me home. He might be angry with me. He might blame me. But he had once loved me. And whatever love he had borne me still shaped some part of him.

I picked up a rock and turned it over with restless fingers. His response to my question had been a challenge. Had *I* ever loved him?

It finally dawned on me why he felt so angry. He could not forgive me for placing my jealousy above his well-being. My love had fallen short of his expectations. I had betrayed the precious trust he had placed in my keeping.

I dropped the rock and buried my head in my hands. What a fool I had been.

Then I thought of how God's people had betrayed him with their flagrant sins. Just as I had done to Jared. In response, God had said, *Your pain is incurable. Because your guilt is great.* That was my life. My truth. The pain I had caused was incurable.

But the story had not ended there.

God had not allowed that wound to be the conclusion of our history. Into our hopeless mess, he had spoken a promise. *I will restore health to you, and your wounds I will heal.* The *incurable* wounds! The ones caused by our great guilt! Even those, he would heal.

That night, I gave God the incurable wound I had created by my jealousy and made myself a promise. For as long as I had breath, I would do everything in my power to win back Jared's trust.

* * *

The Zagros Mountains run from north to south over an extensive stretch of land. Which explained why the mountains that hugged Ecbatana to the north also surrounded Anshan to the south. The peaks and ridges of the Zagros watched over us as we journeyed toward Anshan.

In the north, the foothills spread into lush, green meadows and forests. The farther south we rode, the warmer and dryer the climate became. The verdant landscape of Media with its clove-rich dales had gradually given way to drab wilderness. The world leading to Persia was as barren as the northern landscape had been green.

We had learned our lesson and assiduously avoided the highway. Instead, we kept to the fields that ran parallel to the road, encountering no other travelers. Our pace became painfully slow. Far to our west, we passed the ancient Elamite city of Susa, though we did not dare enter it. We knew Astyages would likely have sent his spies there to watch for our arrival.

Two days' ride south of Susa, the mountains encroached into our path. The only way to cross the range here was by means of the road that had been dug into the bluffs. Though close, we had still not crossed into Persian territory. If Astyages had set a trap for us, it would be here.

Save for the map Harpagus had given us, we had no knowledge of the area. We did not know any safe hiding places. Returning to the road felt like willingly walking into a snare.

Yet there was no other way to Anshan. We simply had to push through.

The road carved into the cliffs of the Zagros was narrow and, in parts, treacherous. Several times, we had to dismount and lead the horses on foot, navigating deep, arid gorges to one side.

On the fourteenth morning of our journey, we awoke to a sultry day and began shedding the last vestiges of our warm clothing. Jared seemed unusually quiet, his complexion ashen. I knew, even though he said nothing, that he was in pain.

That afternoon, we finally crossed through the last of the mountain passes without incident and found ourselves in a hilly wilderness. At its center, a small oasis of trees had formed around a natural spring.

"Let's stop there," Jared said. "Horses need water."

It was not the best spot to defend. Save for a promontory of rocks to the east, the landscape offered no real shelter. I thought we could water the horses at the spring and rest there for an hour before heading for the promontory. The rocks there offered cover from the road, making it an ideal place to spend the night.

I could see Jared had reached the end of his strength. He staggered as he dismounted, remaining upright only by clinging to his horse. I rushed to his side and helped him to the spring. That he did not demur told me how bad the pain must be.

Cyrus and I tended the horses as Jared slumped in the scanty shade of a tree. I managed to give him a few sips of water before spreading his bedding under the tree. Wordlessly, he crawled inside, eyes pressed shut, his jaw locked.

"Are we spending the night here?" Cyrus asked as the two of us sat down to eat. I cut a slice of stale bread and loaded it with rider's cheese. Jared had bought a skin of milk in the village where he had purchased supplies and had secured it under his saddlecloth as we rode. The movement of his body on the horse had churned the milk into a buttery curd known as rider's cheese. I had learned to like the taste, seeing as I had no choice. We almost never lit fires, knowing the light could act as a beacon to anyone looking for us, which narrowed our options for food.

"I hope to move to those rocks after Jared has had a chance to rest," I said, taking a long drink of water.

"What's wrong with him?" Cyrus whispered.

"He's ill. He needs sleep. Think you can take a watch tonight?"

Cyrus shrugged. "I'm eleven now. I can stay up late."

"When did you turn eleven?"

"Yesterday, I think. Or maybe today. Not sure. I lost count." He played with the flatbread he had rolled around the cheese. "We can ask this Mandana woman. She ought to know."

I frowned. "She's a queen and your mother. You ought not to refer to her with disrespect."

"She may be a queen. But she is no mother of mine."

"Cyrus!"

"Artadates!" he hissed.

"You must make peace with who you are."

"You say this queen might not even accept me as her son. I don't care. I have a perfectly good mother at home."

I saw, in the tight line of his mouth, that he did, in fact, care. He cared so much that he was preparing himself for the coming rejection.

We both fell silent. In the distance, I heard a sound that made me turn cold. "Riders."

I climbed a barren sycamore tree and stared at the road.

Three horsemen trotted steadily in our direction, their armor and swords glinting like icicles in the sinking light of the sun. They might have been ordinary travelers. Persian soldiers returning home. But I knew in my bones they were Astyages's men.

I knelt by Jared. "We must leave! Riders to the north."

He opened bleary eyes and nodded. Pushing the blanket aside, he tried to stand. Lurching, he fell heavily to his knees. I put an arm about his waist and pulled. He staggered again and almost brought both of us down.

He might be able to hobble a little way, I realized, but he would never be able to ride like this.

If they found us in this open place, it would be over in a flash. Cyrus and I could not defend against three trained soldiers on our own.

Quickly, I tied a few of our bundles together and added a handful of thin rushes from a broom plant to the top. Arranging Cyrus's cloak around it, I secured the humanlike figure to the back of the packhorse, all the while barking instructions at Cyrus.

"I'm not that fat," Cyrus said as he observed my handiwork.

"You are now."

Throwing a felt saddlecloth on my mare, I grabbed my sword and leapt on a rock so I could mount. I had never learned to vault on the back of a horse the way Cyrus and Jared did.

"Look after Jared," I said. "If anyone but me comes near you, use your bow."

Cyrus gave me a fierce smile. "Don't worry. I'll keep him safe."

I took one last look at the map Harpagus had given us before galloping out to the open field that paralleled the road.

CHAPTER FORTY-THREE

We had passed a particularly sharp bend in the road on our way to the oasis. I headed back toward it, knowing if I converged with the road at that point, our pursuers would not be able to see that I had been traveling from the south. As long as I managed to get there before them, from their vantage, it would seem as though I had appeared on the road from thin air. They would have no way of knowing that I was doubling back and conclude that I had found a narrow pass that fed into the highway.

As soon as I spied the bend, I led the horses into the road and reversed direction to head south, urging my mare into a trot. It wasn't until I heard a shout behind me that I leaned close to her neck and the horse shot forward in a dizzying gallop. I held tight to the packhorse's lead, and it managed to keep up. Jared had trained it well.

The sun had finally set, and the falling darkness worked to my advantage. Behind me, my pursuers saw two riders. A woman and a boy.

I held my breath as I passed the wilderness where the oasis was located, praying that Cyrus had managed to follow my instructions. The knot between my shoulders loosened when I saw no sign of my friends near the spring.

My pursuers paid little attention to the oasis as I and my broom-plant companion hurtled past. I could only hope that Harpagus's map was accurate. I pressed my mare to increase the distance between me and Astyages's men.

The horses were tiring. I needed to reach my destination soon, or the men might see what I was up to.

Ahead to my right, I spied an outcropping of rocks. According to the map, after this, there would be another sharp bend in the road. I slowed our pace to a trot. I needed to be attentive now. My plan could go awry a hundred different ways here.

When the horses navigated the bend, vanishing from view of our pursuers for a few moments, I decreased our speed further. Saying a short prayer, I swung my leg over the side and jumped.

I came to a rolling stop in the dirt. To my astonishment, I seemed to be still in one piece. Confused, the horses almost came to a stop. I slapped their rumps hard with my whip, wincing as I did so. Unused to harsh treatment, they took off in a cloud of dust.

With no time to waste, I crawled into the rocks. Somewhere nearby, there was a goat track that led back to the oasis. I hoped to find it in the dark. If not, I would try to hide amongst the rocks until sunrise, and then head back.

Of course, our pursuers would find the horses long before that, and they would come back in search of me.

I clambered blindly over the rocks, praying I would not step on a snake in my mad scrabble. At every turn, I came upon more rock, finding no tack. My foot hit a ledge and I began to slip. Tumbling on my rear, I could not find a handhold anywhere to slow my slide down. Finally, my body came to a jarring stop at the base of some dry brush. Everything felt bruised and scraped. But when I stood, to my relief, I found no broken bones.

That is when I saw it. A narrow trail at the base of the rock before me.

Apparently the good Lord had to topple me off the high ground in order to show it to me. I wasn't about to argue with his methodology. Grateful to have escaped with my neck intact, I began hobbling toward the oasis and the promontory of rocks where I had sent Cyrus and Jared to hide.

By the time I found them, the moon had risen high in the sky. I fell to my knees beside Jared. "How are you?"

He groaned. "Useless." When he spoke again, his voice was gruff. "You placed yourself in danger to shield me."

"Just a fast ride. Now, we have to move you. We must hide in the goat track. They won't find us there, even in the daylight. The crags hide the path. We'll go slow and steady, all right?"

I don't know how, but from somewhere within, Jared dragged out the strength to accompany us into the goat track. By the time the sun rose, we were ensconced in the cleft of a large rock, hidden from everyone but goats. We had food, water, fodder for our horses, protection. And we had God.

* * *

After a day of rest, Jared felt well enough to return to the road. But we decided to linger several days in our hiding place in case our pursuers were still patrolling the road in the area.

Bored in our rocky shelter, we decided to put our time to use. Jared began to prepare Cyrus for a royal visit. He taught him how to bow, how to address the king and queen, how to eat at a formal table.

"Whether you are a general or a prince," Jared told him, "you will need to mingle with the aristocracy. In either guise, you must learn to fit in. Be at home whether in a palace or a tent in the field. Make friends of common soldiers or the sons of kings."

Under Jared's tutelage, Cyrus started to show interest in matters beyond horses and warfare. He grew absorbed in the workings of justice and began to realize there was more to leadership than mere excitement.

He came to understand the weight of responsibility.

Jared proved a brilliant teacher—patient, knowledgeable, and inspiring. It dawned on me, as I watched him in awe, that he had been born for this. More than a teacher, he knew how to counsel. Every good king needed a few men like Jared at his side.

One night, when it was my turn to be on watch, I climbed onto the flat rock that gave us the perfect vantage point and perched on my favorite spot. Cyrus had already gone to bed, asleep before his head touched the blankets after a full day of training. I assumed Jared would do the same. To my surprise, he followed me.

He settled next to me, one knee tucked into his chest. For some time, he watched the stars quietly. Without preamble he said, "You saved my life."

"I'm glad my ploy worked."

"You risked your neck to protect me." He had not mentioned the night of our escape until now.

"I would do it again," I said.

"Why?"

I wanted to prevaricate. To avoid the hurt of having my heart thrown in my face again. But I had learned love did not prosper in self-protection.

"Because I love you. And I would rather die than see you hurt again."

He took a shocked little breath. If I had hoped for a similar declaration, I was sorely disappointed. I *was* grateful that he did not counter my words with a sarcastic denial, as he had the last time I had intimated at my feelings. Instead, he sat silently next to me for a while longer before jumping down from the rock and disappearing into the dark.

I assumed he had gone to sleep. But at the end of my watch, when I crawled into my pallet, dizzy with exhaustion, I sensed him draw near to throw an additional blanket over me. His hand lingered for just a moment as it tucked the folds of the fabric against my shoulder.

Forcing my lids open, I saw Jared gazing down at me, his brows knotted in intense thought. I could not decipher the strange expression I caught on his face. It was not longing. I could see that. Closer to war, I thought. But then, he was not at war with me this time. Only with himself.

* * *

I had had to sacrifice my beautiful mare and Jared's horse. It seemed a small price to pay for our survival. Of course, Jared and Cyrus still had their Nisaeans. We had also held on to the two horses we had confiscated from Astyages's men. I mounted the smaller gelding, an awkward ride after the velvety smooth strides of Harpagus's mare. We used the larger beast as a packhorse and set off on the two-day journey that would bring us to Anshan.

To my relief, we navigated our way to the Persian capital without further adventure. Just outside the city walls, we guided our mounts into the courtyard of a travelers' lodging. After bedding down the horses in clean stables, we headed indoors, where we ate a hearty bean and bone stew, bubbling hot from the ovens.

I paid the innkeeper for a second helping. The taste of warm food was so delectable on my tongue, I would have paid for a third if I had not been embarrassed before my companions who stopped at two bowls.

Many of the travelers spread their pallets in the courtyard and slept under the stars. We splurged on a room, where we took turns washing the filth of long travel from our bodies. After Jared and Cyrus completed their ablutions, they headed for the stables, where we all planned to spend the night, concerned for the horses' safety. The Nisaeans, especially, were valuable enough to tempt many a thief.

When my turn came to have the chamber to myself, I stripped the layers of dirt from my skin, using jugs of hot water the innkeeper had provided. It took me a whole hour merely to comb the tangles out of my hair. I thought longingly of Daniel's luxurious bathing chamber as I washed my hair in a large basin. When I finally joined my companions in the stables, I found them too restless for sleep.

We had survived our trek from Ecbatana and arrived safely in Anshan. Now we would have to face our greatest challenge: convincing a king and queen that after eleven years, their lost son was very much alive. In spite of our exhaustion, everyone felt too agitated to settle down.

When Jared had traveled from Babylon to Ecbatana, he had brought along a game board called twenty squares, a two-player game of strategy and luck. I pulled it out of one of the bags and set up the black and white pieces, challenging Jared and Cyrus to play against me. The game of twenty squares is a race. Its object is to move all seven of your pieces through the course and finish before your opponent.

We spent the rest of that evening pouring our pent-up energies into the squares. As we rolled the dice, finding our way out of traps and dead ends, laughter slowly replaced the dread of the coming day. Eventually, we all slept a few steps away from our horses, safe in the knowledge that we were together.

PART THREE

Anshan

CHAPTER
FORTY-FOUR

Can a mother forget the baby at her breast
and have no compassion on the child she has borne?
Though she may forget,
I will not forget you!
Isaiah 49:15, NIV

The three people who approached the palace at Anshan seemed entirely different from the ragged troop that had arrived at the city gates the day before. I had donned my Median tunic, its short cape dancing about my arms as I walked. Jared, looking grand and mysterious in his Babylonian finery, wore silver ornaments in his ringleted hair. But of us all, Cyrus was the most transformed. I had never seen him in anything other than a simple tunic or hand-me-down riding clothes.

That morning, Jared had arrayed him in a dark-green tunic, which had a thick band of gold embroidered at the hem. It looked so new, you would never guess it had once belonged to Harpagus's son. Cyrus's hair had been combed for once, and curled, thick, inky swathes held off his forehead by an embellished leather band that circled his head.

He had insisted on wearing his hunting trousers under his finery. "I'm not flashing my legs before the whole Persian kingdom when I dismount," he said fiercely. "I may be a shepherd boy, but I have my dignity."

Anshan, an ancient city built by the Elamites long ago, had fallen under Persian rule a hundred years earlier and served as their capital. It lay southeast of Babylon but, by some trick of topography, enjoyed more temperate weather.

We found the palace, as the city itself, simpler than Ecbatana, and smaller. But everywhere there were signs of new growth. Whereas Media, for all its riches, seemed to have come to a standstill, Anshan was booming.

The Persians had a genius for using underground springs to their advantage. While the area around Anshan looked dry and barren thanks to the rainless climate, the city and its surrounding lands had been made verdant with an abundance of vineyards, orchards, and carefully planned gardens.

Harpagus's seal on the ring he had given Jared, as well as on his letter, gained us entry into the palace. I caught a glimpse of a long, shallow pool, covered in turquoise-blue tiles, at the center of a manicured garden before the guard led us to a waiting chamber outside the royal reception hall.

We had asked to meet with the queen, knowing her our most likely ally. If anyone would recognize Astyages's features in Cyrus's face, it would be Mandana, not Cambyses.

I sat down, preparing for a long wait. But the stone bench was still cool against my skin when the door opened and a bodyguard came to fetch us. We followed behind, walking three abreast, Cyrus ramrod straight between us, a slight flush the only sign betraying his inner turmoil. I placed a hand on his shoulder and felt him tremble.

We processed down the rectangular audience hall, passing the curious faces of the courtiers who had gathered there. Upon a short dais sat two thrones made of carved wood, decorated with gold leaf. The larger throne stood empty. A woman occupied the other.

I had the impression of very white skin and pale brown eyes under a tall, fluted crown. When the guard stopped, the three of us bowed in unison as we had practiced, one hand before our mouths in the Persian manner.

Mandana signaled for us to rise. "You have a message for me from Lord Harpagus?" she asked brusquely in Median.

I bowed my head. "Yes, my queen."

"I must say, Lord Harpagus chooses strange messengers." Her eyes snagged on Cyrus for a moment.

"For reasons beyond his control, we are the only ones able to deliver it."

"You make me curious." She held out a hand.

Jared bowed and handed Harpagus's sealed letter to the bodyguard. It was one of two letters he had addressed to her. This one, short and to the point, merely begged her to allow us a private audience, as we had extraordinary news to impart. *Difficult and yet wonderful* was how he had phrased it.

She read the brief note and arched a brow. After a short conference with her chief bodyguard, she waved, and the waiting courtiers emptied the chamber. I noted the lingering presence of several guards in strategic locations. She was willing to humor Harpagus so far as it did not place her in unnecessary danger. Given the father who had raised her, I could not blame her caution.

"Now . . ." She frowned at us. "What is this about?"

We had always known that I would have to be the spokesperson in this moment. Jared did not speak either Median or its cousin language, Persian. And Cyrus could not be expected to be the champion of his own cause.

Which left only me.

Since the hour I had reconciled myself to the necessity of the task, I had dreaded its coming. How do you tell a woman her dead child lives? It may sound like happy news. But before she can smile, she must mourn eleven years of needless loss. Strive with eleven years of betrayal.

And before any of that, she must first believe my story.

"My queen, there is no easy way to discharge this task."

"Out with it. Has someone died? Is it my father?"

I blinked. "No, lady. No one has died. Quite the opposite, in fact." Slowly, I told her the story of her father's treachery just as Harpagus had related it to me.

Her back grew stiff when I described the fateful conversation between Harpagus and the king. I sensed she thought that exchange to be the end of my story. That I had come to reveal her father's hand in the demise of her child.

Her hands gripped the armrests of her throne until her nails turned white. "You accuse my father of this heinous crime?"

"I accuse no one, lady. The crime was not committed. At least not as he expected."

As the story developed, she grew paler until I feared she might faint. I drew Cyrus forward when I came to the end of my tale. "This, my queen, is that same child whom you thought dead. This is your Cyrus, saved by the hand of Lord Harpagus."

Cyrus stood with a grave dignity far beyond his age. She studied him for a quick moment, not long enough to truly see him. "What calumny is this?" she cried. "What heartless deceit do you spew? How dare you stand in my presence and weave such lies?"

"Lady, by all that is holy, I speak truth. I overheard Lord Harpagus conversing with the shepherd Mitradates myself."

She came to her feet. "My child is dead! And you think to gain advantage by supplanting some shepherd's baggage at my bosom? You think me such a fool?"

Before I could say another word, Cyrus lunged forward, fierce as a lion cub. "Enough!" he cried. "I don't need you to want me. I have a sweet mother at home who adores me. I would be with her right now if your poxy father hadn't been trying to kill me."

Mandana's piercing gaze left me to settle on Cyrus. I had thought her face bloodless before. But as she watched the boy, she grew paler still.

"Come, Keren. Let us take our leave." Cyrus pulled on my hand until I was forced to take a step backward.

I hoped the queen might object. She seemed cast from stone, however, and said nothing. "Please, my queen. Would you at least read this letter from Lord Harpagus? He tells the story in his own words." I handed the second sealed message, this one longer and containing Harpagus's regrets as well as explanations, to her bodyguard.

Mandana took the missive and whispered something in the man's ear before waving us away.

"Where are you staying?" the guard asked as he accompanied us out of the audience hall.

"The inn outside Anshan," I said. I was not fooled by his casual tone. He did not intend to let us go without establishing how to lay hold of us again.

"That went as well as can be expected," Jared said cheerfully when I had translated the queen's words. "I never supposed she would accept our story upon first hearing it. She will need time to digest everything."

"What kind of mother doesn't know her own son?" Cyrus said with a scowl.

"The kind who is flesh and blood, Cyrus. Jared is right. She needs time. Time to hear her heart speak."

"I bet she doesn't even cook." Cyrus sniffed. "Well, I'm sick of palaces. Every time I go into one, someone accuses me of something bad I didn't do."

I ruffled his hair. "Let's go for a ride."

He grinned. "Finally, someone makes a sensible suggestion."

CHAPTER FORTY-FIVE

Thus says the LORD, your Redeemer . . .
"I am the LORD . . .
who says of Cyrus, 'He is my shepherd, and he shall fulfill all my purpose';
saying of Jerusalem, 'She shall be built,'
and of the temple, 'Your foundation shall be laid.'"
Isaiah 44:24, 28, ESV

"We have sprouted a tail." Jared pointed his chin at two palace guards lounging in a corner of the inn's courtyard.

"Good," I said as I threw a felt saddlecloth over my stallion. In truth, I would rather have settled down with my Jeremiah scroll to enjoy a peaceful morning as far away from a moving horse as possible. But I knew Cyrus needed activity.

"Why good?" Jared frowned at the soldiers.

"If the queen wants to keep us under close observation, it means she is interested in him. She can't quite bring herself to let him go. A part of her wonders if our story is true."

"Or she wants easy access should she decide to separate our heads from our necks."

"Or that." I grimaced.

The innkeeper had told us of a farmer who opened his land

to riders and hunters for a small fee. It was not far, thankfully. As soon as we arrived, I dismounted and found myself a delicate pomegranate tree to sit under while the boys cavorted on their mounts. I noticed one of the palace guards left discreetly. To report on our activities, no doubt.

I was half dozing when the sound of chariot wheels drew me out of my torpor. The queen herself was driving a light war chariot, two faultlessly matched Nisaean blacks pulling her in perfect unison. I came to my feet in surprise. It had never occurred to me that she would come herself, and so quickly.

With a deft movement, she drew the horses to a smooth stop a few paces from me. Without bothering to dismount, she stood rock-still and watched Cyrus. The boy was doing tricks, riding without hands so he could practice archery from horseback.

"He is very good for one so young," Mandana said without looking at me.

"He thinks himself quite grown up, especially since he turned eleven a few days ago."

Her mouth tightened. "Boy!" she called. "You, boy! Come here."

Cyrus wheeled his horse toward us. At the sight of Mandana, his grin faded. Jared whispered something to him, and surrendering his bow and arrows, Cyrus signaled his stallion to trot toward the queen. The line of his back had grown stiff. Sensing his tension, the chestnut threw his head. Nimbly, Cyrus reasserted control and came to a stop before the queen.

The two stared at each other, the queen from her chariot and Cyrus atop his horse.

I motioned to him, and after a short hesitation, he dismounted. I took the reins and, under the watchful eye of a palace guard, tethered the horse to a branch.

Cyrus approached the queen's black stallions. "Good-looking. Never seen a pair so well matched."

"I noticed your own chestnut is quite majestic."

Cyrus grinned. "Harpagus gave him to me. He had promised me the choice of any of the horses in his stable if I studied hard." His grin widened. "This is his own horse. Keren said Harpagus would never give him up. But he keeps his promises."

The queen's eyes narrowed. "What did he want you to study?"

"Lots of things. Aramaic. Numeracy. Archery. Sword craft. He even made me study a little Akkadian. Avoid it if you can, lady. That's a poxy language."

The queen switched from Median to Aramaic. "Why did he make you study Akkadian?"

Just as smoothly, Cyrus switched his own speech. "That's what I said every time Keren pulled out her clay tablet. But the chestnut was worth it."

"How did you meet Lord Harpagus?"

Cyrus shrugged. "Don't know. He was always there since I was little." He hesitated. "He even tried to teach me Persian for a while."

My head snapped up. He had never shared that bit of information with me.

Mandana adjusted the leather lines she held in her hands. "Perhaps he is your father."

The easygoing smile on Cyrus's face vanished. "Just because you are a queen does not mean you can insult my mother."

Mandana's hand fisted about the lines. "That's exactly what it means, boy! No less because of your outlandish claims." She loosened the driving lines, and without another word, she turned her chariot in a neat semicircle and galloped away in a trail of dust.

Cyrus scowled after her. "That woman is worse than a crick in my neck."

I took a deep breath. "She is in a hard place. Either you are deceitful or her father is."

"I saw that fellow only once." Cyrus crossed his arms. "When it comes to lying, I would bet on him, every time."

Jared sauntered over. "She left in a hurry."

"For all her haste, she made sure two of her royal guards keep us company." I pointed my chin at the burly soldiers she had left in plain view.

* * *

The next morning, Mandana sent for me. Alone.

This was an unexpected development. Jared was quiet as he brushed my horse. "I don't like it," he said. "I don't like the thought of you going into that palace alone."

"I don't either. But what choice do we have?"

"We can say no."

I thought for a moment. "She is caught between rage and longing. I sense she may be hanging by a thread. If I ignore her, she might snap."

Jared pulled a hand through his hair and nodded. Looping his fingers, he bent to accommodate my foot and tossed me gently onto the horse's back.

He and Cyrus accompanied me as far as the palace gates. Instead of leaving me to dismount on my own as he usually did, Jared came to stand by my horse. Before I could speak, his hands wrapped around my waist, and gently, he lifted me down. For a long moment, he allowed his hands to remain, their warmth seeping into me. A great herd of cattle went stampeding through my chest.

His head bent toward my ear so that his whispered words stirred the hair at my neck. "Have a care. I'll be waiting." It took me a moment to pull myself together enough to make my feet take something resembling a step.

Mandana's personal guard led me not to the audience hall as I expected, but to a smaller chamber that backed onto the garden. The queen was lounging in a nook by an open window, her gaze glued to the dying leaves climbing a pretty arbor.

"Is he Harpagus's natural son?" she asked as soon as we were alone.

I froze mid-bow. Slowly, I straightened. "I thought the same when he first hired me. I assumed his unusual interest in the boy could mean nothing else. Then he told me the story of Cyrus's birth."

Her lips tightened at the mention of her supposedly dead child. "How do you know he did not lie to you?"

"For what purpose? I was nothing but a hired servant. Besides, I've met Cyrus's mother. She is a simple woman. Very loving and dedicated to her child. But there is nothing fascinating about her. Cyrus is sure to tell you she is pretty. In his eyes, she may be. In truth, she is one of the plainest women I know. Lord Harpagus is an elegant man with an eye for beauty. There is no way you could convince me that he would ever have been so tempted by her that he would forget she already had a husband."

"Perhaps he was in his cups, one night. Or he has odd tastes in women. Or he sired the child on another woman and had the shepherd and his wife raise him."

I sighed. "Lady, have you looked at him? I mean really taken the time to look upon him?"

"The green eyes were clever, I grant you. Then again, my lineage is not the only one to whelp green-eyed boys."

"It's not only the color of his eyes, or the shape of his eyebrow." I studied the simple stone floors, so different from the opulence of Ecbatana. "Do you know why I believed Lord Harpagus? Beyond all this evidence—which is no proof, I suppose, unless your heart tells you different?"

She turned from the window. "Enlighten me."

"My people, the Jews, were taken into captivity by Nebuchadnezzar."

"I have heard tales of your continuous rebellion and ultimate enslavement."

I nodded. "The Lord our God made us a promise that after seventy years, we would be set free. Not by our own hand. But saved by a king of the Medes. One of our prophets named our coming rescuer. The king of the Medes who will one day set us free from the yoke of Babylon is called Cyrus."

The queen turned bone-white.

"When I overheard Harpagus speak to the shepherd, he used the name Cyrus. It was the first I heard of it. He never spoke it in public, fearful that it might lead to his death, not to mention the boy's. He could not have known what that name meant to me. A Jew.

"Your father, O queen, believed your son would one day grow so great that he would snatch his throne from him. I believe he is right. Cyrus will one day be the king of the Medes. And he will conquer Babylon."

She rose. "You're mad!"

I shook my head. "I merely believe that God is able to fulfill his promises."

"Have you filled the child's head with all this nonsense?"

"No, lady. He knows none of it." I laced my fingers together. "Did your father ever tell you of his dreams?"

"Don't be daft. He would never reveal them to me, of all people. I knew of them, nonetheless. We have . . . friends . . . at the palace in Ecbatana."

By which she meant spies, I assumed.

"But what you are implying . . . what you are accusing my father of . . . is monstrous."

"Yes, lady."

* * *

I emerged from the palace gate and spied Jared and Cyrus leaning against one of the fluted columns. I had barely taken half a step when I found myself enfolded in Jared's arms.

"I thought you were never coming out." His voice was gravelly. At my waist and back, his hands felt safe, like an unbreakable shield. Disappointment roared like an irate elephant when he stepped away.

Cyrus inserted himself between us. "Who did she insult this time?"

I laughed. "Harpagus, mostly."

Jared gave me an uneven smile. "She's still not convinced, then."

"There is only one person who will convince her."

"Who?" Cyrus asked.

"You."

"Fire and lightning! What does she want from me? I don't remember being abducted when I was a week old!"

"Hopefully it won't come to that," Jared said.

Cyrus kicked a stone, making it fly and twirl. "From my short career as a dodgy prince, I can tell you it's a lot less aggravating being the son of a shepherd than the son of a queen. Let's go and eat a big bowl of stew. All this excitement is sapping my strength. I need my sustenance."

"I'll buy you two bowls if you let me sleep late tomorrow," I said. The long days of travel and the uncertainty of the past couple of days were beginning to wear me down. "I feel like a wet rag used to clean a henhouse."

The corner of Cyrus's mouth tipped. "You don't look at all wet."

I tried to kick him. That boy moved too fast.

CHAPTER
FORTY-SIX

The queen ignored us for three whole days. Her royal guards followed us wherever we went and did not bother to be too discreet about it. I felt grateful for the respite and spent much of the time dozing. The long hours of riding and constant night watches had pummeled my body. The enforced rest finally gave my sore muscles a chance to recover.

During the day, Jared took charge of Cyrus while I recuperated. In the evenings, we ate together and tried to grapple with the Persian language. The Medes and Persians were cousin races, and their languages were closely related. This made it easier for Cyrus and me to pick up its nuances, although to my astonishment, Cyrus already possessed a remarkable fluency in his mother's tongue.

"Harpagus used to drone on and on at me in Persian," he

explained. "It was supposed to be our big secret. I got used to hiding my knowledge of it."

Jared, who had betrayed a touch of warm emotion after my long audience with the queen, withdrew back into his shell. Whatever affection his anxieties had loosened had been shoved back down some dark hole in his heart. He remained kind and polite. But he betrayed no evidence of the feelings I had sensed when he held me that day.

Having tasted a few moments of his ardor, I found it especially hard to return to his cold indifference.

Three days after my private visit, Mandana sent for us again, this time requesting the presence of all of us. She had actually used the word *request*. That was a first.

"I did not realize she had it in her vocabulary," Jared said when Cyrus could not overhear.

"I hope it means she is warming to us."

She received us in the same small room by the garden where she had last met with me. This time, she was sitting on the floor, the ruched skirts of her scarlet tunic spread about her on a hand-knotted carpet. Next to her, a leopard cub played with a leather ball she threw at it.

Cyrus forgot to bow. Leaping forward, he fell on his knees next to the cub, a hand's breadth from the queen. Two guards rushed to grab him. Lightning fast, Jared stepped forward to protect the boy lest the guards became overenthusiastic in their defense of their queen.

Mandana raised a hand, bringing everyone to a sudden halt. The only one who ignored her was Cyrus, who scooched closer. "Aah! Where did you get him?"

"His mother was killed at a hunt a few weeks ago. I am looking after him until he is old enough to be released in the park."

The little leopard turned ice-blue eyes to Cyrus and screeched, making us all smile.

"He is hungry," the queen said, and gathered the cub in her arms. Someone had filled a sheepskin with milk and rigged the lip to serve as a nipple, and the leopard cub latched on to it greedily.

Cyrus watched as though mesmerized. Delicately, the queen untangled sharp claws from the warp and weft of her tunic. "Hold out your hand," she told Cyrus.

He held it out to her without hesitation. Pulling the skin of milk away from the distracted cub, she poured a bit of milk in Cyrus's palm. She turned the leopard around in her arms until he faced Cyrus. Smelling the scent of milk, the cub found its way to Cyrus's hand and began licking it.

Cyrus's mouth fell open. He began to giggle. "That tickles!"

When the queen dropped the leopard into his arms, Cyrus held the cub securely and offered the queen one of his irresistible smiles. "You may not know how to cook. But this is almost as good."

Mandana's lips twitched. "Who said I don't know how to cook?"

"You do?"

She sniffed. "I have not tried."

"That means you don't know how."

He tickled the cub on the belly. The leopard wrapped his paws around the boy's wrist and pressed his nose to Cyrus's fingers. Cyrus threw his head back and laughed aloud. Something about that gesture—the shoulders raised, the green eyes sparkling and narrow, the bird-wing eyebrow raised—caught Mandana. She sat as though utterly paralyzed.

Pain flashed across her frozen face. Pain, shock, hope. It became a mingled portrait too intimate to watch and I dropped my gaze.

Everyone had grown quiet. Everyone except Cyrus, whose chortles mixed with the kittenish shrieks of the leopard cub.

"Leave the boy with me," the queen rasped. "You may go."

I took a hasty step forward. "But, lady!"

"I said you may go!"

Gently, Cyrus set the cub back on the carpet. Coming to his feet, he approached and gave my hand a quick squeeze. "I'll be all right."

"You want me to leave you here?"

He glanced at Mandana over his shoulder. Something passed between the two. "I won't hurt the boy," the queen said. "You have my promise. He will be safe with me."

Cyrus squeezed my hand again. "I will be fine."

*　*　*

"What do we do now?" Jared asked as we sat to our dinner of lamb and quince stew.

"I don't know." I picked at my food. The heady aroma of quince and fresh garlic would have tempted me at any other time. But with Cyrus in such a precarious position, food had lost all its appeal.

"She gave her word."

I nodded. "Do you believe her?"

"It was the word of a mother, not a queen. He'll be safe." The deep line furrowing his brow told me that in spite of the confidence in his voice, he had his own seed of doubt.

After tending the horses, Jared and I made up our beds on a mound of clean straw in the stables again. With Cyrus gone, something had shifted between us. Although we were in a public place, with other travelers bedded down nearby in the open courtyard, I could not ignore the intimacy of our situation. Without Cyrus sleeping between us, Jared and I were lying within an arm's length of each other. A circumstance that would have once been unthinkable.

I tossed and turned, unable to sleep. Finally, I threw aside my blankets and rose, my movements silent. On tiptoes, I made my way out of the stable, through the courtyard, and into the overgrown herb garden beyond. I sat on the wobbly bench and pulled my knees into my chest to ward off the chill.

"Can't sleep?"

I jumped as Jared's voice came through the shadows. "Pardon," I said. "Did I wake you?"

He sat on the other side of the bench. "I was already awake."

"Does your head ache?"

"No. I have had little pain since that night in the oasis."

I exhaled with relief. "God be thanked."

His mouth tipped up. "I have a theory about it."

"About why you have not experienced another episode?"

He nodded. "I came face-to-face with my biggest fear that night. The paralyzing thought that I would get sick precisely when you and Cyrus needed me most. And that is what happened."

I drew my knees closer to my chest. "How did that help you?"

"What I dreaded most came to pass, and we all survived it. God made a way. He did not need me to keep everyone safe. And even though my presence actually placed you in danger, he managed to save you. That fear had been hanging over me like a savage dragon. That night, God pulled its teeth." He shrugged.

"Without the shadow of that anxiety pressing against my mind, the pain is tamed."

We sat in a silence that was far from companionable. Its jagged edges poked and prodded any peace I might have salvaged from this night.

He twisted to face me. "I did," he said abruptly.

"You did what?" I asked, confused.

"I did love you."

My chest constricted so I could barely breathe. "You never said."

He shrugged. Somewhere in the distance a wolf howled. Crickets chirped. My blood pounded against my temples.

"You were the best thing in my life."

I wanted to weep at the finality of those words. What a privileged place I had once occupied in his heart. And I had not known it. "I am so sorry, Jared."

"I felt nothing for her, you know. I had seen her for what she was. Entertaining, eye-catching. But empty."

I dropped my head. "She was so utterly dazzling. And she had set her sights on you."

"My father wanted me to marry her. I suppose she knew that and felt a little proprietary toward me."

A shaft of pain went through me. I wrapped my arm around my chest. "Will you marry her when you go back?"

He gave a huff of laughter. "You still don't understand, do you? Of course I will not marry her! In spite of all the pressure from my father, I had already decided against it. She is nothing that I want." He adjusted the strap of his leather eye patch. "In any case, she is not in the market for a one-eyed bridegroom. We are equally well rid of one another, you might say."

It proved too much. The knowledge of what I had lost. The

love I had pierced on the sharp point of my jealousy. Regret clawed at me until I felt like I might choke. I snapped to my feet and took a step away.

Jared rose at the same time, his movements fluid. I wanted to run, but my body would not obey. Instead, I remained rooted to the spot, trembling, unable to look away. It was as if we had trapped each other, both of us caught in a net we could not break.

Then Jared took a half step toward me. "Keren," he breathed.

A world of unnamed yearning seemed to flare into life with that one word. Something in me melted. The strength that had held me together since he had come to Ecbatana collapsed. The strength to let him go.

He shook his head as if he could read my thoughts. "No. *No*." Turning, he ran into the darkness.

I fell to my knees, face sinking in my hands. *She is nothing that I want,* he had said about Zebidah. How ironic that by my own hands I had made those words true of me, also.

CHAPTER
FORTY-SEVEN

My heart's desires are broken.
Job 17:11, NLT

———————— JARED ————————

Why could he not cut her out of his heart? What was it about the woman? He had thought, having seen her dirty and unkempt, smelling of sweat and unwashed clothes as they traveled, that she would at least lose her physical appeal for him. Instead, he found himself more drawn to her than ever.

Sitting next to her on that hard stone bench, he had almost pulled her into his arms. Even now, his heart changed its rhythm, turned into a beating drum at the mere thought of tasting those delicate lips with their upturned corners. He could not forgive her. But he could not stop wanting her, either.

For years, he had wanted to make her his bride. Cherish her as his wife. Now, when he needed to keep her at a safe distance,

God had bound him to Keren's side in an indissoluble chain of events. The Lord had finally given him the call he had longed for. The task of a lifetime. But he could not accomplish it without her.

To run from her, he would have to run from this divine assignment.

God, it seemed, wanted them bound together, if not in one way, then in another.

He rubbed his sore neck and rose from the corner where he had hunched down so he could remain within earshot of the stables without being too close to her. He sighed as he headed back to his bed in the straw. Perhaps he could manage to catch a few hours of rest before sunrise, even though she would be lying within reach of his arms.

He felt like he had just closed his eye when a booted foot nudged him in the side. Jared's sword was pointing at the man's gullet before he had a chance to move his boot again.

One of the queen's guards smirked at him and held up his hands in a gesture of peace. Jared dropped his sword to his side.

"What do you want?" he croaked.

The guard shrugged and said something in Persian, which Jared did not understand.

"The queen requests our presence," Keren explained, springing out of her tangled blankets.

* * *

"The king wishes to meet the boy," Mandana said over her shoulder. They had been led to the informal chamber they had visited before, and the queen was gazing distractedly out of the window.

Standing next to her, Cyrus grinned. Keren wrapped the boy in a fierce embrace. "You seem hale and hearty."

He shrugged. "I told her that if I am going to face another king, I want my friends with me. The last time I had an audience with a man wearing a crown, I didn't fare so well."

The queen's lips twitched. "I suppose you are referring to my father."

"I am referring to the fact that I had to leg it out of his fancy big chamber to keep my head attached to my neck."

"My husband is not that manner of king."

Two royal guards appeared at the door and thumped their chests with their fists. "We live to serve!" they cried in unison.

The queen turned to face them. "Yes?"

"The king requests that you attend him with the boy, lady."

Mandana led their procession, two royal guards behind her, followed by Cyrus, Jared, and Keren, followed by two more guards. They were announced in the throne room, where the king awaited them.

Cambyses was garbed in riding clothes, more practical than royal in appearance. He stood to take his wife's hand and led her to the smaller throne next to his. The action, though ceremonial, held an air of affection, further confirmed by the way Cambyses held on to her fingers over their armrests.

Their marriage might have been a political merger, but Jared could see that they had learned to trust and love each other over the years.

"The queen tells me that you are making some extraordinary claims about this boy," Cambyses said in fluent Aramaic. Jared suspected that most of those present in the throne room could not understand him. A useful tactic if he wished to keep this conversation private.

Jared and Keren bowed at the same time. "Neither of us was present at the time these events originally took place, O king," Jared explained. "You have, no doubt, already read the letter from Lord Harpagus explaining his role in those unfortunate circumstances eleven years ago. What I can tell you from personal experience is that we have been followed since we left Ecbatana with the boy. Twice, men tried to kill him. The first two soldiers wore the uniform of King Astyages's personal guard. Why would a king want a shepherd boy dead if Harpagus's claims are not true?"

The king gestured for Cyrus to step closer. "What is your name, boy?" His voice was surprisingly gentle.

"My parents called me Artadates, lord."

"Who are your parents?"

"The royal shepherd Mitradates and his wife."

"But you don't like being a shepherd?"

Cyrus's posture grew even straighter. "I love my parents, and I am not ashamed to be a shepherd's son. I have learned many good lessons from Mitradates as I have looked after the king's sheep. But you are right in saying I do not wish to be a shepherd. If you think that means I would prefer to be a prince, you are wrong, O king. I plan to be a general and to lead armies into victory. You don't need to be a prince for that."

Even the mild-mannered Cambyses seemed taken aback at being told he was wrong. He changed tack. His next question emerged less gently. "And yet you claim to be my son, do you not?"

Cyrus frowned. "I'm eleven. It's not for me to make such grand claims or dispute them. All I know is that if they are true, I have one set of parents who, though kind and caring, lied to me every day of my life. And another set of parents who, though loving and powerful, managed to misplace me for eleven years. For this, I owe thanks to a king. And if everything you have been told is a lie, then for that, you owe thanks to the same king, and perhaps to Lord Harpagus, but not to me."

Mandana's cheeks were suffused with pink. A spasm of some emotion flitted across her face before she stamped it down. At first, Jared thought it might be rage. Then, looking at her trembling lips, he wondered if it was guilt that ate at her.

The king might have come to the same conclusion. He snapped to his feet and turned to Keren. "You come armed with tempting lies, woman. Lies to break the heart of an already grieving mother. My wife will not allow me to harm you, or that boy you have trained so cleverly. Leave with your lives and count yourselves fortunate."

Jared rubbed the back of his neck as they left the audience chamber, Cyrus keeping pace with them. That had not gone as well as he had hoped.

Mandana and her guard seemed to appear out of nowhere, intercepting their path. She faced Cyrus wordlessly, staring at the boy as though her eyes could resolve the conundrum she faced.

She cradled Cyrus's cheek with one hand. "What if I believe you and it's all a lie? What if you are a ploy, as my husband believes? What if my heart fools me?"

Jared felt as though he had turned to stone. He understood her, this grieving queen. Understood her rage and her fear. Because his own heart was fighting the same battle and falling to the dagger's point of the same piercing questions.

"Lady, you can trust your heart," he whispered.

CHAPTER FORTY-EIGHT

If racing against mere men makes you tired,
how will you race against horses?
Jeremiah 12:5, NLT

Disappointment warred with relief as we walked to the inn. I had a hold of Cyrus's hand, refusing to loosen my grip even as he made a restless bid to free himself. I knew he was too old for it; I simply could not let go. He remained the epicenter of a dangerous storm. A storm of emotions in the hearts of those who had the power to destroy him.

Like a pair of pincers, the king and queen sat to either side of him, ready to squeeze with the smallest provocation. Tempers were flaring. I had seen it in Cambyses's eyes. Hot, burning outrage at the thought of us trying to take advantage of his wife's long years of grief.

"You handled yourself remarkably well, Cyrus," I said. "I am proud of you."

"Then maybe you can release my hand."

"Pardon." Reluctantly, I let go.

"And maybe you should stop calling me by that name."

"It is who you are."

"It isn't, if they don't believe it." He shrugged. "I don't care. It would be very awkward to have four parents, anyway. What would I call them all?"

Jared ruffled the boy's hair. "Ride?"

Cyrus nodded.

I watched as they left in a mighty puff of dust, galloping as though chased by bandits. Jared had been pale and silent since we had left the palace. I had begun to suspect he was suffering from another headache. But watching him ride, his lithe body almost flat against the horse's back, moving in perfect rhythm with the beast's elegant form, I realized that whatever ailed him did not have a physical source.

Longing for an hour of quiet, I found my way to the herb garden. A spotted woodpecker landed on the hogweed and began pecking away, digging for worms. I watched it dancing on the branch, its black-and-white body shifting with every jab of its beak.

I felt an overwhelming wave of tiredness as I watched that bird work. "Will this quest never end?" I wondered. It seemed no matter what we did, we could not find a breakthrough.

As if in answer to my lament, God's response to Jeremiah's youthful complaints came to me with crystalline clarity: *If racing against mere men makes you tired, how will you race against horses?*

Those words made me laugh and cringe at the same time. Like a madwoman, I shook a finger at the heavens. "That is not very reassuring, Lord. If you are telling me that what we have experienced thus far is nothing compared to what is coming, I may just run away."

My finger dropped uselessly to my side. "Then again, you would probably send a great fish to swallow me."

With a sigh, I came to my feet. God was reminding me to endure. To trust in him in the midst of so much discouragement. Something in my soul bowed before that invitation. I would limp out of bed tomorrow and be brave. And I would bear the weight of the burden before me.

* * *

That afternoon, the queen came to seek us again. She came veiled and alone, on horseback, which told me she must have sneaked out of the palace, to avoid her husband's censure. Obviously, some part of her felt a connection to the boy. Cyrus had not revealed much about his time with her in the palace, except to say she was not, in his words, *too poxy for a queen*. I understood his hesitation in singing her praises. His loyalty to the mother who had raised him objected to the yearning he felt for Mandana.

"Do you want to come for a ride with me?" the queen asked Cyrus, not including us in the invitation.

"How well can you ride?" he said.

She grinned. "Better than you."

Cyrus gave her a narrow-eyed look. "Really? How about a race? And you better not fall on your head, or the king is going to really get mad."

The queen adjusted her seat. "Are you going to talk all day, or do you plan to actually mount that pretty Nisaean of yours?"

"*Pretty?* He is a stallion! Mighty. Powerful. Handsome. Elegant. But not pretty!"

"I see you have a good vocabulary for a shepherd boy."

"I see yours leaves something to be desired for a queen."

They were still bickering as they trotted off to the old farm where they could race undisturbed. I whirled around to find Jared standing too close.

Something about the way he watched me made me stumble over my words. "Did you . . . s-s-see that?"

"I saw." He took another step toward me.

"She is growing f-f-fond of him, I think."

Another half step. "More than fond, I would say."

For the sake of convenience, he had clipped his beard very short as we had traveled. I could see the strong line of his jaw through the bristles. I had spent so much time avoiding his gaze lately that staring at him now came as something of a shock. His features, lean and arresting, softened.

He reached out a hand. Slowly, gently, his fingers wrapped around mine. My lips fell open, but no sound emerged.

"Shall we go for a walk?" he asked. His voice had turned husky. The sound of it traveled over me like a caress.

I gulped and nodded.

His clasp around my fingers tightened. With a quick push and pull, he wove his fingers through mine until our palms lay flush against each other. The heat of his skin seeped into me through that single point of connection and spread.

I stumbled after him as he began to walk. If he intended for us to experience a pleasurable stroll, it was lost on me. When he stopped, I finally took a moment to take stock of my surroundings. He had brought me to a bubbling spring, enclosed in a ring of crooked trees and puny reeds.

"I found this spring the other day," Jared said, drawing me to a low shelf of rock. With a tug on my hand, he guided us to sit. The shelf offered meager space, forcing us close, so that our legs and arms brushed against one another. Even through the soft wool of my riding trousers, I could feel the hard ridges of muscle along his body. A frisson of shock traveled through me.

"I am glad the queen took Cyrus for a ride," Jared said. "Aside from the implications of such an overture, it allows us a bit of privacy. I wanted to speak to you."

I thought of our last conversation and winced.

"For that—" he pointed at the frown on my face—"I ask your pardon. I have been hard on you."

I shook my head. "I deserved every word."

Jared's hand cradled my chin and pulled so that I would look at him again. "When I was a boy, before I had learned to guard my heart against my father, I would run to him again and again, expecting love. Sometimes he gave it, or some pale version of it. A careless word of praise. A pat on the head. Enough to make me return for more. But mostly, he wounded me with his coldness. His indifference.

"It took me a long time to understand that he was not capable of giving me what I needed. When I finally accepted that reality, a part of my heart closed. Learned to shield itself from ever being fooled again into loving someone who could not love me back.

"It was the queen's words that made me realize why this—" he pointed to his leather eye patch—"felt like my feelings for you were an illusion."

"I betrayed you, the way your father had."

He gave a sad smile. "Do you remember what Mandana said as we were leaving the palace this morning?"

I tried to recall her words. *"What if I believe you and it's all a lie? . . . What if my heart fools me?"*

Jared pressed my hand between his fingers. *"What if my heart fools me?* As soon as I heard those words, I realized why I could not forgive you. I felt like I had landed back into my childhood with my father. I had trusted you with everything. And you broke my trust. Every day since then, I have been screaming at my heart for fooling me again. For making me believe it was safe to love, when it was not."

Tears rolled down my cheeks and made their way past my lips to dribble on the rocky ground. They tasted salty and bitter. "God's mercy, Jared. I am sorry."

He wiped my tears. I felt his fingers shaking against my skin. "No. *I* am sorry. I am sorry to have confused you with my father. You are nothing like him." His hand dropped to his lap. "I told the queen what I needed to hear myself. *You can trust your heart.* As a child, I learned that my heart is untrustworthy. And sometimes, it is.

"But this is also the heart that loves the Lord. The heart that is fixed on him. The heart that has learned to be loyal and to choose right." He pressed his palm, my fingers still entwined with his, against his chest. "This heart, though imperfect, can be trusted. And this heart tells me your love is true."

A tiny wail worked its way up my throat.

Jared covered our entwined hands with his other hand, still pressed against his chest. "Love does not preserve us from mistakes. You made a mistake. But your love is trustworthy."

My lips were trembling so hard, I could barely get the words out. "Forgive me, Jared!"

"I do. I forgive you." He smiled.

It was my turn to confess. "All those years in Daniel's house, neither daughter nor servant, I learned to feel a little less-than. A little less than acceptable. A little less than desirable. Zebidah seemed to be everything I wasn't. To have everything I didn't have. The clothes, the jewels, the dazzling polish. I could not believe any man would be able to resist her. I could not compete with her. I was convinced I would lose you. Our friendship, and whatever was burgeoning just underneath.

"All I could think of as I faced you that day was my desperate desire to keep your attention from her. I . . ."

Jared pressed a finger to my lips, cutting me off. "You were right, you know. I am like the Hanging Gardens. Good things growing in impossible places." His fingers fluttered over his eye patch. "Good things coming out of this. Not merely pain and loss. But faith, and strength."

"Jared," I gasped. Love for him overwhelmed me, spilling over, robbing me of breath so that I sat like a hungry chick, beak wide open, hardly able to think of a single coherent syllable. "Jared, I love you with all my—"

His lips pressed against mine, swallowing my last word. His fingers wrapped around the back of my neck, tipping my head so he could explore my lips more fully. The desperate, pent-up yearning of long months found its escape in that kiss, which was part comfort, part forgiveness, part acceptance, and wholly, entirely love.

He lifted his head and gasped.

I drew a finger down his cheek, still feeling as if I might be in a dream.

"Well, this is a sorry pickle," he said.

"Why?"

"Because I want to marry you, and your father is somewhere over there." He pointed over his shoulder to the west. "Across some tall mountains."

"You want to marry me?"

"I have wanted to marry you since you were a head taller than I was."

I giggled. He cut off my laughter with a kiss so hot and restless, my bones melted.

"Fire and lightning," I breathed. Then he kissed me again, fingers tangled in my hair, and I forgot everything, even the ability to speak.

CHAPTER FORTY-NINE

The queen slipped out of the palace to visit us every day after that. She always came alone. Sometimes, she remained for only a few moments, not even bothering to dismount. At other times, she would take Cyrus, and the two would go off by themselves for an hour or two. They would both return flushed, eyes bright with emotions neither would name.

On the third day, Mandana stopped calling him *boy*.

She had brought the leopard cub, wrapped in a soft blanket. "He fell asleep in my arms as I was riding," she said. "He only just awoke, which means he will be feeling playful." She handed the now-wriggling cub to Cyrus.

"He's already heavier than the last time I saw him!" Cyrus cuddled him against his chest.

"They grow fast," the queen said. "Soon, I will have to start feeding him meat."

The boy's eyes rounded. "What kind of meat?"

The queen shrugged. "Mutton or deer, I suppose." Then apparently without thinking, she blurted, "Watch out, Cyrus. His claws are growing sharp. He will draw blood if he scratches you."

The four of us froze. Surely it had been a slip of the tongue. But she fell into the habit of it and took to calling him Cyrus after that.

*   *   *

A week later, we had a visit from another royal guard. I could tell from the red stripe at the hem of his tunic that he was part of Cambyses's personal squad. He handed me a scroll with the king's seal.

I scanned the short note. "The king has invited all of us to a hunt tomorrow."

Jared and I exchanged a look. Mandana must have convinced him to give the boy another chance. I wondered how she had managed to extract this invitation from him.

"At a royal park?" Jared asked.

Hunting had become the favored pastime of nobility throughout the great kingdoms of the world. In Babylon and Media, enclosed parks had been developed for the express purpose of the hunt. All manner of animals were released into the land for the day of the hunt. The contained nature of the environment and extensive preparations beforehand provided an element of safety for the hunters.

Although the Persians had parks, I had discovered that they considered them too tame. Aside from being a popular sport and a necessary source of food, hunting was a training ground for war. It allowed young men to hone all the skills they would need in the midst of a battle. For that reason, the Persians preferred hunting in the wilderness, a process infinitely more dangerous than its tamer version in a humanly fashioned park.

Wild hunts could take several days to complete and were unpredictable. Severe injuries and even deaths were not unheard of during a wild hunt.

"Not in a park," I said, expressionless.

Jared raised a sharp brow. "A wild hunt."

He understood the implication immediately. If Cambyses wished to be rid of this boy whom he considered a pretender, a hunt would provide a perfect opportunity for any number of convenient accidents to befall him.

On the other hand, he had invited Jared and me as well. If he had wanted the boy dead, surely he would not have bothered to include us. One thing to arrange an unfortunate mishap for a single child, but you could not easily murder three people and make it look accidental.

"We have to take the chance," Jared said. "He may never give Cyrus another opportunity."

I nodded. "Tell the king we would be honored to attend," I told the guard.

Cyrus whooped at the prospect of his first royal hunt. He had met his share of wolves and wild dogs while helping his father guard his sheep in open pasture. His handy use of the sling when we had been attacked gave evidence of his competence.

But a formal hunt provided a different kind of excitement. The sheer number of horses present meant that you had to keep your mount under rigid control at all times. The prey could lead you to dangerous, unfamiliar ground. A dozen things could conspire against the hunter.

"Although I am invited, since I am a woman, I assume I will be relegated to the sidelines merely to watch and cheer. Thank God you are an experienced hunter, Jared. You can protect Cyrus."

Jared tapped my cheek gently. "I assume that is why the queen arranged for us to be present. Now stop your worries. God has watched over that boy for eleven years. He isn't going to quit now."

* * *

The sun had yet to rise when we met up with the hunting party. A still quality lingered in the air. Even the dogs were eerily silent where they had gathered about their master.

I dismounted and bowed as the queen approached us. "Will you be able to keep up?" she asked.

"Keep up?"

She tilted her head. "With the hunt."

I frowned with incomprehension. "You want me to actually participate?"

She gave a short laugh. "Many Persian princesses shoot and ride as well as the men. You will see half a dozen amongst the riders today."

I blinked. I was beginning to really like these Persians. "I can keep up, lady." I sounded more confident than I felt.

"Watch over him." Her voice had a slight tremble to it.

"Will he be . . . in danger?"

Mandana had lived in palaces all her life. She knew the real question behind my veiled inquiry. "My husband would never harm a hair on that child's head," she sniffed.

I exhaled in relief.

"That is not to say he will not be in danger, as you put it." She turned to look through the crowd. "That young man riding the black Nisaean is called Otanes."

I spotted a youth with hooded eyes and regal bearing.

"He is my husband's nephew and the official crown prince. Being from the Pasargadae line like Cambyses, he has many supporters."

"Ah." In other words, although Cambyses might not try to harm Cyrus, Otanes and his supporters might.

"Look out for him," Mandana said fiercely.

I bowed in obedience before mounting my horse. "This ought to prove interesting," I told Jared nervously.

He leaned from his saddlecloth to tuck a loose curl behind my ear. "You are a capable rider. Having braved the elements during our travel to Anshan, you are better prepared than most for your first hunt in the wilderness. As to Cyrus, I pity any man who tries to cross that boy. The hand of God is upon him."

I grinned, feeling reassured by that reminder. "I love you," I whispered.

"I know." He leaned to place a quick kiss on my cheek.

Cyrus rolled his eyes. "You do know she doesn't cook?"

Jared put a hand to his cheek and let his mouth hang open in mock disbelief. "You don't cook?"

I made a face at them. "No. But I can spell any food you can name in four languages. What are we hunting?" I asked.

"Deer. Although the hunters won't disdain smaller game if we happen to come upon it." Jared pointed to Cambyses, who was juggling a falcon on his gloved arm while calming his prancing stallion. "The falcon is most likely trained to go after pheasant and partridge."

"That bird is a beauty," Cyrus said, his green eyes shining.

"Don't get distracted when it takes flight," Jared warned. "Keep your eyes on the terrain before you. You are not familiar with this landscape. One mistake, and you could break your stallion's leg."

Not to mention his own, I thought.

The hunting party was arranged by rank, with the king and queen leading the expedition, which left Jared, Cyrus, and me at the very back. I was grateful for this humble positioning. I felt gawky, afraid that I might make a fool of myself in spite of Jared's guidance. At least here, no one could see me.

Jared, on the other hand, had no such qualms. This had always been his favorite sport. He sat back on his saddlecloth, obviously at home in this complex world. He made a formidable picture in his riding attire, with a short leather tunic that emphasized the expanse of his chest and close-fitting trousers that revealed the hard, long muscles he had recently added to an already fit body.

Since we had arrived in Anshan, his language limitation had forced him into a less visible role in our dealings. He had taken on an unseen position, while I was pushed to the front by virtue of the circumstances. Not once had he complained. Now, he seemed in his element, knowing what to do while I felt lost.

Instead of prancing and preening, he quietly spread the mantle of his strength over Cyrus and me. With an encouraging nod or a simple direction, he gently guided us until we started to learn our way around the etiquette that applied to various parts of the sport.

The sun was low in the east when our small cavalcade set

off into the wilderness. Within an hour, we had left all signs of civilization behind, entering a rocky, gray land. We stopped for short breaks when Cambyses's falcon managed to capture a few pheasants. The rest of us had come up empty-handed by the time we stopped for the midday meal.

The quiet pace of our ride, and the lack of any crisis, had lulled me into a false sense of security. That did not last long.

CHAPTER FIFTY

The lazy do not roast any game,
but the diligent feed on the riches of the hunt.
Proverbs 12:27, NIV

At lunch, we found ourselves sitting across from Otanes, a surprising arrangement given the crown prince's exalted rank. This close, I saw that he was only two or three years older than Cyrus. Though taller by two hands, he was thinner in build and narrower in the shoulders. He surveyed Cyrus through moody eyes, ignoring Jared and me.

A bee was buzzing around us in lazy flight. When it came too near Otanes, the prince flashed out a hand and captured the bee in his palm with extraordinary speed. He closed his fist around the bee and squeezed. A muscle at the corner of his eye jumped, making me wonder if the bee had stung his hand before dying.

Otanes dropped the dead insect on the cloth between us.

"In Anshan, that is what we do with uninvited pests that dare to violate our welcome." Like most of the royals in the Persian court, he spoke perfect Median. The men who sat next to him tittered.

Cyrus bent to examine the dead bee. "Too bad. That was a honeybee. Which means you wasted all the honey it could have made."

One of the young women in our hunting party crouched behind Otanes. She picked up the dead bee by one wing. "Not much of a kill, Cousin," she said. "You might try for some bigger game next time." Over the prince's head, she winked at Cyrus and he laughed.

"I am Artystone," the girl said.

Cyrus stopped laughing. The girl's introduction placed him in an awkward position. For the first time, he had to introduce himself publicly. I held my breath, wondering how he would choose to navigate the charged moment. The sudden hush over the party meant whatever he decided would likely be overheard by most of those present.

He squared his shoulders. "I am Cyrus."

A restless murmur arose in response to that declaration.

"How interesting." Artystone grinned. "Isn't it interesting, Otanes? Didn't you once have a cousin by that name?"

Otanes did not respond. He smiled, but his eyes remained flat and cold. Something about the shift in that angled face made my skin crawl.

* * *

In the afternoon, we picked up the trail of a small herd of deer, and our ride became more purposeful. However, when the sun began to sink and we still had not caught up with our prey, we had to give up the chase for the night.

The Persians had an altogether more austere attitude to life than their northern cousins. Where the Medes surrounded themselves with luxury, the Persian court conducted its affairs in plain simplicity. Even their hunting party reflected this attitude. If we had been participating in a Median hunt, we would have enjoyed a performance by professional musicians in the evening, followed by a good night's sleep in a comfortable tent. There were few tents on this hunt, and those were plain fare made for privacy rather than opulence.

Like half the people there, we slept in the open with our felt saddles for a mattress and a blanket of stars for entertainment. As if knowing themselves on display, a thousand bright constellations put on a better show for us than any human could have managed.

I found myself admiring the plain discipline of the Persians. These were a people who had been under threat on every side. Elamites, Babylonians, Assyrians, Medians. At one time or another, they had all wanted a piece of this little kingdom. And although the Persians paid tribute to Astyages, they had managed to survive Media's constant meddling. Indeed, if the evidence of Anshan's growing construction was anything to go by, they were thriving more than Astyages realized. That made me smile.

Used to the aches and pains of open travel, I awoke before sunrise and resignedly made my way back into the saddle. It proved another long and fruitless morning.

By noon, our little trio fell behind the rest of the party when Jared stopped to check my horse's hoof, concerned that the beast might be going lame. We could still see the rest of the party ahead of us, but quite a large gap had formed between us.

From where I was kneeling next to my horse, I saw Cyrus sit up with a sudden sharp movement. "Deer!" he hissed and, pressing his legs to the sides of the chestnut, thundered toward a dried-up brook to our west.

Jared, who had been crouching next to me, rushed to his stallion and, vaulting on its back in one fluid motion, began to give chase. "Slow down, Cyrus!" he roared.

I mounted my own horse, but it could not keep up with their mad speed, forcing me to watch helplessly as the distance between us widened.

By now, everyone had noticed our rush to the brook, and most of the hunting party was turning back toward us. The dogs finally picked up the scent of the deer and bolted ahead.

I crossed the brook carefully and found a steep hill just beyond. Mindless of the dangerous slope, Cyrus was pushing his chestnut headlong down an almost vertical incline, trying to keep up with a loping young stag, which had been separated from the rest of its herd. So focused was he on his prey that Cyrus almost missed the dip in the slope. I gasped as I watched the boy pitch forward, nearly flying headfirst over his mount.

I heard Jared's shout. Heard my own desperate cry.

How that boy managed to regain his seat, I cannot say. Somehow his slipping legs found purchase, clinging to the chestnut's sides. As the ground leveled out, Cyrus brought the stallion under his iron control once more. It was an impressive piece of riding.

He lowered his speed a touch and, notching his arrow in one fluid movement, took aim and let it fly. One arrow was all it took. The stag's front legs folded, and gracefully he fell and went still.

Cyrus jumped off his heaving stallion and ran to the motionless stag to admire his prey. His grin could have lit up all of Anshan. But I could see his legs were shaking from the physical abuse he had put his body through.

Jared had caught up with him, finally, his chest rising and falling as he tried to drag air into his lungs. He looked as pale as I felt. "Cyrus! You could have killed yourself! What were you thinking?"

Cyrus turned his bright smile on Jared. "I was thinking I would be the first to bring down a deer." He drew a gentle hand down the side of the stag, getting a trail of blood on his tunic. "My aim was true. He did not suffer."

Ahead, I heard rustling. A short, bristly creature with a large head and long snout bounded out of the thicket, headed away from us.

A wild boar!

The commotion with the deer must have agitated the beast out of hiding. But thankfully, it had decided to avoid us.

Just then, Otanes appeared on his stallion, cantering toward us from the opposite direction. As I dismounted, I cried a warning to the prince, worried that the boar, which was headed toward him, might try to attack. But alarmed by the height of Otanes's great black horse, the boar decided to veer away from the prince. I sighed with relief.

To my astonishment, Otanes wheeled his horse to intercept the creature. Wild boars were dangerous. No one in his right mind meddled with one lightly. I assumed, at first, that the prince wanted to hunt the animal. But although he held his spear aloft, he never tried to loose it. Instead, he herded the boar, forcing the beast to turn. Directly toward Cyrus.

The boar snorted, wild with frustration, and charged.

I could see its beady eyes locking on Cyrus. I had never seen anything move so fast, its massive neck and shoulders bunching as it bound forward.

Cyrus had thrown his quiver of arrows on the ground next to the stag. Now, he simply did not have enough time to retrieve it. I broke out in a cold sweat and did the only thing I could think of. I ran to Cyrus's side and shoved the boy behind me. I did not even have time to draw my sword.

Three steps from me, the boar staggered. I saw the long handle of a spear protruding from its back. But to my astonishment, it kept coming. Jared shoved Cyrus and me out of the way and fell on the boar, dagger in hand. The struggle was quick. His spear had already injured the beast grievously.

I looked up to find we had a large audience. I wondered how much of the events of the past few minutes they had witnessed.

"Otanes!" The king's voice rang out.

"Yes, lord?"

"What were you trying to do with that boar?"

Otanes was silent for a beat. "It sprang out of nowhere, my king, and caught me unawares."

"Is that what happened?" Cambyses's voice was cool. He dismounted and came to crouch next to the fallen stag. "A clean shot," he said to Cyrus loud enough for everyone to hear. "Well done."

If Otanes had not behaved so abominably, I doubt Cambyses would have shown Cyrus such public favor, in spite of his success in the hunt. The king still disbelieved our story and merely put up with us for the sake of his queen. But Cambyses was a straight arrow. He dealt with his enemy as he did with his friends. Honorably. He expected those who served him to do the same. Otanes's underhanded trick with the boar had riled him enough to throw a bone our way.

CHAPTER FIFTY-ONE

Mandana came to share our fire openly that night, her back straight, uncaring of who saw her or what they thought. "What kind of riding do you call that?" she chided Cyrus.

"The kind that brought down the first kill."

"I already lost my son once. If you make me lose him again, I will have to kill you myself."

Cyrus grinned. "I hope you like venison, my lady."

"I like it very much." She turned to Jared. "With all my heart, I thank you."

He bowed.

"I have arranged to serve roast boar at supper tonight." She smiled. "I plan to serve the first piece to Prince Otanes."

* * *

The next day, we set off to track the rest of the herd of deer, which had managed, after the excitement with the boar, to get away. The thought that Cyrus and Jared might return to Anshan the only victorious hunters sat ill with the rest of our party. The queen might have made her peace with Cyrus's identity. The others still thought him an imposter.

I had a crick in my neck, a slightly lame horse, and a hole in my belly named Otanes, and I wanted nothing more than to head back to Anshan. Cyrus and Jared, on the other hand, still glowed with the undiminished delight of their success. All the discomforts of a wild hunt could not rob them of the sheer joy they had in the sport.

After a long ride, we arrived at a narrow stream, and although it was early, Cambyses ordered us to break camp for lunch. Water was a rare commodity in Persia, and treasured. Even this meager green flow appeared inviting in an otherwise scorched landscape.

I examined my companions' blood-soaked tunics and curled my lip. "You two need to wash."

Cyrus lingered with the horses while Jared fetched water. My mouth went dry when Jared stripped down to his trousers, and I turned my back quickly to hide my red face from him.

"Coward," he whispered and laughed.

I bunched my kerchief into a ball and hurled it at his head. His hand flashed out, and I found myself pressed against his chest. For a moment we froze, our breaths mingling. He dipped his head, and his lips hovered over mine. My eyes drifted shut.

"You better wed me soon," he said, his voice unsteady.

"You better let me go."

He laughed and released me. I staggered back, wobbly on my feet. His eye had turned golden, like warm honey. "Fire and lightning," I croaked.

"One day soon," he promised. "And maybe a little earthquake too."

When I could finally think straight again, I called Cyrus over and convinced him to strip his tunic so I could wash the blood from it. Over my shoulder, I tossed him a washcloth. "Get to work before the queen decides you're nothing but a shepherd boy after all."

I was on my knees, scrubbing Cyrus's tunic, when I noticed the king walking toward us. He wore a strange expression, as if someone had hit him on the head with the blunt end of an axe. I straightened, Cyrus's dripping tunic hanging forgotten from my fingers.

Cambyses continued to move toward us, his gaze glued to Cyrus. The boy had his back turned, unaware of the strange lure he seemed to have cast over the king. When he was no more than a few steps from the boy, Cambyses closed the gap with two long strides and dropped on his knees.

The movement startled Cyrus and he turned. His eyes widened when he spied the king, frozen on his knees, his lips hanging open.

Cambyses tried to speak several times and failed. "Your back," he said finally.

"What?" Cyrus snapped, forgetting proper royal protocol in his confusion.

"Your back," Cambyses rumbled. "Let me see your back."

I nodded encouragingly to Cyrus. The boy shrugged and turned. Cambyses's finger traced a small, dark-red birthmark at the base of Cyrus's back. I had noticed it before. An irregular wine-colored spot, it looked like the map of some ancient kingdom. Yet it clearly held some great significance for Cambyses. His throat worked.

Noticing her husband's strange manner, Mandana rushed over to us. "What is it, Husband?"

"Look!" He pointed at the mark. "Look!" Then, as if words could not suffice, he stripped off his tunic and sank next to Cyrus, presenting his wide back to us.

Those of us close enough to see gasped.

The same birthmark, though more faded, was stamped on Cambyses's skin. Mandana extended a trembling finger and traced the mark on her husband's back before moving to outline the same mark on Cyrus's. With a strangled sob, she dropped on trembling knees next to her husband.

Gently, Cambyses turned Cyrus to face him. "Most of the men and some of the women in my family carry that mark. My father had it. It skipped my younger brother. But Otanes bears it. And my son, Cyrus—the boy Astyages said had been killed by wild dogs—he had it."

He shifted the boy slightly so he could place his hand on the birthmark, as if he could not quite trust his senses yet. "There, exactly. The babe bore that very mark. I remember I kissed it when I took my leave of him."

"I remember," Mandana breathed, and bending her head, she kissed the boy's back where it had been sealed by a tiny red mark. Plump tears were welling up in her eyes, coursing down pale cheeks, and silently dropping to the scorched ground.

Whatever nagging doubts she had held about Cyrus's true identity must have been washed away with those tears. She pulled him into her arms, no longer a queen, but a mother utterly undone by love. Cyrus's tunic fell from my nerveless fingers when Cambyses also kissed the birthmark. Then without a word, he folded Cyrus into his arms.

"My son." His voice emerged husky and broken and elated, so that it was almost painful to listen to him.

For a moment, Cyrus remained rigid in this tangle of intense joy and grief. Then something in him snapped, and he melted into Cambyses's arms.

Jared reached for my hand and pressed it. Only then did I realize that my own cheeks were wet. He held me against the safe haven of his chest, and hiding my face in his neck, I sobbed. The relief and joy and fear and sorrow of recent months flooded out of me.

Jared caressed my hair and smiled into my eyes when I lifted my head. "You did that. You brought them together."

"The Lord did that," I said, turning to gaze at the three who were still holding one another in a shivering, wet tangle of awkward love.

Cambyses finally noticed the audience that ringed about them, looking utterly stunned.

Slowly he came to his feet, keeping his hand on Cyrus's shoulder. He shook his head as if trying to clear it. "By now, you have heard of Lord Harpagus's letter. Of his claims regarding this boy. The queen told me that the child has her father's eyes. The same peculiar flip at the end of his left brow." He shook his head. "I cautioned her again and again that these similarities were clever ploys. That Harpagus was playing his own game, using a mother's tender heart to plant a pretender on our throne."

Heads nodded in agreement. A threatening rumble began to rise from angry throats.

Cambyses held up his hands. "I was wrong."

The circle of aristocrats grew silent. Most of them had been too far to see what we had observed or hear the content of Cambyses's revelations. The king turned Cyrus around so that his back was exposed to the gathering. "Some of you belong to the Pasargadae tribe, as I do. You are familiar with the birthmark peculiar to my family line. This child bears that mark! Harpagus has not lied. His claims about this boy are true. This is my son, Cyrus."

A shocked collective gasp met that declaration.

"Come and bear witness." Cambyses was all king now, reining back his father's heart to do the work of a kingdom. He intended for Cyrus to be accepted and now took the first step toward that goal. Some of the most influential men of Persia were amongst this hunting party. He might not win their approbation, but he would win their acquiescence.

One by one, according to rank, each courtier came forward to look at Cyrus's mark. Somewhere that eleven-year-old found the strength to stand proud in front of gawking strangers, a prince to the bone. He forced a testimony upon them, though they had no love for him yet.

When the silent procession ended, Cambyses took the boy's hand and raised it in the air. "This is my son, Cyrus!" he cried. "Though stolen from us as a babe, by the kindness of Ahura Mazda, he has now been restored to us."

CHAPTER
FIFTY-TWO

Where there is no guidance, a people falls,
but in an abundance of counselors there is safety.
Proverbs 11:14, ESV

We set out for Anshan immediately after Cambyses's proclamation. Cyrus rode with the king and queen and their contingent of guards, giving me few glimpses of him. Cambyses kept a ferocious pace, so that we all arrived at the capital half dead from the long ride.

Jared and I plodded back to the inn, not having received a formal invitation to stay at the palace. I felt relieved, too exhausted to contend with the pomp and ceremony we would no doubt be subjected to as guests of the court.

I was wilting on the mare by the time we arrived, too weary to summon the energy to dismount. Jared lifted me off unceremoniously and swung me up into his arms.

"I can walk!" I squawked.

"But this is so much more enjoyable." He shifted me against

his chest. His inky curls had come undone from their braid and lay in charming disarray around his face.

I wrapped my arms around his neck. "Your hair is a tangle," I said happily.

He sat on a bale of hay and balanced me on his lap. "I have a problem."

"What?"

"I need to put you down."

"All right."

"I don't want to."

I gasped a laugh and burrowed closer.

"You better stop that at once," Jared ordered.

"Stop what?"

His lips landed on mine, tender and slow, making me forget that I was exhausted. "Stop making yourself comfortable in my arms." Abruptly, he dropped me into the hay. I watched him stride to the well and draw a pitcher of cold water. He emptied the entire thing over his head, making me giggle.

I forced my aching muscles to move from the hay so that I could set up our bedding while Jared looked after the horses. I was asleep in my blankets long before he made his own way to bed.

* * *

An ominous silence met us the following day. I had expected an invitation from the court, but none came.

"It will be some time before they think of us, Keren. They need to adjust to each other as a family. And the court has experienced a seismic shift. Everything they believed about the succession has changed. The dust of that discovery will not settle overnight. They will not want strangers in their midst while they negotiate through the initial phases of this difficult maze."

I wrung my hands. "That is exactly why we should be there. Cyrus will need friends."

Jared cradled my cheek in his palm. "He has his parents now. They will watch over him."

I nodded. But the churning in my belly would not calm. We needed to find a way into the palace.

By the next day, I was getting prepared to march over there, uninvited, when one of Cambyses's guards finally arrived with a summons from his lord. Hastily, Jared and I changed into our formal attire, doing our best to look respectable. One of the innkeeper's daughters helped curl and style my hair, so that I looked less like a wild barbarian.

To my surprise, the audience turned out to be a private one, with only Cambyses and us. I found him shockingly straight-forward for a king, with no patience for the usual lengthy pro-cedures inherent to royal visits.

"You have returned my son to me," he said in his gentle man-ner. "For this, I am eternally grateful. Now I have an important question for you."

Jared and I looked at each other. "Lord?" Jared said.

"Do you serve Harpagus?"

"I did, lord," I said. "Though Jared never has."

"*Did*. And now?"

"I suppose, having fulfilled his command to see Cyrus to safety, I am now free of any commitment to Lord Harpagus."

"Why *did* you help my son? Cyrus tells me that you risked your own lives more than once to protect him." His lips tight-ened. "I believe it, given all that was at stake for Astyages."

I considered my answer. "I helped him because I have grown

to love the boy. You will find, I think, that he has a way of worming himself into your heart."

Cambyses nodded.

"Also . . ." I smiled at him. "I believe Astyages's dream. Cyrus will one day be a great king. More importantly, he will be a *good* king. And because of that, many will find freedom by his hand."

Cambyses's eyes widened. "You are loyal to him."

"With my life," I said without elaborating further.

I had already told his wife about the prophecies. Either Mandana had shared them with Cambyses, in which case there was no need to repeat them, or she had chosen to withhold that information from her husband, in which case I had no reason to tell him.

"I am glad to hear it," Cambyses said. "Because I have asked you here in order to bid you to join us."

"Join you, lord?"

"We are preparing for war. What Astyages has done is unpardonable. We must respond to his betrayal with the severity it deserves."

I swallowed. Jared and I had discussed Harpagus's warning that this would be a war Persia could not win. It would merely weaken them, placing them even more in Astyages's power. I had seen enough of Persian fortitude to know they would strike a mighty blow against the Medes. But it would not be enough.

I fell to my knees. "Lord, I will serve Cyrus wherever he needs me. Astyages's treachery must be dealt with." I cleared my dry throat. "You stand in a hard place, because you are both father and king. Your father's heart demands justice. Yet as a king, you must do what best serves your nation."

"I should think they both serve the same end. My nation cannot lie under the shadow of that viper."

"When I served Lord Harpagus, I was often called into the court as a scribe. I had many opportunities to study the king's army. Since settling their affairs in Lydia, a large contingent of Media's troops has returned home. And Astyages has many mercenaries in his service, men who belong to the nations conquered by the Medes. You can no doubt obtain more accurate figures from your people in the court." I gave him the numbers I had observed or overheard.

Under his curled beard, the king winced.

"As courageous and capable as your warriors are, those odds are not favorable to you."

Cambyses's visage hardened. "You expect me to do nothing? After he tried to kill my son? After he robbed his own daughter of her child?"

I looked into the outraged eyes. "No, my king. I am asking you to trust Astyages's dream. He will be punished. Rest assured of that. But that punishment will come at the hand of Cyrus."

"Tell me, young woman: what kind of father would I be if I left the hard work for my son?"

"A wise one, if it is not your work to do in the first place. Prepare him as best as you can. He already has something you do not."

"And what is that?"

"A special bond with Lord Harpagus. I watched the two together. Harpagus has known Cyrus since birth. And I will tell you, lord: he loves your son. He spent many years endangering himself and his whole family in order to keep Cyrus safe.

"The Medes are growing disenchanted with their king. Astyages rules with a heavy hand. Harpagus himself has no love for him, and he is a man who wields great influence both in the army and amongst the aristocracy. Yet you cannot hope to make a secret treaty with any of them, because you are a Persian king. An outsider. With you, it is either war or nothing.

"Your son, however, is half Mede. The blood of Media's greatest king flows through his veins. He speaks their tongue as a native. There may come a time, in a few years, when Harpagus can turn Median hearts to Cyaxares's great-grandson. Then Astyages would face two wars: one from without, and another from within. And that is a war he cannot win.

"Cyrus can birth a new nation. Persia and Media under one ruler."

Cambyses sat back on his throne, fingers beating a restless rhythm on the armrest. "You have given it some thought, I see. Yet you do not understand the world of kings, girl. If I allow Astyages's outrage to go unchallenged, my people will think me weak. No rule remains stable on such ground. I won't have a throne to pass on to my son."

Jared bent to one knee beside me. "Lord?"

"Speak."

"On the day when you acknowledged Cyrus as your son, I was watching your people. Some believed you. Believed Cyrus to be your true son. But regardless of what they believed about his identity, none of them was happy about this new revelation.

"You have a crown prince already. Allegiances have been made around that position. Years of political and financial investments have been made in that particular future. Now, out of nowhere, a supposedly dead boy comes to life. He has been raised a Mede. A shepherd. A stranger. He may be your son by blood, but your people are not going to receive him overnight as their prince."

Cambyses frowned. "Some have already said so." He held up a finger. "They will grow to accept him."

"Indeed," Jared said with a smile. "But if you force them into a war they cannot win, they will have no chance to learn to love him. They will be required to pay too high a price before they even get to know the boy. Every single one of them who survives the war will resent Cyrus as the cause of it. And he will lose his throne before he ever gains it."

I gave Jared an admiring look. We had discussed what I would say if Cambyses brought up his intention to attack the Medes. Jared's follow-up reasoning had been unrehearsed. I wondered if he had managed to come up with that argument just now. I thought again how perfectly suited he was to counsel a young prince.

Cambyses came to his feet and stepped down from the dais. "What do you suggest?"

"Give the boy time to win over your people. Give him a chance to become one of them. Allow them to choose him, rather than have him forced upon them."

"And Astyages?"

"Let your people know they are more important to you than your personal revenge," Jared said.

"You can be a father to Cyrus, or you can be a father to your people," I added. "Help the Persians understand that your reason for not going to war immediately is not weakness, but rather a long plan. The first step in ensuring that, one day, your people will become great amongst the nations. When they comprehend your intention, your people will think you patient, not weak."

Cambyses was silent for a long beat. "You really believe in my son, don't you?"

"Yes, lord."

"Why?"

"Have you met him?"

The king laughed.

As the sound reverberated around the empty throne room, I realized that Jared and I had averted a hopeless war. I realized again, as I had so many times since the start of this journey, that God's hand was upon us.

CHAPTER
FIFTY-THREE

One who loves a pure heart and who speaks with grace
will have the king for a friend.

Proverbs 22:11, NIV

Jared tightened his hold around my hand as we strolled in one of the royal gardens. "You have saved the boy's life. Delivered him safely to his parents. Prevented a war. Are you ready to go home? I have an important question to ask your father."

I could not help the smile that split my face. "What question might that be?"

"You know very well what question. Now, answer." He shook my arm. "Are we returning home?"

I lost the smile. My head dropped. "What does your heart tell you when you pray?"

Jared stopped walking. "He still needs us."

I nodded sadly. "We cannot abandon him. God has more for us here."

Jared adjusted the strap of his eye patch. "It was good to dream for a few moments."

Gratitude welled up in me. Gratitude that this man, who had every reason to leave me, to walk away into a more convenient life, to hate me even, had committed his future to me. Gingerly I turned and wrapped my arms around him. It still felt strange to take such liberties with him. Even before the accident, I had not felt free to demonstrate my love. After my sword had taken his eye, the boundaries between us had grown so vast I never thought I could cross them.

Now, every time I approached him, I came with shy excitement, tempered with a hint of fear, as if I might awaken any moment to discover I had dreamed it all.

But as I drew close, I found only welcome. I tucked my face into the crook of his neck. "I am sorry, my love. I am sorry that our own desires must wait."

His hands spread over my back. "I have a feeling that if we pick up the bundle of our disappointments and unfulfilled dreams and follow God's plans one wobbly step at a time, in the end we will find our way home."

* * *

Jared and I would have preferred to remain at the inn. For all its limitations, it afforded us a certain measure of privacy. Cambyses insisted that we move to the palace compound, however. Jared found himself sharing a chamber with several palace guards, and I was sent to a room occupied by two of the queen's assistants. We had not been assigned any specific duties yet, though the most natural place would be in Cyrus's household, once it was set up. First, he would have to officially be declared the crown prince and replace Otanes.

For now, Jared and I often found ourselves at loose ends. We spent the time together, learning Persian, going for strolls, riding around Anshan to get to know the city and its surrounding countryside. Jared trained with the palace guards every day. He sang the praises of the Persian cavalry and the astonishing accuracy they wielded with their weapons. Already, he was forming a bond of friendship with two of the guards.

A whole week passed before we had a chance to speak to Cyrus privately. He found us in the orchard, practicing our Persian. From the way the boy kept throwing nervous glances over his shoulder, I could tell he had sneaked out of some duty to be with us.

We had all lost weight during our travel to Anshan. It was good to see Cyrus's drawn cheeks filling out again with health.

"How are you?" I asked. "Do they treat you well?"

He shrugged. "It's all right. They put perfume in my hair and force me to wear this poxy tunic." He lifted his arm to demonstrate the flowing sleeve.

"You look very princely," Jared assured him.

Cyrus kicked a rock morosely. "I would rather look like a general."

"You will." I pressed a reassuring hand on his shoulder. "But you don't have much practice at being a prince. It's important that you learn."

He kicked another rock. "Too many rules, being a prince."

I was not surprised that he chafed under palace protocol. He had lived a relatively free life in Media, bordering on wild, sometimes. "Do you miss home?"

He shrugged. A shadow settled on the good-humored face.

"Cyrus." I waited until he looked up at me. "Just because you are growing to love Mandana and Cambyses does not mean you are betraying your parents in Media."

His eyes welled. He blinked the tears away. "How do you know?"

"They always knew who you were. From the hour they took you into their home."

The day I had discovered Cyrus's true identity, I had overheard Mitradates weep because he missed the boy. I was not going to burden him with that knowledge. His heart already sensed the great sorrow his absence would bring his parents.

"They understood that you would likely leave them one day," I said instead. "That you had a greater destiny to fulfill. They understood that you had other parents who would want you."

I ruffled the perfumed curls. "You are blessed to love two mothers and two fathers when others are only given one of each. God must know you have a great heart, indeed, capable of more love than most, to give you such a blessing."

He frowned at me. "You think it's right that I love all four?"

"Right and good."

Cyrus looked over his shoulder again. "She does not want me to come and see you."

I blinked. "Who? Why?"

"The queen. She always has an excuse for why I should not come to you. But I can see she wants to keep us apart."

This was news to me. I had assumed the separation was a natural byproduct of the hectic schedule the boy had to keep. "Well," I said, lost for words. "Well."

Jared crossed his ankles. "Not a surprise, when you think of it."

"It isn't?" Cyrus and I asked together.

"Use your heads. She lost her son for eleven years. The boy loves another mother, already. Would she want to share him with yet a third woman who has been a mother to him for months?"

"*Keren?* My mother?" Cyrus rolled his eyes. "She doesn't even know how to cook."

"Neither does Mandana," I pointed out.

"Yes. But she has a baby leopard. You have Akkadian." He gave me a mock punch in the arm. "You are more like a pestering sister."

I grinned. "Well, I doubt Mandana is about to adopt me."

"She merely needs time," Jared said, his voice soothing. But I noticed the way his eye slid from mine.

*   *   *

A whole week passed before we saw Cyrus again. He was walking down a narrow hallway in the opposite direction from us, laughing at some comment the queen had made. We approached them with a bow.

"Prince Cyrus!" I said with a smile of pleasure. "It is good to see you."

Before Cyrus could respond, the queen whispered something in his ear. His cheeks turned pink. Ignoring Jared and me, he passed by us without a word.

I stood paralyzed in my tracks. "He scorned me!" I gasped.

Jared took my hand and pulled me out of the hallway and did not stop until we were in a barren garden, empty of other visitors. "He scorned me!" I repeated when we finally sat down, my voice shaking with shock and hurt.

"You sometimes forget he is only a boy. An overwhelmed boy in a new world, desperate to please his parents. To make them proud."

I shrugged. "I want all those things for him."

"Yes. But what if pleasing the queen means walking away from you?"

I pressed a hand against my chest where a deep ache had taken root. "He needs us! He needs true friends. He is too vulnerable."

"I don't disagree. But we cannot force our friendship upon him. He must choose for himself. And Keren, you have to prepare your heart in case he decides to walk away."

I bit my lip, unable to think of a response.

"I don't think the queen is ready to release her leash on him. This might be a good time to return home. Our presence is only likely to goad her into becoming more possessive. Cyrus is not likely to resume a relationship with us if it means alienating his mother."

I shook my head. "Grace means allowing room for someone to grow. If we abandon him at the first painful mistake, what will that teach him? Let us wait, Jared. Wait and pray."

CHAPTER
FIFTY-FOUR

You shall treat the stranger who sojourns with you as the native among you, and you shall love him as yourself.
Leviticus 19:34, ESV

A week passed and then another. We heard nothing from Cyrus. I was starting to think Jared right. Remaining in Anshan had become a waste of our time. But whenever I prayed about returning home, I felt led to wait. Wait on the Lord, if not on Cyrus.

Jared and I were ensconced in a nook off the servants' quarters, writing letters to home, when the rustle of fabric made me look up.

"Cyrus!" I gasped.

He put a finger to his lips.

Jared looked up and down the hallway that led to the nook. "Let's leave this place," he whispered. "Too many ears."

He led us to a courtyard where the guards usually practiced

wrestling. "No one is here this time of day. They are either at their posts or in their quarters," he explained.

I sat on a limestone bench. Gingerly, Cyrus sat next to me, as if unsure of his reception. Jared took a spot in front of the boy, blocking the way in case a casual observer was to look into the courtyard.

The boy's fingers knotted together. "I am sorry," he mumbled.

"For what?" I asked gently.

He looked up. "For ignoring you that day. And ever since." He bit the corner of his lip. "My mother told me that in order to find acceptance as a prince in Anshan, I could not be seen speaking to you." He shrugged. "I am already an outsider. I can't appear to be too close to foreigners."

"I understand," I said.

He sat straighter. "It was wrong, what I did. You two risked your lives to save mine. A man should never turn his back on his friends. I wronged you." He looked up at Jared. "Both of you."

I smiled at him. "I have already forgiven you."

He frowned. "Why?"

Jared dropped to one knee before him. "Keren told me grace means allowing room for someone to grow. She can be wise sometimes, even though her head is stuffed with Akkadian."

Cyrus's face lost some of its pallor as he gave a small grin.

"If we don't offer each other grace," Jared said, "then how will we become the men and women we are meant to be? We forgave you, Cyrus, because we want to give you room to grow into the man you are meant to become. That means allowing you to make mistakes and not loving you any less because of them."

"How are you?" I asked, deciding we had spent enough time on the topic. I had hoped to lighten the conversation. Instead,

Cyrus's fingers began to twitch again, a sure sign that he was troubled.

"I have a problem," he said.

"Tell us."

"My father says that the eyes of all the aristocracy are on me. To gauge if I am fit to be their prince, or if they should throw their weight behind Otanes."

"It must be hard to be constantly under watch."

"Worse than having your hair curled! As if that weren't enough. Now, I am supposed to act as a judge."

"What do you mean?"

"Yesterday, a friend of Otanes came to me. His father had gifted him with a large overcoat, expecting that the boy would one day grow into it."

I nodded.

"Well, Otanes, who is taller, took the new coat by force, saying it fit him better, and gave his own old coat to the boy. He was wearing it when he came to see me. In fairness, Otanes's coat fit the boy like a glove. A good overcoat too, as you can imagine. Otanes has expensive tastes."

"But the boy was not happy," I guessed.

"Not at all. He wanted his own overcoat back and asked for me to intercede." Cyrus slumped. "I can't help feeling that all eyes are on me, judging whether I come to the right decision."

"And what have you decided so far?"

Cyrus pulled on a loose golden thread hanging from the embroidery at his wrist. "Well, both coats fit the boys the way things stand. Why change that?"

"Ah. That's a good, practical decision," Jared said.

Cyrus brightened. "You think I should suggest it?"

Jared rubbed his chin. "That depends on what kind of king you want to become. A just king, or a practical one?"

Cyrus chewed on his nail. "A just one. And when possible, practical, also."

Jared and I laughed. "That is a good answer," Jared said, approvingly. "What does justice look like in this case?"

"Justice?"

"Did the boy willingly give his new overcoat to Otanes?"

"Not at all. Otanes took it from him by force." He sat up. "I understand your point. Otanes took the coat by violence, and that was unjust. Whether it is practical or not, a king must first choose justice."

Jared gave him a pleased smile. "You will make a virtuous king, one day."

Cyrus hopped off the bench. "I am going to give them my answer now. And I want you both to come with me."

I hesitated, not wishing to antagonize the queen.

Cyrus took my hand and pulled. "Come. I want my friends with me." He looked at me over his shoulder as he pulled harder. "I don't have so many that I can start misplacing them in out-of-the-way courtyards."

* * *

By the time Otanes and the smaller boy arrived, the throne room where we had gathered had filled with curious bystanders. Cyrus had not been exaggerating when he said that the eyes of all the aristocracy were on him. He sat on the top step of the dais between the king and the queen, a position that affirmed his relationship to them while also accentuating the fact that he had not been recognized as crown prince yet.

When Otanes swaggered in, Cyrus called to him. "Prince Otanes, your friend has brought a complaint against you."

"He's no friend of mine if he has been complaining against me."

A few of the spectators laughed. Most, however, remained silent and watchful.

"Fair point. Since you forcibly took his coat, perhaps you are no friend to him, either."

"Not that it is any concern of yours. But you can see the boy is well rewarded. The coat I gave him fits him better than the one he had."

Slowly, Cyrus rose to his feet and stepped down from the dais. "My father is the king. My mother the queen," he said calmly. "This makes every act of injustice in this land my concern. As crown prince you should know better than to simply take from your own people because it suits you."

"I said," Otanes roared, "that I gave him a coat in fair exchange."

Keep your calm. Keep your poise. Don't get caught up in his rage. I was standing in the back of the audience hall where Cyrus could not see me. That did not keep me from trying to advise him in my head.

He did not need my advice. Remaining calm, he said, "It is not *fair*, as you put it, if the boy is not a willing participant in the exchange. Now, your old friend has asked me to arbitrate between you. My verdict is that you should restore the overcoat to the boy and take yours back. I have given my judgment. Let the king decide if it should stand."

Cambyses came to his feet. "Cyrus is my son. But Otanes is heir to my throne. I owe both my allegiance. Therefore, I pass this decision to General Arsames. What do you say, General? Should Cyrus's adjudication stand?"

Every head in the hall swiveled in the direction of Arsames. Next to the king, he was the most powerful man in court. A leading member of the Pasargadae tribe to whom the royal family belonged, the general had earned his position by blood and effort, gaining himself a reputation as one of the greatest military men the Persian army had ever possessed.

Cambyses had maneuvered this simple scenario to take on a great significance. If Arsames chose for Cyrus, it would be a major blow to Otanes's aspirations. A public pronunciation before a large portion of the most important people in the Persian court would give Cyrus the advantage he needed in order to gain a true foothold on the throne.

Because Cyrus had handled the complaint against Otanes with wisdom and calm, Arsames would have a difficult time striking down the judgment, which was probably the reason Cambyses had taken such a gamble.

The whole court awaited the general's response in tense silence. He fingered the plain hilt of his sword, salt-and-pepper brows drawn. "I can hardly add anything to Prince Cyrus's pronouncement," he said. The corner of his lip twitched. "He seems to have delivered the perfect decision. Let it stand."

A great murmur arose, its echoes filling the hall.

Cyrus gave the general the bright smile that had wrapped Harpagus and me and even the queen around its charm. General Arsames seemed a little stunned under the force of it.

The boy turned to his cousin, holding out a hand in friendship. As equals, if Otanes accepted the hand, they would kiss on the lips. If Cyrus acknowledged Otanes's higher station, he would kiss his cousin on the cheek.

Every eye watched, wondering how Cyrus would choose to greet the crown prince.

But Otanes never gave him the chance. He curled his lip and ignored his cousin's hand.

For the second time that day, a loud murmur echoed through the walls of the audience hall. Most of those present seemed disappointed by Otanes's behavior, which had proven to be less than princely. I knew as I watched the unfolding drama that the court of opinion toward Cyrus had shifted today. Making my way through the dispersing crowd, I managed to find a closer spot near Cyrus.

He dropped his outstretched hand to his side. "I told you, Otanes, when we were on our first hunt together, that by killing the honeybee, you wasted the honey it would have given you. Seems like a habit with you."

"I don't know what you're blathering on about," Otanes said.

"It shows."

Artystone, the young woman we had met during the hunt, gave Cyrus a friendly slap on the back. "You know, you should meet my younger sister, Cassandane. I bet you would get along."

Cyrus frowned. "Can she ride?"

Silently, I made a face at him.

"Ahem. I mean, yes, of course. I would like to meet your sister. Even if she is a terrible rider. Although that would be a shame."

Artystone laughed. "This court will be so much more enjoyable now that you are here."

As the throne room slowly emptied, Jared and I prepared to follow in the wake of the crowd. But Cyrus waved frantically from the front of the room, indicating we should approach him. The queen bent to whisper in his ear. Cyrus shook his head vehemently and said something to her. Whatever he had said drew the attention of the king, and he joined their exchange.

Jared and I lingered in the middle of the hall, unsure whether to proceed or leave. Cambyses saved us from having to make a decision by sending over one of his personal guards.

"The king requests an audience with you."

We approached the king and queen gingerly, unsure of our reception. Cyrus jumped between Jared and me, jostling us as we made our obeisance.

He grabbed my hand on one side and Jared's on the other. "Mother. Father. Keren and Jared are my true friends. They are loyal, dependable, and wise. I need friends like them in this place." He gave his mother a stern glance. "So I mean to keep them." His lids lowered. "I would not have given that judgment if not for their advice. I knew I could not come to you. The whole court was watching me, and the last thing I wanted was to appear a ninny who needed his mother. But I did need good advice." He looked up. "They were the ones who helped me understand that my duty is to uphold what is right, not what is efficient."

Cyrus released his grip on our hands and took a step closer to his parents. "And what is right is that friends should be rewarded for their loyalty, not discarded because they don't fit in. Friendship is not based on whether you were born here or in another nation. It is based on love. On loyalty. On truth. A palace should be filled with friends like that, regardless of where they are from."

I wiped a tear. Then another. I had never been so thoroughly defended. It came to me as I listened to that boy why God had chosen him to one day release my people from their bondage. Cyrus knew how to love the stranger.

Mandana's face had turned ivory white. Even her lips, stretched tight, had lost color. Cambyses watched her twisting fingers, so reminiscent of her son when he felt anxious, and turned to us. "I see we have been blessed by a wise son. We would ignore his request at our own peril, I think. Therefore, we assign you both to his household—you, Keren, as his scribe, and Jared as his cupbearer and adviser."

CHAPTER FIFTY-FIVE

Arise, for it is your task, and we are with you; be strong and do it.
Ezra 10:4, ESV

I was surprised when Mandana called me to her chamber for a private visit the following day. The morning was young, and the queen had not yet dressed. She sat on a stool, her long light-brown hair hanging loose down her back, a flowing white robe tied under her breasts with a delicate ribbon. Like this, without the pomp of embroidered garments, gleaming jewels, and her fluted crown, she seemed young and vulnerable.

I sank to my knees before her, wanting her to know that I would serve her as faithfully as I did Cyrus if given a chance. She gave me a small smile.

It took her a long moment before she spoke. "I find this difficult."

I did not know how to respond to that and merely nodded in encouragement.

"Queens are not often in a position to seek pardon, only to give it. I suppose I am by nature not particularly good at it, either." Her mouth tipped up on one side. "My father's blood in me flows stronger than I had suspected."

I gave a vigorous shake of my head. "You are nothing like your father, lady."

"But I am." Her hand fisted. "I did you wrong, Keren. I told myself I was protecting my son. The truth is that I was protecting my heart. Like my father, I find I am possessive of what I love."

She gave a bitter smile. "I have been a mother for less than a month, and already I have made a grave mistake. It took my son to point it out to me."

I swallowed hard. "I have tasted the bitter fruit of my own jealousy, my queen. You need not ask *my* pardon for it."

She gazed at me, her eyes interested. "You must tell me that story, one day."

I pressed the bridge of my nose. "If you wish it, though it galls me."

She laughed. "I must definitely hear it, then."

I joined her in the laughter. She held out her hand, as an offer of friendship or an indication that the interview had come to an end, I could not tell. But instead of taking it, I bent my head and kissed the ring on her middle finger bearing the royal seal. "My queen," I whispered.

Gently, she placed her palm on my head. We smiled at each other. In that moment something changed between us. Our shells—my mistrust and the wriggling demand of her jealousy—cracked and fell open. In the days and years to come, more than once we would both be tempted to take up those shells again. But that was the morning we learned to resist the temptation.

That was the morning I became friends with a queen.

* * *

Two weeks later, a hunter arrived from Media, carrying a brace of aged and skinned hare. "A gift from Lord Harpagus for Prince Cyrus," he said.

Jared and I took the pungent rabbits and carried them to the kitchens. We knew if they were from Harpagus, they would be no ordinary game.

Jared pulled the already sliced bellies of the hares open. In the fourth one, he found a clay cylinder, ensconced in an envelope, and sealed. We washed the letter and carried it to Cyrus, who was in the company of his parents, enjoying a private dinner.

The queen stretched out her hand to receive the missive. "May I?" she asked Cyrus.

He nodded. Breaking the seal and envelope, the queen read Harpagus's message silently and gasped. Over Cyrus's head, she gave the king a wide-eyed look.

Cyrus went rigid. "What is it?"

Cambyses gave his wife an encouraging nod. Although the letter obviously contained distressing news, Cyrus had to learn to contend with pain. Whether as a king or a man, he had to build the strength to bear the weight of adversity.

As much as the queen wanted to shield her son from pain, she would do him no service by overprotecting him. Cambyses knew that. He had been a king long enough to understand what his son would need to grow into his future role.

Mandana cleared her throat and read.

Son of Cambyses,

Greetings from your old friend, Harpagus. The shepherd and his wife send you their love. They want you to know that they think of you every hour and rejoice that you are safe. One day they hope to hold you again.

As for me, I have survived. When Astyages received news of your safe arrival in Anshan, he invited me to the palace to celebrate the life of his grandson. After the banquet, the king's attendants uncovered a platter, and I found myself staring at the head of my dear boy. My only son. He was fourteen years old, and already a promising warrior.

I pressed a shaking hand to my mouth. No one who knew Harpagus could fail to understand the measure of such a loss. He adored that boy. Cyrus's body went rigid with horror. His mother exhaled, then began to read the rest of the letter.

"You, I will not harm," Astyages told me. "Bury your boy and learn your lesson. No one betrays me without paying the price."

Know, therefore, son of Cambyses, what Astyages has taken from me. You will be king in Anshan one day. When that time comes, I will ask you to help me answer this outrage. Until then, live well.

Cyrus grasped the silver diadem that circled his brow—a recent gift from his father to publicly affirm his princely status—and pulled it off with shaking hands. "This is wrong! This is too big a price!"

"Cyrus!" the king snapped, the single word a clear rebuke. Cyrus merely shook his head, unwilling to replace the diadem.

I came to sit at his feet. "I know how much Harpagus loved his son. But you must understand, Cyrus, he always knew the risk he took in protecting you. At any time, he could have changed his mind. He could have purchased his own safety with your blood. He never did, because he believed in you.

"Do not waste the opportunity he has wrought for you. Yes, the price is high. Higher than any of us would wish. But he paid it because he believed you were worthy of his sacrifice.

"One day, your people will choose you as their future king and exchange that circlet of silver for a crown. Bear the weight and responsibility of it. Prove to Harpagus that his extravagant sacrifice was not in vain. Live a worthy life as a man and as a prince."

Cyrus stared at the diadem with something akin to loathing. I realized in that moment that God himself had allowed the boy to taste the bitter fruit of human ambition and power. It would have been easy for him, at this young age, to grow too proud of that diadem. Too fond of the crown he was trying to win. Instead, God had taught him the price of it at the very outset.

"I am sorry, Son," his mother said, pressing her hand around his shaking fingers.

Cyrus gulped a deep breath. Dropping his head, he placed the diadem upon his brow again. When he looked up, he no longer had the eyes of a child.

CHAPTER
FIFTY-SIX

I will put my law within them, and I will write it on their hearts.
And I will be their God, and they shall be my people.
Jeremiah 31:33, ESV

───────────────── JARED ─────────────────

The next four months became a hive of activity, with Cyrus at the center. The boy's position in the court needed to be solidified. Not only did Cyrus have to learn the art of being a prince, he also had to establish relationships that would have already been in place if Astyages had not robbed him of the past ten years.

Jared had never expected to find work so satisfying. It felt as though God had cut out and shaped a job to be an exact match to his gifting and ability.

The only blight on this deeply gratifying season was the frustration of not being able to marry the woman he loved.

They had both agreed that they wanted to marry in Babylon,

with their family and friends present. He wanted his brother Joseph at his side on his wedding day. Wanted to receive Daniel's blessing. To watch Keren melt into her parents' arms, glowing with joy.

But every time they tried to ask the king and queen's permission for a couple of months away, something cropped up that needed their attention.

Jared would do nothing to risk the ground Cyrus had gained in the court over the past four months. He ignored the chafing of his own heart every time he crawled into bed alone and waited, if not patiently, then at least obediently.

One morning, as they were preparing for a ride, thinking themselves alone, Jared pressed a kiss on Keren's willing lips. He had just tangled his hand in her soft hair, his fingers on her jaw turning her face more fully into his, when a disgusted noise made him spring back.

"When are you two getting married?" Cyrus complained. "Then you can stop all this poxy kissing."

Keren had turned the color of Persian pomegranates. In spite of himself, Jared cracked a smile. "I am not going to stop kissing when I marry. If anything, I plan to kiss her more."

Cyrus groaned. "I shouldn't have mentioned it, then."

Jared frowned. "I am glad you did. In fact, it is high time we wed. I have waited too long as it is. Which is why I want to ask your permission to go home."

"You want to leave me?" Cyrus's voice emerged high-pitched with panic.

Realizing his mistake, Jared held up a hand. "For two months, only. Long enough to travel to Babylon, celebrate our wedding with friends and family, and then return."

"Two months? I'll be an old man by then."

"Even if you were a hunting dog, you wouldn't get old in two months."

"Why can't you get married here? I bet the king would even hold a banquet in your honor."

Jared placed a hand on the young prince's shoulder. "We would like that, also. A celebration with our friends and family, followed by one here in our adopted country."

"One wedding is bad enough. Why would you want two?"

Keren smiled. "Cyrus, do you love Cambyses and Mandana?"

"Of course I do."

"And yet, a part of you still longs for your father and mother in Media. Just because you love them does not mean you don't love your parents here. It's like that for us. We love you. But we also miss home. I want my grandfather there on my wedding day."

"Grandfathers! Bah," said Cyrus, whose only grandfather had tried to have him murdered.

"They're not all like that."

Cyrus crossed his arms. "You better not take longer than two months."

Keren kissed him on the cheek. "We won't."

With Cyrus's backing, his parents' permission proved easy to gain. The king even sent a couple of his own personal guards to accompany them on the journey, ensuring their safety. Spring had melted the snow on the mountain passes by the time they returned to Babylon.

* * *

Jared never knew a single day could be as happy as the day of his wedding. So many of the people he loved were there. Daniel and Keren's grandfather spoke the blessings over them. Jared took Keren's hand, almost drowning in the love that shone from her eyes as she beheld him.

Cambyses had given Jared and Keren a bag of silver each, in appreciation for saving his son's life. Jared had saved every piece. When he went to Asa's house to ask for Keren's hand, he gave Asa the bag as a bride price. He knew it would pay off the whole family's debt, finally releasing them from their endless money troubles.

Asa had wept, but not nearly so hard as Keren since he had surprised her with the offering. She had looked upon him with this blazing adoration since.

Somewhere between the road to Anshan and serving as Cyrus's cupbearer, self-pity had lost its biting hold on him. Perhaps it had been when his counsel had helped to establish Cyrus's position more firmly in the court, or on the night when he had lain in pain, helpless to protect Keren and the boy. In any case, along the way, he had learned to look in the mirror, eye patch and all, without flinching.

Still, his heart sank when, in their wedding bower, Keren laid her hand on his eye patch. "Can I see?"

His eye widened. In the back of his mind, the memory of Zebidah cringing at the sight of him still haunted him.

"You are beautiful to me. This will not change that," Keren said.

Without comment, he reached behind his head to untie the thin leather straps. For the first time, he showed someone besides the physician his disfigured face.

His bride looked solemnly at the ugly tangle of scars and stood on tiptoes to kiss them. Warmly, without a trace of disgust. "You are beautiful," she whispered again.

As he drew her against him, his arms locking around her

with fresh desperation, he thought for a moment how odd love was, for it made you blinder than he was in his left eye. And then, with his lips on hers, he forgot to think. After all the years of waiting and yearning, his dreams finally turned into reality.

* * *

They had promised to return to Cyrus in two months. Three weeks after arriving in Babylon, they packed their bags, which had grown considerably larger thanks to their many wedding gifts, and headed for home. Because home was Persia, where God had planted them so that they could be used by him to create a future and hope.

Like Cyrus's crown, their calling came with a great price. It required that they leave behind those they loved and depended on. It required that Jared leave his little brother in Daniel's safe keeping, not seeing him for months and sometimes years at a time.

They shed their tears as Cyrus had, and willingly paid the price.

On their last night, they gathered at Daniel's house. Johanan sat between his wife and Jared. "I always knew you would marry Keren," he said to his friend.

"We all knew, dear," Mahlah said, making everyone laugh.

Keren placed her hands on her waist. "I wish someone had told *me*."

Mahlah patted her hair. "You wouldn't have believed it."

"I still don't!" She leaned into Jared's side. "I am certain I will wake up any moment and discover it has all been a dream."

"Would you like proof, my love?" Jared whispered in her ear. His hand caressed her back, making her eyes widen.

"Fire and lightning!"

That night, they shared the full tale of their adventures with their friends. Daniel listened, dark eyes piercing.

"I believe you have found Isaiah's Cyrus. One day, the gates of Babylon will open and our people will be able to return home, because of this young man you have come to serve." Gently, he tapped the ground with his walking stick. "But you know, Jeremiah also said the days are coming when God will make a new covenant with the house of Israel. This Cyrus will set us free from Babylon's yoke. But he cannot give us that which he does not have to give.

"One day, another will come. A true Savior. One with power to write God's law on our hearts. And blessed are those who live under his rule."

EPILOGUE

And he called the name of the first daughter Jemimah.

Job 42:14

Nine months after our return from Babylon, Cyrus was formally recognized as Persia's crown prince, replacing Otanes. The pronouncement was met with such a deafening roar in the crowded palace throne room that one of the precious glass chalices fell over and broke from the sheer vibrations of sound. Our Cyrus had managed to win so many hearts that even Otanes's staunchest supporters had decided to change sides.

It was not merely the nobility who held him in high esteem. The commoners adored Cyrus. Having grown up as a simple shepherd, he understood their lives better than any aristocrat living. The common people sensed that their prince's heart was for them every bit as much as it was for the fine men who haunted the palace corridors. Anyone who witnessed the way the ordinary people of Persia showered Cyrus with affection could see that they would one day willingly lay down their lives for him, whether fighting in his name on a hopeless battlefield or plowing a plot of scorched farmland.

For seven consecutive days, the court observed Cyrus's formal installation as the king's heir and celebrated his investiture in that role with lavish banquets. My former pupil sat upon a small throne, a modest crown upon his brow, his carefully curled hair held in place with rings of gold, as heads of every Persian clan and their leading members bent their knees before him and offered him their allegiance.

I saw only a few hours of the celebrations, and that through the narrow slit in the curtains of the throne room. I was huge with child and forbidden by the physician from exhausting myself. God had chosen to bless my womb shortly after my wedding, so that by the second day of the celebrations, I was in my bed, bringing forth new life into the world.

My son came quietly, his polite cry a welcome sound to our straining ears. We had decided we would name a son Johanan after our beloved friend. I had barely had time to press him against my chest and admire his perfectly formed fingers when fresh pains overtook me.

"Twins!" the physician pronounced with excitement.

"Twins?" I cried with shock, then forgot words for some moments as my daughter made her way into the world. The midwife has declared it impossible, but I swear that she smiled at me the moment I held her in my arms. Jared claims she has not stopped smiling since, and he may be right.

I shall never forget the look my husband gave me when the midwife finally allowed him into our chamber. He goggled at the two beautiful babes nestled contentedly in my arms and turned pale as it dawned on him that he was the father of two children.

"Fire and lightning!" he gasped.

I giggled. Before I could think of a response, I was gathered in his arms with such gentleness, it made me weep. Fierce love filled every corner of my soul for my little family. I never knew I could feel so utterly complete.

My parents had named me after Job's youngest daughter. We decided to keep the tradition alive and called our treasured girl Jemimah for Job's eldest daughter. A year later, Johanan's tripping baby tongue bestowed a shorter version of her name upon his sister: Jemmah. After that, our daughter came to be known as Jemmah by the whole palace.

Cyrus asked me to continue my work as his senior scribe. I would hold my babes, one on each leg, as I dictated Cyrus's letters and trained new scribes to organize his official correspondence. Little did we know that these same scribes would one day become the backbone of his empire, a weapon every bit as acute as his invincible army. We were laying down the foundations of a future none of us could truly grasp yet. To us, it was merely everyday business. The ordinary work of our hands. God knew that brick by brick we were establishing the means to manage the greatest empire the world had ever seen.

But that is a story for another day.

Watch for
the next
Tessa Afshar
novel, coming
fall 2023

A NOTE FROM
THE AUTHOR

History has bequeathed to us several different accounts of Cyrus's childhood. Sources referring to Cyrus's early life are predominantly Greek, and like other ancient Greek histories, they represent an amalgam of legend and truth, and at times it is hard to tell one from the other. For the purposes of this novel, I relied on the most well-known account, which is recorded by Herodotus. Since I am a novelist rather than a biographer, I could not resist this exquisite, though probably mythical, early narrative about the boyhood of one of the world's most famous kings.

Of course, Herodotus's legend does not mention Jewish companions who helped save Cyrus from Astyages's bloodthirsty clutches. Keren's presence in young Cyrus's life is purely fictional, as is the novel's account of Cyrus's return to his parents, starting with his escape from Ecbatana.

After Cyrus created his dynastic empire, the Persian court became populated by many well-respected foreigners, including talented Jewish administrators such as Daniel and Nehemiah. This story attempts to provide a believable narrative that explains, in part, Cyrus's later attitude toward Jews, and indeed, all the captives whom he set free. *The Hidden Prince* tries to capture the beginnings of a time in Persian history when Jews and Persians were friends and nations became better and stronger thanks to that friendship.

Many of the characters in this novel are based on historical figures. These include Daniel, Cyrus, Harpagus, Astyages, Cambyses, Mandana (the Persian pronunciation of Cyrus's mother's name), and Nebuchadnezzar. The Bible is silent on whether Daniel was married or single. Some historians have even concluded that he might have been a eunuch. I saw no evidence of this and chose to give him a family.

While this novel is a work of my imagination, where possible I have tried to remain faithful to historical and archaeological details. If you are interested in further reading, I recommend the classic textbook *From Cyrus to Alexander: A History of the Persian Empire* by Pierre Briant and *Discovering Cyrus: The Persian Conqueror Astride the Ancient World* by Reza Zarghamee. The events of chapter 54 surrounding the disputed coat are based on a story told by the Greek historian Xenophon about Cyrus's childhood, which I found in Zarghamee's book, *Discovering Cyrus*. Although Otanes is a fictional character, the general story felt like a perfect fit for this thread of the novel. Biblical references to Cyrus include Isaiah 44:28–45:7; Jeremiah 51:11, 28-29; 2 Chronicles 36:22-23; Ezra 1:1-11 and 5:14-15. Some of these verses were written decades before Cyrus was born and are considered prophetic in nature, while others describe the return of the Jewish captives to Jerusalem and Cyrus's role in those events.

During my reading of the book of Jeremiah, I was reminded of a riveting talk given by the beautiful Jennifer Kennedy Dean, author of *Heart's Cry* and *Live a Praying Life*. Years ago, I heard

Jennifer speak about Moab "settling on his dregs" (as described in Jeremiah 48:11). While I have no notes from that presentation, I believe I have captured some of its essence in Keren's ruminations in chapter 31. Jennifer is with the Lord now, but her teachings live on as evidenced by this paragraph in my book. Even though this is not a direct quote, it was Jennifer's presentation that birthed the idea.

I'd like to make special mention of my friend Diane Galloway, who during a conversation told me, "Grace means allowing room for someone to grow." I was so struck by this notion that I used it in chapter 53 as Keren's response to a painful situation.

In the timeline of *The Hidden Prince*, Persia is a small kingdom, growing in independence, but nowhere near the power that it later became under Cyrus's leadership. His rise to glory is an extraordinary tale, fraught with danger and sprinkled with the miraculous. But that is a story for another book.

ACKNOWLEDGMENTS

First and foremost, I would like to thank my incredible readers. Whether you have been with me from the start or you just discovered one of my books ten minutes ago, whether you read the novels over and over until your copies start to fall apart or you read them once and pass them on to (I assume) your favorite friends, you are the reason I write. Your grace, support, encouragement, and commitment to these stories keep me going. I have the most amazing fans! Please keep those prayers, letters, and emails coming. Even when I don't have time to answer, I read every word, pray for you in your struggles, and thank God for you. I am also deeply grateful to all the librarians and booksellers who introduce my books to new readers.

Thanks to my very talented editors, Stephanie Broene and Kathy Olson, who help me write better books and always ask the all-important question: "So, what's next?" I am grateful for the gifted fiction team at Tyndale House Publishers, including Elizabeth Jackson, Karen Watson, Jan Stob, and Ron Beers. Special thanks to Cheryl Kerwin and the wonderful sales team who work so hard to place these books in the hands of new readers, and to the lovely Madeline Daniels and Andrea Garcia who find clever ways to let you all know that I am alive and writing new books.

I am forever thankful for my capable agent, Wendy Lawton, whose continued encouragement and dear friendship have guided me along both level paths and bumpy roads. Thanks for taking a chance on an unknown writer all those years ago, even though I spilled my tea all over your tablecloth.

So much gratitude for my brilliant husband who helps me in a thousand ways. He created the map at the beginning of this book. More importantly, he challenged me to make Jared the victim of Keren's sword incident, rather than a minor character as I had first intended. It was one of those jaw-dropping moments when it dawned on me that his suggestion would elevate the story to a whole new level. What can I say? The man is a smarty-pants. Yes, I am blessed and grateful to have him in my life.

The longer I write, the more prayer I need! I want to say a special thanks to friends who have prayed for me faithfully: Kim and Kathleen Hill, Rebecca Rhee, Diane Galloway, Tegan Willard, Kathi Smith, Lucinda Secrest McDowell, Lauren Yarger, Jessica Trowbridge, Donna and Dave Luce, and Pastors Tom and Catherine Johnston.

This book is about the beginnings of the Persian Empire. My parents named me for a queen in that empire and planted a love for its history and culture in my heart. Without them, this book could not exist. I want to thank my beautiful mother, who never ceases to support my writing, and my beloved father, who is home with Jesus and whose sparkling eyes and incandescent humor I miss every day. So grateful for these two people who shaped my life with their love and sacrifice.

DISCUSSION QUESTIONS

1. This type of novel is called "biblical fiction," a genre that sets stories during the time of the Old or New Testament and incorporates people we know of from the Bible (in this case, the prophet Daniel and the prophesied Cyrus). Do you enjoy reading biblical fiction? What are its benefits for contemporary readers? What are its drawbacks?

2. Did you enjoy the historical information about the lands of Persia, Media, and Babylon and their customs? In what ways does it add to or detract from the story?

3. From the time we first meet Keren, it's clear that she is both intelligent and adventurous. How do these characteristics prepare her for the tasks she's called to undertake? Do you have personality traits that have uniquely prepared you for challenges you've faced?

4. When Daniel takes Keren to the famous Hanging Gardens of Babylon, he tells her they are an illustration of God's promises: "Their life shall be like a watered garden, and they shall languish no more"

(Jeremiah 31:12, ESV). Do you find evidence of God's love and provision in nature?

5. Daniel teaches his young students about the word *endure*, which is often repeated in Scripture. "We think of hardship when we think of endurance. But sometimes, when God whispers *endure*, he isn't talking about pain. He is talking about love. His love for you endures." How have you experienced both types of enduring in your life?

6. Jared's father appeals to the ancient Code of Hammurabi, which demands "an eye for an eye." Jesus referred to this in Matthew 5:38-42. What was his take on it?

7. Daniel tells Keren, "Your mistake has not destroyed God's ability to fulfill his will in your life." Have you—or someone you care about—ever made a mistake that seemed as if it might derail God's plans? How have you seen God's restoration and grace in such situations? What encouragement would you give someone who is currently struggling with something like this?

8. Daniel tells Jared about his friends Shadrach, Meshach, and Abednego in the fiery furnace and how they pledged to continue serving God even if he didn't deliver them. (You'll find this story in the Bible in the book of Daniel, chapter 3.) Have you ever had to choose to continue loving and serving God, even though he didn't answer your prayers in the way you wanted him to? What helped you to make that choice, or is it something you are still struggling with?

9. As she is setting out for her new life, Keren remembers the story of Jacob dreaming of a ladder to heaven. (You'll find this story in the Bible in the book of Genesis, chapter 28.) She prays, "Set the foot of your ladder right here, my Lord. Be with me and keep me." How is this image a comforting one? Where would you like to ask God to set the foot of his ladder for you?

10. Jared realizes he has two stories to live—two different ways, both true, to look at what has happened to him. What situations in your life could be viewed from different perspectives? Why is it sometimes helpful to reframe our circumstances like this?

11. What do you think is next for Jared, Keren, and their children? For Cyrus? Are you eager to see where the author takes them in the next book?

12. The book ends with Daniel's reminder of God's promise, through the prophet Jeremiah, that he will make a "new covenant" with his people: "One day, another will come. A true Savior. One with power to write God's law on our hearts. And blessed are those who live under his rule." (You'll find this prophecy in the Bible in the book of Jeremiah, chapter 31.) Jesus referred to this in Luke 22:19-20, during the Last Supper. What does God's new covenant mean for us today? Have you entered into this covenant with him?

ABOUT THE AUTHOR

 **TESSA AFSHAR** is an award-winning author of historical and biblical fiction. Her novel *Daughter of Rome* was a Publishers Weekly and ECPA bestseller. *Thief of Corinth* was an Inspy Award finalist, and *Land of Silence* won an Inspy Award and was voted by *Library Journal* as one of the top five Christian fiction titles of 2016. *Harvest of Gold* won the prestigious Christy Award in the historical romance category, and *Harvest of Rubies* was a finalist for the ECPA Christian Book Award in the fiction category. Tessa also recently released her first Bible study and DVD called *The Way Home: God's Invitation to New Beginnings*, based on the book of Ruth.

Tessa was born to a nominally Muslim family in the Middle East and lived there for the first fourteen years of her life. She then moved to England, where she survived boarding school for girls, before moving to the United States permanently. Her conversion to Christianity in her twenties changed the course of her life forever. Tessa holds a master of divinity from Yale University, where she served as cochair of the Evangelical Fellowship at the Divinity School. She worked in women's and prayer ministries for nearly twenty years before becoming a full-time writer. Tessa speaks regularly at national women's events. She is a devoted wife, mediocre tomato grower, and chocolate connoisseur. Visit her website at tessaafshar.com.

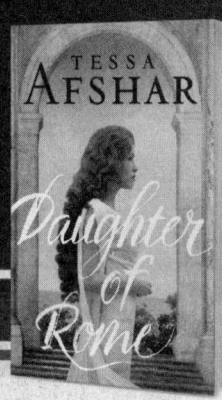

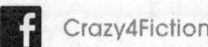
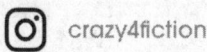

By purchasing
this book,
you're making
a difference.

For over 50 years, Tyndale has supported ministry

and humanitarian causes around the world through

the work of its foundation. Proceeds from every book sold

benefit the foundation's charitable giving. Thank you

for helping us meet the physical, spiritual, and

educational needs of people everywhere!